PRAISE

Praise for *The Usual Silence*

"*The Usual Silence* introduces a dynamic heroine. Arles Shepherd epitomizes the notion of the 'complex character,' complete with a mysterious past and self-sabotaging tendencies."

—CrimeReads

"*The Usual Silence* will frighten, shock, and uplift anyone who reads it, and shows Milchman at the top of her game."

—Bookreporter

"There's nothing usual about *The Usual Silence*. It's a psychological thriller extraordinaire, perfectly conceived and beautifully realized. Milchman's latest fashion[s] a brilliant puzzle we get to watch being assembled."

—BookTrib

"Reigning woman of mystery Milchman crafts edge-of-your-seat suspense laced with bold compassion."

—*Chronogram*

"An emotionally compelling and impressively crafted psychological suspense thriller of a read from start to finish."

—*Midwest Book Review*

"Milchman deftly weaves multiple events, characters, and timelines together. Some novels are an escape . . . Other[s] are complex explorations of the human experience. When you're looking for the latter, *The Usual Silence* should be first on your TBR list."

—The Mystery of Writing

"The various threads of the story come together in very unexpected ways. This is a psychological thriller in every sense of the word."

—Aunt Agatha's

Praise for *Cover of Snow*

"A terrific debut."

—Harlan Coben, #1 *New York Times* bestselling author

"*Cover of Snow* is a luge ride of action and atmosphere, a terrifically suspenseful read. A suicide in a creepy town, clogged with snow and secrets, starts a young widow on a perilous hunt. Soon we're careening along with her as she chases clues and as the full horror of what really happened to her husband is revealed. Reading *Cover of Snow* feels like racing across a frozen lake. Heart-pounding, exhilarating, frightening."

—Louise Penny, #1 *New York Times* bestselling author of the Armand Gamache series

"Everything a great suspense novel should be—tense, emotional, mysterious, and satisfying. Let's hope this is the start of a long career."

—Lee Child, #1 *New York Times* bestselling author of the Jack Reacher series

"*Cover of Snow* is a darkly atmospheric first novel that challenges all sorts of romantic notions we might harbor about small towns and the people we think we can trust. Luckily, heroine Nora Hamilton—and writer Jenny Milchman—has the skill and fortitude to lead readers through a suspenseful story of switchbacks and surprises. A mystery that will draw in fans of darker fare as well, reminiscent of Margaret Maron's work, which is about the highest praise I can bestow."

—Laura Lippman, *New York Times* bestselling author

"In her debut outing, Jenny Milchman has succeeded in a way many veteran writers can only envy. *Cover of Snow* is a tightly plotted, wonderfully unpredictable, and immensely satisfying novel. All the elements—character, setting, pace, language—are pitch perfect. Believe me, it doesn't get any better than this."
—William Kent Krueger, *New York Times* bestselling author of the Cork O'Connor series

"*Cover of Snow* is what every reader wants—a terrific story, beautifully told. Heartbreaking, sinister, compelling, and completely original. I love this book."
—Hank Phillippi Ryan, Agatha, Anthony, and Mary Higgins Clark Award–winning author

"Absorbing from start to finish: Jenny Milchman writes a deeply felt and suspenseful story of a woman whose life is upended by a death and a dark secret. While perceptively reflecting on community and our connections to one another, *Cover of Snow* is also an insightful look at the intimacies and secrets of marriage."
—Nancy Pickard, Agatha, Anthony, Macavity, and Shamus Award–winning author

"Milchman's intricately plotted and aptly titled *Cover of Snow* is layered with suspense, sorrow, and a strong sense of place and character."
—Linwood Barclay

"Jenny Milchman's expertly crafted, dark, and smoothly suspenseful page-turner slowly reveals the layers of terrifying secrets hidden in a small Adirondack town under *Cover of Snow*. I only wish I had written this novel! Watch for this stellar debut on the Best First Novel lists."
—Julia Spencer-Fleming

"Quietly unnerving . . . Milchman reveals an intimate knowledge of the psychology of grief, along with a painterly gift for converting frozen feelings into scenes of a forbidding winter landscape."

—*The New York Times*

"The first-person account told from Nora's point of view thrusts the narrative full force into horror, sadness, and every other emotion Nora experiences as she must start over without Brendan . . . [W]hat makes *Cover of Snow* sing is Milchman's ability to make readers care for Nora as she suffers and starts anew."

—The Associated Press

"When house restorer Nora Hamilton finds that her policeman husband, Brendan, has hanged himself, her image of their idyllic life in Brendan's Adirondacks hometown of Wedeskyull, New York, is shattered in Milchman's evocative debut . . . Milchman expertly conveys Nora's grief in a way that will warm hearts even in the dead of a Wedeskyull winter."

—*Publishers Weekly* (starred review)

"[A] superlative dark, wintry debut . . . These well-defined characters take us on an emotional roller coaster ride through the darkest night, with blinding twists and occasionally fatal turns. This is a richly woven story that not only looks at the devastating effects of suicide but also examines life in a small town and explores the complexity of marriage."

—*Booklist* (starred review)

"Milchman's debut is a chillingly good mystery thriller that quickly picks up momentum and spirals into a whirling avalanche of secrets, danger, and suspense."

—*Library Journal*

"Milchman makes [readers] feel the chill right down to their bones and casts a particularly effective mood in this stylish thriller."

—*Kirkus Reviews*

"But the real triumph of Milchman's first novel is the pacing. The plot unfolds at an excellent clip, stalling in just the right moments, lingering on characters long enough for us to get to know them, ultimately rushing headlong to a series of startling revelations. I found myself completely wrapped up in the story, unwilling to put the novel down until I had reached the fascinating and unexpected conclusion."

—*San Francisco Review of Books*

"Milchman tackles small-town angst where evil can simmer under the surface with a breathless energy and a feel for realistic characters."

—*The Seattle Times*

"*Cover of Snow* is quite dark in tone and mood, which in turn contrasts with the backdrop of ever-present snow literally blanketing every scene . . . This is a memorable debut from an author who promises much and delivers."

—Bookreporter

Praise for *Ruin Falls*

"Milchman shows her chops with this sophomore effort (following *Cover of Snow*, 2013), and she carves out a new niche with this unusual mix of eco-thriller and family suspense drama."

—*Booklist* (starred review)

"Essential for psychological-thriller fanatics, Milchman's second novel trumps her acclaimed debut, *Cover of Snow*. Extreme heart-pounding action follows this determined mother as she risks everything to save her children."

—*Library Journal* (starred review)

"Milchman weaves a complex and intriguing tale, adeptly pacing the narrative as danger escalates . . . Most impressive, though, is Liz's transformation from a meek wife . . . to a strong, capable woman determined to rescue her children at any cost to herself."

—*Publishers Weekly*

Praise for *As Night Falls*

"Electric . . . Jenny Milchman mixes psychological thrills with adventure . . . to shoot her readers with an extreme jolt of adrenaline . . . Milchman's talent for building atmosphere will have readers wondering if they're shivering from the story's excitement or northern New York's winter cold."

—*Shelf Awareness* (starred review)

"Gripping . . . a fast-paced tale that should keep readers eagerly turning pages."

—*Publishers Weekly*

"The suspense starts building right from the get-go . . . The desolation set the hairs on the back of my neck to tingling, [and] there is a shocking twist. Another excellent psychological thriller that should appeal to readers who favor authors like Lisa Gardner and Lisa Unger."

—*Booklist*

Praise for *Wicked River*

"*Wicked River* is partly a who-is-my-husband-really story, partly a horror-in-the-wilderness story, and partly a Manhattan-family drama, all rolled up in elegantly propulsive prose and shot through with sinister suspense."

—Lee Child, #1 *New York Times* bestselling author of the Jack Reacher series

"Suspense oozes like blood from a wound on every page of Jenny Milchman's *Wicked River*. As scary and tense a book as I've read this year."

—John Lescroart, *New York Times* bestselling author of the Dismas Hardy series

"From time to time, I come across an action manuscript that shares my high regard for the [action] genre and the intensity it can achieve. One such book is Jenny Milchman's *Wicked River*, which I urge you to experience. It thoroughly gripped me, not only because of the excitement it creates and the inventiveness with which it does so but also because of the subtext about a honeymoon in which the various stages of a marriage are condensed in a wilderness that's both physical and psychological. *Wicked River* is a wild ride."

—David Morrell, *New York Times* bestselling author of *First Blood*

"On a honeymoon gone terribly awry, two newlyweds battle for their lives in a powerful story of survival told by one of the richest and most riveting voices in today's thriller fiction. *Wicked River* twists and tumbles and roars, carrying readers along for one hell of a thrill ride. Mark my words: This novel will jump off the shelves."

—William Kent Krueger, *New York Times* bestselling author of the Cork O'Connor series

"Jenny Milchman's characters jump off the page . . . *Wicked River* is compulsive reading—I kept holding my breath and turning the pages faster and faster. It's a book that should cement Jenny's place as a must-read thriller writer for fans hungry for domestic suspense in the style of Gillian Flynn."

—M. J. Rose, *New York Times* bestselling author

"Chock full of suspense and danger, *Wicked River* by Jenny Milchman takes you on the journey of a lifetime, canoeing fast-moving rivers and hiking through tangled forests where humans have seldom trod. This is the story of Natalie and Doug's honeymoon; they wanted natural beauty and adventure. They get both, in abundance. You'll be glad you joined them. *Wicked River* is wicked thrilling!"

—Gayle Lynds, bestselling author of *Masquerade* and *The Book of Spies*

"*Deliverance*, meet *Into the Wild*. Jenny Milchman knows how to construct a tautly wound, rawboned thriller that will keep you up like the howl of wolves outside your tent."

—Andrew Gross, international bestselling author of *The Blue Zone* and *The Dark Tide*

"A story about passion and betrayal on the high-stakes stage, *Wicked River* is intensely gripping and perfectly paced—a real standout that pushes the domestic-thriller category to its very edge. With her usual mastery of setting and character, Jenny Milchman has outdone herself."

—Carla Buckley, internationally bestselling author of *The Good Goodbye*

"Milchman has crafted a truly engrossing novel where the river is not the only thing that's wicked."

—Jeff Ayers, the Associated Press

"Riveting . . . A hybrid between John Fowles's classic *The Collector* and Erica Ferencik's *The River at Night*, this novel will appeal to fans of psychological suspense as well as those who enjoy trips to the backcountry."

—*Library Journal*

"A tense exploration of survival and psychological manipulation with a raw, sharply drawn setting sure to please fans of wilderness thrillers like those by Nevada Barr and C. J. Box."

—*Booklist*

"Milchman shakes things up with *Wicked River*; in this author's hands, a babbling brook can become a deliverer of death. The suspense ratchets up steadily, making this a highly satisfying summer read."

—*The Strand Magazine*

Praise for *The Second Mother*

"*The Second Mother* is a gothic unraveling of a novel, as moody and atmospheric as the isolated island on which it's set."
—Jodi Picoult, #1 *New York Times* bestselling author of *Small Great Things* and *A Spark of Light*

"Rich in atmosphere, expertly plotted, and populated by characters who live and breathe, *The Second Mother* is as much a portrait of survival and redemption as it is a harrowing deep dive into the secrets and troubles of an isolated island in Maine. Jenny Milchman writes with insight and compassion, creating a vivid sense of place and masterfully ratcheting up the tension page by gripping page."
—Lisa Unger, *New York Times* bestselling author of *The Stranger Inside*

"With her ever-masterful sense of place and astute psychological insight, Jenny Milchman takes us on a journey from the Adirondack Mountains to a remote island off the coast of Maine, and from the dark depths of grief into the light. This is a harrowing and heartrending story that earns its place in the sun."

—Carol Goodman, *New York Times* bestselling author of *The Lake of Dead Languages* and *The Sea of Lost Girls*

"When Julie arrives on a beautiful, rustic island off the coast of Maine— with a one-room schoolhouse, where people embrace a simple life— she is hoping for a chance to start over. Slowly and expertly, Milchman peels back the layers to reveal what lies beneath the idyllic surface. *The Second Mother* is an atmospheric thriller resonating with the weight and power of secrets. Settle in someplace comfortable, lock the doors, and turn on the lights—you're not going to want to put this one down!"

—Jennifer McMahon, author of *The Winter People* and *The Invited*

"*The Second Mother* is a tense, riveting story about a woman who flees to a remote island off the coast of Maine to escape a tragic past. Starkly beautiful, the island holds the hope of a new life and a new love, but schoolteacher Julie Weathers finds herself facing dangers she never imagined. Told with Milchman's stunning prose, *The Second Mother* is a gripping tale of obsession, secrets held close, and the dark side of island life. Harrowing and addictive, I dare you to put this book down once you've started."

—Heather Gudenkauf, *New York Times* bestselling author of *The Weight of Silence* and *This Is How I Lied*

"A do-not-miss tour de force."

—Linda Castillo, *New York Times* bestselling author

"Jenny Milchman is one of the best suspense writers at work today, and *The Second Mother* is a page-turner extraordinaire. Milchman takes the nostalgic daydream of teaching in a one-room schoolhouse and turns it ever so slowly into an urgent nightmare. That the story is set on a remote island off the coast of Maine—one of the most claustrophobic places a stranger can ever set foot—is an added bonus."

—Paul Doiron, author of the Edgar Award–nominated Mike Bowditch series

"Milchman owns a Highsmith mastery of emotional depth and psychological tension for all her rich, finely detailed settings. She is a true American regionalist artist. *The Second Mother* sweeps us away to an eerie island of complex villains . . . that will chill your blood while it breaks your heart."

—Kalisha Buckhanon, author of *Speaking of Summer* and *Solemn*

"Proving Stephen King isn't the only author who can make a scenic small town in Maine feel menacing, Jenny Milchman's *The Second Mother* is a haunting thriller."

—PopSugar

"Jenny Milchman commands the page the way the best actors command the stage. Milchman brings the suspense from a simmer to a slow boil, as *The Second Mother* becomes an agonizing exercise in escape and survival. This is the kind of book Alfred Hitchcock would have loved to adapt into a film, and for good reason."

—*The Providence Journal*

"Another gripping and satisfying story of suspense from Mary Higgins Clark Award–winning author Jenny Milchman. The author's talent for authentic description will carry readers right along with Julie on the choppy ride in the ferry to Mercy Island. They'll smell the salty air, feel the spray and mist of the ocean on their faces, walk beside her and Depot on the path to an unknown destination. They'll learn along with Julie that this lovely, close-knit community is not as welcoming and tranquil as first believed. *The Second Mother* is a beautifully written page-turner."

— *The New York Review of Books*

"Examines grief, isolation, addiction, social inequality, and legacy set against the background of an insular society desperate to prevent change and growth. Yet this is truly a story about motherhood—the connection between mother and child, and the ferocity of a mother to protect her child at all costs. On every page, Milchman raises the stakes. While grappling with dark questions, *The Second Mother* will thrill and entertain readers who desire a summer adventure."

—BookTrib

"A tension-filled, provocative, nail-biting thriller that will have your heart pounding and your hands shaking as you frantically turn page after page, thirsting for more."

—*Suspense Magazine*

THE FAIREST

OTHER TITLES BY JENNY MILCHMAN

THE FAIREST

AN
ARLES
SHEPHERD
THRILLER

JENNY MILCHMAN

THOMAS & MERCER

Published by Thomas & Mercer, Seattle

www.apub.com

Amazon, the Amazon logo, and Thomas & Mercer are trademarks of Amazon.com, Inc., or its affiliates.

EU product safety contact:
Amazon Media EU S. à r.l.
38, avenue John F. Kennedy, L-1855 Luxembourg
amazonpublishing-gpsr@amazon.com

ISBN-13: 9781662518447 (paperback)
ISBN-13: 9781662518454 (digital)

Cover design by Faceout Studio, Addie Lutzo
Cover image: © Reilika Landen / ArcAngel Images; © Barney Wei / 500px / Getty; © spaxiax, © Lyudmyla Kharlamova, © Karramba Production / Shutterstock

Printed in the United States of America

For Josh. He knows why.

Mirror, mirror on the wall . . .

—*The Brothers Grimm*

Sugar and spice and everything nice,

that's what little girls are made of.

—*Robert Southey*

"Are we lost?" asked Janelle.

Kip turned to her with the helpless look she hated.

"Don't take your eyes off the road!" she shrilled. For once, her tone of voice didn't matter; there was no microphone tucked against her spine, artfully concealed away from her bared stomach. Two thirty-minute core-lift workouts per day to maintain abs as hard and flat as tiles.

Kip—who wasn't good with a car; they usually relied on their driver—couldn't afford any distractions. These roads were treacherous; Janelle had never seen anything like them. The coastal highway back home was different, open to the sea. Here in the Northeast—she couldn't be more specific about their location than that; New York, but not near the city—forests hulked over steep, skinny stretches of asphalt like something out of a goddamn fairy tale.

The pics for tomorrow's posts were going to be amazing. She looked out at a sapphire sky shot through with sun. Bolts of pure gold slanted between breaks in the trees—not that there were many of those. Not many breaks, that is. There were plenty of trees. Enough to sequester all the excess carbon on the planet.

Until now, she'd only seen the location in post. Kip had a producer credit, his first, on the film they were out here to promote, which gave him a say in final cut. But not even the dailies had done this place justice. You had to feel it, smell it, breathe it in.

"We should've taken Jason," she grumbled. They'd left him back at the poor excuse for a hotel, where all of them were being put up. Told him to take a half day off, which wasn't much of an offer, given that there was exactly nothing to do around here.

"It was your idea to leave him," Kip said, pouting like a little kid as he leaned forward to keep control of their rented SUV, now rearing back on an angled pitch.

It looked like he was holding reins instead of a steering wheel. Was that how you held reins? She'd only seen it done on-screen.

Today, Kip was scheduled to put on a show for all the squeal-like-a-pig Deliverance *hicks who lived in these parts. He'd done a couple of gigs after the shoot wrapped last year, shown his face, posed for selfies, but now there were glimmers of attention from the studio, and Kip had been asked to come back. Sure, bring your wife this time. The money people were feeling generous. Two days, then they could all fly home as a family.*

Suddenly, the rental made a giant S across the road, like surfing a wave. Janelle's seat belt yanked her back; she'd been unprepared for Kip's swerve because she was staring at her phone. Not in the way she always did—the thing she looked at most in her day, in her life—but with confusion, even dread, because what she saw on the screen made no sense. Or rather, what she didn't see.

Panic started to set in, filling her like water. She was going to drown.

Kip sat with his hands clenched around the steering wheel, his knuckles whitening.

No car was coming. There was exactly nobody besides them on this whole road. Janelle swiveled to face Kip with rage in her face, heat she knew would definitely skew red as opposed to pleasing-rosy-blush. "What the fuck?"

"Did you see that?" He was panting.

"See what?"

"I don't know!" He looked around wildly, like he was shooting a chase scene. "A deer, maybe? They have those here, right? Something ran across the road. I think I swiped it."

Janelle felt a prickle along her spine. "I didn't feel anything."

"Get out and take a look, will you?"

"Me?" If ever there was a time to make the patriarchy work for her. Plus, she was sure Kip hadn't struck anything, deer or otherwise. He drummed up drama like a teenage girl. No, like a Hollywood actor.

He looked at her, his gaze as brilliant a blue as the sky.

Janelle made an ugly scoff in her throat, a ripping sound, which wouldn't do. Her career required her to coddle her voice, but she was always slipping. She'd hear her mother and startle, looking around for the old hag. Her mother was long dead, but it'd been her high, shrill caw that made Janelle's daddy leave one day and never come back. "Fine."

She opened the door and got out. It felt like she had to drop a long way down to the pavement. The trees here were unreal, their branches like big swiping arms or grins just before the killer swung his ax. She shivered in her baby tee. On what planet was this August? No wonder these people believed climate change was a hoax.

She heard the snarl of an engine, although there was still no car in sight besides theirs. It took her a beat to get it—silly for someone whose husband had started his career in a chain-saw movie as Dead Guy #7. Someone was cutting wood; she could make out a shack through the trees. The realization didn't ignite a flannel-shirt, sexy-lumberjack image. The only thing missing from this scene (Exterior: Hovel in Woods) was the homeowner and a demonstration of his right to bear arms.

"Jane?" Kip had gotten out and was coming to join her in the road.

He was the only person who called her by her given name. Plain Jane versus Fancy Janelle, who'd just cracked three million followers on TikTok and a million on Instagram.

"Car looks fine," she said, completing her lap around it.

Kip had left the driver's door hanging open; she walked over to check it. Not a scratch.

"Yeah, well, that's the least of our problems," he said. "We don't have any service."

Memory catapulted back. Her phone with exactly zero bars. She glanced inside the SUV, but the infotainment system showed only a sea of green. They hadn't downloaded directions, had just been following the map.

"Why didn't Jason warn us about this?" Kip asked in a voice fans wouldn't have recognized. Almost whining. Then he looked up. *"Someone's coming,"* he said in a We're saved *kind of tone.*

He was hot, but dumb as a loaf of bread. She should've dumped him when she'd given up carbs. Except she knew it was fifty-fifty how that would play with her followers. Some would be sure Kip was beating her, ready to pounce and get him canceled, while others would be 1,000 percent against divorce, even if one of the spouses—women more than men, of course—was miserable in the marriage. Who was Janelle kidding, anyway? She would never dump Kip Stratton, not because he was Kip Stratton, but because she knew better than to let go of a man.

He began jogging backward toward the SUV. "Ask him the way, okay?"

"Me?" Janelle said for the second time on this hellish outing.

"I don't think this dude is gonna be the type who buys centering chimes or skin-care products," Kip said, now at their rental. *"He won't have a clue who you are. But he might've seen* Go West *or* Gods & Giants. *"*

Referencing the two (limited theatrical release) films Kip had starred in. The one he'd shot out here last year, based on a blockbuster novel, was looking to be his breakout.

"I can't risk getting recognized," he added. *"Bad enough I'm driving myself around."*

"You're literally out here to be recognized," she countered.

"If we ever find the place, I have to go on and come off. Escorted. Just asking someone for directions like any asshole will ruin the whole, you know . . . mystique." And he eased himself into the SUV, slinking down low in front.

Janelle watched the guy now walking out of the woods, picturing his gaze gliding over her like a pair of skates. But he stopped a few respectful feet away, removing work gloves from his hands.

"Need some help?"

"We're looking for Wucht Road. Our GPS cut out."

"Those things don't work out here," the guy said, visually dissecting their rental as if he'd never seen anything like it. "Just keep going straight and take your third left. Up a hill."

Janelle thanked him, then ran back to the SUV, which shot forward like a cannonball. Kip really might hit something this time unless he watched out. Gravel popped and spit beneath the tires as they left this bend in the road in the rearview. Literally. Janelle began mentally scripting. Anything could've happened. *During her recounting, she'd balloon the time they had spent lost, of course.*

They took the turn, then crested a hill to enter a crowded parking lot identified by a reassuringly bougie wooden sign. A carved beer stein clinking the outline of a book. Their huge rental straddled two of the last available spaces as Kip parked. Pricey late models filled the rest, along with pickups, faded and skeletal, most of their bodies rusted out. Half the size of the ones people drove in LA, even though nobody needed one there. Well, maybe landscapers.

Car doors swung open and slammed shut. People got out, hurrying toward the entrance, excited, chattery. Janelle had just taken her makeup case out of the glove box when she sensed something behind her. She jerked her head up, trying to see. It was impossible, a daymare or something, but she had the impression of a giant spider, a special effect in a movie, crouching in the cargo space. A mile away in a vehicle this size. *Whatever it was had been attempting to hide, but must've been at it too long, so its long, gangly limbs had cramped up, and now it was moving, unfolding—*

The spider-thing had human hair.

Fear encased her like clay. She was at a spa, having a mud mask, not all the way across the country facing God knew what. Janelle didn't have much imagination—who needed it when way more than anyone could ever conceive was continually offered up on-screen?—and she had no clue what was going on right now. But darts of dread penetrated her.

The eellike, slivery guy from the shack. The way he'd eye-fucked this shiny SUV, even if he had been more discreet about looking at her body.

He had gotten past her somehow, evading Kip's notice. Her husband was so self-involved that it wouldn't be hard . . .

Or no, could this be Kip's stalker? Kip referred to him as a superfan, because of course he did, but based on the messages he posted on Kip's Instagram, even though Kip had blocked him, Janelle genuinely believed the guy was nuts. And motivated. How did he find them in this nowhere blotch of land? Well, that was obvious. Kip's appearance had been publicized.

Then Janelle saw a slope of shoulder and let out a long, searing scream. Kip clapped a hand over her freshly glossed lips. "Quiet," he said.

People continued streaming past their car on both sides, parting when they came to it.

ACT I

The Kindness of Strangers

CHAPTER ONE

Kara was being shunted through the bookstore by an older woman with a prominent bow in her back, a spine stuck in *cat* versus *cow*—not that Kara took yoga. The woman had gray waist-length hair and wore dove linen. Tin spectacles shielded her eyes, matching her dun-toned pallor. She looked as dusty as the volumes crammed into shelves and overflowing onto display tables.

Books & Brew had recently taken over Wedeskyull's struggling local bookshop, adding events and microbrews to lure in the acronym set, people flocking to STRs, Vrbos, Airbnbs. But the ailing heart of the former business still beat, like slowly dying roadkill. A sheen of newness paired with a region settled generations ago. That was Wedeskyull circa today.

Although, at the moment, the place held the thrumming energy of a power plant. Clumps of people crammed every available nook and open patch of floor; the electric buzz of conversation was punctuated by sudden, bright laughter and the crackle of an expectant pause.

"What's going on?" Kara asked with a smile she hoped implied self-deprecation instead of self-delusion. "These people can't all be here to see me."

"Oh no, of course not." Her escort smiled back a touch too gaily as she ushered Kara along. "We're hosting two events today—and one is quite a big get for us. That's why I have you here in the back."

Kara felt her face fold sourly, something sluggish fill her motions. She held back, opposing the woman's attempt to hurry. Through a picture window, its lower portion blocked by books, she spotted the WDSK logo on a van with a sat dish angled on its roof.

"Don't worry," her companion said. "You have quite a nice little group gathered."

The woman twisted her gnomic body to edge past a series of stacks, then indicated an area behind them. The space was walled off by movable shelving units filled with horror and speculative-fiction titles, genres typically relegated to the leftover portions of bookstores. A dozen rows of folding chairs, eight seats in each—Kara mentally calculated their total—had been set up, with about half occupied. Kara backed away, keeping out of sight.

Forty-five attendees, give or take, wasn't a bad tally for her, especially on a summer Saturday. This launch appearance was juiced by the hometown contingent, after which three other events were scheduled to take place later this week. One at her alma mater downstate, another at a library where a distant relative worked, and a third with a book club. After that, she was done. She'd told her publicist not to consider her for so much as a podcast or blog post.

Kara intended to avoid interacting with a single soul, even by text, until she turned in her next manuscript. Which pretty much described her level of interaction when she wasn't writing, too.

She snuck another peek at the space. A battered table held copies of her latest—Books & Brew had at least ordered a decent number—with one on a display stand, peacock-strutting its cover. There was a podium but not so much as a bottle of water—maybe the new owners were environmentalists—let alone the beverage that this incarnation of the bookstore peddled.

Too bad. Her talk would've gone down better with a beer. For her, if not her audience.

She realized her companion had been speaking.

"I'll be handling your signing after you finish," the woman said. "I may duck out for a minute or two during your reading"—this with a longing look at the front of the store, where the hum was dying down to a bated, anticipatory hush—"but I'll come right back."

"Uh-huh," Kara replied grudgingly.

"You were scheduled to start five minutes ago, so whenever you're ready," said the woman, a plea peeping out of her tone. "I don't think we're expecting any more to attend." She sent a second snatched look in the direction of the other event space.

Whoever was speaking there *had probably been given a nice cold pour,* Kara thought, sour again. God, she hated herself. Why couldn't she just urge this woman to go enjoy whatever was going on? Something made her stall, leafing through the advance copy of her new novel, which she'd brought with her. This same ugly, balled-up feeling had lived inside her ever since the worst day of her life. All the days afterward had been the worst too; Kara just hadn't been prepared for that first one. At last, with a deep, belly-inflating breath, she stepped in front of her big-but-not-big-enough crowd.

About half the faces were familiar, this being Wedeskyull and Kara having grown up here. A subset of those were extended family—whatever that meant, since the people in question had been of absolutely zero use when Kara needed them. Kara's small-scale celebrity status seemed to rub off on her relatives like glitter. "That's my niece, the author!" someone would crow while standing in line at one of these. Or *cousin* or *goddaughter.*

The rest she didn't recognize. Vacationers who'd probably scrolled through the regional website looking for activities. *Look, a reading by a local author—how adorbs.* One attendee appeared to lack access to a shower, this event providing a place to sit, which, fair, there was a serious housing crisis in the region. The heavy-lidded, unfocused gaze of another suggested he wasn't going to be taking in her scintillating words. There was a third who resembled a real-life demon. Skinny as a length of pipe; dark, slick-backed hair; brows pitched like ski slopes over inky eyes. He exuded danger like sweat from his ruddy, fiery-complected skin.

Kara tapped the mic. "Thanks for coming out on this gorgeous day. I know you could be hiking or swimming!"

Nods of agreement.

She cleared her throat and started to read.

The long, dark street stretched out, blank and empty.

Her editor was always trying to get her to use fewer adjectives, but Kara loved that line. Her sleuth was about to get stopped on this street, a hand on her shoulder from behind.

From between two very old cars, a large, broad man stepped out . . .

There was a sudden gunshot clap of sound, and Kara startled, as did several people in their seats. The others must have realized sooner what it was they were hearing: applause, a furious beat of hands, along with cheers from the front of the store. Kara waited sullenly until the noise abated, her heart galloping inside her, her voice unsteady when she resumed.

She was coming to the best part—where the reader learned that the (large, broad) man had a child trapped in one of the (very old) cars. She paused for a second. Maybe her editor was right about Kara's plentiful sprinkling of adjectives. Something to consider for her next book.

Fragile, slight, he looked too frail to survive such fear.

It was a scene Kara wrote into every one of her books. She was known for it in the mystery world. Children lost, gone, and taken entered her plots every time. She'd done the therapy thing, understood why she kept coming back to this topic, like a dog to a buried bone. But insight didn't change the fact that all the many ways in which a child could go missing was the central conceit of her work.

She finished reading and let the cover fall shut.

The attendees started clapping, a rainfall patter not as rousing as the intrusion from the other event but still nice to hear. As people got up and assembled themselves into a loose line, Kara offered hellos and scribbled her signature in book after book, mentally counting and feeling her eyebrows rise at the number. Maybe she'd make it onto a bestseller list this time.

She cast her gaze down the line, which was finally dwindling.

Four more to go—or was it five? The row of heads, some higher, some lower, took a sudden sharp dip. Like a cityscape with a three- or four-story building at the end of a series of skyscrapers. Without looking down, Kara penned her name in the book thrust before her. She used a particularly elegant hand, going slow so as to make sense of what she was seeing.

The last person in line was a kid.

Kara blinked to make sure she hadn't been fooled by a tiny grown-up. But no. Even though she didn't write children's books—or even young adult—and the scene she'd just read would've earned the literary equivalent of an R rating for violence, somebody who didn't look old enough to get into a PG-13 movie by herself was shifting from one brightly sneakered foot to another, clutching a copy of *Gone Too Soon* to her sunken, heaving chest. Her eyes formed wide, frightened ovals; she kept snatching looks around the store.

The man standing in front of Kara left with his copy, and the kid sidled forward. She placed her book down, open to the right page. But before Kara could sign it—a sale was a sale, after all—the Sharpie she held seized in midflight, its swooping *K* arrested.

Something had been written in the spot where she usually inked her name.

Kara squinted to decipher the words. The excerpt she'd read aloud had been basically memorized, but these words were a mystery—ha—and despite being only thirty-four years old, Kara needed reading glasses already. All those hours spent in front of a screen.

In blocky, childish letters, the first word underlined, was scrawled the message—

<u>I</u> AM A MISSING CHILD

———

Kara looked up, then down at the book, then up again. The makeshift space was empty. Everyone gone, including her host, this little girl the only person left. Kara hadn't registered all the departures, the space clearing out. Her brain felt like fuzz, unable to parse this turn of events.

"What the hell?" It was all she could think of to say, inappropriate as it was to curse at a little kid. "Is this for a TikTok?" She got to her feet, suddenly sure she had the right answer. "Are you filming me?" She peered over the table, looking for a phone.

The little girl stabbed a miniature finger at the book, one perfect teardrop nail tearing a slit in the paper. She glared at Kara, a statement written on her face no less clearly than the one on the page. Feathery blond eyebrows jutted into peaks, pale-blue eyes wide and urgent.

Hurry up, do something!

But what? Kara made up stories like this—she had no idea how to handle a real one.

Who did this kid belong to? Those sharp little brows reminded Kara of the devil who'd been in her audience. Maybe he was an abusive father—like we haven't seen that one before, she thought bitterly—and ran off when his daughter made use of the crowd to escape his clutches.

No, it was never the ones who looked the part.

The scowler was the red herring, so obvious Kara's editor would've struck him from an early draft. And the slit-eyed dude who'd fallen asleep for part of Kara's reading had roused himself enough to leave. He wasn't returning for any kid. Hadn't even bought a book.

At that moment, someone came dashing in, and Kara experienced a squall of hope. But she recognized this woman; they had graduated together. Her former classmate probably hadn't read a book since Ms. Whitman's twelfth-grade lit ended, and she wasn't a mother. She swept up a sweater from a chair and ran back out.

Kara's heart tolled a series of wild, spasmodic beats. "Look, clearly, I have to get help," she said, talking half to herself, half to the little girl. "Let's go find a bookstore employee."

The girl reached across the table and grabbed Kara's hand, shaking her head frantically.

"No, please!" she whispered. "He'll see! He'll find me!"

Suddenly, the whole world had gone dangerous again, fanged. A place and a state that Kara had escaped long ago, terror relegated to the pages of the books she wrote instead of daily life with her father. Who was a threat to this kid? Just about anybody could be the bad guy. The tourists who swilled astronomically priced beer numbered in the dozens if not hundreds, and without a doubt, albeit against type, some of them battered their kids behind closed doors.

She studied the little girl. "Okay," she said, pitching her own voice low and not liking how tremulous it sounded. "Okay."

The kid nodded as if Kara had said something useful.

"Stay here," Kara went on. "Behind the podium," she added, extending a hand.

The little girl gave another nod, scrambling into position.

"And I'll be back," Kara whispered, beginning to turn. She bumped into a movable shelving unit, which rolled, unbalancing her. Catching herself, she wove between the stacks to the front of the store.

The bookstore was filled with hordes of people pressed up against one another. The sight stymied her—how to identify a source of help in the midst of so many bodies?—and also maddened her. She spotted vacationers from her own event, clearly deciding to make a twofer of their trek out for local color. Probably wouldn't even bother to read her book; twenty-eight bucks on a hardcover was nothing to them.

Kara's host was nowhere to be seen, but her petite form probably wouldn't be visible above all the heads craning and angling for a view. She had to be in there somewhere; she'd been so thirsty to be a part of whatever was happening that she hadn't bothered to say goodbye.

What would Kara tell her? *This kid needs help, and she's in your store, so tag, you're it.*

Unless the girl wasn't even there anymore, Kara's initial assumption correct. This had been a prank, a stunt, some challenge or other.

Resentment formed a solid sludge in her mouth as Kara stared into the mosh pit of an audience far more avid and eager than any she would ever command. She began backing away, putting distance between herself and the throng, first a few feet, then the whole entryway aisle.

She wasn't the only person who could help a lost kid, right? Kara hadn't been responsible for another small human since she'd been one herself, and look how that had wound up. She was good at making shit up, but when it came to reality, you'd be better off finding somebody else. *Any*body else. Which was what the girl would do when Kara didn't return. Find another sucker.

Kara wouldn't stay to sign stock. She'd sacrifice those future sales, let the unsold books be returned to her publisher, in return for washing her hands of this burden. Which incidentally proved that real life was nothing like books. If there actually was an Author, a great celestial scribbler, then this kid's message would've been read by someone with greater capabilities.

Rounding her shoulders, head averted so as not to be seen, Kara slunk out of the store.

She trudged through the parking lot in search of her car. Every space was full; the late-model vehicles massive, dwarfing her ancient hatchback. The door made a grinding sound as she heaved it open. She sank down, worn upholstery hot against her, then inserted her key in the ignition. No push-button start for this baby. And no AC. She'd drive with her shirt cuffs pulled over her hands until she got going and a breeze cooled things down.

A head, silky and blond, popped up from the back seat.

Kara jumped in her seat, her own head grazing the padded roof of her car, so much lower than those on the aspirational vehicles around her. She was never going to own an SUV. She wouldn't hit the bestseller list. Her life was about to unravel in ways she couldn't even imagine, payback for things she'd done to her sleuth. No—punishment for something far worse.

The little girl's eyes, so light their blue had an otherworldly hue, met Kara's in the rearview. Perspiration pearled the kid's forehead.

Nobody locked doors in Wedeskyull. Not on cars, not in houses. Although many of the vehicles in this lot, those with plates from Away, were probably secured. Was that how the kid had narrowed down her options?

"Why'd you leave?" Kara asked. *How'd you know what a coward I am?*

"I thought you were calling the police," the little girl answered.

Kara kept her tired gaze on the kid's reflection. "I would never do that. How would they help?" For many reasons, Kara was ill suited to this job, but in one sense, the little girl had come to the right place. Happened upon the right author.

While almost anybody else would've turned to the law, Kara wouldn't have expected assistance from a cop if one appeared in front of her car right now, holding a sign that read: *I know what to do when random kids show up unattended at book events.* In fact, in that case, she'd be even less likely to ask for aid, if you could get less likely than zero. In her experience, the ones who promised to help were the worst.

Onto the next question. "How'd you know which car was mine?"

A shrug of slight shoulders. "I thought a starving artist could afford this one."

Kara's mouth twitched. A second ago she wouldn't have believed she could find anything funny. "I'm not starving. My fifth book just came out."

"What are you going to do?" the kid asked.

Kara twisted in her seat. Where were all the people racing out of the bookstore, the police car screaming up, summoned by panicked parents? Why no mob on the hunt for a kid?

"What's going to happen?" the kid asked again, this time with a whine in her voice.

"I don't know—just give me a second!" Kara instantly regretted barking. She sounded like her father. All that was missing was the *goddamn* if she got lucky and a balled hand if she didn't.

The little girl's face in the mirror appeared stunned. It was as if no one had ever screamed at her before, which made Kara question whether the kid was really escaping anything so horrible.

Then she saw tears wobbling on the little girl's lower lash line and hated herself anew.

She of all people knew wordless could be worse than yelling, quiet more lethal than loud.

"It's okay," she said, dropping one hand over the seatback. "I've got a place we can go."

"You do?" The kid reached over the seatback to thread sweaty fingers through Kara's, sniffling raggedly. "Where? Where are we going?"

Kara withdrew her hand as if wresting herself free. "To see my old therapist."

CHAPTER TWO

It was the nineteenth straight day that Arles Shepherd woke up without any pain.

For the more than four months since she had been shot, pain had served as her warden. Immediately upon her release from the hospital—referred to as *discharged*, but it was an end to a sentence; make no mistake—she had begun refusing anything stronger than Tylenol, and she'd cut herself off from even that after six weeks due to the toll daily dosing took on the liver. She turned then to the mindfulness and meditation techniques she had once coached patients in during her rotation on the psychiatric IPU, and those worked about as well as all the patients had reported. Which was to say not at all.

Then came the first morning when Arles sat up without pain as a stalwart companion. Nobody realized what a violence sitting did to the body—sure, just fold yourself in half, no problem—until they'd been surgically unzipped and Humpty-Dumptied back together again.

Before easing herself out of bed, Arles added a new slash to the tally marks on the wall. Beautiful lacerations of black, like the stitches that left puckered scars from belly button to groin but miraculously failed to involve a single vital organ.

The leaded-glass windows in her room were open on their iron arms to let in the warm August air, and from outside, she caught the rumble of an engine. She started at the sound, and pain dug talons into her midriff—*Did you really think I was gone?*—before she snatched a pillow and pressed it to the slack flesh there, inhaling and exhaling as she had learned to do. The bird stopped cawing. Its talons loosened their grip.

Her SUV sat in a state of quiescence outside, no tick from its engine. An old van had pulled up beside it, curtains on its side windows, remnants of flowery decals on its faded-purple paint, and suddenly, Arles remembered. All these months later, and her mind still hadn't fully cleared of debris.

Moving as if she were a hundred years old, she made her way downstairs. The front door had been rigged to open without Arles having to wrestle with the heavy wood; by virtue of a cable and counterweight, all she needed to do was flick the latch. Taking a step out into the glow of the sun, she readied herself to speak. Turned out talking required muscles too.

"You're off." Words pitched at a lower register than the way she used to speak; it always took Arles a second before she recognized the sound of her own voice. "You're really off."

Stephanie and her daughter had been occupying a cabin on this land for the last four or five months, Stephanie inhabiting a role that blended tenant, employee, and friend. She stepped out from behind the van at the same time that Lissa's face popped up above its roof. The girl balanced on a ladder attached to the rear, dangling before jumping the rest of the way to the ground. Arles watched the child's effortless descent, how she moved like a different sort of bird from the one to which Arles had been introduced by pain. Lissa was tropical, dazzling.

The child raced up the porch steps, dropped onto her knees, then placed both arms around Arles's legs. She had adapted this way of giving hugs when Arles was let out of the hospital, somehow intuiting what would avoid pain. Arles didn't risk bending over, but she placed a palm on Lissa's sun-heated head, feeling the warmth of the girl's scalp through her hair.

"I don't want to leave," Lissa mumbled into Arles's knees.

"Ah, but you're going to see such amazing things," Arles replied.

"There are amazing things here," Lissa said, still low-down.

Stephanie came and stood before the stone steps. "Sure you're going to be okay?"

Arles made a Don't-worry gesture with one arm, stopping before it caused her to wince. "Send me postcards from Yellowstone and Yosemite. I've never been out west."

"But I want Dr. Arles to be there on my birthday!"

Arles patted Lissa's head again. Less distance for her hand to travel than just a few months ago. The girl was growing like a stand of bamboo. "We'll have another celebration when you get home." *Home.* "I'll take a stab at that cake you showed me how to bake."

Lissa cast her gaze upward. "The one with sprinkles in it?"

Arles gave a solemn nod. "Tons of sprinkles. Extra sprinkles."

Lissa got up, whirling around on her heels. "They're in the big cabinet by the fridge!"

"We wouldn't be doing this if it weren't for you," Stephanie said.

Arles made a second, Forget-about-it gesture. "Scales are still tipped in favor of your nursing me through four months of rehabilitation. Not to mention keeping my spirits up with your amazing daughter."

"There are no scales for you and me." Stephanie climbed the stairs to deliver a hug so gentle—not a raptor alighting but a swallow, a starling—that Arles saw more than felt the touch. "Oh, and don't forget it's your turn to choose our next selection."

She, Arles, and Lissa had started a book club, the challenge being for each member to come up with a title that crossed age groups.

"We'll discuss it virtually?" Arles suggested.

"Lis and I will read on the road," Stephanie agreed, backing away to climb into the van.

Then, with a few snuffs of exhaust from the old van's tailpipe, she and Lissa were gone.

Arles was all alone at Fir Cove, the spread of land that had been in her family since they'd settled in the Adirondacks generations ago. It comprised six hundred acres of woods, one of the lower mountains in the range, along with the largest privately owned lake in the region. Plus, the house Arles occupied, sixty-four hundred square feet of stone and beams, and a series of guest cottages, one of which Stephanie and Lissa would return to before the first snow flew, if all went as planned.

Aside from them, Arles hadn't spent time with anyone in person since her discharge. Well, except for Dan; he'd been there at first too. But he was a topic best flitted past quickly. Arles didn't do well with devotion and caring, and during the initial weeks when she was unable to lift anything heavier than a teacup, Dan's presence had proved psychologically intolerable to her. Stephanie possessed a lighter hand, providing assistance while hardly seeming to be there. Whereas Lissa— well, the cruelest misanthrope, Ebenezer himself, could not resist that child.

Arles had encountered people beyond those three, but just on her laptop. On several occasions, Stephanie had chauffeured Arles to Brick Road, where cell signal cut in. There, Arles met via Zoom with the families of victims killed by the man who had shot her, as many as she'd been able to track down with the help of law enforcement and her own online digging. She felt driven to divulge information she uniquely possessed, share it with people whose lives had been lacerated by her would-be killer. Arles alone knew what the victims had experienced. She could deliver finality of a sort. Maybe, hopefully, a kind of relief.

Today, the first and only in-person visit was scheduled to occur.

She shuffled back inside and upstairs to her room, old-woman-moving but able to get dressed at least, even add a polish coat of makeup. She brushed hair whose color was the one element of luster she retained. Her belly was loose, her flesh marred. She might never move with the same agility again, and the spark in her eyes had dulled to a dark bottle green. But her hair was as red as ever, proof of her former fire.

The family she was to meet with were the parents of the one other victim identified in the North Country, a second spot within the radius of nuclear detonation. Arles had spent her whole life not sixty miles away. She pushed the button to start her car—feeling even that small effort—and shifted into drive, heading out along the winding dirt road that led away from Fir Cove.

———

Arles recognized Manille Garcia's parents as soon as they opened the door of their small brick home. She'd never met them before, nor come across any pictures online, but every one of the parents she'd spoken with looked like this, even a pixilated video feed sufficient to convey it.

All reeling, wide-eyed and blank-faced after an apocalyptic strike, staggering to come to terms with a decimated planet. It was not a state for which Arles possessed an antidote, and she knew she couldn't even begin to understand it. She didn't have children herself, and planned never to have one. But that didn't mean she didn't have something to offer.

The pair led Arles into a low-ceilinged living room, where a plate of cookies and mugs of cooling coffee had been set atop a short-legged table. The Garcias took seats on a couch while Arles paused, breathing slowly and evenly. The brief walk to this spot had taken its toll. Each footfall reverberated in her spine, radiating pain to her middle. She fought to conceal her condition, surreptitiously blotting a dew of sweat from her face. She wasn't entitled to pain. She had survived, unlike Mr. and Mrs. Garcia's daughter.

Most of the parents she'd encountered, if their marriages remained intact, chose to occupy seats at a distance, the tiny dot of camera at the top of a laptop struggling to keep both in view. The Garcias were an anomaly, sitting side by side, hands intertwined as they watched her.

Arles lowered herself creakily into an armchair.

On Zoom, she had found that what worked best—provoked the least amount of anguish—was to speak directly, coming straight out with the facts she was equipped to relay.

"Your daughter was not physically hurt or molested," she said, the low tenor and slow pace of her speech now a boon, a way to give parents

23

time to take in her words. "I realize this doesn't diminish the intolerable loss you are living with, but it may help a little to know there was no pain involved. Manille"—saying the name was key—"spent the last days of her life listening, talking a bit, then being sent into a very deep sleep."

The couple's interlocked fingers whitened. Tears like shards of glass obscured their eyes. They both bowed their heads.

Mr. Garcia raised his first. "Thank you."

Arles looked at him, and he went on.

"We had no idea"—a ragged breath—"what Manille went through. Our minds caused us to think so many terrible things—"

"It is true?" Mrs. Garcia asked Arles, speaking over her husband, but less interrupting him than adding her voice to his in a plea. "This is true? You are sure?"

"Yes," Arles said quietly. "I am. That's what he wanted her for. Nothing else."

Mrs. Garcia rose unsteadily. She made the short crossing to the armchair, stooping to cup Arles's shoulders with such force that Arles felt it down to her wound. But Arles didn't shrink back or flinch. Getting shot had been the cost of providing this sort of closure. And it was worth it. Every pierce of talon, each dimple in what had once been smooth skin. All worth it so that she could deliver pardon from one sentence, because, from the other, there would be no release.

The Zoom sessions used to be draining, but virtual chats were a glass of chardonnay compared to the whiskey shot of live. Arles's mouth felt desert dry, and her limbs were limp. Outside again, she leaned a hip against the driver's seat, then manually lifted her legs until she'd achieved a semblance of sitting.

She hadn't brought her water bottle, she realized sluggishly, gaze traveling to the empty cupholder. Since surgery, she was at risk for dehydration. Stephanie had been amazing, keeping track of all the instructions Arles was given upon being sprung from the hospital, but now Arles needed to take care of herself. Which was how she preferred things, except that Stephanie had managed to provide succor and solace—in addition to fluids—at seemingly no cost.

There are no scales for you and me.

Arles stared blearily through the windshield, sunlight staining her vision. These roads were so tangled that she feared getting lost if she went looking for a gas station or grocery. Besides, sleep was coming for her, as it had during her initial recovery—like a punch to the head. She drove a short distance away from the house, curbed the right front tire in a jagged parking job, jabbed the button to turn off the engine, then fell asleep with the afternoon sun glaring.

When she woke, the car was unbearably hot; she hadn't gotten a chance to crack a window before being slapped unconscious. Sweat slimed her skin from the greenhouse effect and a resurgence of pain. She wasn't sure if she'd be able to drive home. Keep her hands propped up on the steering wheel, move her torso to accommodate turns? Just getting into gear felt impossible.

She used both hands to shift, bracing herself when the mechanism engaged with a *thunk*. Eased her foot up on the brake in minute increments until her body adjusted to the fact that it was in motion. Then a slight depression of the gas pedal, accompanied by gentle— achingly gentle—rotations of the wheel.

She arrived at Fir Cove in a brain-numbed fog, not registering the turn onto her private road until its uneven surface caused the tires to jounce. The switch from asphalt to dirt applied voltage throughout her whole body. Her hands squeezed the wheel, worsening the agony, but relaxing her grip would've made her lose control completely.

She only had to make it a little farther. Here, at elevation, the car would stay an okay temperature if she fell asleep again. Or she could summon the last of her strength, nudge open the door, and lower herself onto the grass for a nap.

Cool and green. Like a lake. Her vision swam.

Sweat stung her eyes so that she finished the trip relying on sense memory, the undulating body of the road beneath the wheels. Blinking, she caught a glimpse of another car—some beetle-y rounded body, too small to be the van Stephanie and Lissa were surely miles away in by now—before concluding that she must be seeing things.

Unable to press hard enough on the brake to come to a full stop, she shifted into park, the SUV rocking on its axles. She felt a brutal shake, heard a metallic clank. An auditory hallucination in addition to the visual one? She bore down on the door handle, pain shrieking in her belly as she managed to open the door, letting in some air. She sagged in the front seat, as useless as a withered balloon.

Then she realized she wasn't alone.

CHAPTER THREE

"Your old therapist?" the little girl repeated.

Kara started to drive, catching the kid's eye in the rearview. "Best one I ever went to—and that's saying something, because I've seen tons."

"Me too," said the kid.

Kara frowned. This kid had described herself as missing, but she'd been given therapy? "She left the hospital where I used to see her, and I couldn't go to her new facility because it's way out in the woods. Which might be okay, except it's for families, and I don't have one."

"Don't have one what?" asked the kid.

"Family. Oh, and also, she got shot. So she might not be seeing patients right now."

A pause from the rear. "Your therapist got shot?"

Kara rotated the wheel, holding on tightly to keep from losing her grip. All of Dr. Shepherd's former patients had been notified about the site where she'd set up a new practice, but Kara had never made the trip there. She hadn't seen Dr. Shepherd in almost six months.

The roads here were nuts even by Wedeskyull standards. Thin as thread, bridging chasms, spiraling around the fat middles of mountains. Though at least the temperature was cooling off now that they'd started to climb.

"Yup," she told the kid. "She survived, though. Even took down the bad guy."

This time the pause lasted longer. "Do you mean she *killed* someone?"

"Uh-huh," Kara said again. "Apparently, he was a serial killer," she added, wondering whether that particular piece of info was age appropriate or necessary. Probably neither.

"Your therapist sounds way cooler than any of mine."

Kara laughed without meaning to. "Hey, why don't you tell me your name?" *And maybe why you turned to me for help.* Was it just because of the scene Kara had read from her book?

The kid shifted, straining against her seat belt, her face set in concrete.

"You could tell me, but then you'd have to kill me?" Kara asked lightly, hoping to restore the mood of a moment ago.

The little girl began to mumble something, but it wasn't an answer as far as Kara could tell. It was a strange look, the kid's lips working, forming words in quick succession but inaudibly; it was completely unclear what they were. The behavior reminded Kara of something, but she couldn't put her finger on what.

"Hey," she said, glancing between the rearview and the windshield as she worked to hold the car steady. "Are you trying to say something?"

The kid continued on, a low rumble filling the car, like the hum of a bee. Kara could feel the vibration all the way up in front. She needed to pull over, but where on a road like this? She looked from side to side until she spotted a sign for a scenic lookout. She swung the car over and turned off the engine.

She still had no idea what to do with a weirdly mumbling kid, though. A weirdly mumbling kid Kara had effectively abducted. Sure, there'd seemed to be a good reason, but the act suddenly struck her as past foolhardy and all the way into reckless. She didn't even like kids! Although she possessed enough insight, courtesy of Dr. Shepherd, to know why she'd done this.

The kid's mouth was still moving, emitting low, imperceptible sounds as she laced her small hands tightly together. It suddenly struck Kara what the whole act looked like. Praying. This little girl was engaged in avid, fervent prayer.

"Stop it," Kara said, before it occurred to her that prohibiting a religious observance wasn't very tolerant of her. If that's what this was. The kid didn't listen anyway—it looked as if she *couldn't* listen. Any minute now, and her eyes were going to roll back in her head like the little girl in *The Exorcist*. Kara unlatched her seat belt, got onto her knees, then hauled herself over the console and into the back. She crawled across the seat to where the little girl sat hunched over, muttering. Kara wrapped her arms around the slight form, feeling the thrum of the utterances in her own body and realizing how long it had been since she'd touched another human being.

"Please cut it out," she said, hearing her voice rise in a disconcerting direction. She sounded like her father. "Cut it out, Maeve. Whatever this is, stop it. Just stop!"

The kid's mumbles switched off like a motor. "Maeve? Who's Maeve?"

Kara was floating, suspended beneath the surface of some body of water, glimpsing the kid from below. Encased in sunlight, a golden shimmer of face, a small outline. Then Kara was swimming up, up, up to reach her. Blinking water out of her eyes, shaking off droplets. She had no idea what to give as an answer, but at least the kid had quit her strange behavior for now.

"Um, well, you know what I do for a living, right?"

The little girl nodded. "You write books."

Kara grabbed it as if reaching for a life buoy. Easier to talk about her career than the reason she'd called this kid *Maeve*. "Right. Which means I have characters who all need names. Well, not all of them; there are exceptions for minor ones, like a cop who appears once. Those are called *tertiary*. But most of the time." She was talking too fast, words careening off each other.

"You mean you made up a name for me? Since I can't tell you mine?"

Kara gave a quick nod. "Do you mind?"

The kid appeared to consider. "I like it more than my real one."

Kara eased the two of them apart and clambered back in front. Her voice when she answered seemed to come from very far away, underwater again. "Good. Because I like it too."

The key felt difficult to turn in the ignition, weighty and resistant. BB pellets of gravel sprayed as she fought to get back on the road, which writhed and corkscrewed beside a vast valley, trees as upright and uniform as an army of soldiers.

She'd gone about a mile when the car appeared behind them.

It was following too close for the conditions. Near-right-angle turns cut the mountain pass down to size and threatened to send a vehicle off the road or leave it clinging by two tires. Kara lifted her eyes to the rearview to get a glimpse of the asshole trying to pass in a Don't-even-think-about-it zone. She had to return her gaze to the road before making out whoever was behind the wheel, but he was driving a real beater of a car. Made her own look fancy.

The driver gunned the gas, drawing close enough that his fender butted her bumper, two bucks tangling their racks. Kara bit back a yelp—she didn't want to scare Maeve—and sped up. But there was another switchback coming, with all those skewering trees yawning below. Stakes to pierce the body of any car that sailed over the low stone barrier.

There wasn't a single place to pull over. Nothing besides this curlicue series of turns.

She had to slow down. She'd wreck the car or worse if she didn't.

She lowered her foot, just a tap of the brake, but it was sufficient enough to cause the other car's bumper to squeal against hers again. Then they were speeding into the turn, hovering over the chasm. Kara put her whole body into it, leaning to one side as her car took the curve, wrestling with the wheel.

From the rear, the kid spoke up dully. "It's him. He's driving a weird car."

The hairs on Kara's body stood on end, prickling her skin like thorns. She snatched a quick look at the back seat before returning her gaze to the road. She hoped the kid wasn't about to start mumbling again.

"Who?" she asked without taking her eyes off the windshield. She couldn't think about the car behind them; let it do its worst. She had to fight to keep from soaring over the barrier, that long stone wall, too low to provide any sort of protection. "Who's after you?"

The little girl didn't answer, but at least there was no inaudible murmuring, either.

Kara's mind rocketed back to her book event. Several of her relatives had been in attendance, but while they were each awful in their different ways, they weren't kidnappers. There'd been the devil guy, plus a few other suspicious-looking dudes. And what about the swarm of people attending that other event? Wasn't that the most likely scenario—that when the kid's captor had been a rapt audience member, Maeve took the opportunity to slip away?

Except she hadn't slipped very far. She'd approached Kara.

The turn was finally easing up, the road straightening out. Kara loosened her fists, sensation tingling back into fingers that had gone numb. Her nails had dug ruts into the rubber of the steering wheel.

The other car surged forward. As it roared around them, four arms thrust themselves like swords through rolled-down windows, four middle fingers jauntily flipping her off. A wolf pack of teenage boys leered, then were gone with a howl of engine and a gasoline gust of fumes.

———

"Whoa," the kid said as Kara completed the drive and a peak of roof appeared. "This is like *Game of Thrones*."

"Fantasy fan?" Kara asked, hearing the sour note creep into her voice. She hated when books that had done better than hers came up in conversation.

Kara would've used different allusions—*Wuthering Heights* crossed with *Walden*—but the kid was right. They'd arrived in a forested paradise, an idyll that looked as if time had passed it by. Or had never applied here at all.

Deserted, Kara realized as she parked in a scythe of gravel that lacked any other cars, then got out to mount a series of stone steps leading to an enormous porch. Like, you could play football on it. She knocked on a tall slab of wood, a front door fit for a giant, but nobody answered. The place had the draping feel of inoccupation. She hoped she hadn't made a mistake coming all the way out here, especially since she couldn't think of one other thing to do.

"Now what?" the kid called, voicing the thought in Kara's mind.

Kara returned to the car. "I guess now we wait."

After divvying up every ounce of sustenance to be found in the glove compartment—a torn-apart bag of stale chips and a candy bar melted to its wrapper—she and the kid dozed on the lawn in shade bequeathed by a sprawling tree until the sound of an engine penetrated the silence. Kara recognized Dr. Shepherd's SUV from the parking lot at the hospital, and a cloud of relief settled over her. She got to her feet. Then she registered how the car was being driven.

Wending and weaving across the private drive, tires crushing grasses to a green mat as the vehicle veered sideways. Now steering straight in the direction of Kara's car.

Kara darted forward, crying out helplessly, "Wait! Hold on, you're going to hit my—"

She felt a small hand squeeze a fold of her shirt, the kid holding Kara back, and halted as the SUV soared by. Inhaling a dragon's breath of exhaust, she spun around to check that Maeve hadn't gotten equally close. The expression on the kid's face was as clear as if it'd been written.

This is who you brought us to for help?

A jarring metal clank severed the peace of the sanctuary as the SUV bumped into Kara's car and finally came to a stop.

CHAPTER FOUR

Arles wasn't sure whether she was inside or outside her car. The barriers between physical places, what was real and what wasn't, felt viscous, insubstantial. She must have slid out, because soft ground cushioned her versus a firm leather seat.

She slumped against a cradle of tree root.

"Water—" The word emerged with a wheeze. Too breathy to be detected.

Detected by whom? She had no idea who these people were. Hopefully, they hadn't come to kill her. If so, they wouldn't have to do much, just wait a little while.

"Water. Right, yes," one of them said. "I don't have any. We went through everything in my car while we were waiting for you."

The words didn't fully make sense, but Arles got the gist. "House—"

"There's no one inside. I knocked. Where's your key?"

"Unlocked—" Arles got out just ahead of the cave-in taking place in her mind.

Some unmarked amount of time later, she was lapping from a silvery brook. How had she made it into the woods? Stream water wasn't safe to drink without a UV wand or iodine tab, no matter how pure it seemed, elven refreshment for woodland creatures. Nonetheless, she drank until her belly strained and her sense of awareness sharpened. This water wasn't trickling into her mouth over a series of mossy rocks—it was being poured from a glass. Who held it?

"Are you okay, Dr. Shepherd?"

A patient, then.

"Am I the only one here?" whoever it was asked. "Do you have anybody scheduled?"

Arles's vision had cleared enough for her to take in the woman looking around sharply, her eyes narrowed against the sun, head turning back and forth. She looked familiar, but Arles couldn't place her from a Santa-length list of former clients.

Arles mustered the strength to reply. "I'm not seeing clients these days. Did you think I referred you out but kept others on?"

"I have low self-esteem," said the woman. "You're the one who helped me realize that."

It key-in-a-lock clicked. This was Kara Parsons. An author who wrote under a pseudonym, *Kara Cross*, in an act of alliteration and revolt, a spurning of her father's surname.

"Does anybody else live here?" Kara asked, still snatching peeks at the slope of lawn.

"Just me," said Arles. All this space for one person. "A woman and her daughter occupy one of the cabins"—she gestured in the general direction—"but they're not here right now."

Kara had been maintaining a tense, alert position, like an animal squatting on its haunches, but at that, she sank down onto the grass.

Arles drained the rest of the water. "I don't want to add to the aforementioned self-esteem issues by seeming rejecting, but can you tell me why you've come to my house?"

Kara's mouth lifted in a smile. "I've missed you, Dr. Shepherd."

"Thanks," said Arles. "But I assume that isn't the reason."

Kara raised one arm and curled a beckoning finger. Arles frowned, following the gesture.

A child walked out from behind a clump of trees.

She was wood sprite–tiny with a floss of blond hair, dressed in a way that bespoke wealth. The setting she'd emerged from aside, this girl clearly hadn't been residing in a forest like Victor of Aveyron. And it

34

wasn't just her clothes that were expensive—upon examination, Arles noticed nails manicured a precious pink and buttery hair blown out in sculpted waves.

She wasn't from Wedeskyull. Arles would've bet Fir Cove on it.

"Who's this?" she asked, her tone assuming a practiced ease.

"Call her Maeve," Kara responded, a little too fast.

Not *Her name's Maeve*, or *This is Maeve*. Kara's reply tugged a string of recollection, but most of Arles's mind was still a slurry, and she couldn't dredge up the name's significance from her mental pile of notes.

"She was in the audience at Books & Brew today," Kara said. "I have a new novel out."

"Congratulations," said Arles.

Kara flapped an impatient hand. Arles remembered this too now—how get-to-the-point Kara's sessions had been, not a second wasted.

"And then, during the signing portion," Kara went on, "she came up to me and said she'd been kidnapped."

Arles had lived a life that meant very little threw her, but with that statement, Kara joined the ranks of the few.

"Actually, she didn't tell me. She wrote it. In a copy of my book," Kara concluded.

"In a copy of your book, this child wrote that she'd been kidnapped." When unsure how to react, a therapist should reflect, which amounted to more or less repeating whatever a patient said. It was a basic tool, grad-school stuff. A blunt-force hammer as opposed to a fine chisel.

"Right," Kara said, looking relieved. "Exactly."

Reflection. Worked every time.

The child stood above them, scrubbing the ground with the tread of one fuchsia Puma.

Arles felt strong enough to get to her feet. "Why don't we all go inside?"

Kara and the child trooped toward the house while Arles trailed at a measured pace. When she reached the throat of the driveway, she paused. The hood of her SUV all but obscured Kara's smaller, aging hatchback.

"Shit," Arles murmured. Then louder: "Did I hit your car?"

"Kinda," Kara replied, already on the porch steps.

"I'm really sorry," Arles told her.

"Figure out what to do about Maeve, and I'm prepared to call it even."

———

By then, it was nearing dinnertime, and the child appeared ravenous, a fiery look in her eyes and tense stance that Arles had grown familiar with during Lissa's stint at Fir Cove. Before her departure, Stephanie had laid in enough prepared meals and frozen options that even someone as helpless in the kitchen as Arles was able to put a meal together, which she started to set out on the screened-in deck until Kara stopped her with a look at the mesh walls. Arles took a beat to register the myriad spots from which someone would be able to observe. Her mind, still working sluggishly. She was off her game, months of recuperation dulling her usual prescience bordering on paranoia. She retrieved the plates, forks, and glasses and returned them to the kitchen, waiting to speak until both guests were done exclaiming over the meal. She herself was used to Stephanie's prowess as a chef.

"So, you came to me instead of alerting the police," Arles said.

Kara's eyes widened in alarm.

Arles lifted a reassuring hand. "Which one usually does in the case of a kidnapping, except that you have reasons not to. If I'm recalling your history correctly."

Kara gave two fast jerks of her head.

"Can I have another drumstick?" asked the girl.

Arles slid the pan across the table.

"Really?" the child asked.

"Sure, why not? There's plenty," Arles replied. Stephanie fed people as if they were all adolescents during a growth spurt.

"Yeah, but the calories," the girl said.

Arles smoothed out the frown she felt take hold of her face. "Is that something that worries you?"

"It doesn't worry *me*," the girl replied, tearing a piece of meat off the bone with teeth that looked a tad sparkly-white, even for a child.

The polished nails, styled hair, bleached teeth. And who had raised the specter of calories? Arles watched the child chew, pushing her own food around while taking a mental X-ray. Building a picture of this girl's psychic skeleton. But the child wasn't here for therapy, and Arles was participating in something not only illegal but unethical, which was arguably worse for a psychologist. Definitely for Arles.

"Our current police chief is nothing like the old one," she told Kara.

Kara had been licking sauce off her fingers; at that moment she chomped down hard and winced.

"Tim Lurcquer is someone we can turn to for help." Arles used his first name for additional reassurance, a friend, at least in the collegial sense. There was no choice in this matter, and Kara had to know that, but taking away her sense of control was not something Arles would be willing to do unless forced.

"If you do, then he'll find me," the girl said flatly. "And I'll never get another chance to get away." A ring of barbecue sauce around her mouth gave her the appearance of a clown.

Shivers ran like insect legs over Arles's skin. "Do you mean your kidnapper?" A rookie mistake, the leading question of a psych intern, not a therapist as experienced as Arles. She was thrown by this whole situation, not one she'd had occasion to practice during clinical rotations.

The child frowned at her. "I didn't say *kidnapped*. I said *missing*."

"Oh, right," Kara said. "That's what she wrote. Missing."

An author should be more exacting with words, Arles thought tartly.

She couldn't continue to harbor this child, but she lacked enough information to be sure that even a police chief with as much integrity as Tim wouldn't do more harm than good. *First, do no harm.* Psychologists should borrow the credo.

"Missing," Arles repeated. "Can you say more about that?"

No response.

"Maeve? Is that what we're supposed to call you? Can you say more?"

She looked up from the remains of her meal. "How'd you know it's not my real name?"

Because that name means something to Kara, Arles thought. Throughout her life, Arles had lost things to sunken-in portions of her mind—time, memories, sensations—but this wasn't that. This was simply the overflowing caseload of a clinician at a rural community mental health center. Too many people, problems, lives, for even the most prodigious brain to store. She took in a breath, letting her mind roam freely instead of forcing it, and the connection was made. Pater Parsons, locked up at Dannemora for one of the most horrific crimes Wedeskyull had ever seen.

"Don't push her on this, Dr. Shepherd," Kara said with real alarm in her voice.

Arles looked in her direction.

"She'll start acting all weird if you ask her to tell you her name," Kara explained.

"Weird," Arles repeated.

"Like, mumbling and stuff. Maybe praying?"

"Mumbling and maybe praying instead of sharing her name." Back to reflection.

"I *can't* tell you," the girl said. Her head hung low. "I can't tell anyone. I'm not allowed."

Arles took a mental note. "Okay, then, Maeve, in what way are you missing?"

Silence.

Arles tried a different angle. "Who are you missing from?"

The girl stood up, coming to wrap two sauce-slicked hands around the spokes of Arles's chair. She'd moved so fast that Arles hadn't had a chance to rise. The child positioned herself so that the two of them stared straight into each other's eyes. Her words tolled a more chilling note, a reverberation that shot throughout Arles's whole body, than any answer she might've supplied.

"No one would tell me."

CHAPTER FIVE

Kara began talking then, a rushing stream of information that encompassed homelessness in their community, the meth crisis, and the *devil*, of all things, before she veered in an entirely different direction, mentioning some big event also taking place at the bookstore that day.

"Whoa," Arles said with a glance in the girl's direction. "I tend to talk pretty real around children, but I think you've got me beat, Kara."

"Oh, shit, my bad," Kara said, then paused. "Swearing is probably off-limits too, right?"

Arles was glad to see the child's lips upturn in a semblance of a smile. "Hey, Maeve?"

"Yeah?"

"Would you mind clearing the table while Kara and I talk?"

"I don't know how," she said.

Arles didn't get the feeling this child was being obstructionist or deliberately obtuse. "To clear a table?" The pricey clothes, hair, nails, and teeth. A lack of familiarity with chores.

The girl took a look around. "Do I just, like, bring the plates over to the sink?"

"And the glasses and forks and leftovers too," Arles replied warily, wondering if she were being made fun of. "The food can go in the fridge. With those covers on top." She pointed.

"Oh, okay," the girl said, and got to work.

Arles led Kara into the parlor. It was the room where group had been held, back when Fir Cove served briefly as a therapeutic enclave for families. Four months slash a lifetime ago.

Kara let out a low whistle. "You never told me you were rich."

Arles was beginning to recall Kara's bluntness, the way she came out and said things most other people only thought. "Sort of. My great-greats were. Or great-great-greats."

"Whatever," Kara said. "Now you get to be queen of the fucking castle."

Arles took a seat on a plush embroidered chair, indicating that Kara should do the same. "Tell me about this other event at Books & Brew. It was going on at the same time as yours?"

Kara nodded. "Which is why I can't tell you much about it—I was focused on my own thing. But whoever was appearing attracted a crowd. Made my audience look like a group of stragglers who wandered in off the street."

Arles now also recalled the way a vein of bitterness ran through Kara—a rich, dark rivulet that permeated the woman's perceptions about the world and her place in it. "Well, we can figure it out easily enough. *Easily* meaning one of us drives to where there's signal."

Kara took a look around, her expression growing uneasy. "No Wi-Fi? I tried to get on a network while we were waiting for you, but nothing came up."

Arles nodded, confirming. "I'm off the grid."

Kara's features assumed a look of faint mockery. "Briar Rose in her castle."

Engaging in banter had helped Kara open up back when she'd been a patient. "She's my second-least-favorite princess."

"Who's the first?"

"Ariel," Arles replied. "Neither of them talk, but—"

"That fucking mermaid volunteered it," said Kara.

Arles laughed. "Does Maeve have a phone? Just what's stored would be informative. Contacts, pictures, downloads, search history."

Kara sat tensely, perched on her chair. "I didn't ask. I just saw her in my car and bolted."

It was a response so impetuous, so out of societal bounds, that if anybody else had confessed to it, Arles would've questioned their mental status. Coming from Kara, though, the behavior almost made sense.

"How old are kids these days when they're allowed to get phones?" Kara asked.

"Young," Arles replied. "And I suspect even younger in this child's case."

Kara looked a question at her.

"She appears to come from privilege. The latest upgrade wouldn't be a major purchase."

"Yeah," Kara said, the one word a grunt. "I noticed that. Do you have a guess as to her age?"

Every minute that ticked by added to the distance between this child and the help she needed. "A precocious ten or slightly delayed thirteen. I'm going to go with eleven," Arles said.

The girl had come walking into the parlor, picking up objects on an antique sideboard before setting them down again in different spots. She gave a satisfied nod.

Arles had guessed correctly. "Food all put away?"

"I forgot that part," the child said.

Arles let it go. "Different question, then. Do you have a phone?"

Her parents might be identifiable from pictures, or listed in her contacts. Unless her parents were the ones she was missing from. Who forbade this child to reveal her name?

The girl shook her head. "My dad won't let me."

The *my* spoken automatically, a casual presumption of relationship.

Was he the one who took the girl? Earlier, she had referred to a *he—he'll find me—*and domestic kidnappings were the most common variety. Often by controlling fathers.

The parlor lay in shadows. Arles needed to turn on some lights, drive out the specter summoned by whatever situation had caused this child to seek help from a total stranger.

But the girl went on before Arles could stand up.

"One time my mom agreed to get me one, and my dad went ballistic, wouldn't talk to her for a week. He smashed the phone to pieces, flushed them down the toilet in her bathroom. They had to have the plumbing ripped out."

One couple, two bathrooms, was Arles's first thought.

Before the obvious reaction, which Kara voiced. "K, so your dad is clearly nuts."

The girl seemed to take Kara's inexpert—if accurate—assessment in stride. "Totally."

"Did you run away?" Kara asked. "Is that what you meant by *missing?*"

The child's expression transformed. "No way!" She shook her head in a wild spasm. "That would never work. And I couldn't leave my dad. Even though he's what you said."

Arles rose to her feet, crossing to flick on two table lamps in a brisk, enough-is-enough manner. There was complexity in the hazy landscape of this child's family situation, a sufficient enough amount that neither Arles nor Kara had any chance of sorting it out. And even if they could have, they possessed no authority. Although Arles rarely did this, especially when it came to children, she was going to have to lie. "I have an idea. It doesn't involve the police, don't worry."

Tim could do his thing at the barracks, set parts in motion, while Arles returned with a nice, unofficial-looking CPS worker, no uniform or holster or tricked-out car to set Kara and the girl's alarms blaring.

Kara trailed Arles to the front door.

"Signal cuts in at Brick Road," Arles told her. "I'll be back as soon as I can."

Night was falling outside, the sky navy and splattered with stars. A chill in the August air; Arles ducked back to grab her jacket from a hook on the wall. Then she shut the door behind her, taking the stone steps off the porch at a faster pace than she'd moved in some time.

Meeting someone young and in need had instigated more bodily healing than months of rest. Which didn't surprise Arles. She'd become a child psychologist for a reason.

It wasn't until she reached the throat of gravel in front of the house that she was reminded of the condition of her car.

CHAPTER SIX

Maeve wasn't in the kitchen, but the food had all been left out on the table, and Kara huffed an exasperated breath. Kids were so lazy. She remembered this from trying to get her sister to help around the house. Both of them had been parentified children, as Kara had learned from Dr. Shepherd, but since her sister was younger, Kara took on an overlarge share of the inappropriate roles. Resentment still simmered inside her, banked like a coal, at least until she thought of her sister's fate. Then guilt would toss a handful of cold, dead ash over the flames.

Kara replaced covers on storage containers with firm clicks that sounded like tsks of the tongue, stacking them in a refrigerator big enough to fit three regular fridges inside it.

Maeve wasn't in the room where Kara and Dr. Shepherd had spoken. Kara began checking elsewhere on the first floor. There were multiple corners made murky by shadows, resistant to the few lights she found to turn on, in addition to hulking pieces of furniture, any of which could've obscured a small form. But Kara couldn't bring herself to look too closely, duck down low. It wasn't as if Maeve would be playing hide-and-seek, and there was a haunted quality to this hunt that kept Kara from straying too deep into hidey-holes.

She had grown up in a double-wide that sat on its own plot of land, not in a trailer park. Acres and acres at the base of a mountain. She was used to large swaths outdoors and cramped spaces within. By contrast, just crossing the length of Dr. Shepherd's kitchen required two trips, the second to double back and bypass an enclosed pantry. At the end of that leg was a door. Kara forced herself to flip up an eye hook, unlatching the door, then pulled on a loop of string attached to a bare bulb. The string swung slowly back and forth like a hangman's noose above a flight of crooked steps leading to a basement.

She shut the door, relocking it for good measure. No way was she going down there, and there was no need to anyway. What kind of kid voluntarily went into a creepy-ass basement?

Maybe it wasn't voluntary.

Voices spoke inside Kara's head all the time—it was how she came up with her best plot points—but this wasn't a mystery novel. There would be no creaking joists, unexplained banging, or sibilant rushes of wind that sounded like breaths. Those were devices, and clichéd ones at that, although Kara relied on them to up the creep factor in her books.

Still, now that she was in a real-life spooky mansion, it came as a surprise to find herself surrounded by silence, a mummifying wrap. The quiet made things all the more frightening—she'd have to remember this when she wrote her next book. Why couldn't she hear Maeve? How would the kid not be making any sounds? Footsteps, doors opening or closing, one of the heavy pieces of furniture accidentally bumped. Kara called the kid's name—*Fake name*, corrected the voice, *the one you gave her*—and her cry shattered the stillness like a pane of glass.

But no reply came.

Standing in the hall, Kara swiveled slowly, feeling a presence, a disturbance in the molecules of air. "Maeve?"

For a moment, a laughing little girl seemed to stand there. *Tricked ya!*

Kara gave her head a hard, painful jerk. Whose voice was that this time? Not her inner supplier of plot twists, and Maeve wouldn't talk like that, either, so taunting. Kara's little sister had been a real tease, as their father used to say. But this kid that Kara had saved was more solemn. Probably because she was *missing*. Although her disappearance now in this house called her sudden advent in Kara's life into question. Maybe she had a habit of vanishing.

Or maybe the person she was so scared of had gotten inside and grabbed her. Without Kara even realizing it, so intent had she been on trying to catch hold of filaments in her mind.

Toward the rear of the house was a room Kara hadn't checked yet. She placed one hand on a tortoiseshell doorknob—everything in this place was built for the ages—and rotated it.

"Maeve?" she called, not liking the wavery quality of her voice. "Are you in here?"

She located a switch on the wall, feeling around gingerly, as if the plaster might be covered with spiders. The answering light cast dull illumination, just enough to highlight a mass of enormous boxes, higher than Kara's head. Dr. Shepherd—or perhaps her forebears, people long dead—had packed up their possessions and stored them in this extra room. If Maeve were having fun with Kara, playing a game, then a cornfield maze of cartons was the perfect site for it.

Kara took a few steps toward the rows as if she were sleepwalking.

"Maeve?" An eerie silence had settled, along with veils of dust motes brought to life by Kara's movements, glinting in the lights she'd turned on.

"Kara!" a little girl sang out. "Over here! I'm here!"

But that had to be wrong. Maeve hadn't yet called Kara by name. Nonetheless, Kara followed the singsong notes, as if a puppeteer controlled her.

She entered the collection of cartons, like being swallowed up in a fun house. The scant light proffered by the old-fashioned sconces was damped within the tunnel of boxes, and Kara could no longer hear the little girl, not the soft slide of a body brushing against cardboard, nor any voice. All was quiet for a while as Kara shuffled forward, making her way through canyons between the boxes.

Then someone demanded: "Look for me! I'm here!"

Kara whirled around so fast that she smacked a towering carton. It must've contained only light objects, for it teetered and pitched, then fell, striking the floor with a harsh *whap*.

"Maeve!" Kara cried out in alarm, picturing the carton as bigger than it really was—storage for a giant and impossibly heavy, holding on to a ghastly weight. If it had struck the little girl, she'd be crushed beneath it. Buried.

A light, lilting giggle arose from deeper inside the nest of boxes.

Kara turned in the direction of the sound.

The maze grew darker as she got farther from the light fixture at the front of the room, and she had to use her hands as a guide. Both arms stretched out to either side, palms planted against the cardboard walls that had become either her shelter or her prison.

Another tinkling series of laughs, like drops in a goblet.

"Maeve?"

The laughter stopped. Cut off abruptly.

Porcupine quills stood out all over Kara's skin. The cartons were even taller here and had not been sealed. Their flaps looked like wings overhead, great soaring birds of prey. Kara hunched over, protecting herself in case one of them dove, while navigating the remaining aisles. She was approaching a dead end, one final box hemming her in.

This was where Maeve would be, hunkered down, concealing herself.

Kara walked in a slow succession of steps, drumlike, pulsing. Five boxes before the end. Then four, three, two, one. Her heart pounding as if she were sprinting when in reality she moved with a steady, metronomic beat, squinting to make out the last portion of her enclosure. She had no choice but to come to a stop. Panting, shoulders heaving, she stood with one hand clapped to her chest. There was nobody there.

Had there ever been? Or had she imagined that laughter, those calls, just echoes from deep within her past? Brought forth by seeing her therapist again, or perhaps because a little girl had been placed in her care, given to Kara for safekeeping. Kara had done one thing right—told Dr. Shepherd not to go to the police—and now she was all out of game.

Thrusting out her arms, she pushed at the box that blocked her, and unlike the one that had toppled over, this wasn't filled with anything light. She had to really shove, put her whole body into it, like a linebacker. The carton started moving by inches, in tiny increments, shushing against the wooden floorboards and catching when one was uneven.

At last, she had shifted it enough to allow a gap into which she wedged her body.

Wriggling first one way, then the other, she was finally free.

She raced toward the entrance to the room, slamming the door shut behind her. She had to pause and fling one hand out for balance, closing her eyes against a feeling of wooziness, as if she'd been hanging upside down. After a minute, she blinked, taking in the shadowed hall.

She stood before a massive staircase, each step so wide that three people could've mounted the flight side by side. She had just started to climb when suddenly, she yanked back her foot.

Something was moving around upstairs, this time for real.

She heard a rushing sound, then a series of metallic clanks, just like in one of her books. But instead of dashing up to the second floor to determine the nature of the disturbance, as her sleuth would've done, Kara sank into a crouch. Arms wrapped around her knees, chin tucked to her chest, eyes clamped shut so she didn't have to see. Even with her hands clapped against her ears, she was unable to block out the noises.

Sounds that weren't the tics of an old house but horrifyingly human. Groans as if someone were in terrible pain, or experiencing a hideous sort of pleasure. This—whatever it was—could not end well for the kid anymore. Not with something that disgusting going on upstairs. But whatever role Kara had tried to play was sapped. She hung her head while her body went still. She knew she should go up and locate Maeve—pure evil had to account for those groans—but Kara couldn't budge from this spot.

Overhead, still sloshing. A terrible sound, a liquid gush, the slide of fluids, which kept going on and on and on, from up above and also inside Kara's brain, until at last she opened her mouth and let out a high, shrill scream.

CHAPTER SEVEN

First, Arles made sure the ignition of her SUV still fired, then she climbed back out. Using the flashlight on her phone, she circled the pair of vehicles, kneeling down and taking a peek beneath the chassis before concluding there was no way hers could be freed without doing severe damage to Kara's, possibly hobbling it completely. The bigger car had come to a rest partially atop the hatchback, mounting it like a lion did his mate. The configuration might've looked comical if it hadn't spelled so much trouble.

Eleven miles to Brick Road along a stretch of blacktop as twisted as a skein of yarn. Too far to walk, especially in the dark. But this child couldn't be sheltered here overnight. Arles would be a criminal herself at that point, no matter which one the girl might have fled.

It was too bad Arles had severed things with Dan. Permanently, like a scalpel removing an organ. In the short time they'd been together before she'd gotten shot, he'd had a way of showing up when help was needed, in addition to possessing a few other great traits.

Put like that, it almost seemed as if there'd been no reason to break up with the guy.

Aside from the fact that Arles had never made a personal relationship work, romantic or otherwise.

Her mind continued to roam and amble until she reached down and pinched her arm through the fabric of her jacket. Not a hard pinch. Just an old habit for kicking herself into gear.

Gear. Biking had been part of her PT, and it would get her to Brick Road.

She'd only ridden on a stationary bike, however. With Stephanie and Lissa nearby in case Arles, say, fell off. She could already feel the lumps and bumps in the road jarring her body. Although at the moment she felt fairly okay. Also, there was no other option.

She retraced her steps across the porch to the house to fetch her helmet and headlamp, then halted abruptly on the doorsill, a huge slab hewn from a log.

Save for the handful of reliably warm weeks in the Adirondacks— late June, July, and early August—the interior of Fir Cove was sealed off like a cave, sounds muted thanks to walls built of muffling materials and heavy drapes at the windows. So it wasn't until Arles had gotten the soaring front door open in a sequence of slow nudges to protect her recently resected insides that she was greeted by screams.

She didn't take time to tug the cords on lamps even though the front hall lay in darkness, just ran in the direction of the pitiful cries. At the foot of the stairs, Kara hunched over, sobbing on the floor like a child. Initiating any sort of touch with a client was typically off-limits, but this wasn't therapy, and during her months of rehab and recovery, Arles had been forced to grow more comfortable with physical contact. She bent down to pat the rounded shell of Kara's back.

Kara jumped as if receiving an electric shock.

"Dr. Shepherd!" she shrieked. "Somebody's got Maeve!"

"What?" Arles was already straightening. "Where?"

No vehicle had arrived while Arles had been investigating the condition of her car. Whomever Kara meant either left their means of transportation somewhere along Fir Cove's private road—to camouflage their presence, to be able to sneak inside—or else had come on foot, which would entail serious woodsman skills. The grounds of Fir Cove consisted of mostly untouched wilderness bordering state land.

"Upstairs!" Kara began to take a look before instantly dropping her head. "I heard them!"

Arles could now recollect the reasons Kara had for not going up there herself. The woman had overcome substantial internal barriers today just by bringing the child here.

Spine rigid with fury—this was her home that was being invaded—Arles took the stairs as fast as she could, dashing toward a thin trickle of light spilling out from underneath the door of one of the guest baths. She traveled quicker than she had in months, this child delivering a more potent numbing than any drug Arles had been given in the hospital.

Her heart tolled a hard, painful beat as she covered the length of hall, no idea what she was going to find when she opened the door, simply lunging at it. Taking no time to scruple over the modesty customarily required in a room such as this—

Arles bucked to a stop. Averted her gaze, walking a little way back down the hall.

"Kara!" she called out loudly to penetrate the woman's distress. "It's okay! Come up here!" She turned around, retracing her steps.

The bathroom was fragrant and steamy, a clawfoot tub filled to its brim with bubbles. Beneath the foam lounged the girl, nothing visible besides her dreamily shut eyes and the tip of her nose. Kara arrived at Arles's side, and they stood in the doorway together.

"Maeve?" Kara whispered.

The child jolted in the bath, sending up a wave of petal-scented suds while her eyes flashed open. "My hair! I didn't mean to get it wet!"

Kara was still talking, largely to herself, as if putting pieces together. "The sloshing. It was water. And these pipes are old. They clang. But that doesn't explain . . ."

She went quiet for so long that Arles said, "Doesn't explain what?" Her reply iced Arles's insides.

"That *groaning*."

Just then the child slid back down under the cap of bubbles with a spa-day, get-away-from-it-all moan of pleasure that struck Arles as performative. Not a childlike sound.

"That clear things up any?" Arles asked.

Kara's voice was tremulous as she raised it to get the girl's attention. "Were you all alone up here, Maeve? Have you been up here all along?"

"Uh-huh," the girl said, her voice hollow and echoey from beneath the rim of the tub. "I wanted to take a bath."

"You wanted to take a bath," Kara repeated. "In a strange house that doesn't belong to you. Sure, why not?"

Arles didn't disagree with the sentiment. This child displayed a sense of fit and entitlement, as if she'd be comfortable at Buckingham Palace. Arles herself didn't feel this at home at Fir Cove, a familial property passed down matrilineally in a region riven by class division and strife. She experienced a degree of guilt living here, whereas when the girl popped up, hair slicking her head like a cap, tendrils sticking to her back, she looked around with an expression of disdain.

"This isn't as deep as my one at home. And I've never felt such scratchy towels." She pointed to a length of terry cloth draped over a chair, ready for when she made her watery egress.

"Well," Arles said, suppressing a flicker of a grin. Rude children normally irked her, but this one's uncertain plight called for some indulgence. "I'm sorry the accommodations don't suit."

Kara turned toward her. "Did you do whatever it was you figured out, Dr. Shepherd? Time got a little funny for me down there—" She waved in the direction of the hallway. "But aren't you back kind of fast?"

"Our cars," Arles reminded her. "We're going to need a tow. I might be able to ride my bike, though."

Kara flapped a hand again; this time the gesture looked impatient. "Stay put, Maeve. Enjoy your you time." Relief seemed to have restored the woman's habitual snark. She led the way down the stairs, speaking over her shoulder. "I just got the third portion of my advance, and my car is beat to shit anyhow. Hell, if my book does well, I'll buy us *both* new cars, as thanks for saving Maeve. No police, right? You said you remember why."

"I do," Arles replied over a thrum of tension in her throat.

She detested deceit, especially where children were concerned. But she wasn't going to argue or try to convince Kara of something that would only terrify the woman. Arles had resurrected the details of the crime that had sent Kara's father to prison for life, and indeed, the authorities had failed miserably in that instance. But there was no better alternative.

The two of them went outside, Kara rattling her keys in one hand.

"I had time to study this while you were dead on your lawn," she told Arles. "If we both shift into reverse, I think you can get off my bumper or I can get out from under yours. And I'm pretty sure that hulking thing you drive will still be operational."

They climbed into their cars and ignited the engines, Kara's sputtering and wheezing before evening out.

Then, with a grinding *scritch* of metal that Arles felt in her teeth and her ears, her SUV was free, and she was speeding down the road that led away from Fir Cove, taking its curves and coils too fast so she could do what should've been done the instant Kara had encountered the child.

CHAPTER EIGHT

Signal cut in at Brick Road. Arles drove over the speed limit through dense forest that had been pummeled into submission where blacktop was laid. The twinges and twangs in her midriff stayed at the sparrows-pecking-at-seeds level rather than raptors-tearing-meat-apart-with-their-beaks. Parking along a narrow rim of dirt shoulder, she swiped her phone to life.

Three bars pulsed like a beacon.

But the chief's number went straight to voice mail. Arles asked for a callback without leaving much in the way of explanation. The situation was too muddy, too uncertain to offer any details. That meant 911 instead, although being routed through the state police would require relying on LEOs likely less capable and trustworthy than she knew Tim Lurcquer to be.

She was about to place the emergency call anyway when something about her phone, motionless in her hand, its screen as dark as a stone, caused a stitch right where she'd been shot.

Something was missing. Or hadn't happened that should've.

Her mind creaked, trying to figure it out. Arles hadn't practiced in months, but when she'd been employed at Wedeskyull Community Hospital, emergencies concerning children occurred regularly. Arles was familiar with the systems and mechanisms for dealing with such.

The second she'd gotten within range, her phone should've woken up on its own, vibrating like a trapped wasp. She stared down at the reflective pool of her screen again, black and still. Why no Amber Alert?

It was the inevitable step when terrified parents summoned help in a situation like this.

Arles began calling up sites, hyperlocal to national to global, until reaching a point of absurdity, as if Interpol would've been alerted. But time was of the essence when it came to child abductions, everyone knew that, and Arles couldn't find one mention of a girl going missing near Wedeskyull or anywhere close.

She dialed Tim a second time. Voice mail.

He was probably busy working this case.

You're telling me you've got her? he would bark once Arles finally reached him.

Then why no Amber, not a single story hastily bolted together by media starved for content because this region's last murder was the one Arles committed herself four months ago?

Arles opened her contacts, finding Dorothy's direct line. She was the dispatcher at the barracks and the ex-wife of the former police chief. Arles had known her forever; the chief had been lifelong friends with Arles's stepfather. Best buds, the two. Thick as thieves.

"He's out on a call," Dorothy said when Arles asked for Tim.

"Oh, thank God," Arles replied. Relief suffused her, melting her bones. "I'm calling about the same thing."

"Makes sense," Dorothy said in her terse way.

At times, she could get all the way to gruff, but she was a woman possessed of deep integrity. Her world had been toppled when her husband lost his standing; yet she faced up to what he'd done, making curt apology for the blinders she had worn. So the dispatcher's grunted response didn't faze Arles. She was stuck on figuring out what about this made sense to her.

"You treat the wife?" Dorothy went on abruptly. "Who called in the domestic?"

Relief was replaced by a sudden shock of cold.

Tim was working a domestic complaint. Not a child abduction.

Arles parted her lips, about to correct Dorothy, then brought them together again.

Because what if this constituted a pair of hands pulling Arles back from the brink of doing what Kara had tried to prevent? As soon as Arles presented this child to police, they would determine who her parents were and in all likelihood hand her over, unless they could be certain the parents presented a danger. But this child clearly came from privilege; her parents would be persuasive and have resources available to them. Tim, the staties, whichever arm of law enforcement got involved, would have to adhere to regulations. There would be no further choice in the matter, none of the wiggle room Arles now had to ensure a good outcome. And how many children fell not through cracks in the system but into big, gaping holes?

Kara's younger sister being one.

If you do, then he'll find me. And I'll never get another chance to get away.

Who was the *he* in that sentence? A parent? Somebody the girl's parents knew? Perhaps even someone connected to the police?

"I have to go," Arles said, and ended the call.

The woods all around looked lush and creeping, eating hungrily in their most verdant season. They seemed to have grown in the short time Arles had been parked here. If she stayed any longer, trees would envelop the SUV. Suffocate and bury her.

She shifted into gear with a hard thrust.

She would drive to Books & Brew. Where all of this had started.

———

The bookstore was locked up tight, which presented its own reason for bafflement. The lights should've been turned on, doors left open, people kept behind for questioning. But instead, this was just a shop, ye olde shoppe, closed for the night. Nope, nothing wrong here, as the cereal professor said in *Cujo*. A disturbing tranquility since a child had disappeared from this very spot.

Arles aimed the flashlight on her phone to examine two posters plastered to the front window. A smaller one with Kara's headshot and book cover on it, the date and time of her talk, then a large version depicting an actor Arles kinda, sorta recognized against a backdrop of wilderness, the shot clearly faked. There were no wolves in Wedeskyull, nor snow on summer peaks. Arles googled the guy, scanning as pages downloaded.

A hand clasped her shoulder from behind, and Arles went very still.

"You a fan?" asked the person who had her cornered.

The voice spoke almost too softly for her to make out the words.

Male. And tall, the sound coming from several inches above her head.

Arles swiveled slowly. The man didn't let go of her, simply lowered his hand till he had her by the wrist. She'd been right about his height. He had a crown of lush black hair culminating in an inverted peak on his forehead. She scanned for any weapon he might be holding in his free hand, then looked upward. His eyes would reveal what her next move should be, and in this man's gaze, Arles detected a fierce ardor, as if he were starving.

"Love him," she ventured.

"Right?" he said, letting go. "He doesn't get what he deserves. Not even close."

"Sucks," Arles said, taking a step in the direction of her car.

The man leaned forward, as if seeking a confidence. "Did you see the little girl?"

She halted. *The* little girl. Not *my* or even *a*. Of course, he could've meant someone else; the child who had landed on Arles's lawn today wasn't the only one in the world. From the looks of that big, snazzy poster in the window, all the chairs still set up visible through the glass, there had been a lot of people at the bookstore earlier today.

Arles chose to hedge. "I'm not sure. Who do you mean?"

The man closed the distance Arles had managed to put between them. His eyes were leaking tears; his nose had reddened at the tip.

"I did," he said, almost panting. "I saw her and every single other person there." He tapped the side of his head with a praying-mantis finger, lengthy with articulated joints. "I have to protect Mr. Stratton. Make sure his appearances go smoothly."

This guy didn't seem like the bodyguard type.

She had no choice but to call 911 now. The staties could get two for the price of one. Crazed fan, missing child. Just possibly both would turn out to be connected. Low by her side, arm hanging down, Arles tilted her phone to bring it to life.

Suddenly, the man canted himself forward, a swaying, unbalanced move, and she reared away from him. He was looking beyond her— staring down from his great height—while holding up a long, skewering finger as if signaling someone to wait. Arles half twisted, keeping an eye on him while assessing who might be there. Nobody, as far as she could tell.

The man settled back on the flats of his feet. "She was cute, right?"

His oddly pleasant tone sent a queasy swell through Arles's stomach.

"Really adorable," he went on.

The only kind of patient Arles refused to treat was men who spoke, looked, and acted unnaturally interested in children. The dark sky pressed down overhead like a suffocating canopy. Branches hooked sharp tips in her direction even though the woods lay yards away.

Then the man's voice dipped. "But that doesn't mean I didn't tell on her."

Tell what? This man was clearly too unstable to be interviewed in an uncontrolled setting. If he'd shown up at the hospital, Arles would've ordered a psych eval, stat.

She might be able to locate the phone icon on her screen without looking, but she would never find the right sequence of numbers to hit. The man tracked her motion, and rage suffused his face, turning it plummy and somehow viscous, like jam.

"You going to call the cops?" he said, his tone a taunt, a *dare ya* instead of the sickly-sweet slide of earlier. "Go right ahead. I'm friends with the cops. I tell them all the things they need to do to keep Mr. Stratton safe."

He pitched forward, and she stepped back abruptly, feeling it in her belly when she came down hard. The man glared at her, a furious stare that caused adrenaline to fizz inside her.

"You don't know him at all," he said with wounded surprise. "Do you?"

Arles looked down at her phone. Emergency services took forever to arrive this far outside town, and it wasn't as if she were going to try to keep this guy hanging around. But it didn't matter anyway. Before she could call up the keypad on her screen, the man had turned and raced off into the woods. She snapped pictures of him from behind as he ran.

———

She backed away toward her car, tracking the man's trajectory to make sure he didn't return. With one hand behind her, she opened the door, then sealed herself inside and engaged the locks. Was the fan the girl's father? Psychologists knew better than to rule anything out. Even if he wasn't a relation, he still might've encountered the child in the crowd—*I saw every single person there*—and frightened her as he'd just done Arles.

That wouldn't give the girl reason to flee with a total stranger, however.

Who else had been in that crowd? People from Away, outsiders, so-called flatlanders, to a large extent. Before the maniacal fan had grabbed Arles, she'd been scrolling the bookstore's feed, and the mass of people was way more Instagrammable than Wedeskyull locals tended to be. Pricey clothes, recent blowouts, wings of color at their eyes and gloss-slicked lips, architecturally constructed beards.

The girl's appearance and disposition, entitled and at ease, suggested that any one of those wealthy attendees might be her parent. Many dozens, maybe over a hundred to choose from. People would be willing to travel distances for a glittery, spangled event involving a star.

How to identify them? In therapy, Kara used to talk about how big, bestselling authors had ticketed events. The bookstore must have a list of attendees, although it wouldn't include those who had just been driving by, seen an interesting crowd, and walked in.

Could the girl be part of a movie entourage, maybe a child actor? Arles googled the film but found no kiddie role in it. Kip Stratton—*Mr. Stratton*, Arles thought with a ripple of gooseflesh—appeared to carry most of the film, aside from a few bit parts. It was called *The Ascent*, about a solo thru-hike gone wrong.

Also, if the girl belonged to someone involved in movie production, there would be not just an Amber Alert but a full-court press, instead of a hush so profound around this place that Arles felt as if she might've been the last person left on Earth. Hollywood types would summon the police the second anything went wrong, content in the knowledge that they were the *served* and *protected*.

But then another take occurred to her. Hollywood people might spurn local cops in a town they would think of as backwater, a place they'd been exiled to support their film. Maybe they'd bring in some kind of high-end private security firm, keep things quiet until they were resolved. Avoid headlines. That could explain the news vacuum.

Arles made one more attempt to reach Tim. Got voice mail again. He was out of range, probably still seeing to that domestic. It must've gotten complicated; somehow domestics always did. Unless the girl's parents had come forward, and he had switched to working the case?

Arles's thoughts of before assailed her.

Tim would enlist help from the FBI, and Arles could call the Albany field office herself. But something inside her continued to shy away from that prospect, as if her hand had drawn too close to a flame. She, like Kara, knew what could happen when children got ensnared in the sticky spiderweb of law enforcement. Sometimes, as with Kara, the police tried to help and failed. In Arles's case—her stepfather buddies with the chief and all—they didn't even try, the child sacrificed on the altar of their sanctified systems.

Arles fired up her engine.

For the moment, the girl was safe—always Arles's number-one priority when it came to children. Away from the deranged fan; whichever polished, shiny, Facebook-faced parent whose clutches she'd escaped; or a person whose identity Arles couldn't yet begin to imagine.

Soon enough, Tim would listen to Arles's message, see the missed calls, and when he couldn't reach her, make his way out to Fir Cove. And in the meantime, she would oil the joints of her former self and do what she'd been trained to do.

Get the girl to open up.

CHAPTER NINE

Fir Cove looked as if it were on fire, every window blazing. All the lights had been turned on, even ones in seldom-used dormer rooms. Arles parked and went inside to find Kara sitting at the kitchen table beneath the glare of a ceiling fixture. The girl occupied a chair beside her, the two of them sharing a pair of earbuds and a heap of snacks. Arles made sure to approach slowly, giving Kara plenty of warning.

She saw Arles and jumped up, placing her phone in the girl's hands.

"Decided we both could use a little music," Kara said. "Luckily, I download all my playlists, and Taylor spans the generations."

Arles led the way to the parlor, checking to make sure Kara followed.

They took seats, and Arles spoke before Kara could start asking questions.

"Why did you tell me not to call the police?"

Kara frowned. "You said you know why. Shit, please tell me you didn't—"

Arles interrupted her. "But why'd you have to warn me in the first place?"

Still frowning. "Because calling the cops is what most people would do. Except ones like me."

Arles hesitated. "Let me put this another way. How'd you get way out here to see me?"

Kara dropped her head into her hands. "I'm lost, Dr. Shepherd," she mumbled.

"How were you able to make it this far from Books & Brew before the cops descended, whether you wanted them to or not? A BOLO put out, some book-launch attendee saw you with the girl, roadblocks put in place. Et cetera."

Slowly, Kara lifted her head.

Arles waited until understanding began to stain Kara's eyes. "An eleven-year-old child, maintained like this one is—no way does she vanish without an outcry."

Kara stared at Arles, her gaze hard and elemental now. As the planet had been before it split apart. "My next book's gonna be called *The Mystery of the Appearing Girl*. Get it? Instead of *Disappearing*."

Arles offered a semi-grim smile.

"Okay, so what now?" Kara asked. "What'd you do while you were gone?"

"Went to the bookstore. Which is empty, by the way. Sealed up tight. I also did some checking online." No need to reveal that she'd attempted to contact the police. As for the demented fan—Arles would leave him for later.

"Have you heard of the cult that's cropped up here?" Kara asked. "End Timers, they call themselves. Preppers digging escape tunnels. That would explain why Maeve said 'no one' would tell her who she's missing from. Cults don't have parents. They share the kids."

"Could be," Arles replied. "Although she seems a little polished for a cult. How does she take part in the aforementioned tunnel digging and stay so clean?"

Kara let out a short, hard breath. "I dunno. But I definitely thought she was praying at one point. And in this really weird way too."

"I think the best thing will be for me to talk to her," Arles said.

"You mean, force her to tell you the truth? Say what's really going on?"

"Well, no. Pushing children to open up almost never works. As you know better than anybody else."

Kara gave a reluctant nod. "But you'll have a session with her?"

"More of a targeted interview. Would you mind bringing her in?"

———

Arles believed in playing things straight with children. She would lead with what she'd seen, or hadn't seen, an absence of information that turned out to be terribly informative, before introducing the fan. But the girl launched into conversation first.

"Thanks for all the cookies and chips and stuff," she said as she took a seat in the parlor, legs crisscrossed under her.

Kara sat down in the chair she'd originally occupied.

"Seems like you might not get to eat a lot of that stuff at home. Or wherever you live," Arles added, mindful of Kara's hypothesis.

"How'd you know that?" the girl asked suspiciously.

"I guess I just put a few things together."

"But I haven't told you anything about me."

"Except that you take baths with really comfy towels."

"Oh yeah," the girl said, looking surprised. "Other than that, though."

"Sometimes people say things without telling the other person anything," Arles said with a look at Kara. "That's pretty much the whole reason why I'm able to do what I do."

"Be a therapist? Kara told me that," said the girl, also looking in Kara's direction.

"That's me," Arles agreed. "Kids your age usually call me Dr. Arles."

"You want to therapize me," said the girl.

Arles offered a small smile. "Maybe just a little?"

The girl smiled back. "Okay. Do your thing."

Arles took in a breath. "I went to Books & Brew. Where you met Kara."

"Love that place," said the girl while Kara nodded agreement.

"It has a new look now, right?" asked Arles. "Used to be dry and dusty."

Kara gave another nod. "Got a reno. Bookstore 2.0."

"I'd like it either way." The girl put a hand to her mouth. "Oops. Just told you something else about me, didn't I?"

Arles put a finger to her temple, miming a *Let me think about that*, and saw the deranged fan make the same gesture with his overlong digit. She took a breath before replying. "That you enjoy reading. Probably do well in your studies, whether at school or home or someplace else." Still keeping the cult thing in mind. "You don't object to time spent alone. Making friends isn't easy for you, but that's okay. At least it used to be okay. Something changed recently."

"Wow," the girl said. "You got all that from dry and dusty?"

Arles let out a totally spontaneous laugh. When she spoke again, she gentled her tone, removing the sting from her words as much as possible. "Nobody was looking for you at the bookstore. That surprised me."

"Not me," muttered the girl.

"I came up with a theory about it," Arles went on. "An idea."

"I know what a theory is."

"Of course you do," Arles said instantly. "Because you like books, dry and dusty or not."

"The opposite, even. Wet and clean."

"Which makes me think of baths," said Arles. "So we've come full circle."

It was the girl's turn to laugh, an utterly delightful giggle, a trill.

"I noticed that another event went on at the bookstore today," Arles said. "A movie star appeared, right? Talking about his new film."

Kara's face reflected a glint of *aha*. "Explaining why hardly anyone came to see me."

Arles noted the sulkiness in her tone, a pity party with just one guest.

"I didn't even know what was happening," Kara went on. "Too focused on my own thing. My own *small* thing."

Arles sent her a look intended to be reassuring, a Don't-be-so-hard-on-yourself smile, before refocusing on the girl.

"So, perhaps you're connected to someone in the audience?" Arles suggested. Putting things together in real time, based on flickers in the child's eyes, twitches on her face. Building a plane as it took off. "Or no, the movie?"

"Oh my God, totally," Kara said with a gasp. "Child actors get abused all the time. Did you guys watch that documentary? Well, you probably wouldn't have, Maeve. If it's your life—"

The girl's easy speech from before had been replaced by a steely sort of silence.

Arles used the same technique herself—minus the steel—to encourage clients to speak, and should've been immune to its impact. But something about this child made her keep talking.

"You could be the daughter of one of the what-do-you-call-it staff that works on a movie. The director, say. Or the star himself." Arles knew the latter to be untrue based on her googling; Kip Stratton and his wife lived their whole lives online and referred frequently to their child-free status. But throwing things out there sometimes cracked open a sliver in a client.

The girl's expression conveyed the dead end Arles had reached. "Uh-huh, yeah, and I walked away from all that to ask *her* for help—" With a look flung in Kara's direction.

"Hey!" Kara objected.

Arles sent her an empathic wince before offering her trump card. "There was also this strange man hanging around the bookstore tonight. Tall. Red in the face. Very dark hair."

"The devil," Kara said with a visible shudder. "He sat in my audience for a while. My not much of an audience."

Arles had to ignore her this time because the girl had ceased talking, as if a switch had been pulled. She was crying, but this was no histrionic display of emotion like her moan of bliss in the bath. No wailing, her eyes simply seeping, the slow, steady leakage of grief.

Arles, who'd been privy to an array of emotions in her career, knew this couldn't be faked. Even if her guess had turned out to be correct, and the child was an actor, she couldn't have put on such a show at this age. Most grown professionals didn't perform at this level.

"What are you feeling right now?" Arles asked softly, the tone she adopted with people edging up to the shoals of some buried trauma.

The girl lifted her head, pinning Arles with a fierce gaze. "I *wish* Kip Stratton was my father. Not because he's handsome and rich and famous—anybody on the crew would do. Just about anyone could be my parents. Except the ones I've got."

Silence reigned, and then: "So maybe you're not as good of a therapist as Kara said."

"Maybe?" Arles echoed. "I'm positive I'm not. And I'm sorry I haven't figured this out yet."

She wasn't aggrieved by the child's accusation. She had dealt with therapeutic ruptures, negative countertransference, and the occasional client who just plain didn't like her. That wasn't what made her neck jerk sideways or her chair tilt over as she shoved it back and shot to her feet.

The vicious head turn and fallen chair were prompted by something else.

The unmistakable rumble of an engine, tires crunching in the drive.

CHAPTER TEN

Kara felt welded to her seat.

"Take the back stairs," Dr. Shepherd commanded. "You know where they are?"

Kara gave a swift nod, finally rising.

"Make yourselves scarce on the second floor till I come get you." Dr. Shepherd paused. "Third floor, even. Lots of places up there."

To hide. Kara got the message. They were off the grid here, far away from anything, not a place someone would just happen by. And Dr. Shepherd hadn't mentioned expecting any guests.

For the first time, it occurred to Kara that she might have put Dr. Shepherd in danger.

She's dealt with danger before, an inner voice consoled her.

Cold Kara. Bitchy Kara. Selfish Kara.

All her father's taunts and accusations and name-calling had been right.

Kara led the kid through the kitchen, away from the front of the house. That level of precaution, coming from a professional therapist, sent a trickle of ice water through Kara's spine. From the second floor, she and Maeve mounted another flight before accessing a narrow boxed-in stairway that gave out onto a big dormered room. Kara had discovered this attic earlier when she'd gone on a hunt to turn on all the lights in the mansion.

Should she shut them off now so that she and Maeve couldn't be seen? Or would the sudden extinguishing of even just these two little lamps, yellow gone to black, attract more attention?

Bending over, Kara ducked beneath the bat wings of a sharply pitched ceiling. She approached a window, although it was nearly impossible to make anything out. But she caught the outline of something broad and bulky, black against the night. A vehicle, even bigger than Dr. Shepherd's SUV, moving slowly without any lights on. The lack of headlights in the coal-dark night went past *strange* to *terrifying*.

No car door swung open, and no one got out. Black began to merge with blacker in an unbounded, horizonless sea until Kara couldn't be sure she had seen a car in the first place, that she was looking at anything at all. Dr. Shepherd was probably okay, then. Dr. Shepherd was fine.

Maeve crept up behind her, and Kara jumped.

"Jesus, you scared me!"

"Sorry," Maeve mouthed, and the soundless motion pierced Kara like a spear.

Four stories up, and the kid didn't feel safe enough to whisper.

Kara navigated the two of them deeper into the guts of the house, winding up in a darkened cleft. Sliding her fingers into her back pocket, she fished out her phone. Before leaving the bookstore, she'd downloaded a map in order to be able to find Dr. Shepherd's house once the signal cut out. Now she wanted to view their surroundings. She made a cave with one hand to shield the sickly green light, seeing untrammeled wilderness and little else. But Kara's car had conked out after being disentangled from Dr. Shepherd's. Leaving in it wasn't an option.

Lit up by the phone, Maeve's eyes were big and watchful, her hair no longer done just so. It'd gotten tousled from her bathtub submersion, the strands so pale, they looked ghostly.

Why was Kara faced with this dilemma? What compelled her even to stick around? The alternative wouldn't have been anything much, just another night of Netflix and too many carbs. Still, that sounded pretty good right now, and whoever had come here had no interest in her. She could skirt his car, avoiding any risk of an exchange, then walk all night to her apartment.

Unless he caught sight of her and was interested in having more than an exchange.

The possibility Dr. Shepherd had raised when she'd been questioning Kara floated back.

Someone at the book launch saw you with the girl.

She couldn't bear to look at the kid, who appeared younger and more helpless than ever. Kara stared down at her phone instead. Traced a line through all the green, connecting two dots, a bridge from her past to right here in the present. Separated by a fair distance. But doable.

The place she was thinking of didn't just open its door to any stranger, though, and ones in uncertain, precarious situations presented an especial risk. There were safeguards in place, and arriving out of the blue with Maeve in tow would blow past every one of them.

Not true, said that damnable voice inside Kara's head. Maeve is the type of person they're there to help. You just want to be rid of the responsibility. Rid of her.

Was that so wrong? From the moment the girl approached Kara at the bookstore, Kara had known she was out of her depth.

She powered down her phone. She would need charge for the walk.

Witnessing Dr. Shepherd at work had been like being in the presence of a sorceress. Chanting incantations, drawing out information like a cobra from a basket. Kara had scarcely gotten Maeve to reveal one thing about herself, while Dr. Shepherd had made a decent start on the kid's life history. Plus, Dr. Shepherd obviously liked Maeve. Nearly as much as Kara did.

Kara blinked, the darkness so impenetrable that the only way she knew if her eyes were open or closed was when tears spilled down her cheeks, no longer held in check by her eyelids.

"I'm going to leave you here, Maeve. You'll be in good hands with Dr. Shepherd. She's smart—I have no idea why you think she isn't a great therapist. She's a wizard. How the hell did she figure out you don't have any friends?"

The little girl winced; Kara could tell by the movement, a ripple of cold air around her.

Mean Kara.

Not someone anybody should entrust with a child.

"It's not like we even know for sure there's a threat." Kara went on talking into the void. "You might be in no danger whatsoever. There's just a car parked outside. No one's getting out."

"Yeah, you know why?" The tone shrill. Maeve was no longer taking pains to keep quiet.

"No!" Kara cried. "I don't know why!"

"Because he's the Extricator," the kid said.

Kara heard it that way anyway, with a capital letter. The Extricator. Like the name of a WWE champion.

It felt as if a strong wind had begun to blow, or a hand had come down, big enough to shake this huge house. If a floodlight went on right now, the upper aerie cast into brightness, Maeve would look as if she were being electrocuted, her whole body jolting, lips tremoring as they began to form those uninterpretable words again, her prayer, her chant.

"Fine," Kara muttered, low. "I'll take you with me."

The attic turned out to be a repository of everything they'd need, packed in cartons stowed beneath the hunched shoulders of eaves. Boxes of clothes in descending-age order proffered items in roughly Maeve's size. Kara asked her to change out of her too-nice clothes, worse than useless where they were going, potentially endangering. Cotton. And not warm.

A foot locker contained outdoors supplies. Headlamps, batteries that still worked, water bottles that took forever to fill from a sink running at a trickle in a half bath beneath a sloped ceiling. Thermoses, really, not light plastic vessels. The aesthetic was definitely before-we-knew-how-to-survive-in-the-woods core without a shred of microfiber to be found. But it would do. There was even a knife among the gear.

They should get some rest, no chance of making the trip in the dark. When dawn broke, they'd sneak out. Dr. Shepherd had done a lot for them, but her willingness to steer clear of the police, operate the way Kara would, couldn't last forever. For now, she was capable of tending to whatever was happening in her own home, which might be nothing despite Maeve's assertion. Come morning, Dr. Shepherd could go back to not seeing patients and living in her castle.

Kara had just zipped up the canvas pack she'd unearthed when Maeve sucked in a breath.

"It's the Guarder. He's here." Her tone bleak, as endless as a desert.

The Guarder. Going up against the Extricator for the title in a colossal head-to-head.

"Now there'll be no stopping him," Maeve said.

Tiny hairs stood up like miniature antennae all over Kara's skin. "Stopping who? Who are these people?" Would he do something to Dr. Shepherd? Maeve was the one he wanted, and Maeve was safe, Kara keeping her that way no matter what.

The kid stood by a warbly pane of glass, and although Kara didn't think anybody could see inside way up here, she nevertheless hissed, "Stay away from there!"

Fear plastered Maeve's face as she turned and faced Kara, her eyes so wide that Kara flung a paranoid look behind herself as if someone might be standing there. Maeve started skip-stepping backward, slapping at her shoulder as if a swarm of bees were descending. Her mouth moving again in that damnable prayer. Forming words that Kara had no hope of understanding. What was she supposed to be, a lip reader?

She was the scared one. Some fount of adult assistance Maeve had stumbled across.

That explained why the kid was praying so hard. Seeking divine intervention because Kara had nothing to give, not a thing she could do. Right now, she wanted nothing more than to hunch over in a ball, close her eyes, and cover her ears to block all this out. But she forced herself to take out her phone instead. Aimed its flashlight so she could peek into dark corners and hidey-holes, all the spaces from which danger liked to beckon.

Attic clear, but she'd already known that. She needed to go look elsewhere in the house.

But Kara didn't do things like that. She let the hand holding her phone fall to one side.

Maeve stood in the dark, small hands bunched, face blotchy, muttering so rapidly without taking in breath that Kara worried the kid might pass out. Kara herself was at risk of doing the same thing, minus the muttering. Because Kara Parsons hid. And sometimes left, especially when she was most needed.

Kara Cross didn't, though.

Dragging in a breath, Kara tiptoed over to the doorway, taking a step over the threshold as if it were made of knives. She peered out. The landing at the top of the steps sat in shadows; no light shone from below. The house was quiet, as if draped with heavy cloth. What was Dr. Shepherd doing? And if she wasn't doing anything, then what had happened to her?

The Guarder had gotten her. That was the only thing that could explain this absence.

Kara pictured a man sidling slowly up the staircase, staying out of sight until the last second. Not the Guarder or the Extricator, though. This was someone else, a shadow figure from deep in Kara's past. Somebody who, in reality, could never reach her again.

Anyone else she could deal with, so she started down.

Shining the light from her phone, she set her foot on the top step. It cracked, the gunshot slap of wood, and Kara reared back, then sat down hard. Wind was stolen from her; she had to huff to regain it. For a moment, she remained statue still. Not a sound came from downstairs; no one had been alerted by her half tumble. She rose to her feet, placing first one shoe, then the other, on the next stair before seeking the one after that. Like descending into a dark pool.

Maybe Dr. Shepherd had fallen asleep down there. Who the fuck knew?

Kara had gone far enough for now. There was nobody there.

Kara Cross made up bad guys. She didn't face off with them.

She turned and scurried back into the attic, air raking her throat.

"Maeve," she said as soon as she could speak, "I think it's okay."

The kid drew in a deep, shuddery breath, squinting to make out Kara.

Kara shone the light at her own face, made a *woo-woo* sound, playing ghost.

Maeve smiled shakily.

Kara nodded. "We're okay."

People had fallen down in the take-care-of-Kara department all her life. Meaning she was owed. She would leave this to Dr. Shepherd. She slid downward, her spine against the wall, adrenaline draining. Maeve came and sat beside her on the rough, unvarnished floorboards, the grit of a hundred years beneath them. Kara couldn't bring herself to give the kid a hug, but she extended one hand, laying her palm flat on the dirty wood. Maeve grabbed it and held on tight.

And then she fell asleep, slumped against the wall, her hand enclosed in Kara's.

Kara must've drifted off as well, because the next thing she knew, silvery daylight illuminated the rooftop slats of the attic, faint streaks coming in through cloudy squares of glass.

Still no appearance from Dr. Shepherd, and Kara had grown sick of cowering up here with the kid like Cathy and Carrie in *Flowers in the Attic*. Last night, she'd acted as the grown-up for once, and it had ignited in her a desire to move, to take action, like her sleuth would have.

She gathered the things she had assembled last night, woke Maeve, and hustled the two of them toward the attic doorway.

CHAPTER ELEVEN

As soon as the car—an Escalade, or maybe a Suburban, something big and shambling—reached Fir Cove, it slid out of sight, coasting to a stop behind a sweep of pine branches. Rolling in neutral until it was concealed.

Seated in the dark on a chair in her front room, Arles could just make out the vehicle's shape. Headlights off, engine muted. She considered making a trip off her porch, crossing her own goddamn property to confront the driver, but decided that remaining still was the power move. Much as silence could coax a buttoned-up client to speak, she would use inaction to force this guy's hand, compel him to act.

It could've been the girl's mother, of course, but Arles didn't think so. Lying in wait, lurking in the shadows, was such a male thing to do. A quintessential dick move.

At daybreak, the next car arrived, and at that point somebody got out. He emerged from door #1, though, the car that had stayed put all night. The second vehicle matched the first, big and bold, a chunk of obsidian breaking up the symmetry of her driveway. Arles continued to sit still, staring through a window, the world light enough now that she could see. Her stepfather's Winchester stood at her side, as sleek and lithe as a panther, although less of a threat since she kept it unloaded. She wasn't the best shot.

Based on appearance alone, the man who'd emerged didn't look like much of a threat. Small, unassuming. Dressed in a ridiculous outfit:

stiff, shiny jeans and a Carhartt jacket so new, it practically stood up upon him. An approximation, she imagined, of what he believed locals to wear. Trying to blend in. He stood in her driveway, stretching out kinks in his back as he took a long, searching look around.

Arles rose to her feet, unhinging her own joints. Since getting shot, she sometimes forgot to move. She left the rifle behind. Always best to begin as if things weren't going to get nasty.

Pausing to listen at the bottom of the stairs—Kara and the girl still seemed to be sleeping—she walked over to the front door. She descended the stone steps, then stood with one hand visoring her eyes against the rising sun, her other arm hanging at her side in a relaxed manner.

"I'm looking for a little girl," the man called out, walking forward.

His slow pace, the casual call, made something inside Arles retract, her body shunting blood away from the extremities to protect its core. The demented fan had telegraphed his issue, blared it from his heated red face. Pretend to love Kip Stratton and you'd be okay. Whereas this man hid his ugly. It was coiled like a snake inside him, no warning as to when it would strike.

"She might've been accompanied by a woman." Maintaining a distance, respecting Arles's personal space, he extended one hand with the latest iPhone on his palm. "These things don't seem to be worth shit—I'm sorry—aren't worth much around here, but I've got a photo."

Arles's face could do anything; it was a tool of her trade. Mirror expressions, be a blank page for patients to write on, her features as moldable as bread dough. She went for open and guileless now, just a bewildered woman, living out here on her own.

"I've never seen that child," she said, closing the distance between them. "I'm sorry."

Keeping it concise. People who were lying tended to chatter.

The man regarded her, and Arles gazed back. She'd faced down many an unbroken stare in her career, although this one was peculiar. Empty, without anything filling the eyes. If you peeled back the skin around them, a mesh of net and wires would be revealed instead of flesh.

77

"The woman she's with used to be a patient of yours," he said after a drawn-out pause.

A frown crawled across her face, slivery and cold. She didn't bother to mask her emotion; it was entirely appropriate given the circumstance. "How on earth do you know that?"

He didn't answer.

"Which client?" Arles asked. "They're protected by confidentiality, you know."

"It doesn't matter," the man replied. "You're saying there's no kid here? Because I have a reliable report that the one I'm looking for is on the premises. Or was until recently."

"A reliable report from whom?"

The man's head turned, just a notch, toward the other car, still cloaked by trees.

Arles made sure not to follow his gaze when it flicked, to keep playing her simple-woman role, clueless as to the goings-on of men. *Nope, nothing wrong here.*

"Don't worry about that, either," he told her.

Arles camouflaged her bristle. "Is she your daughter?"

"Look, none of this matters," the man said neutrally.

"Actually, it does," she replied. "Because if you know I'm a therapist, then you also know that people in my profession are mandated reporters. Which means if a stranger shows up, I don't just hand over a child to them. Even if I knew where said child was. Which I don't."

"I was told that you do," he said, and his voice was no longer easy. Something hard ran through it, like a length of rebar.

He shifted and Arles spied a slight lift of fabric, the gleam of metal nestled against the knobs of his spine. His body had a dense force to it, like clay. He moved suddenly, seamlessly; he'd intended her to see the weapon. Arles had decades of practice at intuiting when a man was about to get too close, and took a step back. As she did, she detected some sort of strong soap or deodorant, something formulated to cover up odor, and felt a humid musk coming off his compact frame.

"I'm here to offer you a way out, Dr. Shepherd," he said, caressing her name with his tongue. "Can't imagine why you wouldn't take it. You have no interest in this child. And the people who do are not anybody you're going to want in your life."

Arles widened her eyes, forcing out a small laugh. "I have no idea what you're talking about. It all sounds a little . . . movie-ish. I'm telling you I haven't seen that girl."

His hand migrated around to the small of his back, and a mental image arose, the open cave of a gun's maw. A spasm clenched her gut. She drew in a breath that rattled, hunting for a play here. Jenga pieces stacked themselves in her mind. "Listen," she said, "I'm under absolutely no obligation to do this, but let me show you something."

The man frowned, pausing in the midst of taking another step.

She reached to touch her back pocket. She didn't often have her phone on her at Fir Cove, but it'd been a long night, and Arles had kept herself awake like a cop on surveillance with Noah Kahan and boygenius.

"A woman and young girl do live here," she said, scrolling to find the best pic for her purposes. One with Fir Cove on display and Stephanie and Lissa clearly situated. "But they aren't the ones you're looking for." She tilted her screen. "The woman was never my client. And these two are gone now anyway. Perhaps somebody got confused."

"That's quite a coincidence," he said, looking down. "I'm trying to locate a little girl who's in the company of a woman, and such a pair just happen to reside here."

Arles gave a shrug, feeling every twitch of the muscles required to do it. "Doesn't sound that strange to me. You should hear some of the stories I get told."

"Where are they? Your . . . houseguests? Or did you say they're your tenants?"

"On vacation," she said. "In the Southwest." She wasn't about to sic this man anywhere near Stephanie and Lissa, whose route lay to the north of the lower part of the country. He had discovered Kara's connection to Arles swiftly enough that he clearly had skills beyond normal reckoning. How did he do it?

He took a look around, tilting his small head and breathing in so deeply, his nostrils flared. Fir Cove acted its part, staying silent and still, only chirps from songbirds for company.

After a long moment, time pulling in a way Arles felt in her gut, he spoke.

"I apologize for the intrusion. Somebody got something wrong."

A silken ripple of relief flowed through her. She nearly offered an apology herself in return—*I'm sorry for the long trip you had to make*—before she bit it back, appalled. Women apologized far too often, and to do so when she'd just been interrogated, her property encroached upon . . . But probably this man wouldn't even have noticed, just taken her regret as his due.

He headed in the direction of his car.

Arles stood at the base of her porch, arms folded across her chest, watching his progress.

Then he stopped and turned, wearing a half smile empty of feeling. "Mind if I take a look inside?"

CHAPTER TWELVE

When Kara and Maeve reached the third floor, the kid stopped.

"Where are we going?"

She spoke at a normal volume, the trademark note of demand back in her tone.

The kid didn't seem scared any longer. *Dr. Shepherd must've handled whatever danger had come in the night,* Kara thought with a relieved exhalation. But then why hadn't she come upstairs to get them?

Because she was letting them sleep.

She'd probably checked on them, saw that they were okay.

Or because she was dead. Killed by the Guarder or Extricator.

A serial killer hadn't managed to off Dr. Shepherd, but Kara seeking her out had done it. A second death on Kara's hands.

No matter what, she needed to get out of here with Maeve. All she could do now was keep this kid safe. She pitched her voice low. "On a walk through the woods."

The kid swiveled toward her, face all scrunched up. "What?" she said. Loud.

"Shh," Kara hissed.

Maeve turned toward a window that looked out on a battalion of trees: dense, dark firs, spiny-backed laurels, others Kara couldn't name.

"I'm not going in there," the kid said, as if Kara had proposed entering a dungeon. "There's probably bugs. And other stuff."

"Haven't you ever been out in nature before?" Kara asked, exasperated.

"No."

Dr. Shepherd probably would've been able to complete Maeve's life story based on that nugget of information, but Kara passed it right by, overwhelmed by a sense of helplessness. She'd never been able to convince a kid to do anything—her own personal life history proved that.

All she had, she realized, was the truth.

She peered over the railing, studying a long, carpeted corridor on the second floor. The stairs to the ground floor of the house lay at its end. From there, it'd be a straight shot to the front door, and freedom in the snarled mass of woods.

Kara crouched down, the backpack tilting her awkwardly forward.

The kid looked at her.

"Look, Maeve," Kara said, "I don't know why Dr. Shepherd hasn't come to get us yet."

Still that bland stare. Maeve seemed pretty smart—Dr. Shepherd had said so, anyway—but she wasn't getting this. "Maybe it's not because something happened to her last night," Kara went on. "But if it is, then whoever did it could still be hanging around. Waiting for you."

Maeve's expression finally changed, her face seizing. She took a wild look around, her body whirling so fast that she stumbled. Kara reached out to stop her from falling.

"It's okay," she said softly. "I could be totally wrong. It's quiet down there, and nobody's come up here after you yet. But I still want us to leave. It'll just be a short walk." A long one.

At last, Maeve gave a nod.

Kara gestured to the stairs with her chin.

When they got to the second floor, Kara paused with the kid beside her. Because there was a choice here, and the kid's safety might depend upon it. *Two roads diverged.* Continue on to the main staircase, or retreat to the back stairs they'd taken last night? Kara shifted the weight of the pack between her shoulder blades, trying to get comfortable, trying to decide.

Maeve shuffled backward, then forward, then backward again. She kept stuffing her hands into her pockets and taking them out. At any minute, she would probably launch into her prayer thing; you didn't have to be a therapist to deduce that it was a coping mechanism for when she got anxious. Kara's own stomach felt loose, gurgling with nerves.

If someone *were* here—the Guarder, the Extricator; she heard Maeve's voice pipe in her head, too sweetly for words as malevolent as those—what would he do? Station himself on the first level, assuming the kid wouldn't think to conceal her whereabouts, just dash brashly down the main way? Or guess that she would try to be sneaky, and head her off at the rear of the house?

Stand in the driveway, or huddle in the backyard?

An impossible guess to make with impossibly high stakes.

Kara didn't know these men, couldn't predict their actions.

She could walk Maeve right into the arms of the person she'd escaped.

Or nobody might be here at all.

The staircase to the first floor beckoned only a few feet away, presenting wide, easy passage. They could be down it and outside in seconds. It was the more accessible route; the back stairs were narrow, and they creaked.

Twisting to see past the pack, Kara looked over her shoulder at Maeve. "Can you run really fast?"

The kid nodded.

The backpack would unbalance Kara, but she could compensate for that.

"Like a race, okay?" she said, and Maeve nodded again.

Side by side, they started forward.

CHAPTER THIRTEEN

Should Arles say she certainly did mind?

A woman alone, he understood; she couldn't just let a stranger inside her home.

But he had already crossed a line, issuing that warning—*the people who do are not anybody you're going to want in your life*—and Arles had a feeling that her best play was to continue acting her part. She had nothing to hide, could put up with a few more moments of weird. If instead she chose to bar access, provoked a confrontation, he had the upper hand, given the gun. But being in the house would even the odds—there were places she could lead him from which she might be able to get away.

She extended an arm, allowing the man to proceed into the entryway.

He was several inches shy of her own five foot six, with a mugginess emanating from his skin. Odd—it wasn't at all warm out. His heat had to come from within. When his body grazed hers, it felt like slug tracks upon her, a slippery trail.

Stay put, stay put, stay put, she mentally begged Kara and her charge.

She'd looked in on them once or twice in the night, sleeping in a tangle together in the attic. Not a room Arles would've imagined providing comfort—unfinished, dark, and cold, filled with the leavings of bygone generations—but the two had looked snug.

It was early yet. They might still be asleep. The spot they had chosen was relatively concealed and four floors up. This man probably wouldn't think to check all the way in the attic.

"Quite a place you got." He trailed short, stubby fingers across an antique sideboard.

Arles felt the motion as if he were stroking her body and shuddered.

"You say a kid lives here? With all this nice stuff?"

Arles had a sixth sense for men whose voices dropped in register, or rose—hitting high, squeaky notes—when talking about young girls. Whose gazes skittered away like small, frightened animals, or homed in like birds of prey. But this man seemed as soulless as a machine, a robot that'd been tasked with some job.

He strolled over to a pair of pocket doors and wrenched them open.

Arles fought to camouflage a wince, not to look overhead. That must have disturbed Kara and the girl; opening the set of doors had shaken their framing to its bones. But Arles was attuned to every quake and quiver of Fir Cove, and nobody stirred on the upper floors.

The man turned and headed toward the kitchen. Arles hurried after him in pursuit, although there seemed to be no urgency to his search. He might've been browsing in a store.

"Look," she said, catching up to him at the pantry, "I have no reason to lie to you. As you pointed out yourself, I don't have any interest in the child you're looking for."

The man walked over to the back door, lifting a panel of curtain at the window.

"I'm a psychologist," she continued. "If I encountered a strange child, I would contact protective services. That's my ethical duty." *Stop chattering, dammit.* It implied guilt.

The man drew open the door and took a step outside onto a stone stoop, inhaling so deeply, his narrow chest rose. "Never smelled air this fresh before."

He comes from a city. Arles cobbled bits together to pass along to Tim. Who still hadn't made it out here. What could be occupying him all night?

The man came back inside, closing the door with a quiet *snick*.

Not a big man. But even minus the gun, she knew he could overpower her.

Those pocket doors had been stuck fast for months—Dan had been planning to fix them before Arles told him to leave, then ghosted him like a random hookup—and this man had parted them as easily as turning pages in a book.

He stepped so close, she could see tiny hairs springing from his ears. *Late thirties at least,* she thought. Probably more like early forties. She stared at him, willing her gaze not to flicker.

From outside the kitchen, a tiny nodule of noise. Arles couldn't parse what it was—nothing as clear as footsteps or even a door being eased open. Ripples of disturbance in the air.

The man whipped around, and although his legs weren't long, he covered ground fast back to the entry hall. He paused at the stairway, looking upward while holding on to the newel post. His hand wasn't large enough to encompass the entirety of the polished wooden globe.

It was quiet up there, the stillness of ages. As if no one had walked through this house since it'd been built, the upper floors sheeted and draped. The man tilted his head, tidily cut hair not moving with the motion. His focus had a preternatural feel, as if he might possess an antenna capable of picking out the invisible presence of the child and woman who'd sought refuge here.

"What are you waiting for?" Arles asked.

He shifted his glance, eyebrows knit in confusion.

"A woman on her own, living off the grid. I saw your gun." Pain bit deep in her belly at the mention. "You're holding the cards here, and you know it."

His frown neutralized, expression back to a sheen, as if his entire soul were shellacked.

"There isn't a soul here but us," Arles continued. Alone, alone, alone. Planting the suggestion. Convincing him subliminally. "You could do anything you want, and there's nobody to stop you. So, if you're not going to, then why are you sticking around?"

He stared at her levelly, just below eye level, a moment or two longer. Then he turned and stalked to the front door, opened it, and left.

She watched him get into his car, reverse in an arc that threw a swarm of gravel into the air, then take off back down the private road.

She waited for the other car to follow before sagging down onto a settee.

"Kara!" she called without moving. "You can come out now! Both of you!"

She was limp from her performance, from challenging him to a psychological duel at the end. Though the morning air was chilly, patches of sweat stuck her shirt to her skin.

"Kara!" she shouted.

No answer from above. No sounds at all. Arles got up and dragged herself over to the staircase, placing both hands on the railing and hauling her body upward, aware of every ounce of force gravity applied. The upper floors were empty, including the attic.

Cartons sat with their flaps unsealed; a storage trunk had been plundered. Drips from a leaky faucet plinked into the basin of a cracked sink.

Kara and the girl were gone.

How long ago had they left? How much of a head start did they have?

Kara's hatchback rested, mortally wounded, in the spot where Arles had reversed her trample off it last night. A little later that night, she had told Kara to take the back stairs with the girl. They must've gotten out of the house that way too.

Arles moved as quickly as she could to the backyard, pain at the dull-yellow reminder level as opposed to blaring-red agony. The August soil was dry, holding on to shoeprints, and Arles spotted one regular-size set with another notably smaller forging a trail into the woods. The missing outdoors gear from the attic, she recalled. Kara had outfitted herself and the girl.

People familiar with the region, whose families were old-timers like Kara's, usually had a decent level of wilderness knowledge, could function pretty well out here. The trail Arles started to follow laid itself out straight and true; Kara clearly knew where she was headed, had a destination in mind. Arles felt tugs and strain in her midriff, as if things were a little too loose, but the sensations were faint, and her feet were lent speed by familiarity with her task. Tracking was a skill she'd picked up from her stepfather.

The ground was punctuated by gouges, brush matted down, with broken branches bleeding sap. Arles had just caught the scent of mossy water, felt a fine spray in the air, when she registered something. The twinges in her midsection had lessened. As she ascended a ladder of rocks, she reached overhead, testing. Her body was being used again—and didn't seem to object.

The trail she'd picked up ended at a rounded hump of boulder where a creek burbled, relatively shallow at this point in the season, crossable. But Arles found no signs of disruption on the other side, not so much as one muddy footprint. Kara and the girl could've stayed in the water, taken it upstream or down before emerging. If so, Arles had no hope of finding them.

She splashed back across the creek, leaning against a tree to rest. Kara seemed to be taking good care of this child and clearly had her welfare in mind—a little too much in mind, if anything. If Arles had been treating Kara, she would've probed gently to find out whether Kara was overlaying this girl with another child long gone. But no matter how good a job Kara did at caretaking, she couldn't be allowed to go on the run with a strange child. Arles had to find them.

Something protruded from the tree; she felt it against her spine, with none of the referred pain she'd grown accustomed to experiencing at that site. Arles wriggled out of the way, twisting around to look. Not one twinge as she executed the motion—amazing.

Also amazing was the object she saw clamped to the trunk.

A camera.

CHAPTER FOURTEEN

Maeve had caught the thud of the front door a split second before Kara did.

The kid had cut off her motion so abruptly, she'd had to grab hold of the railing to stay upright, teetering one stair from the top. If Kara had stopped like that, she would've toppled down the flight of steps, so unwieldy was the backpack. Luckily, she had let Maeve go first in order to be able to watch, make sure the kid got safely outside.

Dr. Shepherd's voice could be heard, so uncertain, it sent a bolt through Kara. That wasn't her therapist, sharp-witted, kind in a clipped way. Dr. Shepherd sounded intimidated.

A short, slanted shadow had passed across the landing at the bottom of the stairs. Then a pair of sliding doors rattled open, sending up a vibration to the spot where Kara and Maeve huddled, unmoving. Kara took advantage of the clatter to grab Maeve's hand and yank her in the opposite direction. They went flying down the back stairs, exiting the house through the kitchen with a slow, nonchalant patter of footfalls only a second or two behind them.

After an hour or so of trudging through the woods, Kara was pretty sure they were lost. Maeve didn't know what was happening, just kept blithely walking in circles, kicking at rocks, pushing past tall, clinging stands of brush.

She even felt entitled enough to whine.

"Is it going to be a lot longer?"

Two days. That was how many Kara would be able to grant them given her lack of survival skills. After their supplies ran out, she couldn't forage, fashion a water purification system, or build a shelter in case of rain. Kara liked her wilderness pursuits to go down easy. Well-marked trail, plenty of gear. She was a lazy outdoorsman.

So what was she doing bushwhacking through land where her phone was no use, unable to make the map line up with what she was seeing? Dr. Shepherd's house turned out to be farther from the place Kara was trying to get to than it had looked.

She quickened her pace, gaining altitude to get a better sense of their bearings. Continuing to walk was a recipe for entangling themselves further, like pawing through a ball of yarn, but no one had any idea where they were. It wasn't as if she'd signed a trail log.

Kara had been sent out into these woods years ago, but nothing about them felt familiar. The topography had changed. Young trees had grown taller while old, tired ones fell.

"*Kara!* I asked how long it'll be."

The demand snapped Kara's last nerve like a tendon. She spun in the ill-fitting boots she had borrowed from Dr. Shepherd, smack into the kid who was following too close behind.

"Look, Maeve!" she burst out. "I don't know where you come from—because you won't fucking tell me—but based on the way you've been tripping and stumbling around—"

"I haven't been tripping and stumbling!" Tears jumped to her eyes, glistening like bits of glass in the sun. "That much, anyway."

But Kara could not stop herself. "I'm gonna go ahead and conclude it's not anyplace like here. Which means your safety is my problem, which means we're royally screwed, because in case you haven't noticed, I have no idea where we're going." And she plunked herself down on a knob of tree root, spent. She rolled her shoulders, relieving herself of the pack.

Maeve dropped beside her on the ground. Her face didn't display the fear Kara's announcement should've elicited. She just appeared hurt by the assessment of her survival skills.

"I'm sorry, Maeve. You're actually doing pretty well for a flat-footer on a hike like this."

Maeve sniffed in a string of snot. "What's a flat-footer?"

"It's someone who comes from away," Kara replied. "Doesn't know this land."

"Arizona," Maeve said after a moment.

"What about Arizona?" Kara broke off half a candy bar and handed it over.

Maeve accepted the offering. "That's where I live. You said I wouldn't fucking tell you."

Kara flinched. "Don't curse."

"I was just saying what you did."

"Yeah, well, I'm not someone anybody should copy."

"I think you are," Maeve said. "If a kid ever comes up to me when I'm all grown up, I'm going to do what you did. I'm going to save them."

Kara had to blink, hard and fast. "Arizona, huh?" Maybe Dr. Shepherd wasn't the only one who could learn things. "Is that why you're so tan?"

Maeve had a spun-gold glow that now made sense. It stood out in the Northeast.

"Um, yeah, exactly," Maeve said. "The sun is really strong there."

"So, how'd you get so far away?"

But at that, Maeve set her chocolate-smeared lips together. On her, the brown managed to look like a sophisticated shade of gloss.

Kara didn't want her to start praying again, so she gave a cough, her throat rough and dry. She was conserving their water for Maeve. "I'm really sorry I got us lost."

"It's okay," Maeve said cheerily. "I like it out here. Way better than I thought I would."

She had no idea of the danger they were in. What being lost in the Adirondacks meant.

Maeve's head turned. "What's that?"

Kara blotted her eyes dry with her dirty shirt. "What's what?" But then she heard it too.

She shot to her feet, continuing to listen as she pulled Maeve upright. Kara swung the pack off the ground and set out running, hard on the trail of a series of snapped sticks and broken branches. Sounds made by a large mammal—a deer or a bear most likely, but possibly a human.

At the bottom of a slope, Maeve's eyes sparked. She looked as if she had been wandering across an alien planet for eons and finally laid eyes on a member of her kin.

Or had just gotten invited to a slumber party.

A little girl, Maeve's size more or less, stood below them, stooping over a thicket of blackberries. Kara felt the practiced movements in her own hands, the quick flick of the wrist to avoid thorns, a gentle pressure applied to each bejeweled vine.

Maeve opened her mouth, apparently ready to call out a hello, commune with her compatriot, but Kara clapped a hand over her mouth. Maeve struggled to get loose, her eyes narrowed with outrage.

"You can't just talk to her," Kara whispered.

Now the kid's eyebrows formed a V of protest. Because of course they did. She believed she had the right to talk to anybody.

"I thought making friends was hard for you," Kara snapped, still low. "You have to keep quiet. I mean it. Then I'll let go. Okay?"

The kid's head bobbed.

Kara took her hand off Maeve's sticky face.

The two of them ducked behind a screening of leaves.

"She's been taught not to respond. And what to do if anyone approaches. We can't just walk up to her or even call out," Kara went on, observing the little girl tug a last cluster of berries loose and give her basket a jog to settle its contents.

She delivered the same satisfied nod Kara once would've felt such a haul deserved.

"Gotta tell ya," said Maeve. "That sounds super weird."

Kara pulled Maeve's hand to get her going. "We can follow her, though."

CHAPTER FIFTEEN

Arles's stepfather had strewn the property with game cameras, one of which was aimed right where the tracks she'd been following ended. Peter used to use the images for hunting season, and to find Arles as a child if she fled. He kept the data password protected, as if hiding state secrets, and she wasn't sure whether anything was being captured by the equipment anymore, if Peter had kept it operational after being forced to hand over the keys to the kingdom. But his reign hadn't ended very long ago, which made it seem possible that the footage still lived somewhere. It'd be worth a visit to the monster's lair—a.k.a. Serenity Acres—to find out.

Hopefully for now, Kara was hanging out with the child somewhere in this acreage, doing summer camp–type stuff, splashing in that creek. Based on the supplies Kara had taken from the attic, Arles could tell she possessed wilderness acumen, while the creepy little man with his huge SUV stood no chance of succeeding out here. His freshly purchased clothes didn't scream *outdoors enthusiast*. If Arles could get hints from the video feed, she'd be able to identify the direction Kara and the girl had taken from this spot and go after them.

She pocketed the SD card and headed back to Fir Cove for her car.

Only the rare, lucky few got to exit the world with any grace or dignity. Peter's wealth had bought him some protections, allowed him to hedge against the inevitable degradation. Serenity Acres was the most luxurious memory-care facility between Wedeskyull and the state capitol, sitting at elevation to command striking views, on a large enough piece of land that nothing disturbed its peace, save for the ravaged minds of the residents.

Arles hadn't seen her stepfather in nearly five months. Peter hadn't called or sent so much as an Edible Arrangement after she had been shot, and his lack of social graces wasn't due to the fact that his mind was going. His interest in and use for her had dried up like a fig in the sun as soon as she passed adolescence.

Nothing besides a child in need could've made Arles seek out her stepfather.

"Hello," said a pleasant-faced man standing behind a half wall of burnished wood. "Welcome to Serenity Acres."

Arles stumbled over the name as she identified the person she was there to see.

"How lovely," the man said. "Peter doesn't get many visitors."

"Surprising," she said, brief and bitten off.

The man swiped an icon on an oversize LED screen mounted to the wall, and after a moment, a woman in cheery peach scrubs appeared.

Arles's stomach clenched like a fist.

"You're Peter's stepdaughter?" the aide asked with a smile.

"That's right." A whistling breath, air escaping her lungs as if through a puncture.

"I'm Valerie." The aide led the way to a hall walled with windows. Bright, sun-filled. This place was nice. Much, much too nice.

"So, the good news is," Valerie said as they walked, "your stepfather's mind has been quite clear of late. In fact, if we were doing the intake now, I'm not sure he'd even qualify for our memory-care unit."

It took Arles a second to realize she was supposed to answer. "Wonderful."

They entered another wing of the building, and Valerie's voice grew less upbeat. "Unfortunately, his cancer markers are up. Our oncologist diagnosed him as stage four last week."

Arles glanced down at Valerie, and something must've shown on her face.

"I'm so sorry!" the aide exclaimed. "I should've realized you might not have been told—you haven't seen Peter since he moved in." She took obvious care to neutralize her tone.

You don't know him, Arles thought, fairly shaking. *You think of elders as precious heirlooms worthy of protection and care and places like this. You think Peter is a sweet old man.*

"No one informed you of his secondary diagnosis?" Valerie asked.

Arles managed a headshake. "What kind of cancer is it?"

"Prostate," Valerie replied. "Which can be slow going. Some of our family members are more likely to be struck by lightning than die from prostate disease. Something else will get them first, whether old age or their dementia. But your stepfather's type happens to be aggressive."

"Aggressive prostate cancer," Arles repeated. Suddenly, she swerved toward the wall of glass, resting her forehead against it. The pane clouded with her exhalations.

Valerie waited patiently. Arles hoped her reflection in the glass couldn't be seen, features contorted to hold back a peal of laughter, or maybe a deep, wrenching sob.

"Is he in a lot of pain?" Arles asked once she was able to return.

"Oh no," the aide replied. "Don't worry about that. Due to the improvements in Peter's cognition, we have him on a PCA."

Arles showed her unfamiliarity with the term, lifting her brows.

"Patient-controlled analgesic," Valerie supplied. "It's a godsend in terms of patient comfort. Only they can feel their level of pain and when the meds address it. That's why the *patient-controlled* part is so important. No one else can dose them. They know their bodies best."

Arles nodded vacantly.

Valerie gave a laugh. "There was an incident where this poor grade-schooler accidentally dosed Grandma. Guess the handheld looks like something for gaming." The aide shook her head, laughter shriveling. "Our devices aren't the absolute latest, and we don't use pulse oximeters.

Too many false alarms; they drive the nursing staff crazy. So now we make sure to issue warnings."

But Arles could no longer respond. They had come to a stop outside Peter's room. Valerie pushed open the door, giving Arles a quick smile and nod before departing. Arles chose to take both gestures as encouragement, setting her legs in motion.

Once she stepped inside, Arles saw the PCA, resting like a pet by Peter's side on the cushioned seat of his wheelchair. A smallish box with what looked like a remote control connected by a curlicue cord, reminiscent of one on an old rotary phone except with more generous loops. Peter's quarters resembled a cross between a titan of industry's study and his boudoir, but even if the new terminology ran to *elder-care facility* versus *old-age home*, the odor gave away what this place really was. Cleanser strong enough to destroy the plague mixed with the remains of school-cafeteria food. The sick, sweet smell of disease.

Peter swiveled his wheelchair around with a surprising show of strength given his thinness, the whittled shape of his body, and his eyes lit with recognition. Arles would've preferred him demented, though she needed him copacetic to provide the info she'd come for.

"Back to demand property rights again?" he said. "I don't have another house to give you. Sold the one in town to pay for my occupancy here at Senility Acres. Might not have been necessary, given how brief it looks as if my tenancy will be."

"I don't want anything from you," Arles told him. "Fir Cove wasn't yours to give. Call it an intestate glitch on my mother's part that I forced you to correct."

"Then why have you come?"

"The cameras in the northwest woods," she said. "Are they still capturing footage?"

He wheeled a few feet closer. "Having a problem with poachers?"

It was as good an excuse as any, and Arles wouldn't have mentioned a young girl around Peter under threat of torture. She nodded.

"I told you it's not safe out there for a woman alone," he said, resting his gaze on her.

Peter would forever make her feel like a six-year-old child. That was the age she'd been when he and her mother had married, Peter's eyes crawling over Arles throughout the wedding. Until then, she hadn't known eyes could behave like that, the pupils a pair of beetles.

She fished out the sliver of plastic. "I just need your password; then I can figure out the rest." She walked over to a leather-topped desk. A copper cup bristling with pens stood next to a framed picture of Arles at the wedding she'd just been recalling and a laptop.

"You think I'm going to give you my password?" he said.

"Would you rather enter it yourself?" she asked, flipping open the laptop.

"I don't intend to do either," he said. "It's time for my lunch. I take it in the solarium."

"Lovely," Arles bit out. "Let's lunch."

Maybe she could use something to incentivize him. An extra serving of dessert. Treats when he deserved to be spending his dotage in a prison cell.

The solarium looked out on a swell of lawn, green at this height of summer and speckled with dandelions. Willow branches dangled over a brook by which benches had been stationed. Inside the room, plump sofas opposed each other in pairs, and shelves held books for all ages: illustrated children's volumes, popular novels, nonfiction tomes. A row of mysteries reminded Arles of Kara, the urgency of this errand.

Arles jammed the foot brake on Peter's chair and left him facing the wall.

When she reentered the room with a tray, a killing cold swept through her, turning her insides to ice. A child had wandered into the room, no more than four or five. She crouched by the shelf of storybooks, running one miniature finger back and forth across the spines.

The tray tilted in Arles's hands. A plastic-wrapped sandwich and bag of chips slid free. An overripe plum split as it struck the floor, revealing its pulpy interior. A bowl disgorged a lurid serving of fruit sorbet.

"Do you like stories?" Peter's voice croaked. He cleared his throat wetly.

Every cell and bit of tissue had frozen inside Arles; she couldn't move a muscle.

The girl looked up and nodded.

Oh, Lord, why was nobody else in this beautiful room with its beautiful view? Resident, nurse, orderly? Were there that many spaces in which to while away aimless stretches of barely segmented days? Even as she posed the question, the answer grew clear. Pitched and humped forms roamed the grounds, accompanied by upright companions in scrubs. No one wanted to be inside on such a glorious day. Except Peter, a creature who dwelled underground.

Arles longed to beat her fists against the glass, seek protection from the elderly and infirm. If she called out, screamed, would anyone hear through this thick, expensive glass, insulated against harsh Adirondack winters? It didn't matter. Her vocal cords were encased in ice.

"Do you like people to read stories to you?" Peter asked.

The girl offered another nod, still studying the row of books.

Peter's neck notched as he took a look around.

Arles wasn't standing within view. He missed her as he searched the confines of the room. Not that she could've opposed him in this state. She'd never been able to fend off Peter.

"Are you visiting your grandma or your grandpa?" he asked.

"Granny," the girl replied, rotating on her heels to face him. "But she's having one of her very hard days right now, so I have to find something to pie myself with."

"*Occupy* is a grown-up word," Peter said. "You must be a smart little girl."

The girl plucked a book from the shelf. Something Disney. A princess movie tie-in.

"I can even almost read," she said.

"That so?" Peter said. "I guess you don't need me to read to you, then."

"Yes, I do!" The girl jumped to her feet. "But only the big words."

How could it be this cold inside a sunroom? Arles's flesh had turned to marble, so pale it seemed no blood coursed beneath the surface. She was too cold even to shake.

"Come over here." Peter patted his lap. "And I'll read just the big words."

The girl trotted in his direction, clutching the book. She had trouble climbing up, and Peter's arms lacked the strength to lift her off the floor. For a moment, it seemed that his rapid-fire grooming attempt would fail.

Then the child asked, "Can I stand on top of your feet?"

Peter's old-man shoes rested on a pair of ridged metal flaps. The girl balanced atop them, then scrambled into position. Peter touched the book, his hand emerging out of the sleeve of his sweater, as pale as the underbelly of a lizard. His skin looked flaky and dry; there were limits to the care one received even at a place like this. Or maybe nobody could stand to touch him.

Arles watched him stroke the translucent webbing between the child's tiny thumb and forefinger as he freed the book from her grasp. Then the room wavered, and the girl on Peter's lap no longer had blond pigtails; her hair was a brush of flame. Strands Peter used to wrap and weave around his thick fingers. Sometimes, when Arles would squirm to get down, he'd give that hair a vicious tug. The air warped and blistered like a heat mirage, unfreezing her.

She crossed to the wheelchair in four long strides and swooped the child into her arms, snatching the book from Peter's gnarled fingers. "Can you find your granny's room?"

The girl nodded. Not a *little* girl. Arles had refused to apply that qualifier ever since she'd ceased being allowed to be little herself. Girls were girls. Till they were women.

"Go. Take the book with you." She set the child on the floor. "I'll watch till you get there." Once the girl had knocked and the door swung open, Arles turned on Peter. "Come on. You're skipping lunch today."

She rolled him back along the hall so fast, his wheelchair tilted and pitched.

"Slow down, Arles," he commanded.

She entered his room, scooting the chair over to his bedside, then checked underneath the laptop. A label printed in an oversize font displayed his password. She should've predicted such a Boomer move sooner; Peter was nothing if not a product of his generation.

She keyed it in: *KINGOFTHEHILL*. All caps.

She felt her face contract with hatred. Self-hatred. If she'd looked at a mirror right now, she would've appeared demonic. She was a demon: howling, righteous, deserving.

The laptop demanded to update.

She felt Peter's weight from behind, outsize given how the cancer had eaten him up.

Your update is 3% complete. Please do not shut down your computer.

She palmed the SD card, concealing it from sight. Sleight of hand, the games she used to play, lies she used to tell to keep Peter away. Since escaping his clutches, she tried never to lie.

29% complete.

Mom's gonna be mad if we don't get home in time for dinner, Arles would say.

48% complete.

Uncle Vern asked you to meet him at the barracks, Arles would say.

64% complete.

It was agonizing, watching the line drag itself across the screen like a razor blade.

83% complete.

"Arles," Peter said from behind, "I know why you're not talking to me."

She jumped, jogging the desk. If the computer went dark, she'd have to start all over again. Dark. Like her soul right now. The room a rotting fruit crawling with tiny, feasting flies.

Because she hadn't known. She'd thought she had been the only one—and what a brutal, disgusting way to describe the person she was to Peter, the role she had been forced to play in his life.

It had never occurred to her that he would move on to other playgrounds.

Success! Your update is complete.

The machine started, and she jammed in the SD card. Its contents were encrypted, but Peter was dumb enough to have used the same password, or else arrogant enough to believe cybersecurity didn't apply to him. She downloaded files without taking time to see if there were any relevant images, emailing herself in a fog, unsure if her fingers were striking the keys. Then she closed the lid of the laptop, extinguishing its light.

"It's because you feel jealous, isn't it?" Peter asked, his tone soothing.

Fumes filled the air, the poison gas of her stepfather's breath.

She crossed to stand over him in his chair.

He cast his gaze upward, lips parting over eroded teeth in a smile.

"Don't worry. You'll always be my favorite."

She stared down at him, feeling heat ignite, burning the corneas of her eyes.

He patted her hand, his flesh scaly and tight, as she reached for the remote control–looking thing. Like streaming channels on TV; any asshole on his couch demanding a beer from his wife could've figured out this device.

Arles did what she was doing with a savagery more suited to throwing a punch than depressing a button as small and smooth and white as a mint.

She caught the moment when panic started to fill Peter's eyes. It looked like his grip had slipped from a rope, and he was being dragged over the edge of a cliff. His hand shot out as he tried to stop her, scrabbling helplessly, not strong enough to take even a divot out of her skin.

Then a look of pleasure contaminated his gaze, and his head lolled to one side.

She wasn't sure if she had done it. She didn't know if it would be enough.

She used her sleeve to wipe the gadget clean, then lifted Peter's slack hand and positioned it. The door to his room had stood open this entire time, Arles saw as she walked out. But Serenity Acres, for all its niceness and amenities, didn't appear to be overly abundant in the human-interaction department. Arles doubted anyone had come by. As she approached the exit, she spotted the girl from earlier, standing beside a woman who must've been her mother, based on the matching hair and delicate frames. The child's face was splotchy; she had been crying.

"I hear that you're very sad and disappointed," said the woman. "I know it's hard when we come to see Granny and she can't talk to us."

Good job, Mom, Arles thought tiredly. She felt as exhausted as if she'd taken apart a whole city, concrete and cement and bricks. Her flesh scraped raw. Nails torn down to the quick.

"But we'll visit again," said the mom. "And maybe see that nice man next time too."

The girl caught Arles's glance, and her face turned sunny with a smile.

Arles couldn't bear to smile back. *No next time,* she said with her eyes.

CHAPTER SIXTEEN

The path Kara remembered taking as a teenager was invisible now. Overgrown, requiring bushwhacking to get through, a real slog. The little girl with her basket was the opposite of a skipping Red Riding Hood, muscling her way among stalks and bushes that grew as high as her head. Pollinator plants, Kara realized, breaking trail while keeping far behind the other child, who, if things still went the way they had when Kara was young, would be alert to followers. Everybody received training, even the little ones. Kara pushed aside a tall stand of brush so Maeve could pass. Pearl wouldn't brook this flora being guillotined; she'd always been back to nature like that, concerned with the environment.

What was interesting was how Maeve took to the rugged terrain, examining without alarm the disinterested bees that alighted on her skin before buzzing away. Hadn't the kid been complaining about the prospect of bugs just a few hours ago?

When they finally drew within sight of the house and Berry Girl trotted off, Maeve turned around with her hands bunched on her hips and a clear expression of *Now what?* on her face. Kara counted herself lucky that the kid hadn't gone running after her would-be pal, just strolled into a strange house with as much aplomb as she'd taken a dunk in Dr. Shepherd's bathtub.

"Let me guess," Maeve said. "Entering houses around here is forbidden too."

Jenny Milchman

Kara exhaled a gust of relief that the same system was still in place, no concessions made to the digital age. Locate the pad in its plastic sheath and write a note stating what you needed. Food, shelter, transport, advice, protection, money—all those and more were on offer. Slide the piece of paper through a cat flap to a spot that was manned—*womaned*, Kara remembered being corrected—at all times, just in case someone slipped a hand through instead of a paw. Or a head. Tried to get a look inside. Necks were vulnerable. So were fingers. Dissuading someone from an attack wasn't hard when the only accessible entry point was sized to fit a kitty.

The front and back doors, though they looked normal enough, were reinforced with steel. The windows were too small to crawl through and had both locks and dowels to seal them shut.

"Kara? Fucking hell, that *is* you. Carol thought it was."

Pearl emerged from belowground, the egress a pair of bulkhead doors adorned with weeds, resulting in a degree of camouflage. Seventeen years ago, Pearl had purple hair that used to make Kara think of grape soda. Now it was blue, but other than that, she looked the same. Straight-backed and unlined, while also unapologetically not young, puffy through the middle with squat, purposeful shoes and loose clothing. She might've been wearing this exact same outfit the last time Kara saw her.

"Let me get a look at you," Pearl said.

The director shied away from casual touches, offering neither a hug nor a pat. But she examined Kara in a way that might've felt creepy except for the depth of affection in her eyes.

"You're all grown up," she said.

"I became a writer."

"Oh, I know that. I've kept up with you, Kara Cross. You never did strike me as a *Parsons*, by the way. The pen name is superhero badass. You've done every one of us proud."

Kara looked away, her eyes filling. "I chose it because of having a cross to bear."

Pearl gave her a moment, then said: "And you've brought someone with you."

Kara couldn't introduce Maeve by name—especially not this one—to Pearl. The director had plenty of experience with false identities, but the moniker Kara had bestowed would blare an instant warning. So she just said, "She's in trouble, Pearl. Don't know if that means I am too."

The director snapped into immediate can-do, a mode Kara recognized.

"As you know, we don't wait around here to find out," Pearl replied grimly.

Kara reached for Maeve's hand.

"Come inside," said Pearl. "Both of you."

Carol was on message-retrieval duty; she stood at the back door watching Kara's progression with Maeve. Kara smiled at her as the three of them entered, but Carol didn't respond in kind. Kara remembered this about her—Carol wasn't a smiler. She was nice enough, but her mouth seemed permanently soldered in an inverted horseshoe.

Carol walked over to the stove and fired up a kettle, then returned to her station.

"Have you two eaten breakfast?" asked Pearl.

Maeve gave a ferocious headshake. "Except for some candy."

Pearl filled two mugs with tea, making one milky and sweet, and set them on a round metal-rimmed table. Fetching boxes of cold cereal, a jug of milk, and a bowl containing the berries the little girl had just picked, Pearl added a tray of doughnuts, and breakfast was served.

"What can you tell me?" she asked Kara, dropping into a chair.

Kara recounted the incident that had taken place on her book-signing line—Pearl clinking her mug against Kara's in a congratulatory toast when Kara mentioned her new novel—then went on to describe going to Dr. Shepherd's house and why they had left this morning. She concluded with: "She won't explain what being *missing* means, and the therapist I just told you about said not to push, but this morning she told me she's from Arizona. The kid, not my therapist."

Maeve was cramming a doughnut into her mouth and didn't weigh in.

Pearl had listened to all this quietly, her fingers woven together in a strong, tight ball.

Maeve started in on the berries, eating them by the fistful.

"I think she comes from a cult," Kara added when Pearl didn't say anything.

Maeve looked away at that, her purple-stained lips pressed tightly together.

Kara didn't want to *say* she could out-shepherd Dr. Shepherd, but it did seem like she'd really made headway with the kid. Pearl still wasn't speaking, though, which made Kara nervous.

We have no place to go after this, she thought. *There is literally no place left.*

"The Sunshiners," said Maeve.

The words popped out like a gumball. It was as if the kid had been preparing.

Kara and Pearl both turned their heads at the same time. Then Pearl went to get a pad and a pen out of a drawer and jotted down two words: *Arizona. Sunshiners.*

"I'm not supposed to tell anyone," Maeve added. "The Misters and Maids won't let us."

Pearl sat back down and added those two to the sheet, her face clenched in an expression that Kara was pretty sure mirrored her own. *Fucking misters always making maids of the sisters.*

Kara was about to ask Maeve to go on—was that the right thing to do? How would Dr. Shepherd have handled it?—when a woman significantly younger than Carol or Pearl strode into the kitchen, snatched a doughnut off the table, then shoved her way into position at the back door.

"My turn," she said, her tone snappish.

"Jeez, Meredith." Carol took a step backward. "You don't have to act so angry."

People who resided here tended to be hyperattuned to anger.

"I don't?" the other woman demanded. "When I'm about to waste the next three hours waiting for a message that'll never arrive? Hello, 1990 called. It wants its scraps of paper back."

"I would've received one this morning," Carol said meekly, gesturing to the table. "Except I happened to recognize her."

"I don't give a shit!" the woman yelled, not paying Kara or Maeve any mind. "What exactly *is* our superspy system? Someone who knows this place tells someone else how to leave an SOS, which gets passed along like we're all kids in a fucking game of telephone?"

Carol took a quick check of the woman, as if assessing her likelihood to blow, then sidled past her and scurried out of the kitchen.

Maeve had looked up at the outburst; now she glanced at Kara, who shrugged.

"I'm sorry," Meredith said. "I just know there are better ways to do things."

"Like what?" Pearl asked, rising to turn on the burner beneath the kettle again.

"Like, they've got these so-called public shelters now. Have you heard about them?"

"I have," Pearl said mildly.

"Yeah, well, in one of those, women don't have to be removed from everything we know, leave all our support systems behind. Or our kids, either: their schools, sports, scout troops. Ironic, huh? We run away from our psychopath husbands, then lose the rest of our lives as well."

Kara winced. Meredith had just given a pretty good description of what Kara's life had been like when she was a teenager. When she looked away, she caught Maeve staring at her.

Pearl poured water, dropped a tea bag into a mug, and held it out.

Meredith snatched at the cup, splashing its contents. "The kind of secrecy we've got here—hiding us away like nuns in a convent—isn't the only route to safety! In fact, studies find it may work *against* safety. Think what would happen if dozens of people knew where a shelter was and could be on the lookout for the women who live there. Standing guard in a way."

"That actually does sound promising," Kara murmured.

Meredith acted as if she hadn't even heard her, but Pearl glanced Kara's way before turning back toward Meredith.

"Like a neighborhood watch," the director said, her tone steady.

Meredith used her free hand to push aside the curtain on a window. The gesture looked irritable, a flick, a twitch. She bent down to peek outside, but there wasn't anybody there, at least not as far as Kara could see.

"Yes!" Meredith said. "Right."

"These guardians of mercy being men, I presume," said Pearl.

Meredith didn't say anything.

"You want to hand over your safety—your agency—to a new batch of males," the director went on. "Rely on the kindness of strangers who may not be kind at all."

Pearl turned and faced away then, studying what appeared to be empty space. Kara had been young when she'd lived here, but she was an adult now, in charge of a child. She forced herself to stand, then held a curtain back so she could look outside for herself. Every window in this place was draped. Only now, having listened to Meredith's rant, did it occur to Kara that shutting everybody out also meant shutting yourself in.

She saw nothing through the glass. The land, gardens, outbuildings all looked stationary, still. Of course, the woods couldn't be examined. Anything could be hiding in them. Anyone.

Pearl had begun speaking again. "Did you hear about the incident at the shelter downstate that tried out the alternative model you're so keen on?"

"What happened there?" Kara asked.

Meredith scoured her with a look, then shifted toward Pearl. "That one wasn't built with a safe room. The people who advocate for public shelters all say they need to have panic rooms."

"Don't look at Kara like that," Maeve said. "And stop not answering her questions."

Kara ducked her head, but couldn't hide a smile.

"What?" Meredith snapped, barely glancing at Maeve.

"You act like she's not even here," the kid said.

"Maeve. It's okay—" Kara said, even though the support felt like a warm sweater.

"Just to keep talking about—what's she talking about, anyway?" Maeve asked.

"Public shelters," Pearl responded. "Where women are forced to flee to a bunker at a moment's notice, breathe the same oxygen as their housemates until someone is alerted to the threat, and deactivates it before letting loose the hens huddled away. As opposed to living at a site where we can do what we want, when we want, in the majesty of the great outdoors, and the only price is being on message duty twice a fucking week."

Maeve appeared to have been losing interest although she jerked her head up at this eruption.

"Give me one sec, people," Pearl said.

The director never referred to residents as *girls* or, God forbid, *ladies,* Nor as *guys,* either—members of the group most of them were fleeing. They were all human beings.

Kara clocked Pearl's stance as the director exited the room, and the rigidity and defensiveness in it caused Kara's perennially set internal alarm to jangle. The clop of Pearl's shoes resounded on the basement steps.

From her post by the window, Kara saw the nose of a rifle poke out from between the slanted doors before Pearl emerged. The clumps of greenery on the bulkheads made it look for a second as if the director were dressed in one of those gillie suits Kara's father used to wear when he went hunting. Pearl stood staring out over the land, rifle pointed down at the ground.

Many of the women who passed through here had a phobia about guns, but Kara found the sight reassuring in Pearl's hands. She herself felt paralyzed, standing with her back to Maeve and hoping the kid didn't get up. Kara still couldn't see anybody outside.

Meredith didn't abandon her station, staying put while her eyes welled. She sent Kara a wordless *what do we do?* Kara shook her head; she didn't know.

"Sorry for being a bitch before," Meredith mouthed.

Kara shook her head wordlessly again. It didn't matter. She'd been cast back into the position she'd held as a child only a few years older than Maeve. The times Pearl would stalk across her property, eventually returning to deliver an *all clear.* To let loose the hens. Although on a few occasions that Kara only learned about later—the kids were always shunted away—it turned out that she'd had to neutralize a very real threat. Maybe like the one who had shown up at Dr. Shepherd's house.

A whispered breath from Meredith, a sound of pure torment. "My son's upstairs!"

Kara stared at her, no idea what to say back. Pearl was formidable. But so was Maeve's pursuer, presumably.

"Other kids live here?" Maeve asked joyfully.

Meredith ignored her.

From below came the sound of the bulkheads slamming shut, and Kara, Maeve, and Meredith all jumped. Then Pearl came back upstairs and reentered the kitchen, weapon securely stashed, back in the gun safe, Kara assumed. The director gave a single headshake. Nothing.

"Now finish out your watch," Pearl told Meredith as if there'd been no interruption. "Unless you intend to find one of those public shelters and move out. We may not be at full right now, but I'll have a wait list before too long. Plenty of women who'd appreciate your spot."

"I'm not going anywhere," Meredith said quietly. "Leo's never felt so safe in his life."

The director returned to the table and looked down at Maeve.

"Would you like to take part in lessons with the other children?" she asked. The kid's eyes widened, and she seemed too overwhelmed to get out a simple yes. At last, she gave a rapid series of nods. Pearl smiled at her, then called for Carol, who came to escort Maeve out.

Pearl turned to Kara.

Kara felt air leave her lungs, her body, the world.

"You know I can't let you stay, right?" Pearl said kindly. "Not with the child."

Kara's mouth opened futilely, the protest of the teenager she'd been, railing against perfectly reasonable requests and requirements because the rest of the world had been so unfair.

Pearl held up a cautionary hand. "The men you described finding you at your therapist's private residence aren't what trouble me. Many of our residents are pursued, and I have ways of handling that, in case you needed any reminding."

Kara swiped at her drippy nose. Being here was making her feel like a kid again.

"It's the illegality. And I've taken on the law a time or twenty, but I lose my standing if I participate in felony kidnapping." Pearl shook her head. "I could be shut down. Jeopardize everything I've built—not to mention all the women who depend on it."

Kara stared at the table. Clean, scrubbed daily by an army of women, but clouded with the remnants of all those lives. *The Maids.* "So, you're throwing us out?"

"No," Pearl said fiercely. "I would never do that."

Slowly, Kara lifted her head, sniffling. "What then?"

Pearl glanced over her shoulder, her face watchful, alert.

At the back door, Meredith stooped to lift the cat flap, peering through it before letting the piece of plastic fall back into place. There was no white slip of paper in her hand or on the floor.

"There's a woman," the director said at last. "I wish she'd been around during your time, but her role was created after CPS, working in conjunction with the police, had one too many bad outcomes." Pearl let her gaze rest on Kara, and Kara knew she was checking to see how Kara was tolerating this topic. "She serves as a liaison of sorts between systems. Does everything by the book but is allowed to operate outside certain official protocols when necessary."

Kara drew in a breath, let it inflate her chest.

"I think she's our best option here," Pearl said. "So many unknowns."

Kara allowed time to spool out, hoping for a last-minute stay of execution.

Just kidding. Why don't you two stay, live here like you once did, auld lang syne and all?

When none of that came, Kara at last gave a nod.

Pearl nodded back. "I'll get word to her. And meanwhile, would you like to attend group for old time's sake? It's just about to start, and Erica's leading."

She had read Kara's mind, another of her powers.

For some, it was a bedroom tucked under the eaves, a favorite food, special toy, book, or vacation spot that swept them back to a sense of childhood familiarity and warmth.

For Kara, it was the group room at this DV shelter where she had come to live with her mother after the GAL—guardian ad litem—fucked up, and her father was permitted unsupervised visitation. The police made regular patrols as a favor for a while, but Kara's father was capable of putting on a helluva act. *I've had my nose good and rubbed in it, Officer. I learned my lesson. Sure, stick around as long as you want.* And the cops did. On one particular occasion, the police officer stayed parked outside the double-wide for hours until eventually getting a call and taking off in a whirl of lights.

Kara favored hikes as a way of maintaining distance from her father. She always tried to coax her sister to come along, but if that didn't work, Kara would go alone.

That time, with their dad on the warpath over God knew what, some noise he deemed excessive, Kara got back to find him strangling her little sister. Kara flew at him, and he flicked her off as if he were ashing a cigarette. She'd slammed into the side of the double-wide, wind knocked out as she lay there, bruises rising. Listening to her father huff and puff.

He'd had to work at it; it took real exertion for him to finish off his kill.

Kara rose from her chair and headed toward the hall, her feet remembering the way. But Pearl stopped her before she could leave, reaching out to catch Kara's hand. In all the years Kara had spent here, she'd never once felt the touch of the director's skin.

"This is all going to work out," Pearl told her. "We're doing the right thing."

They freed their hands from each other's at the same time.

"Pickup is at dawn," Pearl said. "You can both have dinner and sleep here tonight."

CHAPTER SEVENTEEN

Dan's apartment was the only place Arles could think to go after leaving Death Acres.

She drove in a state of muscular rigidity, as if lockjaw were setting in. Her hands less wrapped around the steering wheel than set like planks upon it; her limbs as inflexible as metal rods. The possibility that Peter was gone for good had a quality of unreality to it, like hearing a news story about something happening on Mars.

Arles made the turn onto Dan's street. Somehow, she had found the way here.

Dan had been in the level-one trauma center downstate when she had woken up from surgery. She remembered having said his name in the woods as she lay waiting for evacuation, but when he materialized in recovery, she didn't know what she could've wanted him for. She had never been any good at the relationship thing. And now, torn apart, cut open, put back together with stitches and staples? The idea of relating to another human being, especially a man, felt like rubbing hot coals all over her body. Her damaged body.

"I know what you're going to do," Dan had said as he stood in the glistening white room. Instead of asking the usual *How are you feeling?*, for example, or maybe giving her a balloon.

It hurt to lift so much as an inquiring brow, her body reknit and uncertain.

"You'll find some way of pushing me away," Dan said. "Whether that means refusing company, saying you're fine on your own, or being so hostile and prickly, you believe I will run."

Door number three, Arles had thought. Door number all of them.

"But in case you're willing to play things differently, I'm here."

Dan was still by her side at discharge three weeks later. His brothers had given him a leave from work at the family fuel business, and he'd accompanied her back to Fir Cove. She'd gone looking for potato chips; she was on a normal diet then and craving salt. Stephanie kept the snack foods high up so she could regulate Lissa's intake, and the slowly healing crater in Arles's belly made reaching overhead excruciating. She was trying to decide how to tackle a stepladder when Dan grabbed the chips for her. She had asked him to leave.

Now he opened the door to his apartment before she had a chance to knock. He'd been good from the outset at anticipating her needs. For the first time in her life, Arles wondered if that didn't have to be a lethal act.

Give Arles the space she needs; you know how it can get with mothers and daughters.

See how tired Arles looks? Think she needs to go to bed early tonight?

A girl needs to know how to survive in the woods; I'll teach her.

Dan's gaze was level, his body very still. "Am I supposed to just let you in?"

Arles wasn't great at dealing with confrontation under the best of circumstances—she tended to either lash out or retreat. Now her mind was clamped to the events of the last hour or so; she could've found water in a desert more easily than come up with words to offer Dan. Her clients would accuse her of being a hypocrite, trying to guide them in conflict resolution.

And they'd be right. The silence stretched out to snapping.

"You're sorry," Dan said at last.

She frowned at him. *Sorry* was the last thing she felt right now. Tense as hell, wondering what mayhem might be breaking loose at the go-to-die home right now. Or what bloodless, carefully ordered procedures were taking place; they were used to this up there. Well, not *this*, precisely. Mortality events, yes. Not what Arles had done.

Then she realized Dan was talking about the two of them.

"For throwing me out of your house," he went on. "Your life."

"I didn't exactly *throw* you—"

He cut her off. "Don't feed me bullshit, Arles."

She bit back the remainder of her protest. Her—he was right—defensive bullshit.

"You were under no obligation. We'd only met a short time before, and we made no promises to each other. You didn't have to accept my help, my company, my anything."

She gestured him on; he clearly wasn't done.

"But the way you did it fucking sucked," Dan said. "And I need you to hear that."

She swallowed around a cold, hard pellet. "I hear it."

He gazed at her. "Yeah?"

She nodded. "Yeah."

He led the way over to a table with a folding leaf designed to save space. One floor of a house had been carved up to form this apartment, two to a level. Arles found its compactness both cozy and claustrophobic. She sat down, words impacted behind her lips.

A hum came from her bag. There was cell signal in this part of town.

Slowly, Arles took out her phone and placed it to her ear.

Relief flowed like syrup through her veins, her own version of a morphine drip.

"Oh no," she said. "But I was just with him. I saw him today."

Dan looked on as she continued to listen.

"Um, well, my stepfather and I aren't close, as you can probably tell from the number of visits I've paid him." She made sure to swallow audibly, through her best approximation of a choked back sob. "*Weren't* close, I mean. But as far as I know, he wanted to be cremated."

Peter had rarely referred to his death; he seemed to consider himself immortal. Unstoppable. Which explained why, as the person on the other end of the call had just informed her, he hadn't listed any last wishes or instructions. But if Peter *had* grappled with his finitude, Arles knew he would've wanted a big, showy stone at a gravesite prominently displayed on the highest knoll in Wedeskyull's finest cemetery. Maybe a mausoleum. King of the Hill.

Not a fiery erasure, reduced to bits of bone and ash.

Still, she knew it would be the expression of peace on Peter's face at the end, and not his death, that would haunt her.

She took in a breath that raked the tissue of her throat as she ended the call.

Dan sat there, hands splayed on his legs.

"My stepfather died," she said at last.

Dan knew enough not to offer condolences. "Oh yeah? How?"

"Medication overdose," she said. "Self-administered." Arles administered.

Dan gave a nod.

This could stop right here, right now. She'd told Dan enough. Supplied the explanation she would be giving for the rest of her life, as many times as the subject of Peter's end came up.

But Dan had called her on her crap. The way she'd not just pushed him away but ejected him forcefully out of her life like a pilot from a fighter jet. Dan had said he wished things could've gone differently for them. And they still could. All it would take was the truth.

She sucked in a breath. "Psychologists have what's known as a duty to warn. It comes into play if a patient tells us something. Confesses, like. But it only applies when there's a threat of something similar happening again. A repeat occurrence. Otherwise, we're obligated to keep whatever it is to ourselves."

Dan sat motionless, hands laced together on the tabletop.

"Do you understand what I'm trying to tell you?" she asked.

"Not even a little," he replied. "I'm sorry."

He was good at apologies and admitting he didn't know things. He was the anti-male in that way. If he ever traveled to a strange land, he would ask for directions.

Today's event was about to combust inside her.

"I went to see him before I came here," Arles said. "My stepfather."

Dan gazed at her steadily, even though he must've been surprised. But he didn't interrupt with a *Why would you do that?* He had the rare ability to just listen.

"There was a child," she went on. "Visiting her grandmother, only Peter got the girl alone. I sent her away, and then—" She broke off, feeling her way. "I didn't snap like people describe. It was more like I'd been living in a snow cave and came out. Suddenly, I could see what was around me. And nothing was muffled. I knew I couldn't allow it to happen again."

Dan's face creased.

"Confidentiality," she whispered. "No duty to warn."

He got up and went over to a slice of counter with a modest arrangement of appliances. His back was averted; she couldn't tell if he was horrified, condemning, or working things out in his mind. He started the coffeepot brewing, returning a few minutes later with two cups.

Arles drank from hers, the skin on the roof of her mouth burning.

"You weren't sure," Dan said at last. "Until you got that call. Right? Because when you picked up, you looked—I don't know. Worried."

Hopeful, she thought, but *worried* was close enough. She nodded.

Dan sank into the chair across from her. Sipped from his own cup. "You'd better not ever lie to me. I'd never be able to tell."

She shut her eyes. "Don't make me feel like more of a sociopath than I already do."

Dan shook his head. "You're not a sociopath, Arles. I'd say you're a goddamn hero."

He fixed dinner, and she actually ate. Pasta and salad, sauce from his sister's new line of bottled and jarred goods. Elisabeth was a food blogger, cookbook writer, and, of late, a cook-trepeneur. After eating, they sat side by side on Dan's love seat, Arles downloading the images she'd gotten off Peter's laptop.

She wasn't able to provide Dan much in the way of orientation aside from broad brushstrokes. Kara's identity as a former client was protected, and the girl was entitled to rights as well, even if it wasn't as clear which ones.

Arles had watched enough game camera footage as a child to last a lifetime, Peter pointing out what to look for as he sat with his arm curled around her. It was always the same—beautiful but boring. Hypnotic. The woods changed on a micro level; grainy images depicting the life that animals, insects, fungi all shared. The flutter of leaves posed a break in the monotony. A flock of birds was big news.

Now two bodies appeared on the screen, one taller, one diminutive in proportion.

Kara and the girl were there for a few blips before slipping out of sight, the angle no longer right to capture them. Kara's pack appeared bulging; she'd taken plenty in the way of supplies. It was hard to be sure, but the girl looked positively jaunty, a skip in her step, almost as if she were enjoying herself out there.

Arles rewound the footage to study the direction they had headed in, focusing so hard on the images that her vision went swimmy.

"Arles," Dan mumbled, "you're falling asleep."

He didn't refer to the disruption in the feed; maybe he'd been dozing himself.

She roused herself. "A long time ago—in my great-great-grandmother's day—there was a hut on the grounds of Fir Cove. It served as a waypoint for women fleeing violent situations."

"Hey," Dan said, "that's some history."

"One of Fir Cove's prouder moments. It has a lot of lesser ones." Arles went back to thinking out loud, stitching pieces of Kara's past into a larger tableau. The fact that she'd chosen Fir Cove as a source of help, then took off into the northwest woods when it came time to flee. "I can't sleep right now. I have to make a call. Or two."

"Jesus. You know that marketing campaign for the army, how they get more done before eight a.m. than most people do in a week?"

"I'm enlisted?" she asked.

"You're Special Forces."

Arles stood, and the room wavered around her. Her head and limbs felt as if they were wrapped in mud. A yawn overtook her, cracking her jaw. Fatigue like this hadn't been a factor since she'd woken up after surgery. She didn't see how she could avoid sleeping; even just a few hours would help. Besides, if Kara and the girl were where Arles now had reason to believe them to be, they would be all right for a while.

They were safe.

CHAPTER EIGHTEEN

In the glimmer of predawn, silver beginning to limn the horizon, Pearl woke Kara and asked her to get Maeve. Kara had chosen to sleep in a private double like the one her mother had occupied before she'd fled the shelter, leaving Kara behind.

Kara's mother had never lived without the company of a man, hadn't spent so much as a single night without one. She had been forced to share a room with her older brother in childhood. She found the company of so many women at the shelter oppressive, while Kara had experienced the absence of male energy as a balm, a soothing emollient for her soul.

She pulled on pants, the boots from Dr. Shepherd, her shirt. Then, tugging the door quietly shut behind her, she tiptoed down the hall. Maeve slumbered in the bunk room, its walls lined with stacked beds, some of them empty right now. There was a relative lull in occupancy.

Maybe all the men were finally learning to behave, Kara thought.

Yeah, never, she scoffed at herself.

Maeve lay sprawled on her stomach, arms dangling so that her fingertips brushed the floor. At the bottom of the mattress sat a sheaf of papers. When Kara picked them up, a cluster of stubby crayons were exposed, like bugs beneath a rock.

Maeve flung herself over in a tangle of sheets, then opened her eyes.

"What's this?" Kara pitched her voice low to avoid disturbing the handful of other kids.

"A story," Maeve whispered back. "That woman sent me upstairs to sleep way early."

It'd been after ten p.m. when Pearl suggested Maeve go up. "Can I read it?"

Maeve shrugged. "Guess that's fair. I got the idea from you."

Kara sat down at the foot of the bed and flipped over the first sheet. The kid had written a mystery, dead body on the first page according to formula, and everything. The story lacked certain elements of craft, tending toward a superfluity of descriptions, but it wasn't half bad.

"It's good, right?" Maeve whispered, kneeling up in bed.

A swarm of words fought to leave Kara's mouth, but she choked them down. The kid didn't need to hear that Kara had learned something over the past day or so. Which was that clever plot twists made for good reading, but weren't what life was really about. In the end, it was only other people who could save you, and not characters, either, but real, live human beings.

They looked at each other in the dim room, daylight just starting to provide a glow.

"It's great," said Kara.

Maeve gathered the sheets around her, tucking them in with a pleased look on her face.

Pearl met them in the narrow foyer by a front door studded with deadbolts. A white Toyota Corolla—not old enough to be vintage or new enough to be showy—would pull up by a dead oak tree on the road that ran perpendicular to the woods, the only paved stretch for miles.

They set off along a path, Kara feeling a muscular energy in her limbs as she held back branches for Maeve and covered ground with sprightly steps. The sun had risen high enough to tint the sky through the trees and dapple the forest floor with silver coins. Kara peered between a mesh of twigs, then pushed through greenery to clear an opening. She and Maeve stood still, the road strange and smooth beneath the soles of their shoes after their interlude in the woods. The tree they were meant to find was unmistakable: sleek, leafless branches, all as bare as bones.

There was no car. No sign of life whatsoever. The woods had gobbled up the shelter behind them, chewed it to nothing. Kara and Maeve might've been the only two people on Earth.

"Do you come with me now?" Maeve asked in a small voice.

Kara stopped examining the road. "Are you cold?" The kid was shaking; the sun hadn't been up long enough to warm things. "Here, take my jacket."

Maeve shrugged into its oversize arms. "I don't mean for always. But maybe just at first?"

Kara returned to studying the road. Pearl had said this woman was the best, but leaving a child out here in plain view, even in the middle of nowhere, wasn't very smart. This rendezvous should've been prompt.

"Kara?" Maeve said, voice still quaking.

"I can probably get a ride home with y'all," she said after a moment.

They would part ways from there. Kara tested the idea, finding that it hurt.

"Yay!" Maeve said. "I get to see your house."

"It's not much, I warn you," Kara said. "Especially compared to what you seem like you're used to." Did kids in cults live in castles?

"There's the car!" Maeve pointed.

Kara turned, her limbs slackening with relief. Till then, she hadn't realized how on edge she was. A veil of exhaust fumigated the morning air as a white car crested a hill.

The kid took a step onto the blacktop, and Kara gave her a nudge, making her stick to the shoulder. There wasn't any traffic on this road, but Kara was in charge, for another minute anyway, and she wanted to do right by Maeve. She glanced at the windshield to confirm Pearl's description. The driver was short, barely visible above the steering wheel.

Maeve strayed into the road again; again, Kara pulled her back. What was it with kids and crossing streets? The car rolled to a stop a few yards off, door opening to admit a passenger. The driver probably wasn't supposed to get out. That made sense. Her identity might have to be kept concealed, which scotched the prospect of Kara's getting a lift.

Maeve turned and headed toward the car.

Pearl had said the car would park in front of the tree. The dead oak, denuded of bark, smooth and ivory as a tusk. The car was staying put because that was the meeting point.

"Maeve, hold up a sec—" Kara called out, starting to jog.

She should be there when the kid got in. Say hello to the woman. Thank her, even though she was taking Maeve away.

The kid's ride just sat there, engine running, a little growly. Not a late-model car, probably could've used a tune-up. It hulked like some kind of large animal, unless that was just Kara's imagination. Because suddenly, she was seeing events as they would've gone in a book. The cult's henchmen intercepting some woman, a real heroine, dedicated to squiring children to safety. Unless heroism was a fiction and the woman had told them where this handoff was to take place, given up her car and her quarry-to-be without a fight.

Maeve didn't appear to have heard Kara's shout. Probably hadn't been audible with the car's engine gusting. The car drew nearer—willing to leave its station, after all—and Kara saw the driver. Not a trace of expression on small, neat features. And not a woman.

What blisteringly real looked like when it came to evil as opposed to made up.

There were so many unanswered questions. She would never leave so many loose ends in one of her books.

The driver appeared to register Kara's awareness of him, and sped up. She raced forward, lunging at the kid, pushing the small bulbs of her shoulders to get her out of the road. Maeve swung around, confused or maybe annoyed. The woods pressed in from both sides; Kara felt their endless depths.

Land so easy to get lost in. Land so easy to lose someone in.

The car was covering ground shockingly fast now, no time wasted on closing its door. It hung open as Kara leaned down, bending over to get the kid moving. From that position, at kiddie height, Kara was able to yank hard enough to jolt Maeve into action; it felt like she had to rip off a piece of the kid's skin to do it. Without taking a second to straighten up, Kara hollered words she had never gotten the chance to deliver, two short syllables that had lived like poisonous capsules, cyanide pellets inside her ever since the day her sister died.

"Maeve! Run!"

But this wasn't Maeve, not really. This was some kid Kara had given everything to save.

A pair of empty, unfeeling eyes stared through the windshield, as if gauging Kara's position in the road. As one would a traffic cone, some harmless, expendable obstacle, not even as much concern as a squirrel darting onto the asphalt was owed.

The car's brakes squealed. It veered, swerving past her.

No. It hadn't passed.

Its passenger door, open to receive the kid, struck Kara's head with the sound of a ball thwacking a racket. Kara went down, thinking of her third novel, which had been about tennis. A coach father killing off his daughter's rivals. Readers had loved that twist.

The car careened into a ditch, tires whirring amid sprays of dirt as the vehicle fought to free itself. At least, that was what Kara thought had happened; she might've been seeing things.

The world looked different now, full of colors she'd never known existed, an infinite number of crayons on the bunk-room bed. Her gaze remained pinned to the woods. Inexplicably, the trees stood sideways. It struck her after a beat—she was still horizontal. Hadn't been able to get up.

Her vision broke apart into kaleidoscopic particles, the bright lake of blood she lay in spreading out. If Kara had known it was going to be this bright, she would've had no cause to feel guilty about her sister's fate. If people knew what this was really like, no one would ever have any reason to be frightened.

The only regret Kara had was that she'd never learned the kid's real name.

She had vanished into the woods. Unless she was still standing there?

"Go," Kara said on a last sip of breath. "It's okay. Now I'll get to see Maeve again."

This town was so jam-packed that Edwin hadn't been able to find an apartment or even a pair of rooms to rent, paid for in cash, of course, no record of his presence. The only hotel was sold out as well. What surprised Edwin was that none of the visitors dressed in their gear, carrying paddles or packs or loops of rope, had any reason to be here. Why hadn't they cleared out as soon as Mr. Stratton's big show was over?

Until now, Edwin had never gotten this close to Mr. Stratton, had only served him from afar. Learning that he was coming east had been like getting the best combined Christmas and birthday present in the world wrapped up in one beribboned box.

Edwin had brought hammocks; he had experience sleeping rough from when he used to overnight in another, lesser actor's backyard before a TRO was granted. Not that Edwin paid any mind to restraining orders. The first night in this town with the funny name, he had barely slept, anyway, following Mr. Stratton's black Escalade around until a state trooper pulled Edwin over, lights whirling in a giddy blur.

Edwin had steered carefully onto the shoulder. He couldn't afford a speck of trouble with the law. "There a problem, Officer?" Trooper, Edwin castigated himself. Calling cops by their proper titles inclined them to go easy on you.

The trooper had shone his light into Edwin's eyes but barely swept the back seat. Luckily, it looked uninhabited, just a small heap beneath some fabric. "License and registration."

Edwin had forced himself to blink affably and hand over his documents, even though he was roiling inside. No way to catch up to Mr. Stratton now. He fought to hide his fury, glancing up at the rearview mirror with as comforting a face as he could put on.

Then suddenly, miraculously, he was free to go. There'd been a report of a car matching his being driven erratically, but the trooper bought Edwin's demeanor of mild, beneficent confusion, and Edwin returned to the town where Mr. Stratton had put on his glorious show. Mr. Stratton's presence still radiated a glow, but there was a much more important reason Edwin couldn't leave yet.

Now, with the sun a dimple on a new day, he glanced at his phone. Time to start looking again. He clambered out of his hammock—long legs assisting with the jump—then untied it from the tree and bundled it away. The rest of camp could be broken down a little later; Edwin always rose at an ungodly early hour.

His phone throbbed; he kept it on vibrate to be unobtrusive. He walked off into the woods, studying the number, then swiped the call to life. "Hello, Dad."

"Where are you, Ed?"

His father's tone, even when he was being the calm version of himself, could jangle Edwin's nerves like eight cans of Red Bull. The velvety, dulcet strains of Mr. Stratton's speaking voice were so soothing by comparison. "Still here."

"Why the hell haven't you come home? Your mother is worried."

"It's not time yet, Dad," Edwin said, his own voice low. "Tell Mom not to worry."

His father scoffed, the sound of a grater on metal. "When does that ever work with her?"

His father seemed to want a shared laugh with his son in these moments, a women-and-their-damnable-ways mutual acknowledgment, but Edwin was never willing to give that to him.

"What are you doing there?" his father demanded.

"Important stuff," Edwin mumbled. He wished he could howl as loudly as his father. No, he wished he could caress words with his voice like Mr. Stratton.

His father let out a raspy laugh. "That right? So important that you can't do it from the basement level of my house like you do everything else?"

His father's voice rose, filling with explosives like a building about to be detonated. "So important that you have to make your mother whine and fret UNTIL I CAN'T GET ONE LOUSY SECOND OF PEACE?"

A crash loud enough that Edwin flinched, holding the phone away from his ear as if it had burned him. He checked to make sure the racket hadn't been overheard, but camp was still quiet.

From far away came his mother's voice. "Did you break it, Eric? Is it broken?"

"No, it isn't broken!" His father raged in the background, audibly stomping around.

There was a tremulous pause, the very air around the phone seeming to waver like a mirage.

Then his mother came on. "Eddie? When are you coming home?"

The force of his mother's need had always presented a crushing, strangling burden. Only Mr. Stratton's need was greater. "Soon, Mom."

A pause. "You aren't doing anything bad out there, are you?"

Edwin studied the long, angular shadow his body cast across the ground. He didn't know why he was tasting salt until he reached up and touched his cheeks. Crying on command. Mr. Stratton could do that. "It's not like that this time, Mom, I promise. This time, I helped him."

"How can you help someone like that? What would he ever need from you?"

So much.

Mr. Stratton deserved a distraction-free event. If a fuss had been made, a big police clatter, that would've ruined everything. So, no matter what incident had taken place, however bad or requiring of police intervention, things needed to be kept on the down-low. Edwin had helped with that. And of course, Edwin himself couldn't afford contact with the cops. It was lucky the redhead—so attractive, she could've been a movie star alongside Mr. Stratton—hadn't managed to summon the law when she'd shown up at the bookstore later that night.

His mom was still talking, words running together like cars in a pileup, and for once, Edwin understood what his father meant about her.

"But what about Janey? This is no life for a child. Remember what your therapist said?"

In a movie, it was called the All Is Lost moment. This was like swallowing pieces of glass to admit, but Edwin knew he'd go guilty to his grave because losing someone—even someone very important, as important as could be—just didn't matter so long as he had Mr. Stratton.

Edwin stared through the trees at the road he needed to reach. So he could keep looking. So he could watch out. "Janey's fine. Janey's great. You should've seen how nice she dressed up the other day, hair done and everything. I'll send a picture."

His mom had gone quiet, which was a relief.

"You've always said how tough Janey is," he continued, his voice a rubber band stretched so thin, you could see through it. "What's that word you use? Resilient. You say she could parent me. She can handle anything. Whatever happens to her." He believed what he was saying. So why were his eyes leaking again, and he couldn't take in enough air to keep speaking?

"Something's wrong, Eddie." His mother hit that note he hated. The squealy one, like a pig backing away from the farmer, that said she was scared. "I can hear it in your voice."

The Great Reveal, the moment in the movie when all was understood.

"Can I talk to Janey?" his mother asked suddenly. "I miss her."

"She's still asleep," Edwin said dully. Eyes seeping again as he looked off at camp, still and quiet.

For once, his mother didn't say anything. His phone had gone silent, as if Edwin were lost in an endless dark cave, a place from which there was no emerging.

"Wake her up, Eddie. Okay? Just give her a little shake; then she can go right back to sleep, quick as a clam. I'll just say hello."

Quick as a clam? What did that even mean? Sometimes his mother made no sense.

In the background, agreement on that front from Edwin's father who said, "Pipe down, woman! I'm trying to concentrate."

His mother was crying now. "Eric, please, I need to talk to our granddaughter! She's in trouble. Janey's in danger somehow. Oh, I just know it!"

His mother was ratcheting up, or spiraling down, getting her crazy on, so Edwin ended the call, then for good measure, muted his ringtone.

Before the movie had its worldwide release—worldwide!—it was opening in a few select cities, and also right here in this town where it'd been filmed. There would be no better way to view it than in the place where Mr. Stratton had spoken his lines, enacted his stunts, emoted.

Where he'd acted—glorious, magical art, spinning dross out of bleak, colorless reality.

Edwin would fix everything afterward. See to what was needed, make it all better. Yes, even if that entailed bringing in the police. Even if it meant sacrificing himself.

But he would not allow one single thing to go wrong until he had taken his plush seat in that theater, felt the lights go down, and watched Mr. Stratton fill the screen.

ACT II

ANOTHER TO THE MULTITUDES

CHAPTER NINETEEN

The sun sat at a fair juncture in the sky the next time Arles blinked to awareness. Her phone was ringing; Dan handed it to her from his nightstand.

"I plugged it in," he mumbled, climbing out of bed and making for the bathroom. He had a thing about not talking before he'd brushed his teeth. "You were low on charge."

Arles looked down. The number on her screen was a holdover from her days on staff at Wedeskyull Community Hospital, where she'd worked alongside social service agencies and county officials. Her heart beat a thunderclap, and she was momentarily unable to choke down a breath. She had saved the contact simply as *Police*.

It took her trembling finger a while to hit the little green icon.

When Dan emerged from the bathroom, he appeared to register the state she was in. He came and sat beside her on the bed. Waited.

"That was Chief Lurcquer," Arles said at last. "Asking me to come down to the station."

Dan hesitated. "Probably routine, right? You were the last person to see Peter."

She took in a breath. Dan was right. And she needed to talk to Tim anyway.

The only question was whether to tell him about Kara and her unexpected charge before or after being questioned for murder.

———

Perhaps due to her state of mind, the center of town looked strange, off-kilter. Carnivalian, everything overbright and sudden, like the jarring appearance of a pedestrian in her blind spot. She felt like she was driving through a funhouse.

Making the turn toward the barracks, she braked hard enough to jolt the car. Was that the man who had grabbed her at the bookstore, now standing still as a beefeater on a corner of road? She blinked sunspots from her eyes, trying to make out the figure. But whomever she'd seen was gone. She shook her head, trying to clear it of fuzz and calm the patter of her heart. Maybe instead of investigating the death of a pedophile who was dying anyway and deserved a lot worse than what Arles had doled out, Tim should look into this stranger come to town, and whatever strangeness had also brought to Wedeskyull a young girl being pursued by two men.

The barracks occupied a lordly spot high above town. Arles parked in the lot and got out, spiraling in a way she would've worked with a client to correct. *Routine,* Dan had said, and he was probably right. Still, anxiety nipped and gnawed at the still-healing tissue of her gut.

Dorothy wasn't sitting behind the glassed-in front area, so Arles walked on her own to Tim's office. She'd worked in conjunction with him over the years. If they weren't friends, or even colleagues, Tim was at least something more than the head of law enforcement in the town where she resided.

The door to his office was ajar; she thumped it with a quivery fist and entered. Tim sat staring at a laptop screen, hands balled on the surface of his desk. Without a word of greeting, he indicated that she should take a seat, his expression grim. Her legs shook like fabric on a clothesline as she dropped into the chair, assembling an expression of confusion mixed with concern. What anyone would feel if summoned by the chief of police.

Should she tell Tim about the girl before or after he arrested her for a justified homicide?

She didn't get time to decide; he launched right in.

"I'm afraid I have bad news."

Arles began to nod, then froze the motion. Did he not realize someone at Serenity Acres had already contacted her, believed he had to inform her of Peter's demise?

"A woman was killed in a hit-and-run earlier this morning."

Perched on the precipice of her interrogation, Arles was unable to keep her face from transforming. She felt bewilderment take hold of her features, winching up her eyebrows, crinkling her forehead. But her expression either went unnoticed or fit the situation well enough that Tim completed his bleak job without much of a pause.

"It turns out she might be or have been a patient of yours, which is why I called you."

"Who?" she asked, feeling faint vertigo from the readjustment. She wrapped both hands around the flimsy arms of the county-issued chair.

Tim glanced at his computer. "A Kara Parsons. You know her?"

Arles reeled back as if she'd been struck. Her head whip-lashed; a cord bulged in her neck. It felt as if an artery might rupture. Tears, acute and instantaneous, slicked her face.

Tim fumbled with a tissue box on his desk, coming up empty.

She pushed out of her chair, crossing to the window, where she stood with her forehead against the glass, no idea what she was looking at. She fought to clear her vision, to swallow a sob.

Tim approached with a fistful of fast-food napkins.

Arles took his offering, pressed them to her face.

"I, uh, owe you an apology," he stammered. "For just coming out with it like that. I, um, thought that therapists were, well, like us. Have to put up walls."

Arles squeezed her hands together, enclosing wet, shredded balls of napkin. "How did you learn Kara had been one of mine?" Was there suddenly some public database pairing patients with their psychologists? Had the mental health–care system been breached, or maybe world security?

Tim indicated the seat she'd taken initially, and Arles followed his suggestion.

He rolled his chair out from behind his desk and dropped down beside her.

"A jogger found Kara," he said gently. "Saw the car make it out of a ditch, although it raced off before she could get the plate. One of its rear doors open, waving like a flag, according to our Samaritan. I have an accident re-creation specialist coming from downstate. Anyway, apparently the last thing Kara said was: *Dr. Shepherd.*"

Tim thrust out another clump of napkins preemptively, but Arles was done with crying.

No mention of a child. Arles needed to tell Tim about her now, but opening her mouth felt like prying apart a vault with a crowbar. Kara had been sure that involving the police would lead to disaster, and while her reasons for thinking so resided in her own broken past, the worst had happened, and the police were playing catch-up, bringing Arles in for questioning.

Did the jogger not come upon a child because the girl had been taken away in a black SUV? Or because she was hunkered down somewhere, afraid to come out amid police activity?

Did the girl, along with Arles and Kara, belong to the same grisly club whose members had experience with law enforcement in volatile situations? LEOs weren't trained in the art of defusing; and beefy, intimidating men, megaphones, threats, weapons, and ammo were the worst things to bring to a standoff. You might as well try to put out a fire with gasoline.

"Where did this happen?" she asked Tim abruptly.

"A road called Bostock," Tim said. "Abuts acreage extending a long way. You know it?"

Arles shook her head. Wedeskyull was a small town in a big land. There were vast swaths she'd never set foot on, couldn't have named, didn't even realize existed.

"Does confidentiality still apply?" Tim asked.

She fought to follow his train of thought. "No. Not in the same way after a patient dies." The words felt like stones in her throat.

Tim gave a nod. "So, you can tell me about Kara. Can you think of any reason she would've been on a road that remote at such an early hour?"

Arles swallowed around a thick knot, her throat raw and sore.

Because somehow it was supposed to help.

But Arles was too good a psychologist to let her response show on her face, or even the fact that she was having any reaction at all. Tim was an astute investigator and might've noticed her pause, except that just then, his door banged open, hitting the wall behind it.

A clamor came from out in the hall. The handful of times Arles had been at the barracks, the place seemed to function like a factory, busy but orderly. Routines and operations in place to make the business at hand run efficiently and well. But this was a frenzy. Pairs of boots beating down the hall; hard, fast kernels of information spat out; radio snarls of static.

"Chief?" Dorothy thrust her head inside. "Owner of the white Corolla just turned up."

CHAPTER TWENTY

Tim shot to his feet and was out the door with a That's-it-for-now hand signal.

Arles rose, every inch of her body aching, as if she had the flu.

White Corolla, Dorothy had said. Not a black SUV.

Arles crept over to Tim's printer for a sheet of paper. Every version of what she had to say amounted to shining a spotlight on the girl. *I have information pertaining to a missing child* with the subsequent alphabet soup's worth of agencies called in. *A girl might be lost in the woods* would add SAR to the mix, a potential call for volunteers, with a grid search and rescue operation in which someone with malintent could camouflage himself. Including the small man who had invaded Fir Cove. Or the tall and narrow stovepipe guy, who'd clamped Arles's wrist, had a thing for Kip Stratton, and referred to a little girl. Arles settled on *I need to talk to you*, her fingers stiff and cramping.

Maybe she really was getting sick.

Of course she was sick. Kara had survived a brutal, abandoning childhood, then her own misplaced sense of guilt over her sister's death, only to be mowed down in the road and die at a stranger's side. Arles was sickened by every single woman and child who'd met a similar fate or some other version of same—including herself—at the hands of predatory men.

But if the girl were still out there somewhere, alive, then Kara would've died a hero.

Arles dropped the note on Tim's desk and exited his office.

The barracks had cleared out like a ghost town, the front desk area still deserted. Arles went out to her car, swiping her phone to life and downloading the route to Bostock Road. She peered at a hair-thin line in an ocean of green, then sucked in a breath. No wonder Kara had died saying Arles's name. Trek three miles through this stretch of forest, and you came to Fir Cove.

The summer air was still, the parking lot gone soft and gummy beneath the August sun. On her way out of town, Arles spotted the man again, this time for sure. He had positioned himself at the curb like one of those wind puppets shilling for gas stations or going-out-of-business sales. His canted shadow swayed as he gazed up at a banner strung high across the street: COMING SOON—THE ASCENT! STARRING KIP STRATTON. The actor was attired in full backpacking regalia, larger than life, as huge as the mountain behind him.

Arles couldn't see what was so compelling about the guy.

She shook her head, kept driving.

The narrow stretch of road she arrived at bristled with activity, more than it had probably ever seen. People in official dress and badges strode up and down or crouched on the asphalt, took equipment out of trunks, hailed one another, shouted jargon. Some of them were clustered around an enormous bare-boned tree, not a whisper of growth on it.

Arles needed to get past them.

But there was an officer stationed, clearly primed to pull over anybody who drove this out-of-the-way route, ask them some questions. Arles shifted into neutral and rolled back down an incline. When she came to a road running perpendicular to Bostock, she turned onto it, still going slowly in reverse, no K-turn or plume of exhaust to draw attention to herself. She drove until she found an empty driveway beside a darkened house. The property screamed *vacation rental*, but not the shiny, bloated variety, peacock-strutting water and acreage to pump up its price. With any luck, it wasn't booked. What time was check-in at these places?

If it could just stay empty for a while, then her car should go unnoticed. She pocketed her keys, making the return trip on foot.

She lost herself in the dense corridor of greenery at the side of the road. All the flora was thick and fleshy leaved, overgrown at this time of year, but there appeared to be a break ahead in the wall of woods. Arles threaded between trees, then paused at a succession of snapped-off branches, rubbing the juncture between a stub and its trunk.

The wood oozed fresh sap; her fingers came away tacky and scented with fir. She ducked beneath a sweeping bough of needles, broke through a tangle of brush that scored her skin, and then a space opened up, the ground laid bare before her. This deep in the forest, the morning sun had been subsumed by a primeval fog. Gray mist obscured outlines, making everything soft.

Checking the map, she arrived at a slope so steep, her legs strained to mount it, the tendons in her calves twanging. It was hard for any decent-size mammal to conceal its presence in the woods, and Arles attempted to track the girl as Peter had taught her. Her stepfather hadn't needed more prey to corner, but maybe the skills he'd imparted would finally come in useful.

Arles scoured the ground for footprints (those fuchsia sneakers probably had patterned soles), human hair (blond and well maintained), bits of (pricey) clothing torn by a twig or snagged on a rock. There might be a piece of trash; the girl didn't seem the type to have learned carry-in, carry-out principles or the *Leave only footprints* mantra.

But Arles didn't spy a trace of the girl, and a clot of panic rose in her throat; she had to work it back down. The child had a significant head start; she might be quite a ways ahead. Even back at Fir Cove already. Arles continued tramping.

Long after Peter had to stop thumping his chest over his outdoor prowess, the Adirondack wilderness still felt as if it belonged to him. To be his territory. The fact that Arles's mother had been the landowner, Peter's lifestyle owing to her largesse, didn't change anything. Nobody had a right to the land—although thanks to her foremothers, Arles did possess a deed to many acres—but Peter was the dragon breathing over it. Even though he was dead.

He was dead. Arles let the fact of it seep in, as if her body were porous. She checked for guilt, relief, anger, but felt none of those things. She didn't feel dissociated, either, the gauzy sense of disconnection that used to descend whenever Peter approached her. Instead, the world around her felt sharper somehow, made more right, although Kara's death had rendered it wrong in a whole new way.

She dug the toes of her shoes into the soil for purchase. This hill felt nearly vertical, which meant it entailed a good thirty-degree angle. She arrived at the top of the rise, standing on a plateau with her heart galloping. She heard the white noise rush of a waterfall; it would serve as her *panic azimuth*—the proper lingo coming back to her, Peter's voice still alive in her ears—in case she got turned around. It would be stupid easy to miss someone out here, a plethora of potential paths to take through the same swath of land, like spokes on a wheel. And it was pure guesswork on her part that suggested Kara had sent the girl this way. How soulless the birds now screaming overhead would sound if someone were lost out here, in need of help.

A sharp crack came from behind, and Arles ducked instinctively, clawing up a stick from the forest floor to use as a weapon, then rising with it thrust out. But no one was there, only a rainfall sifting of pine needles as a loose branch fell and clobbered the ground.

Her heart heaved; mist mixed with sweat on her skin. She crowned another rise, then broke through a final barrier of branches, twigs razoring her skin as she emerged at Fir Cove.

Air sat hot and dry upon the land; the house cast a lunging shadow. Arles had either failed to accomplish the mission Kara had tasked her with, or had misread Kara's final intent.

Grief as heavy as sand caused Arles's body to sag. First Kara, and now the girl—it was too much. Peter's erasure was not enough to balance out all the lost women and children that men like him stole. Arles gathered breath to make the return trip for her car. Maybe the child could still be found. Tim, the FBI field office, searchers . . . She ticked off sources of help in her mind.

She felt the motion before she spotted its source. Something inching forward on hands and knees, too lumbering and slow and purposeless to pose a threat. Hair swinging, sweeping the ground so that a cloud of grit surrounded the form, preventing a clear look at it.

"Dr. Shep—"

The small body face-planted, collapsing onto the dirt at Arles's feet.

CHAPTER
TWENTY-ONE

Arles felt buffeted by a gale force of emotion, a storm of relief and fright. The girl was alive—if struggling. There was happiness in the mixture too, a sliver of joy. Because Kara had done it.

The child hadn't moved from her prone position on the ground. Her previously coiffed hair resembled fluff from a milkweed pod, so entangled with thorns and burrs that Arles feared it would have to be cut. Why was she focusing on hair right now? She gave her own strands a savage tug, jarring herself into action, and gently rolled the still form over.

The girl's eyes rolled upward, but she didn't come to. Her clothing was wet, her skin clammy to the touch, and her pulse was reedy. Hypothermia combined with shock. If the girl had witnessed the hit-and-run, then in addition to whatever toll the woods had taken on her, she was suffering from trauma. She needed to be brought inside fast, and they both had to get out of sight.

The girl had managed to escape whoever struck Kara. Not the owner of the white Toyota, surely, the person Dorothy had told Tim about. Which meant that the driver of a black Escalade was still out there somewhere. Looking.

Arles snatched a look around. Tall, looming trees, the sickle of driveway, a hump of hill leading down to the lake. It was impossible to be sure she and the girl were alone. She leaned down and attempted to scoop up the child, forgetting momentarily that her body would oppose her. She hadn't lifted anything so heavy in months, her limbs sodden and weak with disuse despite their improvement in the woods just now.

Suppressing a groan, ignoring the tightening guitar strings in her gut, she made a sling of her arms and got the girl off the ground. She staggered up the porch steps, breathing in short, hard spurts, spots dancing across her field of vision. She rested her hip against one of the logs the walls were built from, letting the house support her. What if the reason nobody had ambushed them yet was because they were already inside? She fought down a flare of panic.

Shifting the girl's weight, she placed her in a firefighter's carry, like an oversize baby over one shoulder as she unlocked the door one-handed. Jogging the child up in her hold, she stepped over the threshold. Then, using the benefit of their combined weight, she leaned against the door to close it, the slab of wood too heavy to kick.

She crossed to a couch and laid the child down as gently as possible, although she had to let gravity take her at the end. Then Arles went back to secure the bolt. After brief reflection, she dragged over a table that stood to one side, moving it in slow increments. It wouldn't add much heft to the mountainous door, but its legs would be audible scraping across the stone floor.

She returned to the girl and looked her over. No swelling to indicate a broken bone or sprain, no blooming bruises. Her unconsciousness was a blessing as Arles shucked off her wet clothes and replaced them with a fleece, plus two wool blankets. At last, she lifted the girl's feet and placed them on a stack of throw pillows, above heart level.

It was cold in here, Fir Cove always on the chilly side due to its stone walls and uninsulated panes of glass. But she didn't want to risk building a fire or turning on the heat; smoke or exhaust from the furnace might be seen. Best that this place seem uninhabited, at least from a distance.

The girl was dehydrated, her lips feathered with cracks. Arles went to soak a cloth in the sink, then came back and wiped the child's mouth with it. The girl parted her lips, like a baby bird's beak opening, and Arles squeezed a few drops onto her tongue.

The girl's eyelids fluttered, fell shut, lifted. A look of confusion seized her face.

Arles was ready. "You're at the big stone house that you left the other day."

She watched as the statement was absorbed; then the girl tried to say something. Arles reached for a spoon, dipping it into a cup and trickling a few drops between the girl's lips. When they went down okay, she let the girl sip.

"Is Kara . . ." The words came out raspy.

Arles gave the girl another sip of water.

"Is she here too?"

Arles gathered breath. "No. She isn't. I'm sorry." She waited, unsure how much the girl knew or could remember.

The child lifted her neck, craning for a look, then let her head fall back onto the cushion. "He ran her over with a car," she whispered.

Arles's eyes fell shut briefly. "I'm sorry," she said again. She was desperate to ask, *Who did? Who did that to Kara?* But probing when the child was in a fragile state could do real harm.

"Did she die?" asked the girl.

It didn't do to lie to children, or even soften truths for them, though people did it all the time. Kids were stronger than most adults gave them credit for, but more than that, they had lie-detection systems as finely tuned as a polygraph. "Yes. She did."

The child's eyes welled up. It was a sign of improvement that she had tears enough to cry.

"She told me to run. That was the last thing she said."

Except for my name, Arles thought. Which gave Arles an unfathomable responsibility now.

The girl averted her face, tears like beads on a necklace following each other slowly down her cheeks. In the span of two days, she'd transformed into a different being than the one Kara had brought to Fir Cove. Gone was any semblance of overconfidence or entitlement. This child had been to a place not her own, where no one belonged.

"How did you find the way back here?" Arles asked.

"I just went how Kara took me." She spoke with a whispery breath, fixing her gaze on a window that looked out onto empty land. "Only opposite. And without backing up a whole lot of times and walking in different directions like she did."

"You're telling me that you—" Arles broke off, confounded. Trained explorers, familiar with the geography, would've struggled with that route sans a map. "Most people think this land all looks the same."

The girl tried to shake her head but fell short of a full back-and-forth. "You just have to look really closely."

Arles regarded her. "That's right. That's exactly right. You do."

The girl's eyes were flickering, as if her vision had gone hazy, but overall, she looked better, skin rosy instead of lilac, with a healthy flush. Her eyelids dropped and didn't reopen.

While the girl slept, Arles assembled a restorative, easily tolerated meal from things Stephanie had fixed during Arles's own recuperation. She defrosted bone broth in the microwave, spread crackers with jam, filled a cup with sweetened rice milk. Then she arrayed everything on a tray and carried it up four flights of stairs.

Kara had accessed the top floor of the house to find supplies and a place for her and the girl to hide, but the attic wouldn't have stymied anybody with an ounce of intent. There was one space, however, that nobody would discover. The girl could not be taken back into the woods right now—she had nowhere near enough strength for that—but Arles needed to return for her car. Leaving it would raise questions. And trap her and the girl at Fir Cove.

She went back downstairs with a first-aid kit and set to cleaning the girl's scrapes and scratches. She was glad when the child stirred. No longer unconscious, just sleeping. Arles held up a tube of Neosporin. "Can eleven-year-olds do this themselves?"

The child took the tube. "Aren't you a doctor?"

Arles smiled. "Not that kind."

"Oh yeah. Kara told me." A chin wobble, then recovery. "I just forgot."

"You've had other things on your mind besides what kind of job I have."

The girl squeezed a blob of ointment onto her fingertips.

"Listen, I have to run out for a while," Arles said.

"Hot date?"

Arles tucked away the falsely blasé tone for analysis later. "I left my car behind when I was looking for you, and I have to go get it."

The girl capped the tube. "You tried to find me?"

"Yes," Arles told her. "Very hard."

The girl stared down at her now-glistening wounds.

"Think you can hide?" Arles asked.

"I'm great at hiding," she said.

It didn't sound like a brag. To Arles's ears, it was an admission of defeat.

En route, Arles stopped at one of the bathrooms.

"Don't flush," she instructed. "I need to look at your pee."

"Gross," the girl said, cheerfully enough.

Arles assessed the child's climb to the attic as well, anticipating newborn fawn legs, but instead seeing something closer to sturdy and strong. Children's resilience was amazing. Toward the rear of the attic, where no floorboards had been lain, Arles demonstrated how to walk across a joist.

"That fluff won't hold you," she said, pointing to pink puffs of insulation on either side. "Think of this like a balance beam."

"Never been on one," said the girl, then crossed the length of wood as nimbly as a gymnast.

Coming to a stop with her feet straddling two beams, Arles wrestled a vent cover off the wall and laid it atop a cotton-candy cloud. This had been her own hiding place of choice; Peter never once found her here. Behind the grate was an enclosure tucked beneath the roof. A maze of magazine pictures, snippets of articles, and CD sleeves had been tacked up on the slanted sides of the space, the array making for a museum exhibit now. Earlier, when Arles had brought up the food, she'd traded her dusty old pile of blankets for a stack of fresh ones and added a flashlight, along with a few books and puzzles. She stepped aside now for the reveal.

"Vintage!" exclaimed the girl. "That is the coolest hideout ever. It's like a clubhouse in an old TV show. Like, from the fifties or sixties."

"That is pretty old," Arles responded, taken aback. She'd been expecting the girl to say the nineties. Maybe even the aughts. "You watch classic television?"

"Who calls it television?" the girl asked, squatting to crab-walk into the space.

"People in those shows?" Arles responded.

The girl smiled.

Arles knelt on the joists. "You'll be safe here, I promise. Whatever you hear—even if you think someone's in the house—you won't be found in this spot. Just don't come out."

The child gave a solemn nod.

"It's bright enough out that you shouldn't need the flashlight," Arles added, pointing to sun shafts shining through chinks between the slate roof tiles.

"I won't turn it on," she promised. "Someone might see the light."

"Smart girl," Arles replied. She hadn't wanted to issue that warning. She felt fairly confident that the chances of the men breaking in were slim; there was no reason for them to do so. Even if they drove out to Fir Cove a second time, the house would appear unoccupied.

The girl scooted backward in her nest.

Arles maneuvered the vent plate into place. You could wrest it on and off from inside—she'd done it herself many a time—but the child would be best concealed if Arles got it just so. She took a last look through the slats. The girl lay curled up on top of the mound of blankets; it was warm in the attic. She appeared to be drifting off to sleep again.

"Thanks, Shep," she mumbled.

CHAPTER
TWENTY-TWO

Arles emerged from the woods behind the vacation rental, skirting Bostock Road by a generous margin.

"I can't flipping believe it!" a woman called out in a high, strident voice.

Arles backed up, concealing herself at the junction between driveway and trees.

"We get two days away from the kids, and *this* happens?"

Arles's car sat a few yards off. Her hand twitched, holding the key. She was normally good at maintaining an even keel, internally and externally, but she'd never been responsible for a child before. Something was starting to heat inside her, rising to a boil.

The woman stood with her fists on her hips. She wore frayed jean shorts and a T-shirt that read *Wedeskyull Weed*. A man joined her in the driveway. His clothes were faux lumberjack, and he had a beard so precisely shaped it looked chiseled.

Arles's grandparents had referred to this as *the invasion of the Summerers*. Thinking of that made Arles think of the family manse. She used to retreat to her hideaway for hours; there'd been no other choice when Peter pursued her. But the girl didn't have the same constraints upon her. She might not find staying put so imperative.

"What did you say it cost?" the woman demanded. "Six hundred dollars a night?"

Arles nearly dropped to her knees. This place was a shack.

"A little north of that," the guy muttered.

"And we have to deal with somebody else's *car* in the driveway?" the woman said, sounding as outraged as if they'd found their getaway filled with bugs. Or dead bodies.

"No one's inside the house," the guy said quickly. "I looked through all the windows."

"Great—then the car *doesn't* belong to the cleaning crew like you said. Obviously, because a maid could never afford a car like this. For all we know, the clean wasn't even done!"

Back at Fir Cove, there was an eleven-year-old who had real problems in her life. Arles stepped free of the woods. "I'm so sorry! I finished late. Is it past check-in?"

"By about fifteen minutes," the man said, shaking his phone to life.

Arles wondered whether he knew how useless it was going to be here.

"Twenty," the woman said, sending him a look. "Finished with what?"

"Your property-and-woods clean," Arles replied chirpily. "Which explains why I look like this." She was the worse for wear after her back-to-back journeys through the woods. Clothes muddy, hair frizzed. In need of a blowout from one of the salons these two probably frequented. "It's a service provided where we clear brush and debris from the forest."

"Wow," the man said. "That sounds great. Thanks so much."

It sounded nonsensical, but Arles mustered a smile.

"Is there an upcharge for that?" the woman demanded.

Arles climbed into her car and backed out of the driveway.

She drove to a section of road likely to have signal, close to a school. Pulling onto the shoulder, she sat with her hazards pulsing and fired up her phone. Swiftly, she replied to three missed texts from Dan, the last just a question mark, with an *all-good* thumbs-up. Then she paused, studying the question mark. How did a piece of punctuation, one curlicue and a dot, manage to convey so much emotion? Hope, a smudge of anger, barely contained exasperation. *I need you to hear that,* Dan had said, and Arles had told him that she did.

Her thumbs quivered over the screen, unsure.

Then she tapped out: please dont worry i'll be in touch soon and we'll talk

There. Enough in the way of relationship feeding. She started scanning the news.

Police are looking for leads in a hit-and-run that left local resident, Kara Parsons, dead on Bostock Road at approximately 5:30 this morning . . .

Then a link to a human-interest take on the crime.

Local Writer Dies After Being Struck by Car

The headline was accompanied by Kara's author photo and a cover shot of her latest book. In death, Kara had found some of the attention she'd rued not receiving in life. The piece went on to detail how a couple from Brooklyn had transformed a pokey backwater bookshop into a craft-beer-and-events destination that locals could no longer afford to patronize. Barring the old to admit the new, wrote the journalist. *Walls around Wedeskyull.*

No report anywhere of a missing or kidnapped child, not the smallest searchable mention. There was an internet vacuum around the girl, like a black hole in space.

Arles stabbed the push-button start with her finger.

The police appeared to have nothing. No small man driving a black Escalade, or a tall one making Wedeskyull his temporary abode in order to adulate a movie star.

Even if the police and services they were aligned with would be capable of ensuring the girl's safety—a definite *if*—none of them were particularly suited to getting a traumatized child to open up and reveal information that would lead to the capture of her pursuers.

No more so than Arles, anyway.

She needed to buy a little time to figure out who this girl was and what she had fled. To guarantee there was no chance of returning her to danger. That was the least Arles owed Kara. And this needed to be done in a secure location to ensure that whatever entity was stalking the child could be held at bay. But where would such a place be?

Arles gazed out at the golden apricot glow, the seemingly idyllic summer day. The Escalade driver had already come once to Fir Cove with a gun and his sidling breed of menace. Going to Dan's place, assuming it was even an option given that whatever he and Arles were to each other didn't include being bunkmates, would mean staying in the summer-bloated center of town, where the girl would draw attention. Newcomers didn't escape notice in Wedeskyull, at the very least ire from locals who had a love-hate thing going on with tourists.

Tourists. The shack with its unholy price tag.

Arles knew of another shack.

Her SUV leaped forward like a racer on her mark.

———

She was back home and halfway across the attic before she discerned that the vent cover had been removed. She squinted in the waning light, bits of dust sparkling in hazy shafts of sun. The entry to her hiding space gaped open like a yawning black mouth. Her feet were so fleet on the joists, it felt as if they didn't touch any wood. Many times, she had enacted this race as a child, discovering only later the needle fragments of fiberglass embedded in her skin, how close she must've come to sinking down to the ceiling of the floor below through a frothy cloud of pink.

The girl wasn't in the hideout.

Arles resisted the impulse to call out and risk summoning attention. The girl might be hiding someplace else for some reason. As Arles raced down the stairs, trying to imagine where the child could've gone and why, she heard a muffled groan. There was a half bath at the rear of this hall, and Arles flung open the door.

The girl sat on the floor, her limbs splayed, skin beaded with perspiration.

"I'm sorry!" she said, her gaze skittering around wildly. "I ate that gross soup and got sick! I had to throw up, but I didn't want to get your hideout all messy!" She slapped a hand to her mouth, madly swiping it back and forth. "Ick, I know—I probably reek!"

Arles shook her head. "No, you're good—"

The girl wrapped her arms around herself as she began to move her lips in a quick succession of words that Arles couldn't make out. She was able to catch only hints of sound. Not clanging; she detected no rhymes in the tossed salad of verbiage. Was this a complex vocal tic?

Kara had mentioned the same behavior. She'd referred to it as praying, but it didn't seem like any prayer Arles had ever heard. Then again, she wasn't religious, so really, who knew?

The stream of words continued, the girl's voice dropping until it seemed it might cut out altogether before resuming again. Arles got down on her hands and knees and crawled close, the girl not appearing to register the motion despite the smallness of the space. She seemed lost to the embrace of her speech. At last, an intelligible snatch of sound emerged from the jumble, the most heartbreaking sequence of words about just wanting to be loved.

"Oh, hey—" Arles began.

The child's lament shut off like water from a tap. She blinked at Arles, speaking at a normal volume. "How come you don't have any Listerine?"

Arles decided against pressing the girl on anything now. More important to get out of here quickly. She went to her own bathroom for mouthwash, then came back. The two of them left the powder room after a quick gargle, Arles relaying the plan she'd come up with as she plundered her stepfather's pack—which he'd insisted on calling a *rucksack* as if he were a nineteenth-century Adirondack frontiersmen—for items they were going to need.

"Why can't we stay here?" the girl asked, trailing along while Arles strode from kitchen to mudroom in search of additional supplies.

A welcome strain of demand in her tone, a return to form after her plaintive murmurings.

"This place is awesome," the girl went on. "It reminds me of this one set—"

Arles had been concentrating on coiling lengths of cordage. "This one what?" she asked when the girl fell silent. She tucked a tidy spiral into a carton.

The child gathered a breath. "This one place I went to was all set up to play princess."

"What kind of place was that?" Arles asked, her attention snagged.

The girl shrugged, and Arles accepted it. They'd make progress soon enough. Hopefully.

"Feeling better now?" she asked, and pointed. "Think you can carry one of those?"

The girl hitched a box into her arms. "We can't leave till nighttime, right?"

As they went outside, Arles paused to consider, casting her gaze out across the land. Hummock of hill, private road, woods all around. A shower of sunlight, like Fourth of July sparklers, on the far-off lake.

"That's what they'd think we would do," Arles said at last. "It's maybe the reason no one is here right now. Going out at night when it's easier to escape notice is the obvious move."

The girl stared up at her.

"We should go while there's daylight and most people would worry about being seen."

"That's smart," said the girl. She sounded like she really thought so.

Arles inclined her head. "It's kind of the same in therapy. The less likely move can produce the best result." She closed the trunk manually, avoiding the beep, and muffled its bang.

Perhaps twenty miles to their destination—distances were long in Wedeskyull—and they'd be vulnerable to ambush, a target, at every point along the way. Arles chose to skirt Fir Cove's long, winding drive, go offroad instead. Navigating the tangle of old logging trails wasn't easy, and definitely not an endeavor suited to anyone wearing work clothes as brand spanking new as that creepy little man's had been. She and the girl were alone. They had to be.

Still, she kept envisioning the man's serpentine glide between trees, an impassable obstacle, even though in reality, her car would have no trouble plowing him down. She engaged the locks with a reassuring *thunk*. A few days ago, the idea of someone locking their vehicle while driving in the woods would've struck her as clinically paranoid. But now a woman had been killed. Now, far from locks being unnecessary, they seemed unequal to the task they were designed for.

Her SUV jounced along, tires pummeling stones and splintering wood.

"Whoa!" the girl exclaimed. "What's that?"

Arles turned her head to one side. Blinked as a tree morphed into a man, twin knots in the trunk a pair of cold, dead eyes, before it became a part of the woods again, stalwart and standing.

The girl knelt on her seat, pointing to a high wall constructed of horizontal slats. She pushed the button to let her window down, and the summer day exhaled a balmy breath.

"Raise that," Arles said, low.

The girl did so instantly.

Arles heard the echo of ominousness in her own tone and, recalling the child's display of obeisance in the bathroom, was struck by a sense of remorse. Nevertheless, she located the childproof lock setting for the first time and engaged it.

"It's just that we're better off safe than sorry right now," she said. "You didn't do anything wrong."

In the rearview, she watched the girl nod.

Arles took a turn, then another, checking all three mirrors to make sure they were still traveling unaccompanied. They would be on a real road for a while, more open and exposed than before. She kept on driving, unsure how to answer the girl. At last, she said, "That wall back there encloses a dangerous section of woods. By a ravine."

"What's a ravine?"

The road continued to unfurl.

"A ravine is like a chasm," Arles said.

A pointed lift of wispy blond eyebrows visible in the mirror.

"A steep rocky hill that slopes down to water," Arles elaborated. "If there aren't enough trees, say, they died from a storm or a blight—a blight's a disease." She interrupted herself before the girl had to ask. "Then their roots can't hold up the soil anymore, and it crumbles. The ground becomes unsafe to walk on. Someone could fall."

"Whoa," said the girl again.

"Yeah," Arles replied. She released a long, silent breath. "Whoa."

Some untold span of time later, she braked, easing the car to a halt. They were here.

CHAPTER
TWENTY-THREE

Arles had learned to drive literally at Peter's knee, on his lap with his arms encircling her. She blinked to shutter the image of his corpse, his incinerated body, as she turned off the engine. She knew the purpose her SUV was designed for. Lesser drivers would see this terrain as a solid wall of woods, requiring an ATV to penetrate, but her car had sliced through it like a spear.

The child followed Arles inside a small cabin. It wasn't a cabin in the way great camps were referred to by their owners and compatriots as *cottage*; the understatement intended to deny the wealth disparity required to erect such residences. This place was six hundred square feet, if that. Even for a Realtor, *cozy* would've required some spin. The girl began patting her hand on the bare wood walls. In woods like these, old growth, primeval, time worked differently, and daylight had already started to wane, the interior of the structure dim. Arles stilled the girl's hand with her own.

"No lights," she explained. "I brought lanterns."

She set down a carton on a square of kitchen counter. The ability to carry things again made her feel reborn, like spring shoots poking up through the ground.

The child was looking at her as if Arles had said there were no floors in here.

"No electricity, no heat, and the water comes from a pump," Arles elaborated.

This swath of land was so untrammeled, it made the grounds of Fir Cove seem urban. The cabin had been built by her Uncle Harry, Arles told the girl, who wasn't a relation, but her stepfather's childhood best friend. Alive, though Arles hadn't seen him in years. Small-town word had it that he hadn't yet begun the decline that had eroded so much—if nowhere near enough—of Peter. That part she left out while talking to the child.

"Let's bring everything in," Arles said. "Then you can start unpacking, and I'll build a fire."

Once they had unloaded the car, the girl busied herself sorting through stacks of garments that Arles had found in the attic.

"Are these for me?" the child asked.

It seemed a change that she hadn't just begun trying on whatever she wanted.

Arles nodded.

"I would totally thrift this top," the girl said, examining a shirt.

"The bedroom's there." Arles pointed. "Want to put all the clothing away in the dresser?"

The girl walked in the indicated direction, her arms laden.

Arles poked the flames. The fire was taking a while to catch, Harry's wood unseasoned.

A voice came at her from behind.

"Are you gonna make up a name for me too?"

"No," Arles said, rising. "You can tell me your name if you want to. When you're ready. I figure that choice should be up to you."

"You could guess," she suggested. "My name's like the easiest one ever to guess."

Arles appraised her. "Interesting, but no. I'm not going to do that, either."

"Okay." The girl regarded her with the same look of faint approval she'd worn when Arles made the decision to leave Fir Cove before nightfall. "I still get to call you *Shep*, though."

"I kind of like *Shep*." Arles paused, considering her next words. "The name Kara called you by was special to her. It meant she cared about you. She'd be very glad that you're okay."

"Kara did other funny things." The girl's face puckered. "Besides give me a name."

"Oh yeah?" Arles asked, suppressing her own feeling of sorrow, like a stitch in her side. "Like what?"

The child let out a shaky sigh. "Well, she told the person at the place where we stayed that I came from a cult. So I made up all this stuff and played a girl who came from one."

Arles recalled Kara positing this idea back at Fir Cove. "You don't then?"

The child giggled as if despite herself, the sound like bubbles popping. "Come from a cult?"

Her laughter vaporized. "I just pretended. I've seen cults in movies, and they don't seem so bad. Kinda like summer camp." She took a look around. "Like this place."

Arles had no intention of correcting her, especially since the girl clearly had more to say.

"I wish I did!" she burst out, her voice speeding up. "I wish that Kara had been right!" She plopped down in front of the stove, sitting with her legs crisscrossed.

Arles used a poker to rearrange the logs, sending up a fireworks display of orange, yellow, and green. She nestled one of the punky logs in the opening she'd created and watched it emit a cloud of steam, moisture escaping. The girl seemed mesmerized, her eyes tracking the rise and fall of the flames.

"What happened in the woods?" Arles asked softly. "Do you feel comfortable talking about it yet?"

The girl's cheeks appeared red, heated. "It was okay till the Extricator saw me."

"The Extricator," Arles repeated. "He was in the woods?"

The girl nodded. "He followed me there. That's how come I got lost. Because I stopped paying attention to where I was going and just tried to get away."

"You mean you outran him?" Even hours later, the girl's safety assured, thinking about that troll chasing his prey through the forest made Arles's insides clench with fear.

The child's nod came accompanied by a visible lick of pride. "Kara and me had just gone that way, so I was . . ." She trailed off, uncertain.

"You were more familiar with the terrain. The land. Than he was."

A rapid nod. "Yeah. The Extricator would have trouble running on the grass in a park. He usually goes on the treadmill. Sometimes the rower."

The girl had been unfamiliar with the word *ravine*. She must come from a city or the suburbs, and so did the men pursuing her, probably. They had to live in close proximity; otherwise, how would the girl know which equipment the Extricator used to work out? Was he her father? Distaste curdled inside Arles. But assuming she was correct about the city or suburbs part, then being out here was the first leg up she could imagine having. Home-court advantage.

"Plus, I've been working on my running," added the girl. "It's the best for caloric burn."

Arles tucked that away. "Well, you did amazingly. You should feel very proud."

The girl shook her head. "I didn't do as good as you. You went on the same walk a bunch of times today. Plus, I fell in the river and literally died."

There was no river there. The word *creek* was probably as foreign to the girl as *chasm*.

"That's why I want you to teach me," the girl said.

"Hmm?" Arles said, caught off guard. "Teach you what?"

"You know. How to live like you do."

Arles suppressed a wry grin. "How do I live?"

"You build fires. And walk through the woods. And come to a house that doesn't have a bathroom or a way to get clean even if other times you live in a mansion."

"There's a solar shower," Arles said, amused. "And a composting toilet."

"See?" the girl wailed. "I don't even know what those things are!"

"I get it," Arles said. "You want to learn survival techniques. Wilderness preparedness."

"Yeah," the child said, appearing to relax. "That." She nestled herself closer to the stove.

Damn wood had already almost expired. Some fire starter Arles was.

"How about for every method or skill I teach you, you tell me one thing about yourself?" she suggested. "Anything you want, whatever you're comfortable with. It'll be up to you."

"Like, make it a game?"

Arles gave a nod. The approach was a bit transactional for her liking, but she didn't see much choice. There was no time for therapeutic unfolding.

"Okay. Except not my name."

Arles looked at her in the dimming cabin, the flickering light of the flames.

"You said I don't have to tell you. And it's better that way. For you too. For you most of all."

"Just things you want to share," Arles agreed. Being a therapist entailed possessing a geologic level of patience, the ability to let secrets rise from underground as psychological plates inched apart. But they didn't have the freedom for that kind of process. She gave the fire a prod to cajole it, then rose to her feet. "Let's have a bite to eat and get some sleep. We'll start in the morning."

CHAPTER
TWENTY-FOUR

Arles woke first, inchworming her way out of her sleeping bag before stealing from the bedroom without disturbing the girl. It was a lovely end-of-summer morning, the kind that made tolerable the prospect of another coming winter. Motionless and silvery, the cabin not all the way to chilly yet, leaves and grasses frosted with dew.

Carrying a pot and ingredients from the kitchen, Arles went outside to the pit to start a fire. Once she had water from the pump at a boil, she dumped in a few packets of instant oatmeal and added a hailstorm of sugar and cinnamon, a thing she'd watched Stephanie do.

Arles had only one meal innovation of her own in her repertoire. Years ago, Peter used to bake in a can, and before leaving Fir Cove yesterday, she'd located a box of mix. Now she stirred in powdered milk and a glug of oil, then snuggled the cylinder in among the embers. A short while later, the golden smell of heating batter began to mingle with smoke in the air. Arles realized with a sick thud that cake in a can was as close as she got to childhood comfort.

The oatmeal was bubbling furiously, water hissing as it boiled out.

The girl came outside dressed in a pair of cutoffs and a T-shirt Arles had worn a quarter century ago. Arles averted her eyes, having trouble looking at the clothes.

"Cake for breakfast," she announced, setting the scorched oatmeal aside.

The girl settled herself on a bench attached to a picnic table. "Yuck, these are splintery."

"Weather," Arles replied mildly. "Takes a toll on anything left outside."

The girl stabbed her slice with a fork and took bites as if it were a kebab. "The weather is weird here," she said with her mouth full. "It's cold even though it's supposed to be hot out."

She wasn't from the Northeast, then, but Arles had already surmised that.

Four pieces of cake were gone, so Arles went inside to grab herself an energy bar. When she came back out, no one was sitting at the picnic table, though a scatter of crumbs had been left behind. Arles took a long, searching look around. The girl emerged from behind a stand of trees.

"I saw a bunny!" she shouted. "It hopped away. It actually hopped!"

"Wilderness best practice." Arles gestured toward the table. "Keep camp clean. Animals—and not just cute ones like bunnies—will smell any food from miles away."

"Awesome," the girl said. "This is better than lessons. What's next?"

"Fire," Arles said.

"*Way* better."

Arles led the way toward the pit. "Knowing how to put out a fire is as important as knowing how to build it."

"Otherwise, forest fires," the girl said.

Montana, Idaho, California, possibly Oregon? But wildfires made the national news half the year now. The child really would've had to be buried in a cult not to know about them.

Arles squatted by the dying blaze. She'd used cedar and fir, woods that caught easily but burned fast. "The only time you can leave a fire burning unattended is if you're maintaining coals to get it going quickly again."

The girl crouched beside Arles.

"Four or five inches of sand or dirt is sufficient to stifle the flames but keep the coals alive," Arles said, scooping up a shovelful with a spade and letting it sift down to demonstrate. "But since we don't need to do that, I'm going to ask you to extinguish the fire instead."

"*Me?*" the girl asked, pointing to her chest.

"There's a bucket beside the pump." Arles pointed. "Swing that arm up and down."

The girl ran off, but a few seconds later, complained, "It's not working, Shep!"

The piggish squeal of the pump in the still air was loud enough to drown out other sounds. "Keep at it," Arles called back, raising her voice.

When the pump at last gave a gurgle and water gushed out, the girl let out a jubilant cry, a real rebel yell. She clutched the handle of the bucket with both fists, sloshing a few drops onto the ground as she staggered over.

"Spill that out and then take a big leap back. You'll get a steam bath for your face."

"Ahh," the child said with an exaggerated moan. "So good for my pores."

Arles bit back a smile. "Let's build a new fire using the tipi method."

The girl looked ready to clap but fisted her hands at her sides instead, cool and blasé.

"Oh, wait," Arles said, going for casual herself. "You're supposed to tell me something about yourself first."

The child's expression grew guarded.

"For our game. We're gamifying this. Remember?"

"Yeah, well, I guess I can tell you I told Kara I come from Arizona. But I don't."

Arles had been collecting dead grasses for tinder; now her hands stilled.

"I was there right before I met Kara." The girl's face bunched briefly. "But I don't live there. It's just I've been to tons of places."

That air she had of owning whichever space she walked into.

Still, something gave her away. "Is that a lie too?"

The girl sputtered a breath. "I mean, I *have* been lots of places, but no one knows I'm there. And I'm not allowed to do anything, so I might as well be staying in the same place all the time."

"So, where do you live most of the time? Where are the treadmill and rower?"

"In the pool house," she said, not quite a *Duh* but a *Where else would they be?* in her tone.

"And where's the pool house?" Arles asked.

The girl frowned. "I thought we were going to build a fire. And that I got to decide what I wanted to tell you."

Arles had learned enough for one session, starting with confirmation of the fact that the child was wealthy, such that not just pools but pool *houses* were referred to in a casual aside.

"Tinder, kindling, squaw wood, and bulk wood," Arles began before suddenly breaking off. They both lifted their heads at the same time while the rest of their bodies went still.

From off in the distance came the high mosquito whine of an engine.

Arles spoke with a ferocity she'd never before used to address a child. "Go! Hide!"

The girl took a step backward on trembly, creaking legs.

Arles faced her. "Do not come out until I say so! And if anything happens to me—" She broke off, listening. "Did you watch the way we came in?"

The child gave a single nod, her eyes huge, pupils like inkblots.

"If something happens to me, don't come out till you see the sun at that position in the sky." She pointed to a gap in the leaf cover straight overhead. Noon. Whatever this was would have to be over by then. "Then get back to the road. Flag down the first woman you see driving."

The engine growled, the driver really gunning it. Exhaust fogged the air.

Arles cast her gaze outward, but the trees were too thick to get a good look. When she turned back, the child had vanished.

A mechanical roar and rattle permeated the woods, the ground vibrating beneath Arles's feet. She hoped the girl had run far enough away that she wouldn't be affected by the exhaust now incinerating Arles's throat. Arles hadn't learned enough yet to come up with a strategy to manipulate these men; she didn't know who they were or why they wanted the girl so badly.

Harry stored a gun or two in the cabin, but a deep pinch in her gut told her that a show of bravado wouldn't be her best play.

Which left hiding. A woodpile formed a grid a few yards off; she could conceal herself behind what to anyone else would look like a log wall. Deal with the inevitable insects, even a snake or two. Poised to bolt, she suddenly tilted her head.

That engine didn't sound like it belonged on a car.

From over a rise climbed an ATV, the berm of soil so steep that the four-wheeler reared up like a stallion. No way could the sly, wrongly dressed man she'd faced off with perform a maneuver like that. Arles scrubbed her eyes with one fist, and Uncle Harry swam into sight.

He popped a wheelie, then thudded back down, raising one arm in greeting.

"Jack Krantz is staying out at the pond this summer," he called out once he'd ridden near enough to be heard. "Wife threw him out again."

Harry chuckled, and Arles fought to match the sound, even though her sympathies lay with the wife. The hammering of her heart worked against mirth anyway.

"She'll call him back when it's time to chop wood," he said, still chuckling. "Anyhow, he spotted smoke over this way, came by to investigate."

Arles hadn't seen anyone skulking around. Jack Krantz was a shy man, cowed by his shrew of a wife, in the town's misogynistic assessment. Probably hadn't come close to the cabin.

"When Jack saw it was your car, he left," Harry concluded.

Life in a small town. It was like being part of a fungus, a massive mycelia network.

Arles felt the press of the girl against her. *Stay hidden,* she mentally implored. *This might seem like just a friendly neighborly visit, but anyone who learns about you could potentially light a fuse.* Given the small-town effect, word might get out.

She summoned a smile. "I needed to get away for a while."

He inclined his head sympathetically. "How're you getting on? Is it five months now already?"

"Almost." She nodded. "I'm surviving."

"Can't tell you how glad I was to hear that you did," he replied.

Unexpected tears sprang to her eyes.

"How's my buddy doing?" he asked.

Oh Lord, he didn't know. Hadn't heard yet. So much for the small-town stranglehold.

"Keep meaning to make a trip up there, pay him a visit," Harry went on, sounding uncomfortable. His shoulders jolted in a twitchy motion, a shiver even though the day was warming. "Gives me a goose-walking-over-the-grave feeling. Picturing him in that place."

Well, you can stop worrying about that now, Arles thought, then came out with the news that Peter was gone, hard and fast as a hammer blow. Smashing any culpability she felt.

"Christ." Harry sank onto the seat of his ATV as if his legs had given out. "Can't believe he went south that fast. Or maybe it wasn't fast? It gets harder to mark the days as you grow old. We don't want to see how far we've come. How much less we have to go."

Would the girl stay put for this philosophical pondering?

"I understand why you wanted to come out here," he said. "Stay as long as you like."

Arles wrenched her face into an expression of gratitude just as the girl rose up behind a glacial erratic, a huge lichen-encrusted boulder. She came skipping over in a childlike motion Arles had never seen her employ, which somehow didn't look right on her.

"Is this your stepfather's friend?" she called in a high, sweet singsong.

Arles's heart gonged in her ears, but she spoke smoothly over it. "You've never met Lissa, have you, Uncle Harry? The daughter of the woman who lives with me at Fir Cove."

"I'm Lissa," said the girl as she reached them.

Harry wiped the back of his hand across his wet eyes. "Nice to meet you, sweetheart."

She dropped a curtsy, the abject weirdness of which made Arles's anxiety evaporate.

"The two of you got all you need?" Harry asked. "I'd be glad to shore up supplies."

"We're good," Arles told him. "Thanks, though."

Harry crossed to her in a shaky, almost limping walk, suddenly looking as old as Peter had by the end. She tolerated his hug, but stepped between him and the girl when he went to chuck her under the chin. That had been his signature move when Arles was young. And it hurt.

Arles lifted her hand as Harry climbed back onto his vehicle.

"Wave," she said under her breath, and the girl did.

CHAPTER
TWENTY-FIVE

As soon as Harry disappeared into a veil of exhaust, Arles swung around.

"Why did you come out?"

The child went and sat down at the picnic table. "He seemed nice," she said, a shrug in her tone. "And also, I wanted to practice catching you off guard."

"Catching me off guard," Arles repeated. "Why?"

The girl looked as if she didn't have an answer. Or didn't want to give the answer she had. Arles dropped across from her on the opposite bench and kept quiet. She could do this all day, at the very least for the duration of a fifty-minute session, but the girl sat there too, swinging her legs back and forth underneath the table as if perfectly content to play the same game.

Arles was about to break when the child finally asked: "How come you didn't go get one of the guns? Before you knew it was your stepfather's friend?"

So she'd noticed the gun cabinet. "Because I can't shoot," said Arles.

"You could've acted like you can. Held it out." She mimed with finger and thumb.

Arles shook her head. "Waving a gun around introduces a destabilizing factor. If it's just for show, it could make a bad situation even more dangerous. Those guns aren't loaded. Harry doesn't keep any ammo here."

Momentary silence. Then the girl said, "Can we get back to lessons now?"

"How about having lunch first?"

"Oh yeah. I forgot. I'm starving."

Pumping water and dousing fires, not to mention hiding, had all worked up an appetite, plus the fresh air and mountain living seemed to be doing the child good. She hadn't mentioned counting calories since they got here. Arles fixed peanut butter and jelly sandwiches, doing battle with the jars until the girl took each one and opened its lid with a clean *pop*.

"Nice," Arles said, then mixed a cup of powdered milk. Children drank milk; at least, Lissa did. "What was the hardest part of your walk through the woods?" she asked as they ate—or the girl did. One energy bar in the morning was plenty for Arles. A real food orgy.

"The river was going so fast, I had trouble getting out." The girl sounded aggrieved, as if the creek had wronged her. "And when I finally did, I was so cold. Even though it's summer!"

"Being wet will get you every time. You can die of hypothermia—that basically means getting too cold—on a warm night if you lie around in wet clothes. So you would've been better off taking off your outfit and either hanging it up to dry or leaving everything behind."

"But then I would've been naked!" the girl cried, as appalled as if Arles had told her to wring the neck of something cute and cuddly.

"First thing the wilderness teaches us." She and her stepfather had drawn opposite conclusions from their outdoors ventures. Peter imagined his mastery of bushcraft to have made him superior to other creatures. "We're all just animals."

"That's insane," the girl said.

"The clothing part, or that we're all animals?"

"Both!"

Arles balled up their napkins and tossed them in the campfire. "It may make more sense to you after we bed down like squirrels and chipmunks. Have you ever seen one?"

"Obviously I've seen a squirrel!" The girl paused. "Maybe not a chipmunk, though."

"Think of leaves and grasses as nature's blanket," Arles said, standing up.

"A dirty blanket," the girl replied, wiping her hands off on her legs.

Says the child with purple smears of jam on her shorts. "I bet it wouldn't have felt half bad after you got so chilled."

The girl appeared to consider. "Like a Prancer comforter."

Arles had never heard of the brand. Probably unaffordable.

They spent a while gathering piles of mulch, fallen foliage and brush from the ground, then ferrying the fruits of their labors to a series of natural formations, a rock outcropping, a hollow log, a sweep of low-hanging boughs. The two of them burrowed in and compared various attempts, the gold standard being when they grew overheated enough to throw off a layer of leaf matter.

"I've never felt this icky in my life," said the girl, crawling out to sit atop a mound.

She sounded delighted.

"Want to walk down to the pond and go for a swim?" Arles asked.

"I can't swim," the girl said. "But yes."

Arles lifted her eyebrows. She had her own pool but couldn't swim? The girl must've registered Arles's bafflement.

"Swimming ruins a blowout. It's lucky that river was shallow."

Arles camouflaged her response. "Then this'll be our last lesson of the day."

They stayed in the water till the sun began to drop, and walked back single file, bathing suits dripping. "Cattails are the wilderness equivalent of Target," Arles said, indicating a stand of reeds that grew higher than their heads. "Supermarket, hardware store, pharmacy, boutique."

"No McDonald's, though," the girl said. "Like near my Target."

"Cattail shoots in springtime taste a little like fries," Arles countered.

"I was just kidding, Shep. I've never even been to McDonald's. Or Target."

"Because Big Macs are too junky?" Arles guessed. "Or no—they have too many calories?" Maybe they didn't cost enough.

"Too many people there," the girl said, then didn't speak again.

Arles broke the silence by pointing. "See what's up ahead? An even better treat than young cattails. Your kind of thing, for sure."

Tired as she must've been, hours devoted to mastering a passable float, the child's eyes sparked. "Where? What is it?"

"You really like this stuff, huh?" Arles said. "Woodsmanship."

"I love it. Anyone my age would. It's all *Hunger Games*, survive-the-apocalypse shit. Uh, stuff."

"I didn't," Arles replied flatly. "But you have a real flair."

The girl fairly glowed, her skin golden from the sun, blushing with fresh air and health.

"I bet there won't be too many things that intimidate you like the creek did by the time we leave here."

"Good," the girl replied, her glow replaced by a fervent flush. "Because I never want to be that helpless again in my life."

And suddenly, despite all the differences between them, Arles saw herself as she'd been years ago, and felt something seize her face. She had to look away before the girl saw the same thing. "Here. The nature's candy I mentioned."

"Over there?" the girl asked, trying to see. "Is it like candy you forage?"

"Yup." Foraging had clearly trickled down to the nonwilderness set. Arles held up a *one sec* finger, then walked toward a fallen log, deepening her breath and relaxing her muscles as a perturbed buzz subsided. She slid a stick into a rotted channel, returning with it extended.

The girl sampled the goo. "It's like sweet yak butter! The kind you put in coffee."

The kind who *puts in coffee?* Arles thought, expanding her profile. Rich people, yes, but also bougie. Like the ones who came to that bookstore, according to the article Arles had read.

"What was it?" asked the girl.

"You have to promise not to freak out."

"I don't freak out," the girl said.

She was right. She never had in Arles's experience, anyway. "Bee larvae."

The girl looked intrigued. "How'd you get it?"

Arles indicated the ongoing thrum in the air a few yards off.

"You walked up to that many bees? Weren't you scared?"

"Bees only sting if they're bothered, and they won't be so long as you approach calmly, communicating that you don't intend to take too much from them."

"Bees understand all that?"

"People in past times related to them as if they did. Anyway, I did get stung, but only once." Arles displayed a red welt. "Then they settled down."

"You're kind of a bad bitch," the girl said.

Imagine such regard being provoked by a beesting, one needlelike jab, over and done with. Arles smiled briefly. "Bee whisperer."

"What's that?"

She felt her smile sag. "Just something my stepfather used to say."

"What's he like?"

Arles twiddled a stick between her palms, ridding it of bark. It would come in handy somehow. Things in the wilderness always did. "Not a person you would've wanted to meet."

"You mean he died?"

"That's right," Arles said. *Please don't ask how.*

Luckily, the girl kept silent, either absorbing or sensing something dark in Arles's reply.

They went back to the cabin and built another fire, Arles narrating her steps for the girl, words that became a secret language among those who spoke it. The *char tin*, the *lay*. They settled back against rocks ringing the pit, each one electric blanket warm. The flames chattered cozily, throwing a shower of sparks into the night, like a thousand tiny comets.

The sky was clear and studded with stars. Rarely did you get a run of weather like this in the Adirondacks, long enough to trust or sink into. That almost let you fool yourself into believing easy times were there to be peeled, one by one, like fruit from the universe's orchard.

"You know, you owe me some things about yourself," Arles said, breaking the lull. Psychologists had to cultivate patience—it was nearly as crucial a trait as empathy—but this wasn't your normal therapeutic setting, and there was no chance for gentle unfolding. At the same time, forcing things could crush the fragile shoots of the bond emerging between them. The balance was achingly delicate, almost impossible to strike, except that being out here seemed as if it were helping things along. The girl was clearly in her element, more prone to opening up.

"Four," she said over a yawn. "You taught me how to float, get warm, build a fire, and find candy in a log. So I have to tell you four things."

"Four's good," Arles said. "Get going."

The girl smiled sleepily, reclining against her rock chair. "Can it be in the morning?"

"Too tired to think right now?"

The girl's eyelids were sinking. "Uh-huh."

"Are you too tired for this?"

The child opened her eyes.

Arles held up a chocolate bar, a bag of marshmallows, and a sleeve of graham crackers.

"S'mores?" The girl clapped for real this time, uninhibited, abandoned. "I've never had one before! I've seen them in movies, though. *Tons* of movies."

"Did you think we were only going to eat baby bees for dessert?"

CHAPTER
TWENTY-SIX

Over oatmeal the next morning, the girl relayed her favorite colors. Mauve, then mushroom, which confirmed Arles's assessment that she came from bougie stock, with the muted palette prompting the addition of *millennial.* Her mother must've been young when she had her. Fave food followed. Spaghetti, which the girl rarely got—too high in carbs—and was forever obliterated by s'mores now anyway. Then came her top movie titles and shows.

"I'm up to four things," the girl said cheerily. "What do I get to learn?"

"Clean up camp first, okay?"

"Because we can't leave anything out for the bears to scent?"

"Or coyotes, weasels, and a host of others."

"Yeah. But bears."

The fire flared as the girl tossed their dirty napkins into the pit. Then she rinsed both bowls and spoons in the bucket, which she overturned and refilled with clean water from the pump before coming to kneel beside Arles on the ground.

Arles pushed a mound of material toward the girl, demonstrating how to form a skirted bundle. "Is building a house a good enough lesson for today?"

The girl glanced up. "A real *house?*"

"Well, I suspect it'll seem small by your standards. But yes, real enough to keep you out of the elements, provide a place to stay safe, and sleep. That's what a shelter was for originally." No bathrooms in triplicate, ungodly gobs of square footage, or gym-slash-pool-house tumors.

The girl picked up a fistful of grasses. "How do you know so much about me?"

"What do you mean? I don't know about you at all. Hence this game."

The girl huffed out a sigh and let the clump she was working on fall to the ground.

Arles lifted it, smoothed the strands until they all lay in the same direction, then passed the bundle back. "Give it another try."

The girl began reworking, her face clenched in concentration. "Remember that first day with Kara? In the big room with all the chairs?"

The parlor at Fir Cove. Arles nodded, adding a bundle to the accumulation.

The girl heaved another breath. "How come yours are so nice and neat, and mine look like hair with no product in it?"

"I've been doing this for years," Arles replied mildly. "By the time you're at it for that long, you'll probably be able to thatch a whole roof while I'm still standing on the ground."

The girl's mouth hooked in a smile as she smoothed out a fistful of reeds and rushes.

"Don't hurry it," Arles counseled. "The wilderness teaches patience better than any mentor or guru." She examined the girl's progress. "Be sure to leave the root ends up."

The girl studied her strands. "You knew I loved reading. And that I'm good at school. Also, the thing about not having any friends." Her face pinched.

"Ah," Arles said, arranging her pile into a miniature haymow. "Well, you mentioned loving bookstores." She temporarily abandoned their activity. "Which made reading not much of a leap and suggests you'd be good at school. Pretty elementary, huh?"

The child extended a hand for more strands without looking up.

Arles placed a tuft on her palm. "You're unusual; I could tell that right away. I also got the sense that you come from money," she said bluntly.

The girl's eyes didn't flicker in denial or assent.

"All of those factors tends to narrow the friend pool. Difference. Uniqueness. Wealth." She twisted off another bundle. "Which is why I thought you might not have many. Even so, you still seemed pretty well adjusted. Comfortable in your own skin and with your own company."

Again, no response.

"Except, then something happened to change things. Whatever led you to seek out Kara."

The girl's fingers slowed.

"People say multiple things when they speak," Arles went on. "And psychologists make use of that. We learn to see behind the words and in the spaces between them."

The child's fingers had stilled completely now. "What kinds of things?"

"Well, your favorite color is mauve, right?"

The girl nodded. "Yeah. But I just told you that. You didn't guess."

"That would've been some party trick," Arles agreed. "Or carnival-booth game."

The girl looked blank. Maybe she'd never been to a carnival. Or a party.

"But you told me more than one thing when you revealed your favorite color. Like, that you know the names of colors beyond the basic ones. Which says something about how whoever you live with talks and even what your decor may be like." Arles deliberately didn't use the words *parent* or *home* since the girl had avoided them.

The child returned to fashioning her bundle. "So now you know what my room looks like even though I've never posted a picture? I'm switching my favorite color to red."

Arles laughed, a rarity for her. "That would be telling me something too. I'd hypothesize that you're bold. Not afraid to put yourself out there with a vivid, bright splash."

"I'd be making it up, though. Just playing a role. My favorite color really *is* mauve. Trust me, I'm like the least-bold person ever."

"I don't know," Arles said musingly. "You walked up to Kara pretty boldly."

"Because I'd never been left on my own before!"

Arles looked at her.

The girl startled as if she'd stunned herself with the outburst.

Slowly, Arles began to nod.

"You were right about something changing," the girl mumbled. "That's what it was."

Pieces collided in Arles's mind. A child left unattended. For the first time in her life? Could that be literally true versus an exaggeration, the plaint of a tween craving independence?

"Hey, look at this one!" The child displayed a neatly tied-off bundle. "Is it good?"

"Better than good," Arles said, still lost in the girl's revelation. "Way better."

After lunch, Arles described the features of a good shelter site. Open, with drainage and southern exposure, space for an east-facing entry, close but not too close to a water source, and away from hazards such as dead trees. They set forth on a walk to scout potential locations.

At last, the girl ran forward, peering behind a thicket of immature trees, then pushing past without pausing to hold back the limbs. Arles waited for the sticks to stop snapping and swinging before stepping through herself.

The girl's gaze was aimed upward, checking the sun's position in the sky. "Is this okay?"

"It's perfect," said Arles.

They mixed wilderness cement out of mud and grasses, then collected branches for ribbing and poufs of debris for filling in. Arles used a stick to sketch the ribbed shape of the shelter, which would resemble the bones of a whale.

"First, we need a long, skinny length of wood." She drew another line in the dirt. "Look for a sapling with no leaves. That means it isn't growing, so we won't be taking a live tree out of the forest."

Once they'd found one, Arles instructed the girl to stand a safe distance away.

Peter had practiced a precautionary approach to timbering, if not other blood sports, preaching that you could never tell when an undetected obstacle would alter the path of a felled tree. Arles delivered a two-handed shove, then a few kicks to the base to loosen the roots, and the young tree listed before beginning to topple. The girl sprinted forward with her arms raised and hands splayed, as if trying to catch a football pass.

"I got it!" she screeched.

Arles called out in protest, but the two of them had been whooping and hollering ever since they'd arrived, at the pond, over s'mores, and the girl didn't appear to register the difference between a barbaric yawp and a battle cry of warning. Arles had nothing to call her by, no name to shout. The only thing she could do was dive forward, the slim trunk catching her on the hip—*That's going to leave a bruise,* she thought as the wood clocked her—and shove the child out of the way, momentum sending the girl to the ground and into a drift of leaf matter.

Arles went knobby-kneed, had to sit down on a stump. Her hands were trembling, as were her lips from their shout. Her very mind felt atremble with fear and emotion. Psychologists had training. They learned to put up walls so they didn't fall out of buildings. Built containers so the floodwaters didn't come in and drown them. But here in the woods, Arles had failed to do all that. The child's need had blotted out any semblance of rational thought, driven Arles to a place of pure instinct.

"What were you doing?" she asked once she could speak. *What were you thinking?*

"I wanted to catch it," the girl said, staring unblinkingly up at the sky from her prone position.

"But you could've gotten hurt," Arles said. "Badly."

"By that skinny thing?" The girl still hadn't blinked. Her eyes were beginning to water.

"That skinny thing weighs at least thirty pounds. Could've given you a concussion."

How easily the worst could happen when you were responsible for a child. The distance between here and there was microscopic, the size of a subatomic particle.

"I need something to call you by," Arles said. "If I have to get your attention suddenly for some reason. It's a matter of safety. Are you still refusing to tell me your name?"

"I *can't* tell you, Shep," the girl replied. "It's a matter of safety."

Arles caught the deliberate echo. "Maybe I should give you a trail name, then."

"What's that?" The girl lifted herself off the ground, brushing away a crumble of leaves.

Arles stood up too and winced, feeling her hip. "It's a tradition thru-hikers have. People who're on the trail a long time. You can't give one to yourself; it has to be assigned."

The girl looked curious. "What would mine be?"

Arles regarded her. "Nat. Short for *Natural*. Because—this stunt with the ridgepole aside—you're a natural in the woods, and you obviously love them. Way more than I did. With a little experience, and a heightened sense of caution, you're going to be a real pro."

"Natural," the girl said on an exhaled breath. "That's awesome. Even better than *Maeve*."

CHAPTER
TWENTY-SEVEN

Life out here had a way of making time accordion.

In and out, out and in. Until a day seemed to pass in minutes when you were engaged in some activity, building a debris structure or tracking an animal, whereas seconds lengthened into hours while you examined speckles on the skin of the pond, waiting for them to resolve into a fish or the sun. It felt as if the girl was safe here in the idyll they'd carved out. That slithery man, with his diminutive body encased in stiff clothing, seemed as distant as an ebbing tide.

"Want to spend the night in our shelter?" Arles asked as they applied finishing touches with the sun slipping below its high mark. "That's called sleeping rough."

The child looked as if Arles had suggested they sleep on the moon.

"I mean, only if you think that's a good idea," Arles said.

"I think it's the best idea that ever was," the girl replied.

"We'll need to learn a couple of more things to be really prepared."

"Yay!" said the girl. "More lessons."

She sounded not the slightest bit ironic.

"Which do you think is safer to drink from?" Arles queried as they set out walking. "The pond where you learned to swim, or a creek? It was a creek you fell into, FYI. Rivers are bigger."

"The pond," the girl replied instantly. "Because you could just dip a cup in or even lap from it like a dog. I wouldn't go near that river—creek—again if it got me a million followers."

She shuddered, and probably not because of the noxious spell social media cast over tweens. The fast-flowing creek would've been terrifying before she could swim. She wouldn't have known how deep it was going to get.

"It's a trick question," Arles said, holding back a branch so the child could duck underneath. "No water is safe to drink without precautionary measures. But of the two, a creek is the better option. It's moving. And the rocks filter it to some degree."

She led them over to a stream, barely running at this time of year, so not as fearsome as the creek. Arles dropped down, and the girl squatted beside her.

"It looks so pure," the child said. "Like in a Tinker Bell movie."

"You really love your fairies and princesses, huh?"

"I hate them," she answered flatly.

Arles made note of the tone, at odds with the ferocity of the girl's statement. "But you said something at Fir Cove about liking to play princess."

"I said the princess is the best part," the girl corrected, then closed her mouth abruptly.

"Of the game?"

"Yes! Right!" she replied as if relieved. "The princess is the best part in the *game*. And that's my one thing to tell you. In exchange for our house."

"Okay, well, now I'm also going to teach you that this water isn't really safe. There are microscopic particles, too small to see, which can make a person very sick."

"If no water's good to drink, then what're you supposed to do?" the girl asked. "By the time I got to your house, I couldn't even walk, I was so thirsty. The only reason I didn't drink out of that river, I mean, creek, was because it was slippery, and I was scared I'd fall in again."

Arles gave a nod. "You know how to build a fire now, so if you have a heatproof container, a pot or a tin cup, you can boil your water. Standard practice says five minutes will do, but really, you need twenty to kill spore-stage bacteria."

The girl twirled her fingers through a tannic pool of water that had collected in a basin.

"Or you can purify it using a device you pack in, like a UV wand or iodine tab," Arles went on. "In a pinch, something you fashion yourself will do, a sieve made from fabric or grasses. In a real emergency, you can even filter your own pee."

The girl showed her dismay with her face. "Gross. I think I'd rather drink cow's milk."

This child hailed from a world where dairy barely ranked above urine for imbibing.

"Let's find lunch," Arles said.

"Find it?" the girl said, twisting with her hands squared on her hips.

Arles held an arm out, indicating the great outdoors. "Welcome to Wilderness Bistro."

She had a hard, fast rule against mushrooming; wouldn't touch one unless it came from a supermarket or farmstand. But she'd brought some of Peter's venison jerky from Fir Cove, which she figured was justified since the deer had been taken from these woods. She and the girl also cooked wild onions and greens over a fire, chewed clover to a matted clump and spat it out, and plucked blackberries from a patch missed by the bears.

"Yay! No bears," the girl said.

Time resumed its fuzzy passing.

"Still have to clean up camp," Arles said a while later. "Bears or no."

The girl mock-groaned, then began to groan for real.

Arles helped her walk, a small body leaning upon the part of her own that had been torn apart. By the time they reached the cabin, the child was heaving against Arles's elbow. Arles made a bedroll and laid it outside so the girl could reach the outhouse in time, envisioning a trip to urgent care, other patients in the waiting room, forms that would need to be filled out. What would Arles even give for a name?

As the child writhed, Arles murmured aloud, describing how to start a fire with a bow drill, pound flour from cattail heads, distinguish between the tracks of rodents and lagomorphs. She relayed the definition of indicator animals, small mammals that signified the presence of predator species, and when the girl's face went ashen, the skin on her stomach visibly rippling, quit talking while she dug a hole for the child's latest leavings.

"That's disgusting, Shep," the girl said faintly from the ground.

Arles glanced at her. *I'm burying your vomit and* you're *complaining?*

"I don't want you . . ." the child whispered.

Arles was relieved to see globules of tears in her eyes. She wasn't dehydrated.

"To have to . . ." The girl's voice weakened. "Do that for me."

She turned over, lying face down on the bedroll, her neck beaded with sweat.

Arles rose from her spot on the ground and went to kneel beside the child. She let one hand hover over the girl's head, her back, her shoulders, although she couldn't bring herself to lower it. The girl rolled over again, and her eyelids sank shut.

"It's okay," Arles said, returning her hand to her side. "Get some rest now. Sleep."

As soon as the girl could keep liquids down, Arles steeped an astringent tea made from fir needles and amaranth and coaxed the child to take a few sips.

She made a *blech* face. "That's almost as gross as you scooping my throw-up."

"I know," Arles replied sympathetically. "I think half the reason I used to get better when I was a kid was so I wouldn't have to drink any more tea."

The girl raised herself on one elbow. "This happened to you?"

Arles gave a nod. "I was never as good at foraging as my stepfather. When I ran away, I had to drag myself back for his tea." What did she know about survival, besides everything? It was Peter who had the skills, the know-how, the expertise. The only way Arles had ever bested her stepfather was by snuffing out his life. "I owe you an apology. Packaged food from now on."

The girl shrugged. "I've drunk green juice before."

Of course she had. Yak butter and green juice.

The girl squinted up at Arles. "I bet I just told you a bajillion things about me without even realizing it. Whatever; it won't even count for our game. Just, um, thanks for curing me."

Arles felt herself gape. "Curing you? I made you sick."

The girl removed the damp cloth Arles had lain across her forehead. "You made a *mistake*. Or I did, eating too many berries. Either way, there's a difference."

Arles held out the tea again. "Who's schooling whom?"

"You are still." The girl handed back the cup. "I didn't know it was *whom*."

"How did you make those cool sticks you use in the tinder nest?" the girl asked as they reclined fireside that night.

Arles had decided they should stay in the cabin, not their shelter, a real bed being more suited to recuperation. She mimed a clap for the vocab term. *Tinder nest.*

Fireflies flecked the air with golden sparks.

"The ones that look like—they look like—"

"Feathers?"

The girl appeared to consider. "More like ribbons."

"They're called feather sticks, but I like your term better." Arles hesitated, guessing what the girl would say as soon as she was given this answer. "I used my knife."

"You have your own *knife*? Can I have one?"

"Someday," Arles said. "Getting a knife is a big deal. A milestone in the outdoorsperson's journey. Using it takes a great deal of care, of course. As much as we used for the drinking water—maybe more."

The girl giggled, piercing the plump belly of a marshmallow with a stick. She appeared to be already recouped, her stomach solid enough for s'mores. "Obviously a knife is more dangerous than *water*."

Arles wiggle-waggled her hand. "Think about how you got sick earlier."

The girl rasped a gagging breath.

"But you're right that a knife requires an abundance of caution," Arles went on, with a wince to show she shared the girl's recollection of pain. "You need to know certain things. Where the blood circle is on your body, for example. And the triangle of death."

"The Blood Circle," the child intoned in a movie-preview voice. "Triangle of Death."

She was kind of . . . theatrical. The skipping that looked put-on for Harry. The weirdly quaint curtsy. The girl seemed steeped in a brew of actorly references and lore. What if her father was that superfan? Would that be worse than if she were connected to Slithery and Small?

The girl lifted her stick from the fire, blowing on the charred mush before taking a bite.

"You're learning, Natural. An ounce of prevention is better than a burned tongue, huh?"

"Whatever, Grandma." The girl grinned at Arles in the moonlight. "So, if I'm a natural, can you show me how to chop wood? Till I'm ready to handle a knife?"

Arles rose, brushing dirt from her hands. "Good call. All the wood inside is punky, meaning it doesn't light well. Let's split a few logs so we can leave Harry with a better supply."

Safety out here was an illusion, the idea that they'd created some sort of sanctuary, absurd. There were a hundred ways the girl could get hurt in the woods, and besides, she had a life to get back to, or build, if Arles could figure out a way to make that happen.

She positioned a log on the chopping block, then went over to the woodpile to get Harry's axe. This time when she told the child to stand back, the girl walked off and stayed put.

As Arles lifted the axe overhead, she was catapulted back in time, the damage that'd been done to her interior making itself known again. *Did you think I wouldn't return?* Something threatened to give, to tear. Arles let out a ferocious shout—*Go back where you came from*—then brought the axe down with a mighty *thwack*, sending two spears of wood flying.

The girl brayed her approval. "That was amazing, Shep! Can I try?"

"It's harder—" Arles fought to catch her breath. "Than it looks."

The girl didn't huff out a breath or argue. She simply looked bummed, which was a lot harder to resist. "I think I might be able to do it," she said softly.

How many times had Arles handled it brusquely when parents confessed to overindulging their child? Had difficulty setting limits? "Just say no," Arles would tell them. "Works way better with kids than drugs. If they're eight, take away dessert. Eighteen, take away the car."

It was different when the child was your own. Or—Arles scoffed at her mental blunder—even one you were temporarily taking care of.

"Come here," she told the girl. "You're not ready to split a piece of wood yet, but I'll show you how to hold an axe. Dominant hand at the head, nondominant toward the base." She stood behind the child, making a safety net around her, her arms not quite touching the girl's.

"It's heavy!" she cried. "A lot heavier than it looks."

"It is." Arles had been similarly surprised when Peter taught her to split logs, his arms enclosing her in a vise. She gestured for the girl to raise her hands skyward.

"This is just like that film with Chloe! I mean, that film I saw with Chloe."

More movie stuff.

"Who's Chloe?" Arles asked. A friend, even though the girl hadn't contradicted Arles's supposition about her not having any? Had that been another lie, like the one where she came from Arizona? "Which film?"

"I forget the name. Can I swing the axe?"

"There can be a rebound effect, a kickback, when you strike a piece of wood," Arles warned. "So, I don't want you to split this yet, especially not when it's dark out. Just bring the axe down slowly. Slide the hand you've got at the top lower as you go."

The child moved in suitably cautious increments, allowing the blade to strike the piece of wood with a *clop*. Not as loud as the knock Arles had given it, but as Arles took a step forward, aiming her headlamp down, she saw that the metal shank had sunk in deeply enough for the tool to stay suspended, its handle quivering in the pool of light.

"First try." Arles whistled. "Got your name for a reason, Natural."

CHAPTER
TWENTY-EIGHT

Just prior to dawn the next day, Arles woke with Dan asleep at her side.

She turned her head to glance at the matching twin bed across the room. The girl lay in a curl, inhaling and exhaling soft, ruffly breaths. Apparently undisturbed by the newcomer in their midst; probably because she hadn't been awake when Dan arrived. When *did* he arrive, crawling into bed beside Arles, even though she was sleeping? And how did he figure out where she was?

She was happy enough to see him that she didn't trouble over niggling questions.

She stretched languidly, rapturously, rolling closer to his muscled form while murmuring in a sweet tone that didn't sound as if it could possibly come from her mouth, but which she decided to tolerate, although the voice evoked loathsome roles: wifey, the little woman, worse.

Dan didn't rouse.

She slid her arms around him, then launched herself backward, nearly falling off the narrow mattress. That didn't feel right. Dan's body wasn't firm because it was muscular; it was hard because he was a skeleton, all the flesh sliding free of his bones as she touched him. She'd been hugging a moldering corpse, and it wasn't Dan's but Peter's, except overly small because really, this was the girl, and she'd been dead a while now, both she and Arles out here too long, no one knowing where to look for them, or even that they were gone.

Arles flipped over fast enough to cause a painful wrench in her back, submerging her face in her pillow so that the girl, who was alive—thank God she was alive, and still blissfully asleep—wouldn't hear her scream.

Arles used to have fever dreams all the time. But this one was different because it had involved another child. And because the Dan part, before the horror show had begun, had been nice. Really, really nice. The fact that he had no idea where Arles was struck her for the first time as unconscionable heedlessness on her part. The appalling nightmare had served as a reminder.

Relationships placed holds on a person, and in Arles's case, these had always been choke holds. But that didn't include Dan. He deserved to know why she'd fallen even farther off the map than usual and that she was okay. Arles could also check the news, see if Tim had made any progress with Kara's murder and thus the girl's provenance.

She just had to drive to a patch of road that had signal.

Judging by the girl's prior wake-up times, Arles would be back before the child even started to stir. Best to go on her own. On the slim chance that the little man was nearby—unlikely given the expanse of this region—she'd be alone if he succeeded in waylaying her car.

But just in case the girl earlybirded it today, Arles left a detailed note.

———

She scanned the latest stories about the hit-and-run, which contained no new information, not one updated detail, then confirmed the ongoing news vacuum around the disappearance of a child. After that she composed a semi-explanatory text for Dan, skipping details that made him any sort of accomplice, and added a heart emoji. Hitting send caused a completely untoward, never-before-experienced sensation, a champagne fizzing in her veins.

Starting the engine with a quick, light tap, Arles caught a glimpse of her face in the rearview. She was smiling.

The sky had begun to cloud over as she drew near the cabin. Record spate of nice weather complete; rain coming, accompanied by a break in the heat. Arles could teach the girl how to get a fire going when it was wet out, then steer the information trade-off to yield something concrete. *Why has no one reported you missing?*

The tires ground dirt to paste as Arles cleared the rise, spotting the ATV only after she started to descend. She was torn between being glad that the girl had some company while she'd been on her own and a sense of infringement that Harry had encroached upon them again.

Then she parked and got out and saw that the ATV wasn't Harry's.

Arles's heart clutched inside her, like a rag being wrung out, and her breath sped up.

She went racing toward the cabin, details hitting her too fast to be absorbed.

This ATV was late-model, not a ding or scratch on it, even its mud shiny and fresh, as if the vehicle got hosed off daily. Harry probably hadn't washed his all season. The next bit of proof appeared as she flew past—a metal badge affixed to the flank with some sort of insignia on it. She doubled back so fast, she nearly pitched over. *Wheels on Wedeskyull.* This was a rental.

Arles took all this in, facts coagulating in her mind, before she reached the front door. At the threshold, she stopped short, the grating sound of her boots against the dirt as loud as an explosion. For a second, she ducked, as if there'd been an actual bomb.

A smell filled her nostrils, saturating the space around her. If she'd been able to squeeze the air like a sponge, it would've seeped red. This odor was unmistakable, carrying her back to that day when she boiled in the same liquid during minutes that felt like hours, hours that felt like days, after she'd been shot. It took paramedics time to reach her, so remote was her location.

Now blood had come to the woods again.

———

Arles needed to take a moment to think. Rushing into an unknown and uncontained situation was a recipe for mistakes, and she couldn't afford to make any.

Whoever had come was from Away, judging by the rental. The ATV hadn't been concealed in any way, just left out in the open, as if it'd pulled up in a driveway. Audacious, arrogant, because the rider was confident he wouldn't get any opposition with Arles gone. He must've just been waiting for her to drive off so he could descend on the child with relative ease.

Kidnapper.

Murderer.

Fucking coward.

How long had Mr. Slithery and Small been watching the two of them, observing their actions with his empty, lifeless eyes? Or the fan with his version of same, that deranged, glazed gaze?

The question applied centipede legs to Arles's skin, but the answer didn't matter. The only important thing was where he might be right now, and more urgently, the girl. Had Arles returned in time? Then why hadn't he ridden off on the ATV with the child already?

Because something even worse than an abduction had happened.

Something that explained the stench of blood.

Arles pressed a palm to her gut where she'd been shot, unconscious of doing so until she felt the hard cords of her scars.

Was a second vehicle parked somewhere with easier access to this parcel of land? It would be difficult to transport a resistant child on an ATV, keep her secured on the seat behind the driver. Arles took a look around, hairs rising up all over her body. At this very moment, the girl might be getting shoved into the back of a black SUV. Unless her pursuer was looking around in the cabin right now or elsewhere on the grounds.

The girl knew how to hide.

During their swim lessons, Arles had pointed out the hut in which Jack Krantz was staying. It had been instructional; Jack built his dwelling by hand. Arles had described him as kindly; he'd always been gentle when Arles used to try to escape these woods, even though he never failed to return her. *Little girls get mad at their daddies all the time. Yes, stepdads too.*

But Jack wouldn't do the same thing if the girl arrived at his place with a report of being chased, would he? Did the girl flee to the pond when danger swooped in on its broad bat wings?

Please let her have gone there, Arles beseeched the glowering thunderhead sky. Don't let her be at the end of a red carpet of blood—thinking like the child in Hollywood images—and instead under the roof Jack had fashioned himself out of cedar shakes.

No blood was visible yet. But Arles could smell it, meaty and metallic.

She had to go inside. There were no noises coming from the cabin; the dwelling, along with these woods—the whole world, for all she knew—felt sodden with silence, soaking in more than it could hold without bursting like the clouds. The heavy sense of quiet made Arles's second conjecture seem likely, that the girl was being hunted some distance away. Had she gotten hurt in the cabin, blood drawn, but managed to wrest herself free?

The prospect of the child being wounded provoked a lethal wrench inside Arles, hands pulling on her intestines like rope in a tug-of-war. She needed to find out what had happened. Not knowing was tearing her apart.

Placing one hand on the doorknob, about to enter, Arles spun so abruptly that she fell, went down hard on her knees in the dirt as she narrowed her eyes and peered at the woodshed. The sky glared overhead, muddy gray with backlit clouds.

Something had changed over there.

Arles stood up slowly. She took one step forward, then another.

It wasn't the neat lattice of split logs with a new layer freshly added by Arles and the girl.

Something else had snagged her attention, stubbornly resisting notice.

Splatter vision was the practice of unfocusing your eyes so that they took in a panoramic view. It was important in tracking. Peter had been a master of this technique; he could find Arles anywhere, pick her out from the most camouflaged surroundings.

She worked to relax her eyes, letting her gaze sweep the area, up, down, and sideways, expanding her peripheral vision so that the detail could emerge.

The axe was gone from the chopping block.

CHAPTER
TWENTY-NINE

The sullen sky leached light from the cabin. Inside, all was terribly still, and dim.

The odor overpowering, some meat rich with iron.

Arles walked as noiselessly as possible, the cramped interior suddenly vast, endless. She knew where this floor creaked and sighed, but it would still be impossible to sneak up on someone in a structure this size. Easier to take a murderous madman by surprise in a mansion—just another privilege of the rich.

Arles adopted the fox walk Peter used to favor, rolling smoothly from the outsides of her feet in, lifting rather than sliding. As she passed the gun cabinet, she eased open the glass door and reached for a rifle, muffling the quiet click as she released it from its brackets. The girl had been right—just holding a firearm posed a threat. The Escalade driver was short enough that if he were bent over, maybe tending to a wound on the girl, Arles could brain him with the gunstock.

She had to stop for a second, work something down in her throat.

Then she continued her slow panther stride, cradling the gun.

The blood finally came into sight, a kaleidoscope array of particles on the walls of the room at the end of this short stub of hall. The bedroom.

Details flew through the air like arrows as Arles broke into a run.

In that room, a pair of hands was splayed out, seemingly unattached to any limbs, at least none that Arles could see. And whose hands, she couldn't tell. She also spied a hank of hair, clotted with something, as soaked as if the person it belonged to had just stepped out of the shower.

She gagged, tripped, planting one hand against the wall to catch herself while the other gripped the rifle before she catapulted forward again. The bedroom inching away from her, moving backward, as things did in dreams, unless she was standing still? Impossible; she had never run this fast in her life, her heart clobbering her chest, her lungs screaming for air.

She plunged into a scene of gore and slaughter such as she'd seen only in one of the girl's beloved movies. A river—*not a creek, a true river this time*, Arles thought with a high, hysterical peal of laughter—of red spreading out from under one of the twin beds.

Her eyes were unable, or unwilling, to focus. Splatter vision run amok. She couldn't breathe, all the air stuck in her throat. She was a fish on a dock, gasping and gaping as she threw out one hand, gluing it to the side of the narrow doorway to hold herself upright.

She swung the gun in every direction, left, right, straight, the way she'd seen it done in movies, but even in her panic feeling absurd. The recoil of this thing would send her as far as the cabin entry, if it even fired. Unloaded or loaded, it did no good in this tiny abattoir.

Carefully stooping, she laid the rifle down on the floor, ever mindful of Peter's warnings about an accidental discharge. Then she finally forced herself to look.

There were two bodies in the bedroom.

One seated with its back pressed against the wall, and another, the smaller one, lying face down on the floor, most of it concealed except for a head and two wrists thrust out from underneath the bed, which was why Arles had seen only hands and hair as she'd run in.

It was the girl. She had been trying to get out from under the bed.

She must've hidden beneath it, scrambling forward when her killer came after her.

Only the handle of the axe was visible, sticking up into the air, the blade buried too deep to be seen at the base of her skull.

———

It took Arles a very long time, an ungodly amount, to ask herself why the girl's murderer was just sitting in this bedroom after committing his unspeakable act. Awaiting capture and arrest. Because he hadn't meant to do it? Something had gone devastatingly, irreversibly awry?

She rotated slowly in the direction of the other body.

The man sat so stilly, slumped against the wall, that Arles wondered if he were dead too.

Then she realized neither was the case.

That body wasn't dead.

And it wasn't the man's.

Arles twisted to face the form on the floor, her vertebrae popping as she spun, making sure, seeking absolute, undeniable confirmation. Her eyes and mind had played tricks on her, distorting things in an attempt to find clarity where there was none. And if she were wrong about this, then her heart was going to break once and for all.

One of the hands visible in front of the bed gripped a pistol, all but submerged in the lake of red. A diminutive hand by adult standards, but as Arles made her eyes focus—really forced herself to see—she could tell that it wasn't quite small enough to be the girl's.

Arles drew closer, taking care not to disturb things more than she inevitably had already. She didn't know if the safety was on or off, whether this gun was meant to fire or frighten. And it didn't matter anymore. *He* didn't matter anymore.

Arles dropped down, thrusting out both her arms. She knee-walked, at one point tilting sickeningly, nauseously forward, only to catch herself by grabbing the man's hand, which moved with a jarring ease, unresisting, no opposing force, just sliding loosely in the jelly of blood.

The choreography rearranged itself in her head as she crawled.

The girl must've managed to grab the axe, then ran inside to hide. When the man attempted to drag her out from under the bed, she escaped as he came after her from behind. He'd scooted beneath the bed, trying to grab her by her heels. And then, as soon as she was able to rise but before the man fully emerged, the girl had gone for the axe and swung.

Just as she and Arles practiced together, on another occasion, for a very different reason.

Arles's body was slick and slippery by the time she and the girl joined at the wall. She leaned forward and took the child's hands—as unresisting as the man's, but warm and alive and quivering—between her own. She pressed her cheek to the girl's face, seeing red in her peripheral vision, the color of their skin. Arles let herself sink, sliding downward with the wall supporting both their weights, since she was cradling the girl. She lay in the nest of Arles's arms.

Earlier, Arles had implored some cosmic force, asking for the child to have fled to Jack's.

Relying on a man for salvation when instead the girl had saved herself.

CHAPTER THIRTY

Arles took the girl by the hand and helped her to rise, stiffly, mechanical, as compliant and cooperative as a robot. Walking in short, jerky steps, the child accompanied Arles to the room at the front of the cabin.

After getting her seated on the cracked leather sofa, Arles crossed to the patch of kitchen and lifted the lid of the cooler she'd brought. All the ice had melted by now, but the cans still felt cool to the touch. Caffeine and sugar to restore a few shards of sanity. Arles popped the tab on a Coke and proffered it in the girl's direction. The girl didn't reach for it, so Arles held the opening to the child's mouth, dribbled in a little soda, and waited for her to swallow. After a moment, the girl took the can and guzzled its contents. She burped, long and loudly, a sound that under different circumstances would've provoked a flurry of giggles.

Now she didn't even appear to notice the action of her own gut, esophagus, mouth. It was as if she were disembodied. Symptoms of shock and, if the girl was lucky, dissociation.

She wasn't even doing her mumble thing. Inhabiting a state where she could put words together, even just the sorrowful few Arles had heard back at Fir Cove, seemed as big a leap as a newborn setting off on a jog.

Arles knelt on the floor in front of the girl so as not to crowd her on the couch.

"Natural," she said softly.

She didn't turn her head to look at Arles. She didn't even blink.

Arles tried again. "Maeve."

Nothing.

Arles needed to orient the child to her environment and to what had happened. In as neutral a way possible, factual, without emotion to overwhelm or guide the girl's own reactions, which would have to unleash themselves slowly over time.

"You're at my stepfather's friend's cabin," Arles said. "With me. Shep."

Still no response. The girl sat so still, she might've been hollow.

"Something happened in the other room. In the bedroom at the back of the cabin."

A faint flicker across the girl's face, there and gone.

Arles steeled herself. "But you're safe now. You're okay. And he's gone. He's dead."

The girl met Arles's eyes as if the connection had never been severed. "Who is?"

"The Extricator," Arles said, remembering.

The girl shuddered, a full-body jolt, but spoke in a mild voice. "Oh, right. I axed him."

Arles gave a nod. "Yes. You did."

"Told you I was ready to use it for real."

Arles kept her face expressionless. The girl's statement had made a scenario spool out, an alternative reality Arles hadn't considered until now. "Did you know that he'd be coming? Is that why you wanted to learn how to handle a knife or an axe?"

"No," the girl replied tonelessly. "It just turned out to be good timing."

She sounded years older. As if she'd aged into adulthood in a single day.

All of Arles's therapy and training vanished, and out spewed a spontaneous volcano of words. The dead man in the other room had chased an eleven-year-old child at gunpoint. He deserved every inch of what he'd gotten, each pint of blood that'd been spilled. "You were strong and brave, and you did what had to be done. Just exactly what had to be done."

The girl went voiceless again, taking on her previous inhuman quietude.

It had been the wrong thing to say. To do. Arles should've maintained her professional demeanor, not departed from traditional codifications. She and the girl inhabited roles more loosely defined than they would've held in an office or other therapeutic milieu, but still, roughly speaking, they were psychologist and child in need of help. No more. And also, no less.

"Natural?" Arles said, back to neutral again. "Or Maeve?"

The girl spoke as ferociously as Arles did before. "Lark. My real name is Lark."

Silence suffused the two of them, enveloping the cabin. Arles situated herself more comfortably on the floor, sitting below the child.

"Lark," Arles repeated. "What a beautiful name."

The girl made her *blech* face, astonishingly and reassuringly familiar. "It's a stupid name. But I got lucky. Some of the other girls I've heard about are named *City* and *Thyme* and *Mink*."

There'd been mention of a Chloe too. So, did she have friends or not?

"My mom's first choice was *Field*. But my dad ruled it out."

And a mother and a father, whom, as far as Arles could recall, Lark hadn't mentioned since the first day at Fir Cove. Was the father dead in the other room of this cabin? Why hadn't her parents called the police the instant their fiercely smart and brave daughter disappeared?

But Arles didn't pose any questions. She didn't want to stem the flow of revelations.

"Field Naturals and Organics, because gut health is skin health," the child said in a mocking tone, a perfect rendition of a new-gen hipster. "*Field* is even less real of a name than *Lark*. It's just this product my mom was on about at the time I was born."

This gave Arles more to work with than she had gotten during their game. She composed her best therapy face, adding an inclined head, a *Go on*, with some expenditure of effort. She felt as if she could have slept for a week, and what had she done besides stumble upon a nearly decapitated body? Lark seemed to be winding down anyway. She sank back on the couch.

Arles needed to keep her talking while she was still disposed to it, everything that had been buried inside the girl suddenly flayed. That might be accomplished by skirting around the reality of the horror show just down the hall, tiptoeing in other directions, or by steering straight into it. Impossible to predict which would be right for this particular child.

"You mentioned your dad," Arles began cautiously. "That he didn't like the name *Field*."

Lark looked down at her. Nodded.

"Is he the man you call *the Extricator*? Is the Extricator your father?" Having come out with it, Arles gazed steadily up at the girl, providing a container, an *I'm right here with you*, in case her suggestion of patricide prompted a steep unraveling.

Instead, Lark let out a whoop of laughter, a bray of such hilarity that Arles had to smile back. If laughter were medicine, she'd just delivered an extra-strength dose. Then she realized that maybe this was the spiral, that Lark had become—hateful term—hysterical.

But the girl pulled it back in time. "Why would you think that?" she asked, dabbing at tears that had collected in her eyes. Lark had experienced a release of some sort, anyway. "The Extricator works for my parents. He watches me and does other stuff too."

She hadn't shifted to past tense, the trauma not yet integrated into her consciousness.

"Like . . . a manny?" Arles asked. *Coming soon: The Evil Manny.* Lark could do a preview.

She giggled again. "No, I don't have a nanny. My mom works from home. The Extricator is there for other kinds of things." She stopped, appearing frustrated, the expression of someone who'd been tasked with explaining facts and truisms she'd never had to consider before, just the automatic parts of her life. "Like, anytime I have to go out, which isn't very often, he's there to keep me from being seen. He takes care of all sorts of, um, jobs my parents need done."

He worked for her parents and had also tried to kidnap, maybe kill, their daughter?

That made even less sense than him *being* her parent.

With the suddenness of a slap, the door to the cabin swung open, letting in a wash of rain. Arles bore down on a leg of the couch to steady herself, keep herself from jumping, and the wind grabbed hold of the door, causing it to strike the wall behind it with a furious crack. Arles blinked to see Harry slip inside. He caught the door by its frame and slammed it shut. Arles had missed both the sky opening up and Harry's approach, so lost to Lark's revelations had she been.

Lark.

At the intrusion, she had encased her head with both arms, her back forming a shell, her shoulders bowed. She slid off the couch, her body going loose and jelly-like.

"It's Harry, remember?" Arles murmured, catching hold of the child. "The one you said was nice."

She let Lark stay on the floor where she seemed to want to be—regaining control was a huge aspect of recovery from a traumatic event—and led Harry down the hall without a word of greeting. Whatever had let him know to come out here meant that he was in this with them now.

He frowned at her, equally wordless, as they walked. She registered for the first time how she must look, her skin bloodied where it was exposed, clothes a Macbeth drenching.

They came to a stop in the doorway, Arles standing behind Harry.

There wasn't room for the two of them to fit side by side.

"Oh, Jesus. Oh, fucking hell." Harry's skin went so chalky, it seemed to have been erased. He looked more like a corpse than the man did. "What the hell happened here? Did you do this, Arlesey?"

Her stepfather's baby name for her. It had stuck for far too long, into adulthood.

Life's two diverging roads. Should she answer in the affirmative even though the facts would of course come out? Try to protect Lark?

What kind of messaging would that be in terms of the act the child had been forced, for still unknown reasons, to commit?

"No," she said quietly. "I didn't."

Horror at the slaughter in front of him transformed into disgust as Harry turned to look toward the other room. His expression foretold what Lark was going to face in the public eye. *Kiddie Axe Murderer.* Harry appeared to be contemplating a creature in a sideshow, some miniature monster, instead of the courageous, desperate warrior Arles believed Lark to be.

Arles had to be aware of her own biases, though. If she'd been in supervision, still a trainee, she would've discussed the predator in her own childhood about whom she'd often fantasized killing, and in the end had executed. Was Lark in a similar situation? Had she acted in self-defense, or was Arles projecting?

Harry let out a stifled moan, staring at the floor.

"I need you to get the police," Arles said.

"Right," he answered. "Yes. Sure."

But instead of leaving, he began to talk. He'd been at his favorite watering hole in town last night. Arles knew the place; Dan liked it too. Not either of the pricey ones—Thirty Lagers or Stream—this one didn't have a name anybody remembered, its sign too faded to read.

"I was talking about you," Harry went on. "To Nick, the bartender. You know him?"

Oh yes, Arles knew Nick. Stephanie's abusive piece-of-shit ex.

"I said how you and his little girl were staying out at my cabin. But Nick tells me that's impossible because his baby's on a road trip with her mama this summer. That's when I see this man, the dead one—oh, sweet Jesus, who is he?—sitting in a booth. Strange little guy. Nick says he's been coming in all week, people seeing him different places around town. Standing on street corners, poking around. Anyway, it looked like he'd been listening to what I was saying. Eavesdropping, like. Which kept bothering me off and on all night, so this morning, the wife starts nagging at me to come out here and check on you two. Wouldn't pipe down till I agreed." He swallowed, taking another look at the floor. "Guess I should've listened to her sooner."

"Harry," Arles said hoarsely, as if she'd been screaming, though she didn't think she had, "I really need you to go for the police."

"Right," he said again, this time backing out. "Yeah. Sure."

"Make sure it's the chief. Get Tim Lurcquer," said Arles.

"I could take you both away from here—" Harry broke off, casting his gaze toward Lark in the central room while his skin paled all over again. "Ferry you out one at a time on the back of the four-wheeler. Or go with the two of you in your car if you don't feel up to driving."

Arles shook her head. "She can't leave. And I'm not leaving her." A pause. "I'm supposed to stay here too, come to think of it. I was first on scene. You go. We'll be all right."

At last, he did.

Arles went and sat down on the floor since Lark hadn't altered her position.

"We have to involve the police now, Lark. You know that, right?"

A corpse lying in a sea of blood kind of mandated bringing in law enforcement. In an environment like this, there might've been wiggle room—stash the body somewhere on the near-infinite acreage and let the coyotes and cougars have at it; they'd do a better than middling job of taking care of the crime scene too if the cabin door were left open, right down to removing the blood spatter on the walls with their tongues. But covering up a murder, even if the quote, unquote victim proved to be a person nobody missed at all, probably wouldn't be the best life lesson for Lark.

Upon hearing Arles's question, she nodded once, a sharp jerk of her chin.

Then, on all fours, she suddenly rushed at Arles, closing the space between them, and winding up with her face pressed against Arles's shoulder. "But you can't leave me alone. Not for one second," Lark said, muffled. "Alone on my own, or alone with anybody else."

"I won't leave you," said Arles. It was a vow. "Not till I know that you're safe."

CHAPTER
THIRTY-ONE

While they waited, Arles distracted Lark from her obvious trepidation over what was going to happen next with equal parts food and conversation, which was to say a lot of both.

Lark went from scarcely revealing a word about herself to speaking as freely and vociferously as if she'd just mastered a new language. And in terms of eating, she was apparently ravenous. If they'd been intending to stay at the cabin, they would've had to resupply, so completely did Lark scavenge the remains of their stash. Arles didn't feel hungry herself, couldn't imagine eating ever again. But the talking part she did well, engaging Lark in a chat about the girl's favorite topic—movies—before meandering onto skills needed if you were outdoors in weather like this.

Thunder shook the cabin and rattled its windowpanes.

Then the noise of an engine emerged out of the clamor, a way off in the distance, still, just a low thrum in the air, but growing louder, getting closer.

Lark began fidgeting in her chair, digging her heels into its legs, twisting and turning on the seat. "I wish we could cut him up." She tossed a look over her shoulder in the direction of the bedroom. "Feed him to the wood chipper. Like in *Fargo*. Then nobody would have to know."

She isn't a monster, Arles mentally proclaimed. *She's a terrified young girl.* Refuting Harry's instinctive recoiling, the whole patriarchal, judgmental world that was going to have a field day with an eleven-year-old girl enraged enough to deliver a killing blow.

Arles couldn't take away Lark's fears over what was about to happen, but she could convey her certainty that the girl wasn't the creature—loathsome, baffling—that people would try to make her out to be. Forge an alliance between them. It was a stretch—gallows humor for sure—but children didn't screen off darkness the way many adults did. "If Harry didn't know, I might be with you on the wood-chipper thing," Arles said, injecting her tone with dryness.

Cramming a last bite of granola bar into her mouth, Lark snatched a quick look outside.

Rain streaming. No police car pulling up yet.

"Not for real though, right?" she asked.

"No," Arles said quietly. "Not for real."

Lark swiveled away from the small table as a snake tongue of lightning flickered.

"Hey, why's that gun thing open?" she asked, standing up to look.

"Stay away from there, okay?" The cabinet would require analysis, the first stop Arles had made after entering the cabin. She continued talking in an attempt to engage Lark, avoid having to impose a limitation on the child's movements. "I took out a gun. Before I knew where you were. To have just in case."

Lark stilled in place. "But you said they were basically props. No one gets hurt with a gun that's not meant to be used as a weapon. There're all these new regulations now."

Jarred by what Lark had just said, Arles forced herself to attend to the girl's next words.

"That's why I got the axe. If you're gonna hurt someone, it has to be for real." Lark's face shadowed with remembrance, with doing it for real.

But Arles couldn't offer an empathic response just then. Her mind was elsewhere.

On movies. *Fargo.* New regulations.

"Lark," she said, "who are your parents?"

The authorities had to be nearly here, competing with the storm to be heard. An engine roar and clap of thunder, God's hand smacking the face of a cloud, sounded outside as headlights aimed twin beams through the window. Unless that had been a split fork of lightning? The room shifted with the changing light, altering its confines, its shape.

"Huh?" Lark replied with a frown. "You already know who they are. You guessed the first day I came. Which was crazy smart of you, Shep."

Arles experienced it as parts beginning to move on a machine that had been stuck.

A shriek, a great grinding of gears, before the correct piece slid precisely into place.

It was hard to see Lark in the room, given the low level of light. But when a streak of lightning hissed through the trees, heating the wetness condensed on their leaves, a gleam was illuminated on the child's face, an expression of quiet satisfaction.

A car door slammed, and boots could be heard thudding outside.

Lark didn't seem to notice. "I just pretended you got it wrong," she explained.

"No, that's not right," Arles said slowly. "Not quite. You didn't pretend. You *acted.*"

A hard rap on the door.

Lightning lit up the cabin; it was suddenly as bright as noon on a clear day.

"Yes," Lark said on a long, exhaled breath.

She didn't seem simply pleased or tickled, no state as light or breezy as that. Instead, she appeared replete with something. Deeply, soul-satisfyingly gratified.

"That's what I did, Shep!" she said. "I acted."

Arles looked straight at her.

They traded nods as the cabin door opened, and Tim strode inside.

Lark said, "Just like my dad."

"Jason didn't make his last check-in," Kip announced, entering the kitchen.

Whether Jason had finally chosen to duck out on them for good, escape while three thousand miles away, having finally been given an assignment even he balked at, or had met with a fatal accident in that wild, distant land, didn't matter to Janelle.

Yes, Jason would be irreplaceable. He was 1,000 percent loyal to them and took care of so many tasks, they were uncountable. Luckily, he was on salary, not paid by the job, which included driving, scheduling, babysitting on the rare occasions when Lark had to be out of reach, plus less mundane things, such as hacking into a studio exec's email to find out who the lead was slated to be, and on one occasion, intimidating talent away from a role Kip was up for. Even housekeeping, if Janelle couldn't get Lark to hide on the days the cleaning lady was scheduled.

Almost no one was allowed to know Lark existed. She didn't even have a pediatrician—Troy had trained as a physician's assistant before joining Kip's employ, and Lark never needed the doctor anyway. Her health was due to the lifestyle Janelle imposed. A diet individually tailored to Lark's gut biome, strength training at an early age, aerobic conditioning. Her brain was strong too. Lark was homeschooled—or no-schooled. Even better.

An alert chimed, and Kip's frown deepened as he glanced at his phone. "Make that his last two check-ins."

Janelle would've warned him about the grooves, the valley he was carving between his eyebrows, except she knew lines only added to his marketability. Kip's baby face needed weathering; he had aged into sexy forties male, non-action-star variety, not that he wouldn't sell his soul to book Marvel, despite the franchise being a dying empire, limping along till its final breath sputtered out.

It was early, a pink-and-orange sun just starting to stain the skyline, colors amplified by pollution. They'd been trying to stick to Eastern time, keep up with what was happening back in New York, even though they'd had to fly home to make the last of Kip's prerelease appearances.

"So, where is Lark?" Janelle asked, making sure to vanquish her own vague frown of concern.

Kip studied his phone. "Jason was headed God knows where. Some cabin," he said, scrolling. "Last text says he had intel suggesting Lark met up with that psychologist after all."

The return to the with-a-psychologist theory caused a more severe stab of alarm, a worry line Janelle couldn't erase, than the possibility of Jason perishing back east.

Janelle would've preferred Lark to encounter a kiddie predator than a psychologist. She'd seen the result when Lark had gotten therapy, the therapist forced to sign an NDA and meet with Kip and Janelle's lawyer so she knew she'd be sued into oblivion if she ever disclosed the fact that they had a child. And still, Lark had barely begun participating in sessions before Kip pulled the plug, causing Lark to find additional therapists online and sign up for free initial consultations, playing adults who refused to turn on their video—one had crippling social anxiety; another, body dysmorphic disorder—until her real age was discovered.

Lark always got found out; she was a terrible actress. When she grew up, she'd have to work in one of the lower sectors, some behind-the-scenes capacity, a brand solicitor on Janelle's side of things, camera operator or best boy on Kip's.

Whereas a serial sicko—well, Lark could've handled anyone like that.

When Lark had been a baby, Janelle used to have a recurring nightmare that her daughter turned into a spider. Human size, large and creeping. The site Janelle used to analyze all her dreams said that spiders were a symbol of female empowerment.

Janelle was more like Lark's life coach than her mom. Lark was her project, her biggest one to date. Janelle had helped all the women and girls who followed her improve themselves, selling products and habits and regimens so they could live their best lives. But Lark, she had built from the ground up. Created her out of nothing. No kid of hers was ever going to feel like Janelle had when she was young. Back when she'd been just Jane— inferior, weak, self-doubting.

Janelle still felt that way most of the time, truth be told. None of her millions of followers would believe that. Well, millions less a few thousand due to her absence this week; influencers were gone in a poof of pink dust the second they stopped posting.

Even being married to Kip Stratton didn't change anything. Or this house. Or inhabiting the role she did—a role of her own, the cyber-era equivalent of Virginia Woolf's call to action—in the wellness, beauty, and lifestyle space as one of the most-sought-after influencers. None of it could deliver a tenth of the power and self-actualization she knew Lark possessed.

It was perhaps the one good thing Janelle had done in her life.

She walked across the kitchen toward the wall of glass at the back, flexing her hands. Trying to smooth out wrinkles that the priciest black-market emollient—made from animal byproducts forbidden from import, a concoction that surely would've led her followers to get her canceled— couldn't prevent. Still, despite it being a losing battle, she stretched her hands. When what she really felt like doing was balling them into two knotted, wrinkly fists.

"That little shit," she said. Their daughter, not Jason. Well, him too.

"Jane," Kip warned, his tone like a blade against someone's throat.

He hated it when she cursed around Lark. Cursing at her was worse, and cursing her out apparently worst of all. But that was what you got when you married someone whose mother had used slut *as a pet name for her daughter.*

Before her father had left, Janelle had been a daddy's girl. Her mother blamed Janelle for not having been enough—good enough, sweet enough, smart enough, pretty enough, skinny enough—to have made Janelle's father stick around.

Her mother never lost the mouth she had on her, just aimed it in Janelle's direction once there was no longer a man in the house to harass.

Part of why Janelle only ever had eyes for her daddy, even long after he was gone.

She stared out at the pool with the sun streaming in through the glass, then swiveled to face Kip at the coffee station. With Jason gone, Kip was trying to learn how to use the machine.

"Why did she run away from Jason at that hotel?" Hotel in air quotes, the way she and Kip had been referring to the place ever since they'd checked in. More air quotes for check-in. "And hide in the rental car? She knew we were just going to a bookstore." What kid wanted to hang out at one of those? They were literal dinosaurs.

"Maybe she wants company from someone besides Jason," Kip said, fighting with the coffee pod. "Or us."

"But she's already got everything!" Everything Janelle never had as a child.

She felt an internal tug, though. There was no way Lark could've heard her last week, was there? It wasn't nearly time for that post to go up yet; Janelle had just been preparing in advance. Getting her magnum opus ready, a vlog years in the making. None of the other top influencers would be able to match it, or even conceive of such a thing. Once it finally went live, it would wield the power to bring Janelle far beyond brand proselytizing, keep her relevant for years. A Jurassic Age in internet time.

Lark had been explicitly told not to come near the studio that day. And she was an obedient child—another trait being raised by someone like Janelle instilled. But if Lark had disobeyed—drifted close to the wing of the house where Janelle filmed—then, oh God, Janelle hoped she'd overheard only the first version. The other one was just a worst-case scenario.

She attempted to stifle a yawn—more wrinkles—but failed. She needed a shot of her usual high-octane, yak-butter-enriched morning brew, but she had sworn off caffeine for another of her I'm Me regimens just before they'd flown east. She wondered how her followers were making out in her absence. Without her there to cheer them on and pump up their spirits and sell them things to make it easier, or at least distract them from their misery with injections of consumerism.

Keeping to her regular schedule while the daughter nobody knew she had was missing wouldn't have played well, even if Lark's identity didn't come out for another two years, the age Kip had determined sufficient for Lark to stand the exposure. Posting during this time could get Janelle canceled after the fact, assuming she referenced her ordeal at some point, which she definitely would. Going dark was the right move, but giving up both caffeine and posting had turned her into a hot mess. A hot mess with a massive headache.

Janelle wouldn't cheat, though. She never cheated with her followers, not even over a little thing like giving up coffee or if there was zero chance of being found out. She had actual ethics. She was no Belle Gibson.

She walked back across the kitchen to the refrigerator to get a bottle of her substitute elixir. The gleaming stainless door was heavy, she thought, realizing how rarely she opened it for herself. How much harder life was going to get if Jason didn't come back to do whatever.

She turned around to face Kip. He was still struggling with his pod. He gave a hard tug, and coffee granules exploded, scattering across the poured concrete floor like tiny ants.

This house and its accoutrements were extravagant, absurd, especially by the standards of where Janelle had come from. And also where Kip was in his career, not yet at the top. But in LA, real estate was aspirational, and debt a fiction so long as you stayed in the game.

Kip stared helplessly down at the floor as if he'd never heard of a broom. Maybe he hadn't.

"I don't think we can keep Lark a secret anymore," she said sorrowfully. She lifted her gaze sadly to his; Kip wasn't the only person who could act in this family.

"Are you kidding?" He glowered at her. "You want to tell the world about Lark right before my film drops? That girl is a beauty already. When she speaks, she sings like the bird I named her for. She'll walk into the biz as easily as Colin Hanks."

I named Lark! *Janelle wanted to protest. Also, could you be a nepo baby if your father wasn't Ethan Hawke or Sean Penn but Kip Stratton?*

She couldn't tell if the bolt of pure and shining loathing that flashed across Kip's face as he stared at her was real or put-on. Probably both.

"All the years of work to hide her, and my years of work to get here, will be scrubbed by the time you and I appear at the preview. It'll be the only thing the damn press cares about. Our newly unveiled daughter. 'Kip Stratton's Secret Child,'" he intoned.

Janelle looked at him with the most spontaneous, organic expression she'd worn in years. Surprise and disgust and horror. She scarcely considered how her face must be contorted.

She'd gone along with Kip's decision to keep secret the fact that they had a child, even though she believed Lark would have benefited more by embracing her status from an early age than being sprung on the public in a craftily spun, meticulously orchestrated media blitz after Kip judged her mature enough to handle it. When he'd announced his grand scheme, the unveiling was supposed to happen once Lark aged out of babyhood, then the toddler years, the elementary era. But Lark only got more winsome and adorable, and Kip only pushed harder to hide her.

Following Kip's lead like she always did, Janelle had come up with her own script for the eventual reveal, a version that might in the end blow up her channel even more than eleven years' worth of look-at-my-kid content, lucrative kiddie-product placements notwithstanding.

Surprises played well online.

And sob stories even better, hence Janelle's rehearsing last week.

But never once had it occurred to her that Kip's tyranny over Lark, the lengths he went to in order to keep her out of sight, stemmed not from paternal—and paternalistic—concern over what the industry did to children, how it chewed them up and swallowed them before they were old enough to get high to cope, but terror that her career would outshine his.

"You're jealous," she said wonderingly. "Of our own child."

She was so blown away by the workings of her mind, the insight it had generated, that she forgot not to purse her lips around the straw in her ash and mushroom cold brew.

She'd have to schedule her injection early this month.

Kip turned away from the mess scattered across the floor.

"Come on," he told her.

"Come on?" she echoed. But she was already hurrying after him, the kitten heels on her indoor house shoes crushing coffee grinds to a blackened sludge. "Where are we going?"

"Where else?" he demanded. "Back east to that hellhole."

ACT III

Neither Depth nor Demons

CHAPTER
THIRTY-TWO

That first day in the parlor at Fir Cove, Lark had scoffed at the suggestion that she had a famous actor for a father, dismissed the idea with real derision. Or what had *looked* like real. Arles's mistake had been in concluding that no child could act that well, perform at such a level.

People always got into trouble when they underestimated children.

Age didn't prevent an actor from being brilliant; Lark could probably name all the children who had won Oscars. She had been steeped from birth in the brew of an acting family, sculpted in its image, performance the air she breathed. Which explained why she used its vocabulary so seamlessly—mentioning *crew* when Arles had stumbled over the correct term for people who worked on a film—and referred to actors by first name. How she knew so much lore.

In addition to having been fooled by Lark's stellar acting skills, the child's description of Kip Stratton as *handsome* had also been convincing, because who spoke about their dad that way? And when Lark had lashed out, accusing Arles of not being a good therapist, Arles had allowed herself to be swayed, even though she of all people knew that the best defense was to go on the offensive.

The notion that Lark's rejoinders had been scripted, that she'd been ahead of Arles this whole time, made Arles shiver in her wet clothes. She and Lark had gotten drenched despite the umbrella Tim held up as he escorted them out of the cabin. Neither of them spoke as they rode in the back of his county-issued police-grade vehicle. Lark had said just one thing before getting in.

"It looks the same on set! Sometimes my dad sneaks me in after wrap."

They got soaked anew when Tim parked in front of the barracks and ran with them through the downpour. Dorothy hovered by the glass doors, holding a towel and tutting like a mother bird as she patted Lark dry.

Tim led them down the hall to an interview room. Arles had looked into this room through a one-way mirror when the parent of a client was being questioned. To be inside it was a whole other beast.

Tim bent down, speaking in a respectful tone to Lark, which was to say not much different from how he would've spoken to an adult. "I asked my officer, Mandy, to stay behind here at the barracks because kids always seem to like her best. While Dr. Shepherd and I talk, would you like to go get a snack from the vending machine with Mandy?"

Lark reached for Arles's hand, Arles amazed by how snugly it fit inside hers.

"Thanks, but I want to stay here with Shep."

"Shep," Tim repeated. "Okay. Gotcha."

Lark smiled up at him. "I still want something from the vending machine, though."

She was going to be more junk food than human if she ate another candy bar or bag of chips, Arles thought. To Tim, she said, "I promised Lark we'd stay together." She glanced down. "You'd be okay doing some activity while I speak with the chief, right? Maybe watch a movie?"

Lark nodded eagerly enough that her hair swung.

It was dirty, Arles noticed, neither pond water nor rain equal to the products and treatments that must pamper her at home. She looked like a different child from the one who'd arrived at Fir Cove. Not necessarily worse. In some ways, the opposite.

Tim appeared to be pondering Arles's proposal.

"Lark's a film buff," Arles elaborated. "Could be anything. First-run. Classic."

"To be perfectly honest, I'd rather not grant access to our Wi-Fi. No offense, Lark."

"None taken," she said courteously. She repeated it with a touch of officiousness, as if trying to get the line right. "None taken in the least." Lastly, she went for wasted-on-weed casual. "No worries, you're good."

Tim gave a finger snap. "Bet I can find something in the evidence locker."

"Stolen merchandise!" Lark sang out as he left the room.

"Well, stolen merchandise in police custody," Arles amended.

"That's even better," Lark said. "Means the bad guy didn't get to keep it." Then something seemed to strike her—perhaps the nature of bad guys, be they lying dead in a pool of blood, or the people who had put them there—and her face folded.

Arles held her gaze, empathetic, unflinching.

Tim came back into the room with an ancient-looking DVD player and a stack of disks.

Lark immediately started sorting through the titles.

A few minutes later—just enough time for the device to be hooked up while Lark whooped and crowed over how old-fashioned it was, as if she were about to watch a talkie on a Cinematograph—she was engrossed.

Arles and Tim seated themselves on opposite sides of a battered table.

"So," he said, squaring his hands on the scarred wooden surface, "corpses abound."

Kara. A nearly beheaded stranger. And Peter too. Arles winced.

But she'd stared down worse than the police chief, from sociopaths in her office to her own family members. She watched Tim, making sure to blink at a natural rate while she waited.

He broke first. "My condolences again about your patient. Former patient."

"Yes," Arles said. "That was—is—brutal."

"And your stepfather." Tim glanced at a notepad. "You're aware he died three days ago?"

An instantaneous flurry inside her, a flutter of pulse at her neck.

Tim faced her, unblinking, his face stone.

"Um . . ." Arles gathered breath. No *ums*. They showed weakness. She needn't appear grief-stricken; people knew who her stepfather had been, even if they were never willing to say so out loud. Matter-of-fact should do. "Yes. A staff member at the facility where he is—was—living reached out."

"They contacted me too. It's protocol when they have a bad outcome."

Bad outcome. If she'd tried to speak, it would've been a whistle.

"And the first thing I do is ask for a list of people who were with the deceased around the time of his passing. Nurses, aides, other staff." Tim paused. "Visitors."

Arles's throat was plugged, no air getting through.

"You went to see your stepfather that day," he said.

The scantest of nods.

"Was that a frequent occurrence? Did you visit him regularly?"

Tim would know that from the logs. It was her reaction that mattered to him.

"No, hardly ever." The words rasped, each one a claw in her mouth. "But I was trying to locate Lark." She gestured to the rapt child seated on the other side of the room.

Lark's eyes didn't so much as flicker while she stared at the screen, which probably indicated how intently she was listening to the conversation between Arles and Tim.

"My stepfather has—or had—" Continuing to borrow the page from Lark where she'd referred to the small man in the present tense, even after she had slain him. "Game cameras on the property. I went to ask for access to the footage."

Tim kept quiet, staring at her with steady eyes.

Arles felt things tighten deep within her, as if they were being wound on a crank.

At last, Tim dropped his gaze, speaking as if he'd come to a decision. "I became chief after Vern Weathers stepped down. As you probably remember."

Arles swallowed. Uncle Vern.

"Or was forced to step down," Tim corrected himself. "Anyway, there were rumors back then. Not about Vern, who was a known-quantity, old white dude like I'm getting to be."

Arles mustered a fleeting smile to match Tim's.

"Corrupt as hell and one of those guys who liked things the way they were, preferred them to stay that way."

Arles signaled agreement.

"But one of Vern's cronies didn't hold up even that well." Tim's face darkened. "He was real bad. According to these rumors."

Bad, Arles thought dully. So much bad in this world. Some of it lying on the floor of Harry's cabin. Some recently expired at Serenity Acres. Some had shot her nearly five months ago. And there would be more. There always was. As soon as one source of bad got taken out, another came along to fill it, like water closing over rocks thrown into an infinite lake.

Tim had begun scrawling on his pad. "Deaths at Serenity Acres tend to come down to natural causes or a disease process. In your stepfather's case, he seems to have dosed himself too aggressively." He flipped his pad closed. "That's what my report will say, anyway."

Arles held his gaze.

"Dr. Shepherd—"

"Arles," she said.

"Why didn't you let me know you needed help?"

The question startled her. "You mean with getting the game-camera footage?"

"I mean with anything."

Arles lowered her voice to a level she hoped wouldn't penetrate Lark's false fixedness. "That's something I've never been able to do."

CHAPTER
THIRTY-THREE

The movie hadn't yet ended when Tim let Lark know that a CPS worker would be coming. Lark snatched Arles's hand in a claw grip, shaking her head wordlessly.

Arles looked down at her. "I work alongside Child Protective Services all the time. I'm sure I can stand right out there in the hall." She pointed. "We'll leave the door open, and it'll be like I'm still in here with you."

While a social worker named Angela met with Lark, Tim waited with Arles in the hallway, standing with his back braced against the wall.

"I wish you'd felt able to trust me," he said, maintaining a mild tone. "Deciding to see to the child yourself opens up a world of accountability."

"I know it does," Arles said, keeping watch on the happenings in the interview room. "But even if you'd managed to determine who Lark's parents were—and I couldn't do it myself for some time—you, the staties, or feds would almost certainly have had to hand her over. Trust me on this. Not because any of you are bad at your jobs, but because the system ties your hands. And even though I don't know why yet, I have a feeling that's the worst thing we could do."

Tim hesitated. "Let's just say you skipped a few steps, and leave it at that."

"Will she be remanded into custody?" Arles asked, the question causing an ache of tears in her throat. "While you conduct your investigation?"

"Cursory examination of the physical evidence sets things up fairly clearly," Tim replied. "Small handprint in the blood on the handle of the axe, for example."

Arles flinched.

Tim allowed for a pause. "Crime scene folks will learn a great deal more, of course. But in your professional opinion, is Lark a danger to herself or others? That's what we need to know to decide placement. Angela's report should cover it, but based on how much your girl seems to be giving her, I have a feeling it won't." He indicated the other room.

My girl, Arles heard. A fresh crop of tears pressed against the backs of her eyes.

"I don't think so," she said quietly. "What happened at the cabin was very targeted." For reasons Arles didn't yet know.

"Then no immediate assignment to juvenile justice or pediatric inpatient is required," Tim said. "Assuming the child can be contained somewhere safe and isn't at risk of fleeing."

A geyser shot up through Arles, a great gusher of relief. She was able to focus on things that had been crowded out before Tim laid her most urgent concern to rest. Like Lark's obvious recalcitrance as Angela attempted to interview her. Along with some questions.

"Who was the owner of the Corolla?" Arles asked.

Tim studied her. "A Petra Armstrong."

Arles visibly recoiled; she felt herself do it.

"You know her," said Tim.

"Worked with her once or twice." A heroic figure in Arles's view. "Is she okay?"

"Going to be," Tim answered. "She suffered a skull fracture. Wasn't able to make a report until yesterday. Apparently, she'd been trying to drive away at gunpoint when her window got smashed, and she was dragged out of the car." Tim's gaze continued to rest on Arles.

"By the dead man in Harry Price's cabin, I'm thinking. He appears to match Ms. Armstrong's description, though it's a little hard to be sure, condition he's in."

Arles swallowed. "That tracks."

Her attention was dragged away then by Lark. The girl whipped her head back and forth, making the *lips sealed* gesture with her forefinger and thumb pinched together at her mouth.

"Is there a history of abuse or neglect?" Tim asked. "Does that explain this refusal to talk?"

They both looked at Angela, now asking Lark to lift her sleeves, stand with her back turned and her shirt raised, roll the cuffs of her shorts higher. Checking, Arles knew, for scars, burns, bruises. Thankfully, Lark didn't have any from their sojourn in the woods. A hospital visit might be recommended, X-rays to look for evidence of past broken bones.

"Not physical abuse or neglect," Arles said, thinking of Lark's clothes, her hair. "Some caloric restriction, but that doesn't seem to stem from neglect. Vanity, more likely. But emotional abuse for sure." Parents who hadn't bothered to report Lark gone. Her baffling statement that she was a missing child.

A squawk came from inside the room. "I *said* no more!"

There was the queenly child Arles had first encountered. The CPS worker gave a quick nod and dropped into a chair, focusing fiercely on some paperwork.

Lark sat with her arms crossed over her chest, a scowl disrupting her features.

"There's clearly a great deal we don't know," Tim said.

Arles sighed. "Lark's been through a trauma. And a police barracks isn't the most calming environment."

"You know what is, though?" Tim asked.

"What is what?" Arles said.

"A calming environment. Or was until recently, according to a few people in town."

Arles frowned. She usually stayed a pace or two ahead of people, but in this instance had no idea what Tim was getting at.

Angela could be heard asking loudly, "Ready to give this another go, honey?"

It was not a honey-sounding *honey*.

Lark stalked across the room while Angela went red-faced and began scribbling again.

"I received a call earlier," Tim said. "From a pair asking to remain anonymous. They offered an obvious alias, gave me a fake residence. Said discretion is of the utmost importance."

Hollywood royals, Arles thought with a mental headshake.

"In other words, you were right," Tim went on. "These folks are accustomed to setting requirements. Making demands, and seeing they get met. I made sure they know they're not the ones in charge here. Given what happened in that cabin."

A flash of that crimson-filled room. Arles worked to conceal her response.

"So, what we've got is a child-welfare case," Tim said.

"Best interests of the child," Arles countered. "But tomato to*mah*to."

Tim smiled briefly. "I'm inclined to give these two the anonymity they want while we get to the bottom of things. Why this girl saw fit to leave home, who the deceased was to her. If the situation turns out to require social services—and I can't imagine it won't—then we transfer the case as soon as you have a home address."

"DCF," Arles said, "would oversee. It's what they call children and family services in California."

"She's from California," Tim said as if *that* made sense.

Arles nodded. "LA."

"See? You know more than Angela already." Tim jotted a note. "Imagine how much you'll come up with if you get everyone together in one place."

Arles got it then. The calm environment Tim meant. "You're saying you want me to give the—" She'd been about to say *Strattons*. "Family *therapy?*"

"Isn't that what you do?" Tim responded. "Talk with kids and their parents to make them tell you the truth?"

"I wouldn't put it quite like that. I can't make anyone do anything." Arles paused. "But sort of. Sometimes. When it goes well."

Tim faced her, folding his arms across his chest. "Well, then, we'd better hope this goes well. Because I've got two murder investigations to tie up before I can oversee a youth eval."

"But I closed Fir Cove," Arles protested. "Five months ago. And it'd only been open as a treatment facility for a short time before that." Tim was vastly overestimating her abilities. Either that, or he'd come up with the one solution that had a chance of working.

As if tracking her thoughts, he said, "There are few perfect moments in law enforcement, Dr. Shepherd. Arles. I suspect it's the same in your line of work."

She looked at him.

"A lot of investigations can be reduced to cobbled-together elements. Made up of *the best we can*s. And in a situation with as little precedent as this one, I'd say the bar is set even lower."

Arles dipped her head in assent. "The pieces rarely fit together in just the right way to ensure winding up with a clear answer. Assuming there even *is* a clear answer."

"So, what I'm suggesting is about as close as I can imagine to a setup that will let us determine what this child needs." Tim gave a nod as if it had been decided. Not just decided—set in stone. "And you know what she's up against if we don't."

Juvie. Or foster care with the few caregivers willing to take a child who'd committed a violent criminal act. Lark would be absorbed into the system as seamlessly as a drop of water in a lake. And arguably worse than any of that—unchecked public scrutiny with no way to shape a coherent story that would protect Lark.

Arles glanced into the room as the girl caught her gaze.

"I'll have an officer swing out your way anytime I can spare one. Check up on things." Tim depressed a button on the radio on his shoulder and gave a listen before heading down the hall. But then he turned. "Get this California couple off my back and out to that center of yours. Have a grand reopening."

Arles held up a finger in Lark's direction. *One sec.*

"I'll make sure they understand the conditions and know how to find your place." Tim resumed his stride while continuing to speak. "And you can figure out what the hell is going on."

CHAPTER
THIRTY-FOUR

The world had changed in the short time Arles and Lark had stepped out of it.

Before setting forth on their drive, Arles went online, doing a deeper dive into the Strattons than she had when she'd been at the bookstore. Power couple, in different branches of the entertainment industry, aggressively child-free. The couple continued to succeed in deflecting media attention away from the fact that they had a daughter.

Kara was for the first time bathed in something like fame, reflection from that false sun. Not a constant, faraway star, just light from a million flashing bulbs.

"Mystery Author Dies in Real Life Mystery" read the headlines, along with others more salacious and mouthwatering than that. Kara's latest release topped the Amazon charts, and her previous titles were being featured on book blogs. In death, she'd achieved what had eluded her in life. Imagine what could happen if the truth of her heroism came out. In addition to procuring a safe future for Lark, Arles intended to make sure Kara's full story got told.

"You once said that your name was the easiest one to guess," Arles remarked to Lark on the way back to Fir Cove. She'd let her take the passenger seat. Technically, the age for this was twelve, but Arles figured that anyone who could slay a child predator deserved to sit up front. "Were you acting then too?"

Her head bobbed in a nod. "It's an exercise. You say the exact opposite of what's true."

Arles spun the steering wheel, taking that in.

"You look sad, Shep," Lark observed.

Arles glanced sideways. That was usually her line.

"I guess I wish you hadn't felt you had to act with me," she told Lark at last. "Said who your parents were when I guessed. And other stuff." *Like why the man you killed had to die.*

"I'm not allowed," Lark replied glumly. "They're gonna murder me when they find out."

"Not on my watch they won't," Arles replied, setting her mouth in a thin line.

"I didn't mean for real," Lark said, still gloomy. "Redrum or whatever."

Arles got the reference. She wasn't much of a movie person, but Stephen King had been there for her in childhood.

Lark fell abruptly silent then, her eyes filming over as she stared out at the blue-bright sky. The storm had cleared. After a while, the girl tilted sideways over the console until her cheek touched Arles's shoulder. Arles took her arm off the wheel to lay it beside Lark on the child's seat, driving the rest of the way home one-handed.

Back at Fir Cove, they showered to rid themselves of the smears and streaks of blood, then Arles opened windows to air out the house and defrosted one of Stephanie's entrées for dinner. She looked around, didn't see Lark, and released a long breath. The time had passed when the girl's absence would've caused an immediate spike of alarm. Was Arles's newfound sense of peace due to the dead guy being gone? Or because the child clearly had tools of her own, and sufficient mental robustness, to prevent a bad outcome?

Those two words again.

Fear over what Arles had done to Peter felt like a thing of the past too.

According to Tim, she was off the hook. Legally speaking. The witch was dead—physically, anyway. Psychically, Arles would have to deal with later.

She trudged upstairs. Steam floated in wisps through an open bathroom door. Shower followed by a chaser of soaking? Arles knocked on the adjacent wall.

"I'm in the tub, Shep!" Lark sang out. "Don't disturb me!"

That night, after a dinner a lot healthier—thanks be to Stephanie— than junky snacks or the nonperishable camp food Lark and Arles had been subsisting on, the two of them reclined on twin couches in the main room on the first floor.

Steering straight into the matter at hand—Lark's parents and why they hadn't claimed her—would be too direct an approach, especially given the trauma Lark had just gone through. Besides, Arles was going to meet the elder Strattons soon enough and be able to come to her own deductions, as close as she could get to the inevitably gray-shaded truth. For the moment, however, there were other topics to discuss, plenty more to learn about Lark herself.

"That thing you do," Arles began. "Saying words barely aloud. Are they from a movie?"

Lark jerked her chin up. "You mean my monologue? Yeah, I practice it whenever I get stressed out. So I can make sure I still have the whole thing memorized. It's Saoirse Ronan."

Arles looked blank.

"*Little Women*," Lark said. "Greta Gerwig's version, of course." She spread out her hand like a fan against her collarbone.

Not so heartbreaking, then. Just a line from a script.

"And was that another—" Again, Arles had to reach for the term. "Not a bit."

"Acting exercise," Lark prompted. "A bit is for comics."

"That time you wanted to catch me off guard at Harry's cabin."

Lark had begun winding loops of hair around each of her fingers, making curls as it dried. "Oh, right. My dad worked with his Kowalski coach forever on that one. It's hard because both people know what's happening, really, but with you being surprised for real, it was—" Lark gave a chef's kiss with two of her fingers, which released perfect long coils of hair.

All the different roles she had put on. The skipping child, the elegant curtsy, the officious pardoner of Tim's *no offense*. Was coldblooded killer just another of her acts? Lark was the daughter of two people who lied for a living. Kip convinced viewers he was someone he was not; Janelle convinced them she had a life she really didn't and to buy things they didn't need. How was a child raised in that milieu supposed to tell truth from fiction?

"I think I might be a better actor than my mom," Lark said lightly. "Even my dad."

Her tone did nothing to lessen Arles's tinge of unease.

"I went super method with the cult thing. Totally faked out Kara."

Then memory appeared to return, and Lark began yanking her fingers, disentangling them from her lengths of hair. She did it so violently, the motion seemed an act of self-harm. Unless this too was a performance.

"I did some research about your parents," Arles said.

Lark stopped pulling at her hair to look at her.

"Followed them like a groupie," Arles continued. "Not an in-person one, but still."

"What's a groupie?"

This time Arles had to hunt for the correct word for a different reason. Not because she came from another profession, but because she came from the other side of the Gen Z divide.

"A stan," she said at last, finding it.

Lark jounced her head in a nod.

"Your parents live their whole lives online. Everything is documented and for show. Their settings on social are public, and they tell the world a stupid lot. People write about them all the time too. But nothing anywhere about their having a child."

Still lounging on the opposite couch, Lark studied Arles.

"That's part of what convinced me to stop looking in their direction, back when Kara brought you here. In addition to your superb acting job, of course."

"That's because," Lark said calmly, "they're liars too."

Arles had just told herself the same thing, but coming from Lark, the words chilled.

The light in the room had grown dim, night coming on. Arles got up to turn on a lamp.

Lark bowed her head in the sudden pool of light. "Aren't therapists supposed to be able to tell when people are lying?"

Fair, Arles thought. "People lie to themselves even more than they do to others, and psychologists get very good at picking up on that. But you seem pretty straight with yourself. You face up to some hard truths, and you definitely fooled me. You might still be, for all I know. Deceiving me somehow. In this very conversation we're having tonight."

"I'm not!" Lark cried. "I didn't! I haven't!"

She stood up too, and rounded on Arles, outrage masking a tremble of hurt. It was the same display of opposing emotions that had led Arles astray the first time. So hard to fake that particular defensive process, something hard put on to camouflage the soft molten core beneath. At the same time, the trio of protestations seemed like one or two too many.

"Are you lying now?" Arles asked. "About not lying?"

Silence piled up, a weighty accumulation. It was a full and pregnant hush, the moment before the curtain goes up, a microphone is lifted, or the opening shot appears on a screen.

Finally, Lark said, "Yes."

Arles sank onto the couch, patting the cushion beside her.

Lark came and dropped down. "My mom always says I'm a sucky actor. Guess it's true. If you've already figured out how to make me."

Arles spoke dryly to dilute the poison of Lark's mother's assessment. "I think we should both be offended."

Lark gave a short laugh before falling silent.

"So, what did you just lie about?" Arles asked.

"An actor will never be bought in a role unless they find part of themselves in it," Lark explained, sounding as if she were quoting someone.

"The best lies contain a grain of truth," Arles murmured, translating between professions.

"Right. So, I don't really think I'm a better actor than my dad. Not even my mom. Total lie." She paused. "I just wish that I was. Because then I could trick them the way they've always tricked me."

"Ah," Arles said.

"You know, you lie too," Lark said suddenly.

"I do?" Arles said, surprised. "I think of myself as being truthful. Especially with kids."

"You lie by not saying anything. Just, like, by going quiet and waiting for the other person to talk. Or saying something that doesn't mean anything like you just did now. *Ah.* But really, you're thinking something. You just hide what it is."

At age eleven, Lark had nailed the distinction between a lie of commission and one of omission, and also picked up on the opacities therapists offered instead of requiring of themselves the kind of self-revelation and disclosure they asked of clients.

Lark looked like she was waiting.

"Interesting," Arles said, then paused. "I just did it again. Right?"

Lark let out a long exhale and settled back against Arles, nestling in the crook of her arm. Arles sat stiffly; this was why she liked having a pair of couches. Sharing one with Lark had been a leap already, never mind . . . snuggling. Not even Dan would've chanced sitting this close.

After a moment, Lark said, "What were you thinking before? When you said *Ah*?"

Arles answered without taking time to shape her words. "The truth?"

"The truth."

"I was thinking that I'm scared to meet your parents. Find out who they are."

"Yeah," Lark said. "I'm scared of that too."

CHAPTER
THIRTY-FIVE

"Shep. Shep? Shep!"

The next morning, Lark stood at Arles's bedside, shaking her shoulder.

Arles awakened the way she'd been trained to do as Peter's stepdaughter. Instinctively tightening the covers around her, never demonstrably startling. Outwardly calm and deliberate, but internally roiling, just as she was now. Heart hammering in her chest, mouth pasty with fear. She felt Lark's rough handling all the way to her gut.

The sun sat comfortably in the sky; Arles hadn't slept this late in years. If ever.

"Shep!" It wasn't a demand; Lark also sounded frightened. "Are you okay?"

The child had been flung around this week with no grounding or place to catch her breath. She hadn't yet given voice to being chased at gunpoint, then turning a lethal weapon against her attacker. Arles knew what it took to wall off traumatic events until your mind resembled the rooms of a sealed mansion. She was doing the same thing with Peter's death right now herself. It didn't work forever, she wanted to tell Lark. But it would do for a while.

"Yes, sorry, I'm up." Gesturing for Lark to step to the side, Arles climbed out of bed, sliding her feet into a pair of flip-flops. Luckily, she always spent the night clothed, a lifelong habit. Her pajama shorts and T-shirt were appropriate garb. "Didn't realize I was that tired."

"I slept late too," Lark announced, hoisting herself onto Arles's high bed, then burrowing between the sheets. "But I came in to tell you my parents are here."

Arles swung around, alarmed anew. "They are? Already?"

Tim must've sprung into action fast, and Lark's parents too. Arles wondered if they had access to a jet instead of having to deal with the hassles of flying commercial. She would've thought such luxuries came only once you were stampede-on-a-street famous.

Lark pointed to the window. "They don't usually ride in the first one."

Arles looked out through the panes of glass, visoring her eyes to block the sun. A black SUV had nearly arrived at the throat of the driveway, with two more behind it, triplicate chunks of gleaming metal. Visible only by their roofs now, but minutes off at most.

They rounded a bend, three SUVs to disguise the one Kip Stratton rode in, as if he were the shell in a game of monte. It struck Arles as absurd, Kip putting on airs. He wasn't deterring an assassin. The vehicles continued their serpentine crawl, none of the drivers used to the terrain.

"The Guarder's driving one car, and my dad must be driving another since the Extricator—well, since he can't do it for them anymore," Lark went on. "I don't know who's in that last one. Maybe my mom found an Uber."

Not up here she didn't, Arles thought. Less of a gig economy in Wedeskyull.

"Well," she said, dry-mouthed again, "let's get ready and meet them downstairs."

Lark bounced off the bed and went to get dressed.

Lark's mother could be heard before she was seen.

An unpleasant voice, hoarse and raw, as if its possessor were suffering from a bad cold.

"This looks just like that set," the croaky voice said as the door of the middle SUV opened. Legs wrapped in artfully frayed jeans, feet clad in a pair of the most gorgeous shoes Arles had ever seen. Delicate webbing in a deep, rich navy, with slim heels the same color as the straps. The nails on the toes were polished a midnight blue to match. "Remember? When Kip had that bit part in *Great Expectations*."

Arles couldn't see the person the woman was addressing, presumably whoever sat behind the wheel. She felt mild affront at hearing her house compared to Miss Havisham's, although she supposed Lark's mother had a point. She wondered what the woman would think if she saw the attic in which her daughter had recently hidden.

She emerged from the car, and upon spying Arles, changed as if a wand had been waved. Her voice became instantly lush, a sound you'd be happy to listen to forever and do whatever it said.

"Hello there!" she called warmly. "Our savior!"

Arles snatched a quick peek behind her to see if Lark had come out onto the porch. She was hovering behind a panel of curtain inside the house, looking small and lost.

"Welcome," Arles said, turning to face front. "Lark's mother, right?"

"Janelle," she replied, as if the name had a little flourish.

She looked years younger than she must have been, more like Lark's sister than her mother. As she drew closer, however, Arles revised that impression. Janelle was in her early- to mid-thirties, just extremely well kept. Preened and polished to a gloss. But her hair, makeup, nails, and teeth were only a glaze. As the woman continued her approach, cautious steps across the gravel in her cobalt heels, it became possible to see her eyes.

They were empty. Like sinkholes, shiny and vacant. Janelle didn't look around for her child, and this didn't seem due to being distracted by her surroundings; her gaze appeared to take in none of the beauty.

Only when Arles forced a smile, staying in greeting mode, did Janelle's eyes offer anything back. They became mirrors, twin reflecting pools, and she smiled in return.

The engines of all three SUVs cut out at once, and quiet settled over the grounds. Then the rear door of the last vehicle opened, and Kip Stratton stepped out.

Unlike his wife, he exuded feeling and personality. Despite Arles not being familiar with his career—she thought she might've seen one of his earlier films, nothing recent—his presence made the world go a little swimmy. It was as if he weren't 100 percent human, some kind of being less misshapen and flawed than that. Still, although almost anyone would've called Kip devastatingly good-looking, the sight of him made Arles think of Dan with a fierce pang of longing.

Janelle stood looking down at a phone in a fun floral case. "How do you get on the Wi-Fi? And I'll need a place to plug in and charge," she said, her wide, blank-eyed stare suggesting a degree of alarm.

She still hadn't asked about her child.

"No Wi-Fi." Arles let out a little cough to soften the blow. "And we're in a cell vacuum here." She hadn't had satellite installed since moving to Fir Cove five months ago. This place had been both hell and harbor to her as a child, and predated the internet age down to its very soul. The idea of being able to go online, text someone or make a call, look up a fact or resource, seemed less an improvement, a modernization, than an abomination.

Janelle's features momentarily disrupted themselves before rearranging. "Are you for real right now? How has Lark been coping without being able to watch something?"

She sounded more concerned about Lark not getting her streaming fix than that the girl had sought out a stranger for help, then walked away from her parents without looking back.

Janelle began stabbing the screen of her phone as if kicking a faulty tire.

Kip approached his wife. He almost appeared to glide, as if the earth were moving smoothly beneath him, requiring little of his own effort. "Jane, I think Dr. Shepherd deserves our thanks, not a grilling about her tech. And don't we want to greet our daughter?"

Arles knew Lark was still hiding—the curtain ruffled in a breeze when Arles opened the front door—but neither Kip nor Janelle appeared to notice.

Arles had set out coffee along with a platter of Stephanie's scones, tempting the Californians with carbs. Janelle and Kip steered straight for the dining room without prompting or invitation. Janelle filled a cup with black liquid and gulped it down so fast, Arles wondered if the carafe had failed to keep its contents hot. But Kip blew on his own cup, alternating cooling puffs of air with bites of scone, which he crammed into his mouth.

"Hey, where's Lark?" he asked suddenly, perhaps rejuvenated by the caffeine.

"Asleep still?" said Janelle. "She probably never adjusted to not being on Pacific time."

Arles had seen the child sidle silently by. She wasn't sure if Janelle and Kip were woefully unobservant, or if Lark always lived like a ghost in their presence, hardly even there.

She pointed the couple to the parlor.

CHAPTER
THIRTY-SIX

The night before, Arles had arranged seats in a smaller version of the ring she typically used for FIT sessions, a branch of therapy where multiple families took part in treatment at once. Lark sat with her legs crisscrossed on a chair next to the one Arles usually chose. When Janelle entered the room, Lark slid down and stood in place like a small, obedient soldier.

Janelle met her there, placing one hand around each of Lark's upper arms and giving them a squeeze. It didn't look like a hug or a stroke—Janelle appeared to be taking the measure of her daughter's biceps. As she looked Lark up and down, Arles had the impression of a teacher sizing up her prize pupil versus a mother reuniting with her child. Janelle frowned, assessing.

"Your hair!" she exclaimed, then appeared to catch herself. "I'll braid it," she muttered.

Kip shifted Janelle aside to offer his daughter a less strange hello. He knelt to embrace Lark, although the nudge he'd given his wife bordered on aggressive.

"Larky," he murmured. "I've missed you."

Lark maintained the same robotic rigidity Arles had seen once before, in a much smaller room, with a pool of blood slowly spreading.

"Why don't we all take a seat?" Arles suggested, and everyone did.

"We owe you a debt of gratitude, Doctor," Kip said, turning in her direction.

Arles had the feeling that he would take control of this entire situation, maybe launch into a soliloquy, if she didn't guide things from the outset.

She shook her head. "Taking care of Lark has been my pleasure."

Lark fixed her gaze in Arles's direction, and Arles gave her a smile.

"But I am curious about one thing," she continued. "Well, a lot of things. But let me start by asking why you didn't call the police as soon as you couldn't find your daughter?"

Lark switched her gaze, watching her parents with interest.

Janelle and Kip traded glances.

"Because we were told not to!" Janelle cried, appearing to catch herself and modulating her voice. "Someone sent us a message. It said they would hurt Lark if we involved the police."

"I have a stalker," Kip added, as if stating that he had a dog, or a sweater. "The intel that's been gathered, IP address and such, put his location close to here, so we assumed he was the one who took Lark. And neither of us was willing to call the bluff of someone so unhinged."

It was a good story. But Kip Stratton was a good actor. A decent one, anyway.

"So, the men who came to my house," Arles said. "You sent them to find Lark as opposed to involving the police? Including the one who is now dead."

Peripherally, Arles saw Lark react, a minute tremble.

"Did we send them?" Janelle echoed.

She sounded genuinely perplexed. But her line of work made her an actor too.

"That's right," Arles said steadily. "They work for you, right?"

Janelle let out an ugly laugh, which she massaged into a throaty chuckle. "Does the home invader *you* allowed into the place where you were supposedly looking after my daughter—my poor, tough, brave daughter, who then had no choice but to *murder* someone—*work* for us?"

It was the first reference either of them had made to Lark's act.

"Yes," Arles said simply.

"Um, no, Dr. Shepherd," Janelle said with disgust. "Not that you seem to be any kind of real doctor. He does not."

I play one on TV, Arles had the impulse to say. Janelle's insult reminded her of Lark accusing Arles of not being a good therapist. The best defense was a good offense.

"Told you they were liars, Shep," Lark said. They were the first words she'd spoken.

"Larky," Kip said, no longer smooth. Awkward now, really. "What does it matter? He's gone. You can come back. Be with us again. At home."

Looking at her father, Lark's eyes welled. "You don't know what he does. What he did."

"Lark," said Janelle, a warning note, "your dad's got a ton on his plate right now."

She was silencing her daughter, and a flame licked at Arles, anger on Lark's behalf.

Lark twisted in her chair. "Give me your phone, Mom. I'll prove the Extricator works for you. He's in a million background shots."

"What the fuck is an Extricator?" demanded Janelle, back to raspy.

Lark fell abruptly silent, her hands trembling until she fisted them.

"That's what she calls Jason," Kip said softly. "Called him, that is. And Troy's the Guarder. I don't know why, but Larky likes him better."

Lark looked as if she were about to say something except that Kip spoke over her.

"We're made, Jane," he said like a character in a Mafia movie. "Be better to come clean." He cleared his throat, a low, pleasing rumble.

Arles half expected him to let out a series of nonsense syllables, or start exaggeratedly rolling some *r*'s, one of those voice exercises actors did to get ready.

"We didn't call the police, Dr. Shepherd," he said, planting her within his sights, "because we've kept Lark's identity a secret. For her sake. We didn't want her to have to live the life of a big star's offspring. And once she ran off, we knew Jason could handle things, take care of the matter. A lot better than that Andy Griffith sheriff you have out here."

Chief, Arles thought crossly. *Tim is the chief of police. And Wedeskyull isn't*—what was the name of the town in the show Kip was referencing? She would've googled it but for the lack of internet Janelle was probably still inwardly grumbling over. Then it came to her. *Mayberry.*

"Lark wasn't even supposed to be with us at that dog and pony show at the bookstore," Kip went on. "We never let her out in public for things like that—for anything, really. We'd given Jason the night off, and Lark was supposed to hang with him. But she snuck into our rental car."

Lark flinched, a visible jolt of her slight body, and Kip looked at her.

"You're breaking my heart, Larky. What did Jason do? I've kept you far away from everything all these years to make sure nothing like that ever happened to you. I know what this business is like. I've been teaching you about it since you could talk."

"It wasn't like that." Lark spoke so softly, she could hardly be heard. "That isn't what the Extricator used to do." Her words settled with a thunk, for once and for all into the past tense, the over.

"Well what then? Just tell us already!"

Lark crossed her arms over her chest—her vow-of-silence stance.

In his worry—or less charitably, frustration—Kip had spoken in a whine that Arles had a feeling fans wouldn't tolerate. She needed to guide this process, but there was nothing keeping the couple here with their child beyond an order from the police chief Kip had just scorned. No tactics Arles could employ, if it came to that, to ensure she got the time necessary to determine who these people were and why Lark had fled from them. Then she wondered whether the techniques she'd been taught to use as a therapist would engage them, same as any regular client, their wealth and status notwithstanding.

An open-ended question to start. "Kip, what did you mean about what the business is like?"

He focused his gaze on her, and dammit to hell, Arles felt a ripple. Kip's eyes were cerulean blue; they looked like chips of a rare jewel.

"They have guardians on set for two groups," he said. "Children and animals. Because both need protecting from the biz. It's brutal. I don't want Lark having anything to do with it until she's mature enough to cope."

"Who wants your stupid business?" Lark demanded.

Arles nodded her on. "Can you say more?"

Lark shrugged, two sharp points of her shoulders. "I don't want to be an actor or director or producer. And especially not an *influencer*." She said the last word as if it tasted bad, avoiding her mother's glare. "They're all monsters."

Janelle reddened with something that resembled shame, her face and neck aflame.

"That's what I've been saying," said Kip. "The industry is filled with assholes."

Lark aimed a look at him that he should've been able to interpret even without a script.

And you think you're any different?

"All right," Arles said neutrally. "Why don't we take a break? Lark can show you where she's been staying while I see to some food."

Arles decided to serve sandwiches; Lissa had taught her how to fix ones that actually tasted good, as opposed to the paste between planks Arles remembered from childhood lunch boxes. You had to include a crunchy element, chips or pretzels, which you placed against whatever condiment you were using. Bonus points for something fresh and green between the meat and cheese; Arles went outside and harvested some late-summer dandelion greens. She remembered to add a smear of jam to offset the bitterness.

Kip and Janelle took seats in the dining room, arraying their plates and glasses across a good share of the table—which was long enough for a banquet, let alone a meal for two—before launching into a heated conversation.

Arles gave them privacy, but not before getting the gist. Janelle demanded to know what they were going to do. Kip offered up some hotheaded reply, *I'll tell you what*, while not really saying anything at all. The two were helpless without the infrastructure they'd put in place to make their lives run, their extricators and their guarders. Maybe Arles didn't have to worry about them picking up and leaving with Lark. They didn't seem as if they would know how.

Lark had wandered outside without any food, so Arles filled a plate and joined her.

"Oh. Thanks," Lark said, looking up at Arles from a porch swing. She took a big bite of sandwich. "Yum. It has potato chips."

"Would I serve anything less to the junk-food queen?"

Lark smiled around her mouthful.

Arles settled into a rocking chair. The two of them moved gently back and forth on their respective seats for a while. Then Arles said, "What you said in the parlor before. That's yours, you know. You don't have to share it with anyone till you want to. And you may never want to."

Arles had revealed her own abuse history just once as a child, to her then–best friend. When that hadn't gone so well—understatement— she kept the truth to herself for decades. Now only Dan had heard the truth by Arles's own telling. Unexpectedly, in that moment, she realized something. Psychologist, heal thyself. Peter had made Arles a collaborator in his secrets all the way until the bitter end. His death would be the last secret Arles kept—but it was for her sake this time. Not his.

Lark wiped her mouth with the back of her hand. Arles had forgotten napkins.

"You think the same thing they do," Lark said, jerking her thumb sharply toward the inside of the house. "That it was stranger danger, except not from a stranger. That the Extricator touched me in a bad place."

"A private place," Arles amended.

"Okay, that," Lark said, accepting the correction. "But nothing like that ever happened."

Relief flooded Arles, though she didn't display it, in case whatever *had* happened turned out to be its own breed of bad. Which it'd have to be, wouldn't it? To justify the axe?

"Why'd you think so, anyway?" Lark asked, picking up the other half of her sandwich.

"The truth?" In one short night, it had become a code between them.

"Yup," Lark said, chewing.

"Well, it happened to me when I was a child. So now I'm always scared it's happening to somebody else. We psychologists call that *projection*. I try to guard against doing it, but . . ." She gave a Humans-are-flawed-especially-me kind of hand wave.

Lark was gazing at her. "Harry?" she guessed.

Arles stared off into the distance. "No. Not Harry."

"I'm sorry. Because that's . . . yours. Right? I won't try to figure it out."

"It's okay," Arles said softly. "He's gone now."

She and Lark had that in common.

"I guess I could tell," Lark said, tilting her plate for the final shard of chip. "I guess now is the right time."

"Is it?" Arles asked her. "Are you sure?"

Lark appeared to consider, then nodded once, decidedly.

"All right," Arles said. "Okay."

They both got up in unison and went back inside.

CHAPTER THIRTY-SEVEN

But back in the parlor, before Lark could get a word out, Janelle spoke up. It was the gleaming version of her voice; even Arles—knowing what Lark had worked up the courage to do—grew momentarily diverted, finding it difficult to resist the woman's unique tonal delivery.

"Kip wants me to tell you something, Dr. Shepherd," she said. "He's worried you might think we're bad parents or something."

Why on earth would I think that? Arles thought. But she bit back the rejoinder.

"First, I want to apologize for complaining about the Wi-Fi. Or lack of it." Janelle held up her phone in its flowery case, the screen as dark as lead. "I'm kinda finding it nice to be offline. I feel free," she concluded, and the claim sounded truthful.

"It takes some getting used to," Arles replied with more generosity than she felt.

"I have a confession to make," Kip put in smoothly. "Since you know that we have—ah, *had* two men in our employ. Buddies of mine. Old friends from back in the day."

One of whom your daughter killed, Arles thought. But she gestured Kip on.

"Jason was able to get information out of some of the locals. Your name and address, the connection the author at my event had to you. I realize that was a violation, and I apologize."

It was the first utterance Kip didn't deliver well. He very palpably was not sorry.

Still, the couple was clearly in placating mode, and Arles intended to make use of it.

"How did Jason do it? The people who live here aren't inclined to open up to strangers." She wondered which of the people she orbited around and who orbited around her, in the way of small towns, would've sold her out.

Kip looked as if he couldn't comprehend such ignorance. "All Jason had to do was offer some merch," he said. "At most, a quick FaceTime. I smile at them. Say hello to their kid."

"People will do anything to get close to us," Janelle added.

Unlike Kip, regarding his invasion of Arles's privacy, she at least sounded apologetic.

Arles both should've anticipated the answer and also couldn't wrap her head around it. Such flagrant infatuation with fame. A desperate desire to stand even just at its periphery, be the tiniest bit a part of what it was. People were obsessed not just with the famous person but with the notion of fame itself.

"There's one other thing you should know," Janelle said. "Which is that neither of us has ever exploited Lark. As you've heard, we don't let her near either of our careers. If anything, that might be our biggest flaw as parents. We protect her *too* much."

"So, Lark left home because she felt controlled," Arles said. "That's your conclusion."

"Exactly," Janelle said, settling back in her seat.

Kip offered a nod with grandeur to it; Arles was reminded of queenly Lark. At the same time, Arles sensed what the concession was costing him to deliver, and that he didn't really mean it. Over lunch, he and Janelle had obviously come up with a script. Now Kip was acting his role.

But there was a part that gave the lie to this story, blew the whole thing up. Arles wished they could just leave it at a tween chafing at parental overreach and restraint. Nope, nothing wrong here. But Lark had become more than a client. And understanding what had really made her approach Kara that day was essential.

Janelle seemed to intuit a threat. She stood up, coiling her prettified hands into fists before relaxing them. "Do you have any idea how much money I could've earned if I'd made Lark part of my brand? BodySculpt alone would've covered the down payment on a second home like everybody else has! It's the only method approved by the FDA for children. Lark could've sculpted before she's even started on her cycle. Not an ounce of cellulite on her."

"Mom!" howled Lark.

Arles experienced a heated flush on the girl's behalf. She was all for period positivity, but Janelle wasn't being open and communicative; she was shaming. The woman was a psychopath, in layperson terms at least. If she didn't meet the clinical criteria for the diagnosis, she definitely fit the diluted way in which the word had come to be flung around today. The streaks of antisocial behavior Arles had observed in Lark had been arrived at honestly.

Kip opened his mouth, and Arles looked at him.

"Don't worry, Larky. I wouldn't have let Mom do that to you. If I'd decided to reveal who you were, we would've faked the Before and After." He gave an easy-peasy snap of his fingers.

Arles shifted to try and help Lark process her parents' contributions.

The girl sat with tears rolling down her cheeks like clear glass beads.

"Larky?" Kip said.

Janelle heaved a sigh. "What the hell is wrong with her now?"

It was hard to get either older Stratton to interrupt themselves once they got going, but Arles finally succeeded, holding up a palm, half rising out of her seat.

A silence fell, suffocating, stifling everyone in the room.

Then Lark smashed it.

"The Extricator was going to marry me," she said. "He talked about it all the time. He said he wasn't one of those sickos—he knew we had to wait. But I was getting closer every year. Every month." Her voice machinelike. Monotone. The verbal equivalent of how she sometimes held her body. "He said that we were meant to be together, told me all about what it was going to be like. How we'd never have to say goodbye anymore when he got sent out to do something. I would come with him. He complained how now he had to settle for looking at me or talking to me, but soon I'd be his for everything. He'd have a real-life movie star's daughter for a wife."

She seemed to be winding down, her words ending in a trickle. But then she swung around to face her parents, and there was finally some life to her tone, a vein of venom. "It was all he ever talked about. Right in front of you sometimes. He said you'd have no choice but to give me to him because of everything he'd done for you. Or else he'd tell. Get you canceled."

Both parents looked queasy, though it was hard to be sure whether that was due to their daughter's disclosure or the prospect of getting canceled.

"But we tried to protect you, Lark," Janelle responded hollowly, her own version of the robot voice. "I lost BodySculpt because they wanted a kid to trial it, and they knew I didn't have one." A pause. "I mean, they thought I didn't have one."

"The snake was already inside our house," Kip said, the line so perfect, it sounded scripted. His eyes filled, and the tears shimmered just shy of falling. "He stayed with us all the time. The guest room was basically his."

Well, Arles thought numbly, *this explains the axe.*

Kip wasn't done. "If Lark hadn't killed him already, I would've beaten Jason to death myself."

Lark turned to him, her own eyes brimming. "No, you wouldn't've. You've never even been in a real fight." She shoved a fist against her nose, sniffing in raggedly. "I already said. The Extricator used to do his thing when you were right there."

Kip didn't miss a beat. "Then I would've hired someone to take care of it."

"Yeah," Lark said bitterly, her eyes still refusing to overflow. "Like, maybe a stunt double?" She gathered in a breath. "You know what, Dad? I did it myself."

Arles allowed a pause, for the room to breathe along with everyone in it. Then she said, "I think we all deserve a rest. Kip and Janelle, let me point you to your room. Lark—"

"I'm going outside," the girl said, and got up from her chair.

No one tried to stop her.

———

The mental anguish and torture Lark must have lived with every day.

It was impossible to comprehend, except perhaps for someone like Arles.

And although Lark had proved herself an adept weaver of tales—and had good reason to come up with one now, given her murderous act—her disclosure had a factuality to it, a weight like a stone sinking to the bottom of a lake. People basically didn't make up this crap. The only lie was that they did. Because the accusations were almost always, tragically true.

Arles went upstairs to check on Kip and Janelle—who sounded like they were slumbering behind their closed door; Arles heard a few ruffly snores and no murmurs—then left the house to find Lark.

The child was stacking logs in the woodshed, bending over to heave splits into the sling of her arms before assembling them in intricate formation.

"Thanks," Arles called, giving notice as to her approach. "Hadn't gotten to those yet."

Lark turned around. "You'll have more for winter now."

Her voice so sad, it caused an ache.

Chopping wood was one of the seasonal tasks Arles had been putting off—laying in a cord could test a ravaged gut region—but the prospect no longer felt daunting. She proposed an activity that she hoped might proffer Lark a little healing of her own.

"Want to go on a hike?" she suggested. "While your parents settle in?"

Lark brightened instantly. "We haven't been in the woods in forever!"

It'd been less than a full day, but Arles felt the same. "There's a great climb out to a ledge." Arles pointed to a mountain, sloth-shaped and full-bellied until its bald peak. "With a wicked scramble at the end."

"An evil scramble," Lark translated, squinting up at the sky.

"I thought kids your age would say a scramble that *slays*."

Lark grinned. "Yesterday, Grandma."

Arles handed Lark the daypack she'd brought, then donned a second one herself.

But just as they were ready to go, Janelle shouted both their names.

"Thought you two might be doing something rustic!" she said, drawing near.

She had changed into sneakers that didn't look any less pricey than the heels, and had put on a hoodie. She carried a branded water bottle—Arles had never heard of the product it was shilling—that would be impossible to hold on to during a hike that required both hands at points.

"Mind if I join?" Janelle asked. "Dad is staying back in our room—"

There was a vague presumption of ownership in her tone.

"To rest before the spate of interviews he has coming up. But I'm ready for an excursion." She mock-boxed the air, bouncing from foot to foot as if to demonstrate her fitness.

"Can I wear your hoodie, Mom?" Lark said with a whine. "I'm cold."

Arles had never heard that particular tone from her before, a childlike griping.

"Lark Angel Stratton, I'm not going anywhere with you unless you start talking like a—" Abruptly, Janelle cut herself off, regarding Arles with wariness, the way she might've examined a beast behind bars. "Of course you can, honey. Here you go." And she stripped off her hoodie.

Lark looked ready to drop the unneeded garment on the ground—she was flushed pink, her face still beaded with sweat from log stacking—but tied it around her waist instead.

She sent Arles a *Well, I tried* look.

Arles considered the methods Lark must've perfected to get space from her mother—misbehaving in ways she knew Janelle wouldn't stand for, evasion, and finally, escape. But this time at least, Janelle did not seem about to be deterred.

"Don't worry," Lark whispered once she and Arles had gotten a little way ahead. "My mom thinks nature is a park bench. She'll turn back as soon as she has to step over the first rock on the ground."

Arles paused to let Janelle catch up, watching as the woman ducked between trees as if their branches were knife blades. She understood why Lark had been so eager to learn survival skills; her mother would be as useless as a dusting of sugar out here. Also, Lark had had her efficacy robbed—by Jason, by her parents—in enough ways that the wilderness was one venue she could truly make her own.

Lark grabbed Arles by the hand and pulled her ahead.

"I'm getting the feeling you have something you want to talk about?" Arles asked, making sure to keep Janelle in earshot, which wasn't hard, given the woman's frequent verbal expulsions.

"Jesus! Fuck!"

"Now who's whining?" muttered Lark.

With every step Janelle took, she set off a cacophony of cracked sticks, skittering rocks and raining soil. Arles and Lark reached the ledge and kneed their way out, then sat with their legs dangling as they watched Janelle struggle below. She was more dogged than her daughter had given her credit for.

Arles shrugged out of her pack just as Lark slid free from the straps of hers. They unclasped the outer bands in unison, then drank from their water bottles, draining the liquid to the halfway squiggle before leaving the remainder for the trip back down. Arles had stowed a sack of M&M's nut mix in Lark's pack, a protein bar in her own, and they opened their snacks at the same time, while Arles tried to figure out how to formulate her next question.

There was a piece here that went beyond Jason's mental torment and psychological warfare. A *missing* piece, to use the word Lark had. During the session after lunch in the parlor, Janelle had taken the stage before Arles could ease into this topic, but she knew she shouldn't delay any longer. Not if she wanted to fulfill the duty with which Tim had tasked her.

"Look," Arles said around a bite. Food always tasted odd in her mouth, as if it were some substance she didn't habitually consume. Her mother had weaponized cooking when Arles was a child, and Arles wasn't sure if she'd ever experience eating as anything less than noxious. "I get that Hollywood might not be the glam life so few of us know but we all think we would love."

Lark cracked a smile, disrupting the chocolate ring around her mouth.

"But that isn't the reason you walked away from being royalty. You left to get away from the Extricator. And also"—Arles mustered a breath—"for some other reason."

Lark swung so abruptly in her direction that she pitched forward on the ledge, and Arles shot out one arm to clutch the back of her shirt.

"How do you know there's anything else?" the girl asked.

Arles was breathing hard. "Move back a little, okay?"

Lark did, Arles maintaining a grip on her as she scooted.

They both studied the drop while observing Janelle's progress. Where her daughter had bounded over the scramble like a mountain goat, Janelle crawled from rock to rock, casting her gaze upward and wiping sweat off her brow. Arles took her eyes off the rim of rock.

"You told Kara you were missing," she reminded Lark, then watched her, waiting.

"Oh, right. Well, mostly I left because I found out my mother is planning to kill me."

CHAPTER
THIRTY-EIGHT

Arles had heard plenty of shocking revelations in her time as a therapist, but the way Lark shared this one caused Arles to shrink back, although not until ensuring that the two of them were situated squarely on the ledge. There had been no exaggerated quality to the statement. And Arles was relatively certain that this time, the child wasn't acting. She had sounded matter-of-fact, her voice stripped bare. A flat accounting of some future, unspeakable act.

How future? What act?

Arles couldn't find out.

Janelle was nearly there.

Waterless—she must've forsaken her bottle at some point, choosing between hydration and a plunge off rocks—and dripping with perspiration. Arles thought she looked better, more real and robust than she had upon first stepping out of the air-conditioned cool of her shiny SUV. But she had a feeling Janelle would've been horrified had she looked in a mirror.

"Oof," she said, plunking herself down beside them. "I was worried about Lark being given therapy, but it seems you and I are more like-minded than I'd thought, Dr. Shepherd. You have done some serious coaching with my daughter."

Wordlessly, Arles handed over her water bottle. Why would Janelle be worried about something as benign as therapy? Because she had a secret she needed kept, sinister and dreaded. That would explain the leeriness with which she'd been treating Arles all day.

The woman gulped down the remainder of the water with a grimace. "You don't realize how gross water is till you've gotten used to Vita brand. They add this juicy taste—and all these electrolytes—but zero calories. It's amazing."

"Look around, Mom," Lark said, gesturing out at the lace filigree of treetops. "There're no cameras here. No audio."

"I wasn't doing a sponsorship!" Janelle said, outraged.

"Yes, you were," Lark replied blandly. "You always are."

Did Janelle's internet persona, her *Always be selling*—such a farce that it was a caricature of itself—have to do with what Lark had just revealed? Arles had noted plenty of faults in Janelle; she was vapid, self-focused, unseeing of her daughter. But was she capable of infanticide? What would be her motivation? The accusation seemed baseless.

But although Lark could lie with agility, Arles was on the lookout for such behavior now, and Lark hadn't seemed like she was being duplicitous.

Arles intended to probe further on the way down, but after supervising Janelle's retreat from the ledge, offering a hand before ultimately having to place her arms around the woman's waist and lower her back to the trail, Janelle seemed disinclined to give Arles and Lark any time alone. It was as if she knew peril was at hand. She aimed a laser beam of chatter at Arles.

"Well, you're totally gorgeous, obviously. Stunning, really. Amazing things could happen for you if you came on my channel. Maybe a tie-in about mindfulness?"

"Don't let her do it, Shep," Lark murmured.

If Janelle heard her daughter, she didn't react. "It'd be amazing! You'd get referrals from all over the country! How do you conduct video sessions without internet? Do you have an office in that, um, town? The one with the freaky name?"

It was all a diversion, Arles realized, Janelle trying to snake-charm her, mesmerize her into turning her attention away from Lark. Janelle was plainly incapable of grasping the idea that what she had on offer might hold no allure.

When Arles finally made her disinterest clear, Janelle switched tactics, acting helpless and dependent as they made their way down. She walked in mincing steps behind Lark, holding on to her daughter's shoulder until Lark shucked her off.

Arles picked up a fallen branch, stripping it of twigs to create a makeshift hiking pole, and handed it over. But when they came to a tricky juncture with a sheer overhang, Janelle lost her grip on the branch, which plummeted with an unending clatter. Arles could've sworn she'd seen the woman open her hand as she held the branch out over open space.

She looked at Arles with a pout of regret.

They went on in a tight chain of three, Janelle taking staggering steps to bring up the rear while complaining vociferously—*Are we there yet?*—as if the tilt of the terrain didn't give a pretty clear indication as to how close they were to its base. Perhaps to distract herself from the misery of their descent, Janelle began offering Arles tips on maintaining her hair color once the natural tint started to go. "Those auburns and reds don't stick around forever, you know."

"Shep?" Lark said, louder than she normally spoke.

"Oh, thank God," Janelle said with a heaved breath.

The slope was evening out, although having reached level ground didn't encourage Janelle to go on ahead. She clung close, matching her pace to theirs.

"Yes, Lark?" Arles said, modeling responsiveness for Janelle.

"Did you really mean that about a girl's mom being the most important person in their life?"

The taken-off-guard exercise. Only this time, Arles was a little less so.

"Now, that isn't quite what I said, Lark," she replied.

Lark's face fell. She clearly thought Arles wasn't keeping up, hadn't gotten it.

But for the first time during the whole wretched descent, Janelle ceased her litany of complaints, interrupted her patter. She went quiet, listening while trying to hide her interest. She studied each tree as they passed, running her hand over its bark.

"I said it *can* be, depending on the mother. Mine, for example, was not someone you'd want to connect with." The best lies contained a strain of truth. "But having met yours—" Arles pretended to have lost track of Janelle, then catch sight of her again, making deliberate eye contact. Psychologists had to be actors too. "I'd say you fall into that lucky camp. Of potentially deep connection with your mom." What Arles said next would contain no deceit. It was entirely true. "But being a kid can be hard, and you have issues you need to work through to build those kinds of healthy relationships. Things best expressed in therapy."

"Yeah," Lark said with a flawlessly delivered sigh. "I guess so."

"Well!" Janelle said.

The house had come into view.

"We're home!"

Laying claim to the place again as if it were hers.

"You've definitely put me through my paces, you two. I don't even need to ask if you have a home gym. Got all my steps in. Now, Lark, you and Dr. Shepherd keep up the good work while I go shower before dinner, okay?"

Arles had distanced any sense of threat and aimed the responsibility for change in Lark's direction. Fear assuaged and ego suitably stroked, Janelle pranced off, having made what seemed a full recovery from her exertions. She offered a jaunty, pleased little wave over her shoulder.

And Arles and Lark were on their own.

Arles had given no thought to dinner. She'd never fed this many people for so long. Having a child in your care made a difference. Left to her own devices, Arles would've survived on bleaker rations.

She decided to build a fire in the pit. They could roast hot dogs on sticks, follow them up with s'mores. And she and the girl could talk while gathering kindling and arraying logs.

Words pent up inside Lark exploded out. "Have you ever heard of Munchausen's by proxy disease, Shep?"

"Yes," Arles said tentatively. "I've heard of Munchausen's syndrome." She gave the name its German inflection. "And Munchausen's by proxy. Also known as factitious disorder imposed on another. If you want to be fancy."

"'Course you have. You're a therapist."

"It's rare. I've never treated a case." Arles paused. "Are you saying your mother has MBP?" She was stumped. Aside from engaging in some food deprivation—and even that seemed to apply mainly to unhealthy kinds, just as well skipped—Arles couldn't identify any symptoms of the disorder in Janelle. Lark seemed very healthy physically. "Which is another thing to call it."

"I know that, and I also know it's rare," Lark said. "I watched two movies about it. This girl—oh my God, it was so sad."

Arles was pretty sure she knew the case Lark meant. It bore no resemblance to what she'd seen of Lark or Janelle, as far as she could tell.

"Are there different kinds?" Lark asked.

Arles brushed wood dust off her hands, examining their work. The sun was going down, lending an orange hue, a red stain, to the sky. It would soon be accompanied by an invading army of insects, but the fire should help dispel them.

Arles went for the stash of matches she kept in a waterproof box in the crook of a tree.

"Different kinds?" she said, returning. "What do you mean?"

Lark sat down on one of the stumps encircling the pit. "Like, most people with it, they want attention from doctors and nurses and people who work in medicine. But my mom wants attention from people who follow her online. Oh my God, there isn't anything she wants more. And she's planning something big for when my dad decides it's okay for them to admit they have me, which is in two years when I'm a teenager." Lark took a breath. "He thinks he's gonna come off a real hero, going this far to keep his daughter from growing up in the shadow of the biz or entering it as a child. You know, like Miley Cyrus or Demi Lovato. Meltdowns and addiction and rehab and bankruptcy or whatever."

Arles didn't actually know, got only the most vaporous sense of Lark's references, but they weren't the crucial part right now. "You were talking about your mother," she said gently.

"Oh, right," Lark said. "My mom has her own version of why they had to hide me. Conceal my identity. Her post is all scripted. She's going to say the reason is because I'm sick, and it was, like, too sad for her to talk about. I forget the name of the disease I have, but sometimes you die from it. And that's what's going to happen if her audience doesn't like that my mom didn't share me just because I was sick. Nothing gets more sympathy than a dead kid. Even I know that. Imagine all the weepy faces and prayer hands! Her followers will forgive her for keeping me a secret, and then she'll get even *more* followers after I die."

Arles felt air leave not only her lungs, but her whole body, oxygen gone from every cell. She dropped down as Lark had, except less gracefully, nearly missing the stump, and hitting the wooden surface hard enough to hurt her spine.

MBP for the internet age. Attention showered on the parental caregiver in the form of comments and emojis and purchases instead of office visits and scrips and consults. Lark was a native diagnostician; she'd identified a new subcategory for the next DSM.

And Janelle presented a whole new variety of evil. An online variety.

Had she *told* her daughter this plan?

Lark appeared to be tracking Arles's thoughts.

"I wasn't supposed to go near her studio that day, but I was getting away from Jason. He won't be around my mom when she's filming because he doesn't like all the makeup she puts on and everything she does to her hair, so that part of the house is the best place to hide." Lark's face crumpled. "Except I heard her rehearsing. Two different ways. One where I stay sick, and she comes up with a bajillion posts about my illness and everything that's needed to treat it and help me live with it and try and make me better. Wellness stuff. And the other where I die."

Although Arles used silence judiciously when called for, she'd never been at a loss for words before. Her superpower was coming up with not just any words but the right ones. Utterances to apply a balm, coax a person to open up, talk them out of a threat or down from some ledge, literal or figurative. But as Lark ended her relaying, Arles had nothing to say. Her jaw was locked; she couldn't unhinge her mouth. Nor could she rise from the stump, go offer comfort in one form or another. None of her bodily mechanisms seemed to be working.

But as horrifying as Lark's story was, it didn't explain why she'd told Kara she was missing. Had she meant it more symbolically? Her mother was going to make her disappear?

"Ahoy, the lawn!" Kip called in his deep, rich voice. "Dinner ready yet? I could eat one of the bears I hear live in these parts. And what else do you have here? Mountain lions? Wolves?"

Janelle let out an unappealing *eek* at the mention.

"It's so dark out," she complained.

One of the projects Arles had been meaning to get to was having exterior lighting installed. Fir Cove had always rested like a great, slumbering beast in late nineteenth-century dimness. Part of Arles liked being acclimated to the shadows, able to walk and move about without benefit of sight except for that bequeathed by the moon or the stars.

Lark dashed forward, snatching the matches out of Arles's flexed, unfeeling hand.

The girl struck a blooming bundle of sulfur-tipped sticks and hurled them into the pit so that the coarse nest of tinder erupted in flames.

CHAPTER
THIRTY-NINE

Confronting Janelle was unlikely to work; Arles needed to keep in mind that the woman was an actor herself of sorts. Was she a physical danger to Lark? Did she intend to really make her daughter sick, or would it all be fakery, just for show? The latter would cause enough emotional damage to have Lark removed from her mother's care. If Kip had no role in the sham, and was willing to separate from his wife while she received treatment, then he might be allowed to maintain custody. But failure to meet those criteria would mandate seeking out another relative, assuming one existed. And if one didn't, then Lark would become a so-called ward of the state. It was an unlovely maze with few good outlets.

Despite the warm cloak of evening, Arles shivered, imagining Lark caught within the grip of that system. She did a bit of acting herself, painting on a sheen of jollity as she prepared the fixings for a fireside meal. She pointed to a cooler of soft drinks and wine, handed out paper plates. As if she were throwing a summer grill session instead of gathering adversaries together in an attempt to arrive at the best interests of a child.

The nighttime temperature stayed balmy, the air as soft as a blanket. Fir Cove put on its own sort of show for its guests. Lark ate heartily at a ratio of three s'mores to each hot dog. Her mother winced with every graham cracker tower Lark constructed, refusing any hot dogs herself and nibbling a single square of chocolate instead. The woman seemed to subsist on air. If you cut her open, she'd be empty. No organs, blood, or bones.

Kip polished off four hot dogs, yanking each one out of the flames before it'd even started to char, was hardly heated through, until Janelle finally called a ceasefire.

"Range will put you on a cucumber cleanse," she said.

"My trainer," Kip told Arles.

"I watch him with my dad sometimes," Lark added. "They don't even know I'm there." She mock-curled a weight, letting out an exaggerated macho grunt.

Neither of her parents appeared to hear her, leaning forward to get closer to the fire with their arms extended, burnishing their hands in the heat.

"It's lovely here," Janelle said after a silence had fallen. "I can see why you like it, Lark."

Arles wouldn't have expected the woman to have picked up on that.

Lark looked a bit surprised herself.

Could a happy ending still be had? How could a psychological malady that didn't even have an official name be addressed? Plus, there was Jason, admittedly dead but to whom Kip and Janelle had given free access to their daughter. What ensured that the other one—the Guarder, or what was his real name? Troy?—didn't present a risk as well?

Kip moved away from the flames, his face red and heated.

Somehow he managed to make being a few shades away from burned to a crisp look good.

"So, what's supposed to happen next, Doctor? The police chief wasn't real specific. And while I agree with my wife that you have a helluva location here, could definitely make bank if you rented it out to studios, this mini retreat isn't well timed. I have a film about to be released."

Arles couldn't defer any longer. Based on what she'd already learned from Lark, she knew the Strattons weren't going to be allowed to simply drive away with their daughter.

"When Lark left during your event at the bookstore, she told Kara something," Arles said, forming words into a strand. Or a noose. "Wrote it in a copy of Kara's new book."

"And what was that?" Kip asked casually, propping his feet up close to the flames.

But Janelle looked the opposite of casual. Wary. On edge.

Of course, she had reason to, if she suspected that Lark might've overheard her rehearsing her vile conceit. But the Munchausen's script wasn't what Arles was getting at.

"She told Kara she was missing. A missing child."

Kip shook his head. "That doesn't make any sense. Missing from who?"

"Whom," Lark said perkily. "Right, Shep?"

Arles sent her a brief smile. "I don't know. Does anyone?"

She looked around the ring of faces, illuminated by orange and gold.

"Not a clue," Kip said easily.

After a moment, Janelle shook her head.

Lark's quip had clearly just been an act. Her lower lip was vibrating like a jackhammer, tears wobbling on her eyes, their shine detectible in the firelight.

"I heard you guys," she said.

Something else? Arles thought. Different from her mother's MBP plan? How many blocks had been stacked to enable Kip and Janelle's teetering life to reach nearly to the stars? And how many more would they accumulate to ensure they made it the rest of the way?

Janelle flapped a graceful hand. "What's that expression? Water under the bridge." She looked brightly in Arles's direction. "They used that slogan when I endorsed Mountain Valley Spring Water. There was the sweetest little bridge over the spring."

"I thought that bridge got blown up, Mom," Lark said.

Janelle's face looked flushed in the firelight. "Well, yeah, the first one." She glanced at Arles. "It had to go when the company began bottling. But they built another for my shoot. You couldn't walk on it, though; it wasn't structurally sound. We just shot reel. If you'd stepped onto it, the whole thing would've collapsed."

Now there's a metaphor, Arles thought.

"That's great," Lark muttered. "A fake bridge because they destroyed the real one."

"Ugh, reality. So glad we got rid of that, right?" said Janelle. "It was never any good. Lumpy and bumpy. Messy and ugly." She extended her legs as if to admire them, scrunched her hair with her fingers, plumped her lips in a series of gentle bites. "The packaged version is a lot easier to create." She leaned forward, taking her daughter's hands in her own, and although Lark struggled, Janelle didn't let go. "Why would anyone choose the old way?"

"Because it's messy," Arles murmured, as much to herself as to them. "And sometimes ugly."

Lark wrenched her hands free.

Janelle pulled a sad face. "Come on, Lark, you know how well an adoption story plays these days. And yours is kind of cool, unusual, at least the way we'll make it sound. We'll hire a screenwriter."

Lark stared at the fire until her eyes began to water. "Actually, Mom, the way you did it doesn't play well at all. Your followers are gonna hate you."

Janelle reared back. "What? They would never! What're you talking about?"

"You're not supposed to hide the truth about who gave birth to me, Mom. I was supposed to know that before I was even old enough to understand everything you said. Full disclosure. Transparency. Not letting me learn it wasn't you because, I don't know, some bill was late?"

Arles was trying to keep up. "You adopted Lark?"

Janelle leaned back on her block of wood, defying gravity by engaging her core, and lifted her tank top to display a taut stomach, belly button pierced by a hair-thin hoop. "Not even a scheduled C-section and a tuck the same day could preserve this."

"Lark's mine," Kip said, as if describing a possession of middling but not surpassing value. "But my wife didn't want to lose her body." This time, he did sound apologetic.

"Families get created in all sorts of ways," Janelle added, straightening back up.

It was the first thing the woman had said that Arles wholeheartedly agreed with. But Janelle would've been in her mid-twenties or so at the time. Not an age you would necessarily think she'd decide to adopt a child and start her family. And if she did choose to become a young mom, then why go to such lengths to keep Lark's existence a secret?

Lark turned to Arles. "They've been paying for me for years—"

"That little bitch said she'd report Lark stolen from her if we didn't keep the money coming—" Janelle started to explain.

"We haven't been *paying* for you, Larky." Kip spoke over both his wife and his daughter. "And watch the swearing, Jane. What we did is make an arrangement—"

"Please let Lark finish," Arles ordered.

"Except they skipped a payment accidentally," Lark said, flashing her father an *I was right* look. "And then my mom reminded my dad I could be reported missing anytime if they didn't stick to the schedule. Something like that. Which would be terrible PR, especially with my dad's release date coming up." Her face wilted, and her small shoulders sloped. "It's like they pretended to the world I didn't exist for so long that they forgot I did."

"We'd never forget that," Kip told her. "Everything we've done, it's been for you."

Well, Arles thought, *not* everything.

It had gotten late, the nighttime temperature finally beginning to plunge.

She rose from her stump of wood. "Lark? Would you like to extinguish the flames?"

Lark got up and went for the bucket of sand at the rear of the pit. "Step back," she said to her parents. "This throws up a lot of dust."

Both did. They watched their daughter put out the fire in a swift succession of moves.

"Good job, Larky," said Kip.

"You've lost weight," Janelle added. "I saw it when you raised your arms."

Ash from the cinders and dying flames brought forth a new variety of darkness, life after a nuclear fallout. Everyone turned to start making their way to the house.

Arles spotted the intruder first; her vision was attuned to picking out disruptions in the shadows. This wasn't an animal such as Kip had referenced, not even one of the large ones, meaty and muscled. The outline in the trees assumed the unmistakable upright shape of a man.

CHAPTER FORTY

The Guarder, was Arles's first thought. *Troy.*

The man stood so motionlessly in the border of woods, he appeared deserving of the moniker Lark had bestowed. As if he were watching over them. Kip had said that Troy—along with the late Jason—were buddies of his in addition to employees. Would he just station one of them on private property without even mentioning his presence to Arles?

She was responsible for Lark in addition to the girl's parents. Getting everyone sequestered had to be top priority. She spoke in a low tone. "You three go up to the house, okay? Use this flashlight." She handed one over. "I'll just see to the last of our campfire."

"I put it out, Shep," Lark said, no reason for her not to speak loudly. "See?"

But Arles was too focused on the gap in the woods to examine Lark's job well done.

The figure hadn't moved an inch. One arm was crooked at a sharp angle, fingers spread against a tree trunk as if webbed, the skinny digits of an amphibian. The hand attached to them extended as far as a high notch between branches. This person was tall.

Lark was tracking Arles's gaze.

"Someone's out there," the girl said, dropping her tone.

"What?" Kip yelped. "Where?" He craned to look in the wrong direction. "Who?"

"There!" Janelle thrust out a hand to reorient him. "I told you it was creepy as fuck here!"

"Is it your employee?" Arles asked them low, with a thrum of urgency in her voice. "Troy?"

Kip's head wagged wildly. "I sent the other drivers away."

Both he and Janelle began backing toward the house, keeping their gazes plastered to the woods. Janelle stumbled, a clump of earth catching her foot, and flung one arm out to stabilize herself against Kip. He shunted her away, turning around so as to walk a straighter path himself.

At the last second, he called out in a high squeal, "Come on, Larky!"

"Who is it, Shep?" Lark asked.

"I don't know," Arles said, though by now she had an idea. She reached for Kip, snatching at his shirt to keep him from leaving. The sculpted borders of muscles shifted, rearranging themselves beneath the fabric as he moved. "That stalker you mentioned. What do you know about him?"

Kip barely slowed down. "Oh, shit. That's who you think this is? Call the police!"

"We literally can't," Janelle told him, hurrying to catch up.

"Fuck, that's right," Kip said. "I better get out of here."

And he ran for the house with his wife at his heels.

"Lark," Arles said, "please go with your parents."

"But I want to be here if you need help!"

Arles had just placed her hand on the bulb of Lark's shoulder to nudge her in the right direction when her gaze was arrested by motion behind the girl. The figure had come striding out from the woods, his long legs covering ground unspeakably fast. Too late to send Lark across the expanse of lawn on her own; both her parents were gone, concealed within the confines of the house. Arles shifted Lark, blocking the child with her body.

Illuminated by moonlight, the man was visible now—definitely the one Arles had seen around town who'd grabbed her at the bookstore. Then from behind him emerged someone else.

A young girl.

Despite the undeniable creep factor of the situation, Lark instantly blossomed. Her mouth formed a smile, and she waved a hand in impromptu greeting before seeming to catch herself and lowering it. Making friends wasn't hard for Lark, as Arles had originally surmised. She'd just never been given the opportunity, kept like a rare hothouse flower apart from others of her kind.

The presence of a child made Arles's task both easier and harder. If handled correctly, it could render the man less of a threat; however, it gave Arles another person to look out for. The pleasant, muted greeting the man offered as he drew closer seemed to affirm the former scenario, his voice melodious enough to give Janelle a run for her money.

"Don't mean to alarm," he said, stopping a few paces away. "I'm just here to see Mr. Stratton." His body did a strange thing then, a ripple up and down its long length. He glanced down at the child beside him. "Here to see Mr. Stratton," he said, repeating his own words and giving them a trill. "Can you believe it?"

The girl looked up at him. "Cool, Dad."

He was her father, of course. And why not bring your daughter out after nightfall on this bizarre errand?

Arles forced a smile. "I'm Dr. Shepherd. Can you tell me your names?"

The man appeared to be weighing whether or not to comply when his daughter spoke up.

"I'm Janey."

"Hi, Janey," said Lark.

The girls traded smiles.

"Lark," Arles said, "why don't you show Janey something on the grounds? Would that be okay?" she asked both father and daughter. Get the children away from the unknown quantity, the least-stable factor. If not quite Psychologist 101—a tad debatable—it was close.

The man's gaze was fixed on the house where a series of lights was going on; Arles detected their brightness from behind. Rooms lit up one by one like fireflies winking to life on a summer night.

"Sure," he said vaguely, as if he wasn't giving permission for his child to head out into unknown land with a stranger.

"Not too far," Arles cautioned, providing reassurance he clearly wasn't seeking.

"We'll go look at that tree," Lark said. "The one with the abandoned nest."

"Perfect," Arles said. The tree Lark meant was within earshot but out of eyeshot. Arles could hopefully keep things from getting weird— weirder than they were already—but it would probably be better for the man's daughter not to have to see her father in action. "Take this," she added, and handed over a flashlight.

The girls walked off side by side, already starting to chat.

Then Janey stopped. "Dr. Shepherd?"

Arles took her gaze off the man momentarily. "Yes?"

"My dad's not bad, okay? He just really, really loves Kip Stratton."

—

"Who's the other little girl?" asked the man once they were alone.

Arles deflected. That was definitely Psychologist 101. "Why don't we go have a seat?" she said, indicating the Stonehenge of stumps around the smoldering fire.

"Yours, I gather?" the man asked, sitting. "She doesn't belong to Mr. Stratton. There's nothing I don't know about that man." His face puzzled as if he were trying to figure out something nearly unsolvable. "Did you go back to the bookstore that night to claim her?"

So, it was indeed Lark this man had meant when he'd accosted Arles. She despised the way he was speaking of children, of daughters in particular, perhaps, as belongings, possessions.

She kept silent, and the man spoke into the space, an irate harangue.

"Why'd you let your kid go out on her own and sneak into a car? Do you even know that author? A stunt like that could've ruined Mr. Stratton's whole show. Some man started looking for her right away. He was about to make a fuss, I could tell."

Arles allowed a couple of words, paying them out like rope. "Some man."

The fan's arms lifted in a sharp shrug, points like two mountain peaks. "A little guy. I told him what I'd seen. I couldn't let people start running around, asking about a child, and yours clearly didn't belong to Kara Cross. That lady isn't anybody's mother."

Arles experienced a pang of hurt on behalf of Kara, who'd sacrificed her life for Lark. And none of this clarified how Jason learned that Kara had gone to Fir Cove, or where she'd spent her teenage years such that he'd been able to locate the road by the shelter. But Arles supposed Kip had already provided that explanation. Kara's relatives would've attended her event, some of them privy to intimate details from her past, including the name of her therapist and the place she'd lived after her father was sentenced. It was a logical leap that Kara might seek out either or both sources for help when approached by a child in need. Maybe Kara's traitorous uncle or cousin made a cash exchange for the information. Or settled for merch, as Kip suggested.

This man clearly would not consider it *settling*.

His complexion was hectic, ruddy, as he sat forward. "I'd like to see Mr. Stratton now."

The heavy force of the statement, like a blow from a battering ram, made Arles dig her fingertips into the wood of the stump until a splinter lodged in her skin. She'd known better than to try to contain this man at the bookstore; now they were in an even more isolated setting, with two unattended children nearby, and this man's target within his fevered sights.

The front door to Fir Cove opened and slammed shut again, heavy enough to provoke a rumble through the ground. Arles rose, and the man did too, looming over her even with his body bowed. Janelle had changed into warm clothes, a jacket with a fur-rimmed hood and woolly boots. She approached with one bejeweled hand extended, rings on four of her fingers, equally sparkly nails. She was holding out a sheaf of glossy papers.

"Kip sent me," she told the man, looking way up. "He hopes you'll be happy with these."

The man studied an autographed headshot and what looked like stills of Wedeskyull, scenes from the movie, maybe, and while his expression clouded over, he still spoke wondrously.

"Kip," he said. "Kip."

Janelle gave an eager nod, but Arles was focused on that cloudy expression. It had the barometric pressure of an approaching storm.

"Dad? Are you okay? I came to check on you."

Something clutched inside Arles's chest. This poor child, assuming oversight for her father.

"Shep's on it, Janey," Lark said reassuringly. "Everything seems fine."

All three adults rotated to see the girls approach.

"Goddammit," Janelle muttered under her breath before rallying. "Look at these cuties getting along!" she said in a sprightly tone. "This one must be yours," she said, indicating Janey and speaking to the man. "She looks just like you." She then made her tone weighty, portentous, sending Arles a significant look. "And, Dr. Shepherd, I've already met your daughter, of course."

"I knew it," said the man. "No way does Mr. Stratton get anything past me."

Arles didn't respond to either of them. There were so many potential actions and interactions in play, two severely compromised parents, two children in need of protection, that she was having trouble anticipating scenarios. They came at her like targets in a shooting gallery.

Janelle walked up to Janey. "You're pretty," she remarked, lifting a lock of the girl's hair. "Put tourmaline in to control the frizz—it's the safe one, don't worry—" She tossed a look over her shoulder at the man. "And get rid of this pudge—" Now her gaze flicked up and down over Janey's body. "And you'd totally have a look."

"Mom!" bellowed Lark, her outrage heated, fiery.

Arles experienced a flash of alarm upon Lark's identification of Janelle, but the fan didn't even appear to pick up on having been fooled, his focus distant and faraway. And it served Janelle right, Arles thought. Teach the woman to deny her daughter's parentage. As for Janey, Arles fought to come up with an antidote to Janelle's poison, although she knew there was none to be had. A statement like that shaped a person more than any diet ever could.

The woman still hadn't stopped talking to Janey. "I'm going to let you in on a secret, okay? You and I have the same name, only I changed mine. Swapped it out for better. You could do the same thing. Janetta? Like Janet but pretty. Or do a real pivot. Maybe Oak?"

Janey wrenched her head so that Janelle let go of her hair.

"That's okay. I like my name. And my hair. My stomach . . ." Her voice trailed off as she looked down at herself in the dark.

Suddenly, she was cast into brightness, with Lark illuminated beside her. Headlights appeared, bobbing and weaving along the private drive. Fir Cove was a veritable street fair tonight. Tim had promised to send a patrol car around, but when Arles looked, she could tell this wasn't one of his prowlers. The car braked, with a red alarm flare at its rear. Then the driver's-side door opened, and a woman got out. All five of them turned to look at her, including the man.

"Emma?" he said, his skin reddening in an unhealthy, lurid way. "What are you doing here? You've never seen a single one of Mr. Stratton's movies. You don't even follow him!"

Janey's face squeezed, a sad clenching in the glow of the headlights, which hadn't yet shut off. "I shared our location with Mom today, Dad. Our camp in town and this place after we came to find it in the daylight. I'm sorry."

Arles recognized the aching maturity, uncanny for a child Janey's age—twelve at most—that stemmed from being raised by a man as empty and wanting as this.

"I've been driving all day," said the woman, walking up from her car.

She stooped to give Janey a hug, then rose with her daughter enclosed in the half-moon of one arm, facing off with the man. Her features reported a panoply of emotions, a recipe made up of warring ingredients. Anger, pain, pity, even some love.

Janelle began edging toward the house, on her face a clear *See y'all*.

Lark didn't even appear to notice her mother's departure.

Emma gave Janey a tap on the shoulder. "Wait in the car, okay, sweetie?"

"Can I get Lark's Instagram first?" the girl asked.

"I'm not on Instagram," Lark said with her *blech* face.

"Yeah, it sucks," Janey agreed. "Maybe just trade phone numbers?"

"I can't," Lark said. "I don't have a phone."

Janey looked impressed.

"Sweetie," Emma said, this time with some heft to it.

Janey and Lark traded hugs; then Janey trudged off toward the driveway, kicking at clods of dirt with her shoes.

"How could you do this again, Edwin?" said Emma, swiveling. "I've been going out of my mind! You know what the judge said. The only reason I didn't call the police was because it would've meant you going to prison. Prison, Edwin!"

He stood with his arms swinging, Emma subsumed by the elongated shadow he cast.

"Drive back with us," she said. "If you come right now, tonight, then your mother says she'll supervise visitation. You'll still get to see Janey, even if she can't stay with you anymore."

The girl reached the car, Edwin watching her progress in a fatherly, not fanatical, manner.

"You're coming, right, Dad?" Janey called back. "I can visit you on weekends?"

Edwin glanced down at his wife, who gave him an encouraging nod.

He lifted a broad hand, fingers splayed out in his daughter's direction. Arles couldn't tell whether he was offering reassurance—an *Of course*—or a wave. Perhaps he was signaling Janey to wait; they would get in the car together. He started striding toward the driveway.

Arles and Lark exchanged smiles. A happy ending, or at least as close to one as this entangled knot of lives was going to get. Arles should introduce herself to Emma now, make a referral to a therapist wherever they lived, if they didn't already have one.

As Arles mustered breath, Edwin swerved.

Before anyone could do anything, even call out, he lost himself again in the woods.

CHAPTER
FORTY-ONE

"Clearly, it's not safe for us here," Kip said.

Arles and Lark had reentered the house as soon as Emma and Janey drove away.

Kip stood in front of a window, having apparently watched the proceedings with no inclination to help. Janelle reclined on one of the sofas, yawning languorously, in her own way as attention-getting as her husband.

"That man is still out there, and you've got about the least secure location on the face of the planet. Your liability must be ruinous." Kip shook his head, a gesture that appeared practiced, meant to convey absolute certainty. "Go get your things, Larky."

"I'm sorry," Arles said. Normally, she didn't do apologies that rang as hollow as that one, but this man was used to getting his way, so she was willing to soften the blow. "But a few things need to be decided before you can go." She would explain the permutations in the bright light of day. "Everything will be locked down for the night, I promise. And we'll talk things over during breakfast." Cold cereal would have to suffice. Nut milk since it was shelf-stable, and there was some in the pantry. It'd probably suit the celebrities better anyway.

Kip faced her with a blue blaze in his eyes that said *villain* not *hero*. He never could've played the good guy in this state. "I intend to take my daughter home, Doctor. I can keep her safe better than anyone."

Someone made him unsafe. The insight jumped into her head, an explanation—if not a justification—for his dominance displays and the extreme lengths he'd gone to in sequestering his child. Arles saw Kip register her awareness, some tweak or twitch that must've taken hold of her features, and his own face closed as smoothly as a lake over a stone.

He would do whatever he wanted, abscond with Lark like she was his prized racehorse, if Arles didn't come up with some way to stop him. The *right* way to stop him. Her mind reached, stretching and straining.

At last she said, "What you've tried to do is brave."

He glanced in her direction, the word *brave* like catnip to a tom.

"It's an imperfect battle, keeping a child out of harm's way," Arles went on. "Impossible to cover all the bases." Mixing metaphors, but the latter bought Kip out of his failure vis-à-vis Jason. "But you made a more valiant attempt than most parents. And I've seen a lot of them."

"We have resources," Kip said, going for modesty. "The people you treat likely don't." An unlovely shadow passed over his face. "Like my own parents didn't."

"That may account for some things, like how well Lark has been educated so far. But not all of it. Part of who Lark is comes down just to you." Which was true. "And what you felt compelled to do because of your unique history." Less true, but not a total lie.

Lark's gaze flicked between the two of them like she was watching a show.

Kip's broad shoulders settled. "Let's give this a night," he said, as if it had been his idea. "No reason to take your tricky road in the dark."

Arles gestured. "I think you'll find everything you need in the closet in your room."

All four of them trooped upstairs in a soldierly row, Kip at the fore.

Though she expected to toss and turn for hours, Arles fell asleep before even flicking the switch on her bedside table lamp.

She woke in the middle of the night, a cone of light on the floor from the lamp.

From childhood, she'd always slept like a soldier in battle. Part of her brain alert, primed, ready to spring to life. Knowing to suppress her startle response, hide the fact that she was stirring. Registering every single sensory stimulus: sighs, grunts, creaks; shadows moving, shapes shifting; the temperature of the air on her skin.

Or a thin golden thread now shining into her room from underneath the door.

The hall sconces had been turned on.

Arles rose silently, jamming her feet into the boots she'd worn by the fire, not taking time to find socks or trade her pajama shorts for a pair of pants.

She drew open the door, muffling the noise its catch made with her hand.

She needn't have bothered; there was nobody in the hallway to hear.

Arles ran for the staircase. She should've known Kip was not the type to take no for an answer. Had he been lying, or had he changed his mind? She suspected the latter, but perhaps that was just self-flattery, imagining herself immune to the manipulations of a master.

The Strattons were at the bottom of the stairs, walking three abreast toward the front door. Janelle clutched Lark by the wrist while Kip's palm lay solidly on his daughter's shoulder. The two adults towed sleek wheelies; Lark's arms hung stiffly at her sides.

She was moving with her robot walk, her legs as rigid as stalks. She appeared nonhuman, no emotion to her face or bend to her body.

Approaches arrowed through Arles's head.

Stop! Where do you think you're going? I told you not to leave!

Give me Lark.

None of them seemed likely to work, given that her first injunction and massage of his ego had not. Once Kip grew impatient or frustrated, he took what he wanted with blunt, brute force, a kindergartener's grab for a cookie. Arles went dashing down the steps, missing some, grasping the railing for purchase, hauling herself upright when she started to trip.

They didn't detect her presence until she'd made it out onto the porch.

Then Kip and Janelle turned around in the drive, halfway to their car.

Panting, Arles ran to catch up to them.

Kip raised one arm like a sword, extending his hand, and dammit, Arles actually stopped.

"Thanks for everything, Doctor," he called in a ringing tone. "But I'm afraid we won't be needing your services after all."

Arles's brain finally sent an order that got her legs to move. "As I mentioned, there are a few things left to be decided." Massive understatement. A Hollywood-level lie.

Kip ignored her, cheeping the locks and tossing their suitcases into the trunk as the hatch sailed upward. He opened the rear door, and Lark walked forward in a series of automaton steps.

Lark had become a different child from the one who'd warded off Jason's assault with one lethal blow. Led by her parents like a lamb across a field. Perhaps everyone became different in the company of their parents; certainly, with Peter erased, Arles felt a sense of unfurling, of new roads being laid. But this was one road that couldn't bring Lark anywhere good.

"Janelle!" Arles shouted. "Going rogue will throw Lark's life into chaos. And both of yours too," she added, figuring that this argument might stand a better chance of swaying the woman. If Kip's publicity campaign were jeopardized. Or Janelle's channel.

Janelle turned to her. "Kip isn't somebody you can oppose, Dr. Shepherd. I've never been able to, anyway. And he's only gotten worse with the upcoming release."

Lark stood with her back to them. Arles couldn't tell if she were listening. Hearing.

"That's not true," Arles protested. "I've seen what you can do, Janelle. I watched you climb a mountain without ever having taken a hike in your life." At least, it looked that way.

Momentarily, Janelle brightened. "Yes, you're right. But my strength doesn't matter when it comes to our daughter. His Larky," she hissed, her face stiffening, as if it'd been shot full of some numbing agent intended to defy age while really turning its recipient into a monster. "Who do you think decided to hide her away like a goddamn princess in a tower?"

"Into the car!" Kip roared, dropping onto the driver's seat while Lark dove in back as if a rope had yanked her. Janelle began backing toward the passenger door. "And don't make me yell again," he added amiably. "I have to protect my voice for next week."

"Janelle," Arles said, "this isn't up to Kip. It's maybe the one thing that isn't. The state is going to step in and take the decision out of your hands. Out of all our hands."

"I'm sure you know how tricky it'll be, coordinating something like that at a distance," Janelle replied, still walking backward. "I didn't realize, but Kip clued me in. Especially when the states are as far apart as ours."

She was right, or he was. Child welfare operations were some of the most difficult to get right, and the responsible agencies were notoriously unconnected, the opposite of a countrywide web. Nonetheless, Arles tried again. "Please let me help Lark. Let me help all of you. Before none of us gets to decide anything anymore."

Janelle gazed at Arles with an expression that at first Arles couldn't parse, perhaps because it was a totally authentic, organic look, Janelle's feeling naked on her face with no adornment or smoothing. She felt pity for someone. Arles? No, Lark. Or was it herself?

"But you have no way of getting them here, do you? Any of those people who are supposed to decide." She held up her dead phone, the pops of color on its case washed out by the night. "And by the time you do, we'll be long gone. Back in Kip's kingdom. You won't find us, and even if you did, there wouldn't be anything left for you to do. Kip will make sure of that."

And she turned and ran for the car.

Before she was able to seal herself inside, her door still hanging partway open, Kip took off in a sputter of gravel and a gale of dust.

Without even giving Lark the chance to say goodbye.

CHAPTER
FORTY-TWO

There was a pass through the woods.

A shortcut that met up with the private drive before the gates let out onto the road. Kip was unfamiliar with the terrain. He would have to drive slowly, and Arles could run again now, felt speed uncoiling inside her.

She raced into the trees with déjà vu trailing like a long cape behind her. Five months ago, she had made this run, and a man had been waiting for her on the other end with a gun. Arles didn't think Kip would, or even could, shoot her. Any weapons he'd fired in his life had probably contained blanks with artfully concealed blood packs to suggest he'd hit his victim. But it struck Arles as a not-insignificant possibility that Kip might plow her down if she tried to block his exit. Borrow a page from his buddy Jason. In fact, she vaguely recalled Kip conducting just that maneuver in the one film of his she'd seen, unless a professional driver had done it.

There had to be some other way. If Kip got past Arles, he would squire Lark away, bar her from services and interventions forever, a princess in her tower, as Janelle had said.

Arles cast her gaze around as she wove between tree trunks, stumbling over roots and bashing her hands against the occasional boulder that reared up as if God above had a temper tantrum and hurled it. Twigs clawed ruts in the uncovered parts of her legs, drawing blood. When she finally reached the section of drive she'd been aiming for, with no grit stirred up or cloud of dust settling—reassuring indication that Kip hadn't gotten there yet—she spotted toadstools sprouting from a downed log, white scalloped ledges glowing in the dark.

The log was decaying, powdery and softened, which made it difficult to get hold of, but light enough to move once she had a good grip, sinking her fingers into the rotting innards of the tree. She felt insects squirm beneath her hands, trying to get away.

She bent lower, putting all her weight into the motion as she rammed the tree forward. Bits of gravel caught in the log's rutted bark, impeding its passage. She grunted as she pushed and shoved, using both arms and legs, her just barely reconstructed abs.

From around the bend came a glimmer of headlights.

Arles lurched backward, retreating into the barrier of woods.

If she stood in front of Kip and confronted him, tried to force his hand, she'd only activate his ire. Janelle was right about that—Kip Stratton was not a man willing to be defied. Whereas if he believed he'd left Arles back at the house, cowed her into compliance, perhaps he would do the wise thing when he caught sight of this obstacle.

The log jutted into the drive, lying about three-quarters of the way across it.

Kip would have to stop. Get out to investigate.

He braked, flashes of red that bloodied the darkness. Arles glimpsed them from her position in the trees. Kip slowed down, lowering his window to poke his head out, craning to see.

"What the hell?"

Janelle must've been leaning across him in the front seat, trying to get a look for herself. Her head joined Kip's outside the window.

"A tree fell down," she said.

"Yes, Jane," Kip replied, in a tone like a scorpion sting. "That is a tree, and it did fall. But not since we've been here. That thing is long dead, and we just came this way this morning."

He had better outdoor wherewithal than his wife, not that that was saying much.

"How'd it get here, then?" Janelle asked in the squeaky, unpleasant version of her voice.

"Hell if I know." He resituated himself inside the car. "Sorry for all the cursing, Larky."

If Lark answered, Arles couldn't hear her.

Janelle looked away from the drive at the same time that Arles stepped out of the woods. Not by much, a few steps at most. But it was enough of a shift that Janelle's eyes met hers.

"You can get past that thing, Kip," Janelle stated, sliding back inside the car and dropping into her seat. "Just steer around it."

No, Arles begged mentally, about to reveal herself. She could put up a decent fight. Kip was stronger, obviously, compelled by his industry to keep his body muscular and ripped. But by the same token, he wouldn't want to risk marring his looks. Arles could land a bruising punch, give him a black eye right before his movie opened. If all else failed, she'd claw his perfect face. Gouge him too badly for a makeup artist to hide.

"C'mon!" Janelle urged. "Remember that time you wanted to be your own stunt driver?"

"I'd have to get halfway into the woods," Kip said doubtfully.

Not so brave when it's for real, huh? thought Arles.

She took another step forward, which Kip didn't appear to register.

But Janelle sent her a look so savage that Arles momentarily faltered. She had been the recipient of many a hateful look in her life, but the loathing in Janelle's felt lethal.

What did Janelle think Arles was going to do, anyway? Throw open the car door, drag Lark across the back seat, and haul her out? With Kip gunning the gas to make his escape? It'd be way too dangerous. A move requiring choreography and practice, crash pads, CGI, all the tricks of the trade that Lark had been educating Arles about.

Lark.

There were official channels, avenues Arles could access, favors to call in once the girl's parents had taken her away. The steps would entail a ton of red tape, forms in duplicate, triplicate, tenthlicate. Proprietary computer programs to learn. All of it taking time. But it was the cautious option. The only option.

Janelle met Arles's gaze again with a cream-licking expression of satisfaction.

She'd gotten what she wanted. She knew, or sensed, that Arles had decided to fall back. Was the woman trying to protect her daughter or possess her? Arles would sooner let Lark leave than risk her safety in any way by trying to keep her here.

Kip tapped the gas so that the SUV moved forward in hitches and starts while he steered as far to the right as he could. But the vehicle was oversize; in order to make it around the log, he'd have to go off-road. Which this car had been built for but might never have done, definitely not with the likes of Kip Stratton at the wheel.

"Wait, let me out for a sec!" Janelle screamed, not in her pro voice, no whiff of restraint or modulation to it now. "I'm going to ride in back with Lark! Make sure she stays put!"

"Good thinking," Kip muttered through his still-open window. A head pat for his wife while he concentrated intently on what was in front of him. He came to a temporary halt.

Janelle climbed out and yanked open the rear door. "Crawl across, Lark! Let me get in!" She heaved a dramatic sigh. "Hold on, Kip, she's being a bitch. I'll go around the other side."

"How many times have I said I don't want you swearing at Larky?" Kip leaned closer to the windshield, his perfect brow crimped in a frown as he assessed the landscape.

So hard to know what to do with no script to follow.

Mad thoughts thrummed beneath that one, stabs in the night—something, anything—for Arles to try. "Janelle," she said softly as the woman went racing around the car. But Arles had no idea how to make

Janelle fail to complete the rest of her mission. Commit marital treason and change factions, join Arles on this side of the fight.

"My real name is Jane," the woman said, her voice nearly drowned out by a gust from the engine. She grabbed Arles's hand and pressed something into it, her curved nails carving scythes in Arles's skin. "Just like that chubby little girl."

My real name is Lark, Arles heard in her ears, an echo from not so long ago.

"I kicked it old-school," Janelle added.

Then she pulled the back door open and wedged herself inside next to Lark.

Arles edged forward to try and get a glimpse of the child, at least wave goodbye.

"I haven't seen her in anything, or looked her up online," said Janelle.

Arles wasn't sure who the words were intended for, herself or Lark, nor what they meant.

"Maybe she's in a better situation now," Janelle added. "Maybe she made it."

Then the woman slammed the door shut, gunshot loud in the still night, and the SUV leaped forward like a horse at the gate. Branches raked the car's flank as it swerved into the woods, twigs snapping off and leaves flying through the air like darts.

At the last second, Arles realized she couldn't just stand there. Couldn't let Lark go.

If Kip hit Arles with his car, injured her or worse, he would get away with it. Rules and laws didn't apply to men in his position. Not even when it came to their children. Which meant that if Kip absconded with Lark right now, she might never be recovered.

Arles crossed the private drive in four fast strides, headed toward its other side.

Kip spotted her, and the SUV zigzagged. But he didn't have the control to do what he was doing. He lacked the skill to miss her and came arrowing back toward the road.

"Get the fuck out of the way!" he screamed through the open window.

Now who's cursing?

"Stop the car!" Arles shouted in her most commanding tone, raising one arm as if she could do this by hand, bring three tons to a screeching halt. The car was maybe thirty feet away.

It surged forward, taking down a row of saplings, one by one like dominoes, as Kip fought to avoid her. But he was nowhere near experienced enough to enact the move. A corner of the hood clocked her as it hurtled by, throwing Arles onto the drive with a punishing blow, the force driving bits of gravel into her skin, piercing and lodging themselves deep within. She let out a bellow of sheer fury and failure.

The SUV skirted the log, then skidded back out onto the road, disappearing into the darkness, a sleek pantherine shadow of black, there and then gone.

Taking Lark with it.

Only once the last plume of exhaust had dissipated did Arles make it onto her hands and knees, checking herself for damage. She thought she would be able to get up. At some point. Not now. Maybe not anytime soon.

Motion came from underneath some tree branches, then onto dirt at the shoulder.

A shape emerged out of the shadows. Arles blinked, trying to see, then began scrubbing fiercely at her eyes. Something was crawling, same as Arles was now. They were both on all fours, moving toward each other. Paying no attention to pebbles, debris, kneed-up swirls of dust.

Lark threw her arms out, clinging to Arles. The girl began muttering, doing her monologue—*world, souls, hearts, lonely*—while crying hard enough to jounce Arles's body. Unless those sobs belonged to Arles? Lark's hold was so strong, it winched Arles's arms against her sides, but Arles managed to unclench her hand with Janelle's offering still squeezed inside it.

A slip of paper.

I kicked it old-school.

On one side of a rental car agreement, just barely visible in the faint light of impending dawn, words had been formed by something gummy. Lipstick.

How had Janelle pulled it off? Arles rewound the tape in her mind. When Kip was focusing so intently on the log and Janelle opened the rear passenger door on the other side of the car. She pretended Lark wouldn't let her in, but really, she must've been easing Lark out. Sending her into the woods alongside the road to hide.

"Lark," Arles said wonderingly. "Lark."

The girl lifted her grimed and tear-slicked face.

"We were wrong," Arles said. "Both of us."

Blinking tears from her eyes, Lark aimed a wordless question at her.

"Your mom turned out to be kind of an amazing actress," Arles explained. "In the end."

They looked down at the piece of paper together. Enough daylight now to read it.

Janelle's tinted scrawl spelled out a name.

CHAPTER
FORTY-THREE

First, there was a stop at the barracks.

Tim agreed to have the department cover the costs and to fill out the paperwork himself, making sure *i*'s were dotted and *t*'s were crossed in the electronic record. "We made you an emergency foster last spring for the Rudd girl. Remember? That applies to this scenario too."

Stephanie's daughter. Lissa had needed a temporary guardian while her mother was in the hospital, courtesy of bartender Nick, now barred from seeing his daughter unsupervised.

"Right," Arles said. So much of that time was still a muck in her mind. Chunks missing she hadn't known had been removed.

Identification was, of course, required; there turned out to be a birth certificate for Lark with Kip and Janelle's original names on it. Nothing linking the child to the people her parents had become as stars, performers, the identities they'd taken on. Arles figured Lark must've been seated with one of her parents' hired guns on the plane ride east and any other times she'd flown, preventing Kip and Janelle from being seen with a child. Arles fervently hoped the seatmate had been Troy, but feared not. The thought of those hours in a contained capsule prompted a sick, queasy swell.

She thanked Tim, then gave Lark a nod, and the two of them turned to leave.

"Arles?" Tim said.

She looked back at him.

"I hope you find what she needs out there," he said, indicating Lark with a jab of his chin.

"So do I," said Arles. She hoped it so intensely, the words bore repeating. "So do I."

En route to the airport—a small local one first, just a runway within a chain-link fence, which would get them to Albany for the cross-country flight, connecting through Denver—Arles parked on the street outside Dan's apartment. It was early enough that he hadn't left for work.

"Come," she said with a smile in Lark's direction.

They unbuckled at the same time.

"There's someone I want you to meet."

Dan opened his door before Arles had a chance to knock.

"Dan! I've heard *so* much about you," Lark said, playing the host of an evening soiree.

"Not one word until today," Arles murmured, biting back a smile.

The encounter was swift, with just enough time between greetings and goodbyes for Arles to offer a quick explanation, then ask Dan if he could arrange something at Fir Cove. And for him to agree; he happened to have the right company on-site now at the LaMora build, a new affordable housing complex, and they could take care of what Arles wanted done.

Dan leaned in through the open driver's-side window while Arles started the engine.

"You haven't been able to get the woman on the phone?" he asked.

Arles shook her head. "I had to go through her manager, and he didn't call back, but then that seemed risky, anyway, so much to lose in translation. I need to assess the situation myself."

291

Dan hesitated. "Half dozen ways things could go sideways, though, no?"

Arles reached out and took his hand. "And one big way it might go right."

She saw it play out mentally. A wish, a longing. Lark's birth mother, whose name Janelle had passed along, had been caught in a vise eleven years ago, one of the many that could make having a baby untenable for a woman. Time had passed, though. And Janelle along with Kip had proven themselves unfit in so many ways. A new adoption story was needed.

Hadn't Janelle's final words indicated understanding of this? *Maybe she's in a better situation.* Was that too much to hope for?

"You're not usually an optimist," Dan said.

Arles felt herself flush, caught out. Time had passed, she thought again, this time in terms of herself. Things were different now. Caring for Lark had changed her.

"It's a good look," Dan added. He bent down to give her a kiss, whose imprint Arles felt as he backed off toward his truck, one palm lifted.

Next to Arles, Lark spoke too softly for him to hear. "See ya, Dan." Then she and Arles were on their way.

———

Arles had considered going alone to meet Lark's birth mom. But Lark had been through so much in her young life, both overall and crammed into the events of the past several days, that taking control away, making decisions without her being involved, wasn't ideal psychologically. Nor would placing her in temporary care with total strangers fit the brief of trauma recovery.

By the time they reached the other side of the country, Arles felt as if her body was being crushed, every cell limp with exhaustion. But they had gained three hours traveling west, and there was enough time left in the day to meet the woman. According to what Arles had been able to glean online about her life, she was in the midst of shooting a film.

LA traffic was as miserable as reputation had it.

Whenever Arles left Wedeskyull, especially for a city, she got crotchety. Itchy. She considered herself allergic to urban environments, and this one felt particularly oppressive. She and Lark sat in a rental car in a long red river of brake lights until the punishing sun lost some of its bite and the hard, glaring sky began to soften.

Arles had been envisioning the fairy-tale ending so few people got, but which Lark surely deserved. Happiness Hollywood-style: a small tucked-away house, enswathed by the proverbial fence, no more or less in size and embellishment than was needed. A Goldilocks-style *just right*. Spare room inside, waiting for a child to make her own. Lark's birth mother emerging from this picture-perfect enclave; she'd never stopped wondering about the child she had given up.

Life should've taught Arles better than to foresee any of that.

Lark spoke up from the rear of the car. "Hey, that's a lot."

"What's a lot? A lot of what?" Arles asked.

The girl smiled. "You know, an outdoor lot. Part of a studio."

"Oh." Arles checked her phone. "Then we're here."

"My birth mom is in the industry?" Lark said. "I'm so surprised."

The girl was nervous enough that it threw off her acting; she sounded sad, not sarcastic.

They parked on a short, stubby street that lay in the shadows of a highway overpass, backing up to a run of low buildings that had seen better days, their paint grubby and peeling. A cracked walkway formed jagged jigsaw pieces. Before, Arles had gone so far as to imagine a window box or two, but nothing had flowered or grown here in a very long time. There wasn't so much as a sad, listing tree. Even the grass had conceded defeat.

Lark pointed things out through the window. "See that? It's a soundstage. The walls come apart on that house they built. And look, there's an equipment shed. A really small one."

Anyone who dreamed of a life in the movies needed to see this place; then they'd decide in favor of a more glam career, like accounting. Lark had been able to identify the shed's purpose because its doors hung open, and since it never rained here—and to Arles's admittedly uneducated eye, none of this stuff looked worth stealing—that presented no problem. In the shed was a motley collection of beat-up cameras with duct-taped lenses, trolleys and carts with mismatched wheels, mikes and audio equipment whose fur looked mangy, pitted foam resembling acne-scarred skin.

This was the underside of the business, the reality behind the curtain, the industry as in *industrial*. No allure, just hard work and mechanisms and breakdowns and sweat.

Arles twisted around with her arm over the seat rest, examining Lark in the back.

"You know I need to go in first, right? Make sure she's here, then have a few words. After that, I'll come get you."

Lark looked ready to protest, opening her mouth, before closing it and giving a nod.

Arles narrowed her eyes. "I mean it. I haven't been able to get this woman on the phone, or talk to, you know, anybody who might be connected to her—"

"Her people," said Lark.

"Okay. Them. And I can't just bring you into something that could turn out to be a total . . ." Arles broke off, searching for a word.

"Shit show," offered Lark.

No cursing, Larky. Away from her parents, Lark was really coming into her own.

"Okay," Arles said again. "That."

Lark gave her a small smile.

"I promise to come get you the second I can. This is about you, and I understand that."

"That's why you brought me. Instead of just leaving me someplace."

The Fairest

Arles's heart squeezed. This child had been left so often. And now that Arles was aware of whose hands she'd been left in, and to what purposes, the statement tasted like a poison pellet.

"Right." Arles swept her gaze around the street—drab, but decently populated, given the buildings—then back toward Lark. Technically, children weren't permitted to stay on their own till they were twelve, but that rule was broken all the time, and quick dashes into stores while the child waited in the car qualified as okay.

What about a dash in to meet the birth mom of said child?

"Shep," Lark said, using one hand to indicate her back-seat quarters, "I'm waiting in a comfy-ass car in, like, the one shady spot LA has, which you actually managed to find, with *Tom Brown's Field Guide* to read and a heap of junk food. What could go wrong?"

"That's it," Arles said. "You're coming with me."

———

Arles hadn't been sure which barriers would stand between Talia Bent and someone walking in off the street requesting to talk to her, how many layers there would be between actor and visitor. The answer turned out to be almost none.

"I take it back," Lark said as she and Arles entered one of the low-slung buildings. "She doesn't have people."

Arles looked at her.

Lark peered around the gray-walled entryway. "This is some low-budget shit."

Arles was probably going to have to talk with her about the cursing.

A security guard pointed Arles down the hall to a communal room and agreed to let Lark sit and read by his podium.

Arles went through the whole rigmarole again. "Stay here. You promise?"

Lark already had the field guide open. "I promise."

"Truth?"

"Truth."

The door to the room stood ajar. A dozen or so women occupied flimsy chairs, sheets of paper on their laps, talking aloud to themselves in various intonations. Trilling, ponderous, meditative. They looked up when Arles entered. All roughly the same age and of what Lark might've called a type. Maybe this was an audition? Either that, or the movie being filmed was about cloning. The group went back to reading aloud and speaking and gesticulating for no one.

Arles set her sights on woman number eight, staring until the woman seemed to sense it.

She looked up, meeting Arles's gaze.

Even in a field of like versions of herself, golden-blond heads like flowers on slim stalks, she was indisputably, unambiguously, Lark's birth mom.

CHAPTER
FORTY-FOUR

Talia had seemingly no compunctions about sharing her story with Arles. She was an actress, used to baring her soul. The two of them stood in the hallway outside the room.

Talia and Kip had been taking the same acting class when they'd slept together once, and Talia fell pregnant. (Only then did Arles detect the faint traces of a British accent, which the actress had clearly worked to erase.) Talia knew a baby would derail her fledgling career and had no interest in having kids at any point, to be honest. All she'd ever wanted in life was to make it in the business.

But Kip had gone off, said no seed of his loins was going to be scraped out or given to strangers to raise. He'd convinced Talia to carry the pregnancy to term, which was okay; she'd been raised Catholic and had been struggling with the idea of an abortion, although she was for choice politically, of course. Kip had apparently also convinced Janelle both to forgive what he called his *oops*—as if he didn't sleep with other women left, right, and sideways—and that momfluencers were blowing up big-time. According to Talia, he'd bought a baby for Janelle like a bag. His payments kept Talia from having to wait tables—or take a position worse than that, like so many others of her ilk did.

"Be careful of him," Talia added. "Arles? Is that your name?"

Arles gave a short nod.

"Be careful of Kip. He's hot and all that, and he seems jokey and genial, but it's just another act. In real life, nothing makes him quit until he gets what he wants. That's how he's made it this far. And one thing he wanted from the second he suspected I was knocked up—never should've left that test kit in the trash—was his daughter. It was like he thought he'd created a work of art, his grand masterpiece. One of those paintings the owner hides away so the sun can't get at it, and it can be looked over and studied whenever the rich arsehole wants."

Everything inside Arles had seized up while she'd listened, the warm softness of imagined homecoming turning to sludge. Talia kept sneaking peeks over her shoulder at the busy room, palpably itching to get back to a thrum that Arles found frenetic and unappealing. People speaking over each other, talking as if no one else was there, as if they were the single only entities on earth. It seemed so lonely. In her line of work, people took turns. Made safe spaces.

But Talia wasn't finished; like many a client, once she'd gotten going, she discovered more that she wanted to share.

"Think about what Kip had to do to get what he wanted in this case," she told Arles. "Make me spend three months puking my guts up, and another six the size of a whale. Force his wife to raise a child she'd never expressed the slightest desire for. And the biggest stretch of all? Keep his kid from making a peep, never show herself once to the world." Talia leaned closer, her breath hot and minty in Arles's face. "Kip can make anyone do anything. Probably even you."

Arles rubbed her goose-pebbly arms with her hands, working to camouflage the chill Talia's warning had instilled. But she didn't want to let the woman go before clarifying one aspect of her story. Because far from becoming a momfluencer, Janelle had hidden from the world— and her millions of viewers—the fact that she had a child.

Talia nodded. "The second I gave birth, Kip grew even more dominant and controlling. Tale as old as time, right? He came into labor and delivery; I barely even got a glimpse of the baby, which was fine with me. I heard he took her home before being officially discharged! It's just how Kip is. When he's on a shoot, he makes all these out-there demands—only red leaves in his salad or whatever, the car he's driven in has to have three rows—and everybody plays along." Her artfully made-up mouth formed something thin and crimped. "I considered exposing the truth a few years ago. Kip's career was taking off, and I thought he could help mine do a little better. But I decided in favor of keeping the money coming over bringing an ugly story to light. It's not like being able to get blokes canceled has really changed anything anyway."

"It's made things worse," said a small voice from behind.

Arles felt her heart sink, her chest cave in.

"Now they know we're coming for them. Now they have warning. That's what my mom says, anyway. My *other* mom."

How much of Talia's speech had Lark heard?

A man pushed past the three of them to enter the room. "Okay, girls—sorry, sorry, I mean *ladies*—we'll meet on set after the supermarket fight, all right? Big changes to go over. Call time as usual tomorrow, so if I were you, I wouldn't expect to sleep at home tonight."

A few moans that sounded more pleased than anything else.

"That's my EP," Talia said proudly. "I'm finally about to get my big break. Don't have any more time for chitchat."

Arles looked down at Lark.

"Executive producer," the girl told her.

Talia went back into the room, kneeing the door shut.

She hadn't given Lark so much as a glance.

In a few years, the two of them were going to look like identical twins, but Talia hadn't even appeared to register the presence of her offspring. Arles wondered whether Kip had been disappointed— felt narcissistically wounded—when his child didn't turn out to resemble him.

The door swung open again, the other women in the room all rising. A few glimpsed Lark in the hall and offered up the smiles and squeals that Talia had not.

"Is the little girl here to get autographs?" another asked. "Or take selfies?"

One woman began digging in her purse, coming up with a pen, while others fired up their phones.

"I'm posting this!" one of them said.

"The kid probably knows we have a night shoot tonight!" another added.

A night shoot clearly being worth some excitement, although Arles wasn't feeling it.

"I don't see a grip truck," Lark responded bluntly. "Where's the gaffer and DP? Is your amperage coming from flashlights?" Her lower lip trembled, then curled. "Or not even. Maybe those things we wore around camp at night. What were they called again, Shep?"

"Headlamps," Arles said softly.

"Yeah," Lark bit out. "Those. Because there's not enough power here to light up a shoebox."

The women shrank back, clearly under attack, although Arles didn't get all the specifics.

"You're, like, Lifetime actors," Lark scoffed. "Right? Or MariGold."

"This is Year-Round Productions," one woman asserted.

She said it as if it were one of the ones even someone like Arles might know—Columbia or MGM. This place had delusions of grandeur; the whole city did. Even Arles could detect the indicators of what Lark had called out as meager, how the company occupied a low rung on a ladder. Arles suspected the view from the top would be more of the same, though. A little glitzier, perhaps, a few more touches of glitter, but still, just another facsimile of real life.

"*Television for women,*" Lark said in an air-quote type of tone. "As if shows shouldn't be for everybody."

"Yeah, well, they're not, according to ratings," another woman said, lower lip trembling.

But Lark didn't let up. "What's this one, another chewed-up *Stepford Wives* reboot?"

"Come on," said a different woman, rising. "We don't have to take this."

"Hold up." One of the women came and crouched in front of Lark. "Did you get turned down for a role today, honey? Is that why you're so upset?"

"Aww," said another. "That happens to everyone."

"You're gonna be gorgeous, you know," said the one still in a squat.

The other nodded vigorously. "Keep at it, and I bet you leave us all in the dust."

The words made Arles go even colder, LA heat no match for her internal chill. Lark had expressed nothing but antipathy for the business since Arles had met her, but what child wouldn't be swayed, moved, mesmerized by such a prospect dangled in front of them, a path laid out like the yellow brick road to lights, camera, action?

Lark had reviled this industry when talking to Kip at Fir Cove, yet she knew it like she knew how to breathe. At least some part of her loved it, was obsessed with its features and flaws.

She lifted her head. "Shep?"

I want to live here. Is there a foster family I can go to? You have no right to stop me.

"Yes, Lark?"

"Can we get out of this place?"

⸻

Lark angled herself on the back seat, her seat belt straining as she stared fixedly out the window. She was the shut-down child who had first come to Fir Cove.

Arles pulled away from the curb. "What do people eat around here?"

After a beat, the girl said, "In-N-Out Burger's good. I get it on my birthday."

Arles drove up an access ramp, then waded into an endless stream of cars. The freeway looked like a thousand used-car dealers had vomited up their inventory. "Well," she said, finding the closest franchise and entering it into the nav before easing up on the brake. The car in front of them had begun inching forward. "Many happy returns of the day."

She booked a hotel room while Lark leaned across the seat to order from the drive-through.

They ate on queen beds with the TV streaming something '90s-era. Set not far away from here.

"You left the security guard's station," Arles said, testing her burger with a small bite.

She was mindful of the fact that within a roughly forty-eight-hour time span, Lark had been forced to absorb slaying a man who had tormented her for years, the revelation about her birth mother, and that same woman's careless rejection, not to mention her parents' unfazed reactions to all of the above. Still, Arles couldn't let this go unaddressed.

Lark poked a fistful of fries into her mouth. "Yeah, so?"

"Well, that isn't okay," Arles said, setting her burger down. "You can't just say you'll do something and then not do it."

Lark looked at her as if Arles had just said she couldn't touch her nose, or take a drink of water, or something equally doable. "Why not?"

Arles gave it some thought. All the standard responses she'd heard parents offer were flawed. *Because it's bad. Because I said so.* "Have you noticed that I never lie to you?"

Lark appeared to consider this.

"If I can't answer something or tell you something, then I say that. But I don't just make it up. I don't make *anything* up."

"I guess that's right," said Lark.

Arles gave a jerk of her head. "So, not lying is a two-way street. As long as both people are truthful with each other, it works. But if one of them lies, or promises to do one thing but does another, then, well, it's like driving the wrong way down a one-way street."

Lark scrambled off her bed, coming over to place her hand on top of Arles's. Arles often had an irrational response to touch, experiencing it as something cold and wet, a mud patty or maybe a toad against her skin. Even Dan could provoke this sensation. But Lark's hand felt small and warm and still. Gentle.

"Shep?"

"Yes?" *I understand. Thanks for being real with me. No more lies.*

"Can I eat the rest of your burger?"

What to do now? A new ending was needed.

Did Arles return Lark to Kip and Janelle, find their house on some tourist map of the stars, since Lark might resist sharing her home address? Her parents' ability to take care of her seemed iffy at best; according to Lark, Mom had plans to do real harm to her child.

Turn the girl over to DCF, then?

The prospect induced a shudder in Arles. Just drop Lark off, leave her three thousand miles away?

Maybe she should bring her back to New York State. Enlist CPS. Arles at least knew some people in the system, as well as its workings. She could advocate for the best outcome.

That idea caused slightly less of a shudder. More like a ripple.

The TV had gone dark. Lark sat on her bed, surrounded by a crumple of fast-food wrappers, the remote in her hand. It looked bloody, its plastic body streaked with ketchup.

"I'm sorry, Lark," said Arles. "I wish this had gone differently."

"You were just trying to get me my happily ever Nemo," Lark said, fiddling with the trash on her bed.

"Is that like *happily ever after?*"

"Only better. No prince."

"Yeah," Arles said. "I was trying for that."

"Maybe it's still out there," Lark said. "The perfect family, just waiting for me."

The child's spirit was irrepressible. "Out where? Here?"

Lark made her *blech* face. "No way. I wish this whole tectonic plate would fall into the ocean. I like it better where you come from. Where that bookstore is. And all the woods."

"I was thinking along the same lines," Arles said slowly, nodding. "Well, minus the tectonic plate part."

Lark untangled her legs and wrestled the blankets down, sliding beneath them.

"Brush teeth?" Arles suggested. "They have disposables in the bathroom."

But the girl had already fallen asleep.

CHAPTER
FORTY-FIVE

In the morning when Arles woke, the curtains had been drawn back, and the room was empty. Lark had achieved a feat no other human could—eluded notice while Arles continued to sleep. Arles hurried to pull on clothes, swept up her key card from the desk, and headed down the exit stairs without taking time to wait for the elevator. Only a small part of her was worried that Lark had fled. Perhaps she'd gotten hungry, last night's meal digested. She was probably gorging on the hotel's breakfast buffet right now. Junky cereal, maybe the kind with marshmallows.

Arles didn't find her in the dining room.

But as she crossed the lobby, figuring she'd ask someone at the front desk if they'd seen an eleven-year-old, she spotted Lark in the business center.

Arles used her key card to enter the glassed-in room.

Lark spun in a chair with her hands still hovering over the keyboard.

"Oh, g'morning, Shep," she said. "I decided I wanted to write something."

Arles took a step forward and looked down at the screen. Tabs to set up a profile and a new email account; Lark had chosen larkintheworld@gmail.com for her address. And a doc attached to a message with a dozen names in the "To" list.

"I found a bunch of the bloggers and influencers my mom's jealous of. She thinks their reach is greater." Lark considered. "Probably is. Their numbers are insane."

———

On the plane back east, a direct flight this time, Lark shared what she had written.

My Momsters, she'd titled it. *The High Cost of Being Sold Cheap.*

It was somewhere between a Reddit post and a school essay from hell.

If Arles had deemed Lark smart back in the parlor that day, now the girl seemed close to genius level. Her piece was heated and horrid and bursting like a ripe piece of fruit. Arles bet that at least one of the outlets Lark had selected would choose to write about it, link to it, something.

It was a helluva piece of writing. Kara would've been proud.

Arles had to rent a car since her SUV had been left at Wedeskyull's tiny airstrip. It was afternoon already, three hours stolen by time zones, with a long drive still ahead, so she made the decision to head straight to Fir Cove. In the morning, after a night's sleep, she would bring Lark to the local CPS office, get things started. Have one of the workers open a case.

A case. She didn't want Lark to be a case. But what choice was there?

The sun hadn't yet started to sink in the sky when she turned in at the gates. Summer was dying slowly for now, although its pace would speed up soon. Daylight lasting into evening wasn't to be for much longer, but the season was putting up a good fight. Arles drove along at a fast clip, glad to be home. Then suddenly, she braked.

Lark had been nodding off, but her head jerked upward.

Arles turned the engine off. She pocketed the keys.

"Shep?" Lark mouthed, not quite a whisper.

Arles swept her gaze around: left, right, front, back.

Lark waited.

Finally, Arles said softly, "Someone's here."

Lark frowned, taking her own look.

Lush, verdant greenery. Woods so thick as to be impenetrable, let alone scrutinized from this vantage point. Fir Cove at the height of its growth and otherwise empty and still. Not a bird twitched. There was no hum of insects or muffled breeze.

"How do you know that?" Lark whispered.

"The truth?" Arles whispered back.

Lark gave an *obviously* jab of her head.

"The truth is, I'm not sure," Arles said.

All her life, she had understood things other people didn't. That Peter was lurking in her closet when her mother came in to say good night. And then, as Arles grew older, she understood that her mother realized where her husband was; she was only pretending she didn't.

Call it second sight, or situational awareness, or just a willingness to strip off the blinders everybody wore so they could live their lives without losing their minds, not claw to shreds this whole ravaged, impossible world. Arles had become a psychologist so she could put the things she knew into words and help other people liberate their own truths.

She checked her memory of the ride in, the section of drive they'd covered before she had realized. It had gotten torn up during Kip's hazardous trip away from the property, but his tire treads were pretty well obscured by now, replaced by fresh ones. Those could belong to someone from the company Dan had sent to take care of the job Arles needed done. Could also be the patrol Tim had allocated; Arles had spotted a prowler on the grounds upon leaving for the airport the other day. But she had a feeling that none of those well-intentioned visitors explained what she was sensing.

Lark tugged at Arles's sleeve. "Do you know who it is?"

Arles hesitated. Had Kip come back to give it another go? Or was somebody else here? "Not for sure," she said. "But I have an idea."

"Yeah," Lark said, settling herself lower on her seat. "I do too."

Arles was thinking, trying to come up with any sort of a plan. Her mind felt like a rubber band about to snap.

Dan had texted her the needed information last night. Said it should work without a hitch, but to call if she ran into any snags.

She'd better not run into any snags.

She took a breath. "Do you know how to get into your mom's—whaddyacallit—show? Not as someone watching. Into it."

"You mean, like, be her when she's recording a post?" Lark asked.

"Or going live."

Lark shook her head. "My mom's dumb about passwords, but that would take two-factor authentication, and we don't have her phone. And phones don't work here anyway."

Arles gave a nod, resigned, the flare of hope she'd felt subsiding.

"I set up my own channel, though. At the hotel. So I could share it when I sent out that thing I wrote. I already have a crazy number of followers. I checked at the airport. My mom would seriously be jealous."

Arles lifted her head. It didn't seem possible what she was picturing. Too perfect. Almost staged. "Really?"

"I told you, I hid out by my mom's studio all the time," Lark said. "I learned stuff."

So Arles explained what they were going to do.

CHAPTER
FORTY-SIX

The two of them sidled between trees, Lark walking as Arles had shown her back at Harry's cabin. Near soundlessly, not a stick cracking underfoot or a stone kicked. Nothing tripped over or brushed against. A tread good for tracking. And for sneaking up on someone.

But as they neared the house, it became clear that any reason for subterfuge had long since passed. What had come to Fir Cove was oversize, giant, an incursion so great, and so out of place, that the property could've finished out its second century without ever brooking such an intrusion. Arles pulled up short, gaping at what sat in front of them. Lark stopped abruptly too.

A final rim of forest, screened by a mesh of leaves, delivered a line of sight on the helicopter that had been plunked down atop a field just upwind of the lake. Its bulbous body dominated the landscape like a tumorous beetle.

Kip and Janelle sat on the grass some distance away. The rotors of the helicopter weren't whirring; four long prongs simply sliced the reddening sky into sections. A wine bottle stood on the ground, twin glasses lying overturned next to it in some bizarre approximation of a picnic.

A black Escalade had been parked before the wide stone porch steps. Just one this time, but its presence had escaped Arles's notice until now, so used had she become to the vehicles invading her turf. Like a permanent fixture, some art installation she'd allowed. The monumental distraction posed by a freaking *helicopter* on her land had probably also contributed to Arles missing the SUV, along with the pair of arms now reaching out from some unseen spot, securing her in a tight, hug-like grip. Lark let out a shriek, then just as quickly squelched it.

Lark's hands had been hanging freely by her sides; now she slid something out of the pocket of her shorts and aimed her palm upward while concealing the object against her thigh.

Invisible to her parents, or at least likely overlooked. Grown-ups didn't let their eyes descend to child height very often, and the item Lark held on to was as unexpected in its own way at Fir Cove as the helicopter.

The helicopter that would squire Lark away; no time wasted driving on the tricky road. Lark would be out of reach in seconds. While Arles was still pinned, presumably by the driver of the SUV, unable to make any sort of move. But she did have her voice.

"Well, you two know how to make an entrance at any rate," she called as she was wrestled out from the woods. On the ground lay a pair of binoculars. Their arrival had been monitored.

"Let the doctor go," Kip said, affably enough, from his supine pose on the ground. "Just keep her under control." Still affable despite the toxicity of his command.

The man freed Arles, shoving her forward so hard that she stumbled before righting herself. Which gave the man time to turn a gun on her, releasing its safety with an audible click, then positioning the muzzle at center mass.

Just a few inches from where her flesh had been torn open before.

Lark shrieked without cessation this time, an unending spiral up to the sky.

"Don't look, Lark," the man said apologetically. "You know I'd never hurt you. This is only for your doctor friend. She took a bullet a few months ago. Won't risk it a second time."

"You know I can hear you," Arles said crossly.

The man's gaze didn't so much as flick in her direction, as if she weren't in fact there. Maybe people had to cross a certain threshold on the fame meter to register for him as real.

"I know she did," Lark said, also angrily. "Shep is a goddamn icon."

Kip frowned before loosening his brows. "No cursing, Larky."

"I'm sorry," Lark said, and she indeed sounded sad, weighted with sorrow.

Arles was going to have to talk with her about the female lavishing of apologies.

Lark didn't appear to be speaking to her father, though. She faced the man whose gun was trained on Arles, keeping her motionless.

"But I don't think you can guard me anymore, Troy," said Lark.

Arles had never gotten a good look at him before this. Bland. Banal. Women passed right by men like him without notice or paying them any mind. Which could cause a host of problems.

"I have to guard myself now," Lark said.

It was both the bravest and saddest statement Arles had ever heard an eleven-year-old make. *Not yet, Lark,* she thought. Give yourself some time on that. There are better guarders than the ones your parents enlisted. There are helpers and guiders and mentors and friends.

"Kip just wants his baby back, Dr. Shepherd," Janelle called out, recumbent in her grassy nest. "Make this nice and easy and you'll never have to think about us again. Although you will, I'm sure," she added, as if the idea of them being forgettable was an impossibility.

Janelle had let Lark go the first time the woman had fled Fir Cove. Because she had no use for Lark, didn't want her around? Was it wishful thinking—Arles trying on optimism again—to see this as a response to King Solomon's challenge? *The mother who loves her child sets her free.* Either way, Kip clearly hadn't been willing to stand for that.

Arles took a look at the gun, which hadn't moved. She swallowed.

Janelle appeared different, changed in just the few dozen hours since Arles had seen her last. Haggard, depleted. But Kip looked the same as ever, slick and smoothly put together. He'd probably had hair and makeup done as his transport touched down.

"I'll be happy to do that," Arles called back, leading with the carrot, the yes these two were so used to hearing. "There are just a few steps to get through first. A sit-down with some people. Perhaps a safeguard or two to consider." That was as gentle as she could make what was going to happen sound. At a minimum, the Strattons were in for interviews, batteries of psychological tests, home visits for the foreseeable future.

"Those things don't apply to people like us," Kip said, as if able to track her thoughts.

And maybe he could. Maybe acting depended on having that kind of intuition.

"Look," Janelle said, rising unsteadily, swaying in her heels.

Arles wondered how much of the wine she'd drunk.

Kip looked as straight as a soldier as he got to his feet.

"We're not saying you can't have any contact with Lark," Janelle said. "Obviously, you care about her."

Arles felt a flutter in her chest. She looked down at the child standing a few feet away.

"We'll figure something out once we have her back home. Maybe you can make a trip out west," Janelle went on.

Been there; don't want to do that again, Arles thought.

Janelle let out a sloppy series of giggles. She really had gone hard at the wine.

"I'll text you our address. Oh, wait, I can't do that. Because it's 1999 here. Maybe you have a cordless phone?"

"Tin cans and a string would've been funnier," Arles said.

Janelle looked blank while Lark let out a loyal laugh. Or maybe the girl truly found Arles's remark amusing. Janelle had age and experience on her daughter, of course, but Lark's body of cultural references was amazing.

"You bitch," Janelle said with a guttural snarl that made Lark let out a yelp and take a leap in Arles's direction. Janelle's shellac of showmanship was starting to crack, revealing where the woman had come from, the person she used to be. And the reality wasn't pretty. "You are not fucking things up for my husband. This is the worst time for him to be dealing with this."

Lark plunked herself down at Arles's feet, coiling one of her arms around Arles's leg.

It took Arles a second to recognize the genius of the girl's position. Not only was Lark tethered—and thus that much harder to extricate— but the object in her hand was partially hidden by a fold of Arles's pants.

"You don't get it," Janelle went on, advancing. "I've already written this script, and you're the villain! The witch who dragged off our daughter. Kip comes off looking great, and fuck if my followers won't eat it up too. They *love* having someone to loathe. Get a load of this place. It's perfect—" Janelle flung out an arm and tripped.

Troy caught her, momentarily swinging his gun away. But it hadn't been long enough. He swept it back within shooting range before Arles could do anything, even if there'd been something to do, a move that would get Lark to safety.

Janelle stood in front of the two of them, panting. "No scout could've found a better location. I took shots before you got here. You brought our kid into the literal woods, kept her at your creepy little castle—"

Now that was going too far. One thing Fir Cove was not was *little*.

Surprisingly, Janelle detected Arles's snark, a curl of lip or narrowing of eyes, maybe.

"You think this is funny? You think I'm a joke?" Janelle raged.

"I think your priorities are in the wrong place," Arles replied honestly. "I think that when you look, you see what you want to see. Instead of what's really there."

Lark clung tightly to Arles as Janelle shook and swayed as if caught in a windstorm.

"There won't be a parent on the planet who'll let you give therapy to their kid." Janelle tossed her hair, which looked more disheveled than sexy-messy at the moment. She extended a hand, letting it waft slowly down until it settled on her daughter's shoulder.

Lark shrank back.

Janelle spoke to Arles in rigid intonation, one beat between each word.

"Give. Me. Back. Our. Daughter—"

"Take a look, Janelle," Arles said. "I'm not the one holding on to Lark."

Janelle let out a piercing shriek. "I'm going to reveal you to be a batshit-crazy hag to three million people." The woman took a breath as if preparing for the reveal, her big finale.

A Kara term, and a Lark one. Two people who deserved Arles's best efforts now.

"You let little girls die, Dr. Shepherd. Never went to the police because, um, you blacked out? And forgot all about what happened? Great trait in a therapist." Janelle's expression melted like wax into a sneer. "Anyway, clearly you've latched on to my kid out of displaced guilt or something. Do I have that term correct? You'd know better than me."

By the time Janelle had completed her first sentence, Arles had already begun wilting. She hadn't felt the motion, but it must've happened because she was on the ground beside Lark. Her legs so loose and flaccid that Lark could no longer maintain a grip on the one she'd been holding. Janelle was right, at least as seen through a certain lens. Arles's history of memory loss—due clinically to trauma and dissociation—was the reason she hadn't returned to treating patients after last spring, and also why she had such an intense, driving need to keep Lark from meeting any harm. Even if Arles had to make sure of that all by herself, not trust a single other soul who might make a mistake. In a weird way, Janelle had nailed it.

Janelle stared down at Arles with satisfaction. "Yeah. I know what happened."

Lark aimed a perplexed stare in Arles's direction.

The truth? Arles could imagine the girl asking later. And Arles would have to tell her.

Slowly, she rose. "So does most of the world, Janelle. So do your worst."

CHAPTER
FORTY-SEVEN

Kip had been hanging back, letting his wife's performance play out. Now he strode forward, coming to a stop beside Troy. Slowly, with authority, he lowered Troy's arm like a lever. "Holster that, okay, buddy?"

Troy did, and Arles was finally able to take in a breath; the land felt as if it contained oxygen again.

Janelle turned to her husband. "Kippie?"

He didn't even bother to look her way. "I've told you not to call me that."

"Yeah, well, you call me *Jane*. Maybe we both knew each other when. Or before."

"Before what?" he groused, a tone of begrudging, barely piqued interest.

"Before you were Kip Stratton, and your name was Kenny, and I thought *Kip* sounded so funny—so romance-novel, bodice-buster hilarious—that I poked fun and called you *Kippie*. And before I was anyone besides plain Jane Finch."

"That's all ancient history," he said, dismissive again. "What're you bringing it up for?"

"People don't know about Lark," Janelle said. "We've made sure of that." It was the version of her voice used for selling, the one that could convince anybody of anything. "No one in the industry knows we have a daughter. And nobody online. So, effectively, she doesn't exist."

At her feet, Arles sensed, more than felt, Lark slump. Arles lowered a consoling hand, but the child didn't reach for it. She couldn't; both of Lark's own hands were busy.

"We could leave her here, Kip," said Janelle, her words taking on force, like a freight train. "Let Dr. Shepherd figure out what's best. Lark can be excised from our lives. Like plastic surgery—a nip and tuck. You and I just feel a little lighter. Younger."

Lark's face pinched, and tears budded in her eyes. The cruelty of her mother's proposition sent Arles staggering backward, as if Troy had fired his gun.

Unless, as Arles had wondered before, Janelle was the true mother, willing to give up her child to ensure the right fate.

"No way," Kip said ferociously. "I'll never let Larky go." He turned to his friend. "Okay, buddy, it's time. Get me my kid."

But as Lark flinched and shied away from him, Troy's steps finally faltered.

"Hey, Kipster?" he said.

He spoke in a different voice than the one he'd used to address Lark after taking out his gun. Deep, bullfroggy. Perfect for the bro-y soubriquet and summons, like a dude at a frat brawl.

Kip half turned. "Yeah?"

"I don't know if I can do this, man. I'm sorry. I'm no Jason. I can't manhandle your daughter. Or do something . . . else."

Kip turned fully to face his friend, indentured servant, whatever Troy was. These men Kip Stratton had managed to rally around himself. If you can't be famous on your own, at least be close to someone who is.

Kip looked as if he were weighing options, how successful he'd be at forcing Troy's hand. Finally, he heaved a put-upon sigh. "This is why some people are made for bit parts and supporting, and others are leading men."

"You've never been the lead, Dad," said Lark, gazing up at him from the ground.

Her hand still angled down low beside Arles's ankle.

317

He didn't glance her way. "That's all gonna change as of next week, Larky." For a second, Kip appeared rapturous, euphoric; then he snapped back to the here and now, confronting Arles with fists squared at his hips. "From what we've learned, you're a decent headshrinker, Doctor. You've got talent—in your own way, you're a lot like me." A studied pause. "If we let the world know who you really are, though—I mean, who we want them to *believe* you to be—then you become a different sort of woman. One who kidnapped a little girl, maybe for nefarious purposes." Another beat while his actor's face folded.

Despite everything, Arles had to marvel at Kip's expression. No, not his expression; something more subtle than that, lying beneath his features. It conjured whole worlds beyond the words he was saying, layers of sickness and horror and disgust less displayed than implied.

"Victim turned victimizer is a great narrative, Doctor. Like my wife said, it's relatable. Understandable. That's why it plays well with audiences today." He broke off while his visage, his entire body, evoked what he meant, the impending losses for Arles. It was a hell of an act.

Arles did a slow clap.

Kip frowned. "I don't think you're getting this."

"Oh, I'm getting it," Arles replied. "I know about people like you. I know your intimidation tactics, the way you believe that if you dangle the proper bait, or wield the right threat, everyone will fall in line."

"They will," Kip said simply. "They do."

"Well, not me," Arles replied.

She looked down at Lark again, aiming a question at her. The girl gave a nod.

Arles nodded back. Then she said to Kip, "I'm not a victim. I'm not even very much of a psychologist these days. So, as I said to your wife, do your worst."

"Our worst will be going to the police," Kip said.

Arles lifted an eyebrow. "I'd say I have less to worry about on that front than you."

Kip stared at her levelly. "You sure?"

Arles gazed back.

"Would you be sure if I told you we'd found a frustrated actor, real old guy, must be close to eighty, who's happy about finally being given his big break?"

I'm about to get my big break, Lark's birth mother had said. How many people all after the same thing, wanting it more than food or air, desperate with desire? Legions. Vast armies. Most of them picked off early, or fallen in combat later on. So few would ever make it to victory.

"His name's Langston Warren," Kip said. "How's that for a stage name? Except I don't think it is. His mother hoped her son would fulfill her own frustrated dream of a life in pictures." An artful pause. "Poor ol' Lang thought he was going to die without having made good on his mother's wish." Another beat. "Till Troy found him. Working as a Walmart greeter."

Arles continued to return Kip's stare, keeping her expression even to hide the roiling inside her. She listened with a slow seepage of dread—for herself and this guileless old man.

"We drove him here, put him up—rented limo, dilapidated hotel, but enough to wow Lang. Gave him the real star treatment. Guy thinks he's about to make his debut, keeps referencing June Squibb. Lang will say he was a friend of your stepfather. Not a close friend; maybe no one even knew he existed. But he saw something upsetting when he stopped by Peter's room recently to say hello. On what turned out to be the very last day of his old pal's life."

This time Arles's legs didn't fold; she refused to let herself go down. But all life drained out, as if her veins had collapsed, sinking in on themselves, unfilled by any life fluids.

Kip gave a single nod. "We've kept an eye on you ever since we were given reason to suspect you had our kid. As much as possible, given the crazy cell situation and poor excuses you have for roads out here. Followed you to that old-age home."

He was bluffing. Didn't know anything.

"One of my men poked around after you left, was still there when an ambulance arrived. Didn't take long; they must have a fleet on standby at that place. Anyway, imagine his surprise when the paramedics took away the body of the man you had just gone to see."

Arles wore her unreadable face, marble smooth and hard. "Bullshit."

"Doesn't matter, Dr. Shepherd." Kip gave a shrug designed to look careless. Or maybe he knew it truly didn't matter. "There'll still have to be a thorough investigation." A wait before delivering his final few words. "My story just sounds so, uh, what's the word I'm going for?"

Line! Arles thought faintly.

"Real," said Kip.

Arles's lips were as frozen as the rest of her face. She couldn't part them. And she would've had nothing to say, even if her mouth had been mobile. The nursing home would have to question things if new concerns emerged. Tim would be compelled to take another look.

Kip finally spared his daughter a glance. "And that," he said with a grandiloquent bow, dropped head and rolled arm at the level of his stomach, which was divided into visible lines and wedges beneath the sheer fabric of his shirt, "is the blow."

"No, Dad," said Lark. "This is the blow."

And she held up Arles's phone.

CHAPTER
FORTY-EIGHT

The screen looked alive, digitally at least. Blinking and flashing in real time.

"Lark Angel Stratton, if you post one single image of me when I look like this—" Janelle said in a threatening tone.

"I'm not posting, Mom."

"Good," Janelle said, starting to turn away. "Delete any pictures you took."

"I'm streaming," Lark said. "Everything you and Dad said."

Janelle's face went waxy, colorless. Her skin looked like it belonged on a plastic doll.

"That's not possible," she said in a nearly airless whistle, an unlovely gasp, as if her windpipe were being compressed. "There isn't any connectivity here. I haven't been offline this long since Myspace. We don't even have our phones on us. Left them on the bird."

It sounded like another line. *The bird.* As if Janelle were some black-ops militia member.

She stood blinking in Arles's direction.

Arles extended a hand toward a small gray dish, tucked discreetly away among the trees at the crest of a hill. The decision hadn't been an easy one for her to make. In some ways, a lot of ways, she preferred Fir Cove as a relic.

Features bunching and clenching with rage—though she instantly ironed them smooth—Janelle turned to look where Arles was pointing.

"I decided it wasn't safe to live as I was." Arles mentally tapped out a beat of her own. "Especially with a child around."

Lark spoke up. "You should see this live, Mom. There are so many frowny-face bubbles on the screen, it looks like an orange tree is throwing up."

Arles imagined viewers, eager to hear and see Janelle after an unusual gap.

The woman let out an anguished wail. "I have to get makeup on! And change my clothes! Where's my lighting kit?" She ducked out of view of the camera Lark aimed into a grove of trees from which her voice could still be heard, however faintly. "Troy! Get that fucking phone."

Troy took two steps forward and plucked it out of Lark's hand.

Janelle didn't pause for breath, visible in snatches as she paced back and forth behind a mesh of leaves. "I know what I'll tell them. I'll say . . . I've been shielding the fact that we have a daughter. The best lies contain a grain of truth." Even at a distance, her voice grew more assured. "It's because Lark has sociopathic tendencies. That's popular with kids right now. I forget the name of the disorder—oppositional something. Have to look it up." Janelle went on talking to herself, for once no hint of an audience in her presentation. "But it's gone too far. She stole my equipment, maybe even tried to take over my feed. That's why I went dark. And then she forced me to say shit. She's gotten abusive, and I have to stop hiding. For all of y'all's sake, not just mine," she added imploringly, as if testing things out, rehearsing. As she stepped out from the trees, she formed a fist and slugged her bicep with a meaty wallop, the sound of a raw steak hitting a countertop. "I'm sick of wearing long sleeves and makeup." She placed a sharply hewn fingernail against her cheek, then appeared to think twice and raked her neck instead. "Come here, Kip! Or Troy, you can do it! Put me in front of a camera!"

Kip gazed at his wife with palpable disbelief. "You?" he stated. "You're worried about your pathetic, pissant career? You perform for female internet zombies. Me—I'm an *actor*."

He and Janelle were in a frenzy, a state of disarray and panic. Helpless when it came to a world without infinite redo's and do-overs, no endless number of takes. They looked like bugs fleeing from a big stomping boot or the flat of a giant's hand.

"I'm going to meet with Elliott," Kip said. "In person—his firm is in New York City. Troy, get him on the phone, will ya? We've got four days to spin this. Let's say Janelle had a mental breakdown. Tell Elliott the copter will have me there in a few hours—"

At that moment, as if rebelling against Kip's command, the helicopter started with a devastating rumble and updraft of wind.

Kip whirled on Troy, who sent a helpless glance back.

"Time's up, man," Troy said. "I booked three hours. You're over budget at that—"

"Fuck, no!" Kip yelled, and set out running.

The helicopter wobbled in an awkward left-to-right loft, grasses blowing sideways on the field like hair on a green, broad-backed beast. Kip raced forward, hunched over, bracing himself to resist the force of the wind. He thrust both arms out, as hard and strong as two lengths of pipe. He was reaching for the skids, finely hewn hands poised to clench them.

Planning to use them like a chin-up bar, pull himself into the helicopter.

Which was ten or so feet off the ground now, and steadily, if unevenly rising.

Kip leaped, not ballet-dancer graceful, ungainly, although his hands managed to scrape the metal of the skids. He bore down, visibly clenching. He was going to make it. Would complete his maneuver. It looked just like that shot in the movie.

Then the helicopter banked left, getting clear of a rise, and his hands were left squeezing nothing but two fistfuls of air. He fell.

"Dad!" screamed Lark.

Janelle let out an ugly squawk of a laugh.

The whole world seemed to vibrate. Arles's body was jarred, her teeth rattling as the helicopter lifted. It buzzed and thrummed, rotors chewing up the air in greedy bites, until it was a speck in the sky, then no more.

The wind must've been knocked out of Kip when he plunged. As he pushed himself up off the ground, he was gasping. He began limping toward Troy, holding out one hand.

"Key—" he said on a sucked in breath. "I can get there myself in four hours."

"I'll take you," Troy said, and it looked like . . . Was he *crying*?

Had Kip's failed maneuver gotten to him? Was he worried about his friend's well-being? Or just worried that Kip's career was about to crash and burn and Troy would be out of a job?

Kip shook his head, thumping his chest with a fist as if to get his lungs working. "I drive faster than you. Call an Uber." He glanced around. "Maybe a cab?" And then he was running for the Escalade, shouting over his shoulder. "I'll come back for you, Larky. Or send someone—"

He took off in a cyclone of grit and gravel, leaving Lark, Janelle, Troy, and Arles all looking on. But before Kip could even round the first bend, Edwin stepped out of a thicket of trees and into the private drive. On his face was a look of such bereavement that, as odious as the comparison was, all Arles could see were Manille Garcia's parents the day she had met them. Edwin's body was dragging, pulled down by gravity. His mournful eyes were watery and filmed.

The Escalade was coming right at him, but he didn't seem capable of moving.

Kip didn't appear to be looking through the windshield. Probably fumbling with his no-longer-useless phone. Of course, Janelle had been lying when she'd said they'd left them behind.

"How did you miss?" Edwin shouted, loud enough to be heard over the engine.

It took Arles a second to parse that he was referring to Kip's ignominious *splat*. In this man's mind, it hadn't been supposed to go that way. Why would it? Such things never did when seen on a screen. Edwin's hero, his lord, his god, had quite literally fallen from grace.

"How did you not make that leap, Mr. Stratton?" he bellowed. "It didn't look that hard!"

Behind the wheel, Kip lifted his head in slow-motion increments. On his perfect, handsome face, confusion, then a clear clocking of the man standing stiffly in the middle of the road. Kip jerked the wheel, and the SUV swerved sideways, heading straight for a tree.

It stood only a yard or two off, a tall, stout oak, no time or space for Kip to turn, go in a different direction. Arles whipped Lark around, pressing the girl's face against her side.

They stayed locked together, as still as wax figurines. At some point in the melee, Lark must've retrieved Arles's phone; now Arles slipped it from Lark's unresisting hand and jabbed 911 on the keypad while the Escalade surged forward.

It hit the tree with a sonic boom, a great clash of metal and wood, and the car's hood pleated. The vehicle bucked to a stop as the windshield smashed in a hailstorm of glass pellets, and Kip's body flew through it like a rocket from a launchpad.

He hadn't been wearing his seat belt. In his world, no restraints were needed.

His body struck the earth, angular and crumpled.

A silence settled after the collision. All the earth had quieted, been erased of sound.

Until Janelle let out a beautiful, pitchy cry, as if she thought someone might capture the audio. Edwin's voice rose up to join hers, thin as a wisp of smoke.

"There," he said. "That's more dramatic."

CHAPTER FORTY-NINE

Lark began to struggle against Arles, who turned her gently aside. She bent down and spoke into the girl's ear, just a few words, only those that were needed, and Lark's legs sagged. Hot tears seeped through the fabric of Arles's shirt.

She eased Lark in Janelle's direction, but Janelle took a few steps away.

Lark sank down on the ground, arms wrapped around her knees.

Arles crossed the road to where Kip lay. She was pretty sure no one could've survived that impact and subsequent flight through the air— even Kip Stratton—although she placed two fingers against his neck to check for a pulse. She felt nothing. It was as if he'd always been this still. His eyes stared straight at the sun overhead, the two orbs wide and unblinking, no less blue or beautiful in death. There came a faint shrill of sirens, disrupting the motionlessness of the day.

Before Arles could think how or if to try and stop him, Edwin took off.

———

After the—unfortunately unneeded—paramedics left and Tim's team finished up, Troy drove Janelle downstate to meet with the studio's publicity satellite. News of Kip's death was going to have to be carefully timed. An announcement made just prior to release day, really get those tickets selling, audiences filling seats. The funeral or memorial service, TBD, would be put off accordingly. Could Janelle let Lark know once things were decided?

Edwin had been swiftly located by police and taken into custody.

No chance of his leaking the story.

Arles brought Lark back to the house.

She fixed dinner, boxed macaroni and cheese, at Lark's request. It was a gastronomic stretch for Arles, but it turned out okay. Kind of good, even; she ate a portion while observing Lark carefully. How much trauma could one girl absorb, a sponge in a vast sea?

Well, a lot, in Arles's experience.

Lark ate hungrily, asking about the sequence of events, not in a pressured way, just as if trying to get everything laid out in order, make sure she had it all right. She didn't seem distanced emotionally, either. At a few points, she cried before mopping her face and returning to filling in holes. A textbook entryway into grief, in Arles's assessment.

At last, Lark sank low in her seat, spent. "I'm too tired to keep talking about this."

"Don't blame you a bit," Arles said. Lark's state of mind would require probing as time went on, like feeling a gash to determine where the tenderness was. But it could and should wait.

"I do want to talk, though," Lark said. "Just not about this."

"Hmm," Arles said. "Wilderness stuff, maybe?"

"Good call, but no. For once." Lark hesitated. "Isn't there anything else?"

Arles thought. "There is one thing you could tell me."

Lark nodded seriously.

"Something I don't know, didn't understand at all, but definitely want to. *Need* to, really."

Lark gave another solemn nod, appearing curious now.

"What's the blow?" Arles asked.

It was an actor's parting line, their exit, the mic drop. End scene.

Kip had gotten his. But Lark's was yet to be.

By nightfall, Janelle had filed a termination of parental rights, which wasn't really a thing, so she'd had her lawyer draw something up to explain the precedent it followed, along with an NDA laying out the penalties Arles, the Wedeskyull police force, and the State of New York would face if they violated the confidential nature of the information contained therein.

> *I am not equipped to care for my child any longer. My psychiatrist* [see addendum] *believes I am a danger to myself and to Lark if she remains in my custody. I ask that the childcare system of New York State* [Child Protective Services a.k.a. CPS] *oversee her next place of residence and all other matters pertaining to her future.*

Arles wasn't sure whether the form would stand up under any scrutiny. But no child services worker would risk defying such a statement. The stakes were too high when it came to the life of a child. People had been fired for making far grayer calls.

While Lark ate cookie dough from the freezer for dessert, Arles sorted through an accumulation of mail. As if the batter had conjured up its chef, there was a postcard from Stephanie in the pile. It'd been sent from Canyonlands National Park, its photo depicting three ruddy red arches captured at sunset. Stunning—Arles tilted the card so Lark could see—but how had Stephanie and Lissa gotten that far south? Arles thought the pair was sticking to the northern route. The message on the back explained it.

In looping script, each word so big and open and unfurled that it seemed the embodiment of joy, Stephanie had written:

I've met someone, Arles! He lives in Utah, and you are going to absolutely love him. Lissa and I are planning to stay out here a while, but we'll be back at Christmastime to see you and, if things go well, get our things!

She'd drawn a pair of tiny crossed fingers, like the emoji.

Lissa's working on writing you a separate postcard, a real letter, actually. She misses you sooo much! But she's doing great.

Arles set the card aside, making sure to keep it separate from the junk to be recycled.

She hadn't even chosen their next book-club selection yet.

She walked Lark upstairs, fetching a toothbrush from the linen closet and watching as the girl climbed into bed. Arles said good night and turned off the light, leaving the hall sconces on in case of middle-of-the-night remembrance, sudden tears, a predawn wakeup, or a bathroom trip.

Then she went back down to the first floor and called Dan.

———

Before the two of them headed off to sleep themselves, Arles let Dan read the postcard.

He handed it back after he'd finished, and when she saw the weight of it in his eyes, tears started in hers.

"It's just . . . I'm really going to miss that child," she said. "And Stephanie too, of course."

"I know you are," Dan said sympathetically. He laid a palm atop hers.

Not toad-like tonight. Kind of nice. Welcome.

"And . . ." Arles pressed the heel of one hand against her face to dam a flood. "I never even told her. I haven't gotten the chance to say what I want to yet. How much I care about her. How happy I'd be if she didn't leave Fir Cove. If she wanted to stay here."

When her vision had cleared enough for her to see, Dan was facing her.

"Are you talking about Lissa now?" he asked.

Arles scrubbed her face, sniffled raggedly. "Who else?"

He gazed at her, and she stared back.

"I mean, I'm no psychologist, but . . ."

"Oh," Arles said after a moment. "Oh."

———

In the morning, Dan slept in; Sunday was his one day off.

Arles spoke with Tim for a long time; he'd stayed on for the overnight, tons to wrap up in Kara's and Jason's and Kip's deaths. He wouldn't be working his normal shifts for weeks. After finally ending the call and texting a *ttyl* because there was much more to figure out, Arles went outside to find Lark eating her way through a box of Pop-Tarts on the porch.

The sun had just begun to limn the sky with berry hues.

Arles sat down on the stone steps. Checked Lark for swollen eyes or uneven breaths or ashen, sleep-deprived skin. But she appeared fairly calm. Well rested, even. Which could be an issue on its own—a delayed response to grief—but one that dealing with could be postponed.

"Hey, Lark?"

Sucking red goo off her fingers, Lark looked at her.

Arles worked to take in a breath. "You can, of course, say no to this. You can tell me it's the worst idea you've ever heard. You don't have to worry about my feelings or anything else. Only yourself and what you believe is best for you right now."

Lark tilted her head, wearing her interested expression.

"How would you feel about staying on at Fir Cove? Living here with me?"

Lark stuck an icing-smeared finger into her mouth.

Arles felt as if her head had been thrust beneath water.

Lark took a last lick. "That's what I've wanted all along."

A spark inside Arles, then a fireworks explosion, sprays of pink, purple, gold, green. Air had vacated her lungs, and she could hardly speak. "It is?"

"Yeah. Didn't you know that?"

The truth? "No," Arles said. "I didn't."

"Do I still get to call you *Shep*? If you're my—if you're my whatever?"

At last, Arles was able to inhale. "*Shep's* the best thing I've ever been called."

Lark tore open another silvery sleeve and reached inside it.

Arles leaned over to still her hand. "Hey, maybe have some oatmeal instead?"

Lark nodded agreeably and replaced the package in the box.

"Oatmeal for Sunday breakfast?" said a voice behind them.

Lark shot to her feet. "Dan!"

He reached down and ruffled her hair. "I was thinking pancakes."

"I was thinking you're right!" Lark said, and ran inside.

Arles rose and walked over to Dan.

He bent to kiss her, but she pulled back, keeping her distance.

His body also rigidified, a clear *Don't do this again* in his eyes.

But Arles couldn't attend to that right now, disgust about to drown her. "And you'd be—what?" she said, feeling her face crinkle. "Some kind of *stepfather* figure?"

Dan's own features unfolded, anger diffusing. He took her hands, and she allowed it.

"I'll just be Dan," he said with quiet force. "While you're Arles. Sorry, I mean *Shep*. And isn't that good enough? Isn't it pretty great?"

Found families. Forever families.

She took a step or two closer. "I guess it is," she said. "Pretty great."

Lark appeared at the front door. "I thought someone said something about pancakes."

Dan crossed the threshold and went inside. "Coming right up."

Lark waited for Arles to enter the house.

"I wonder what's going to happen next?" said the girl.

"What do you mean?" Arles asked.

"I dunno. Just seems like something's always happening around here."

"I think we're going to be okay for a while now," Arles replied. "I have a feeling it's going to get quiet again. For a good long time."

Lark paused as if thinking about it.

The smell of sizzling butter wafted out from the kitchen, and Arles realized that for once, she was hungry. She headed toward the aroma, to the man flipping the first pancake on the stove.

"Shep?"

Arles turned back. "Yes, Lark?"

"That's the line they say in the movie, you know. Just before the monster shows up."

After Janelle had gotten Lark out of their rental car at that creepy-ass castle, she'd twisted around to make sure Dr. Shepherd and her daughter reunited safely. Janelle hadn't been able to see all that well in the dark, but the image of the two crawling toward each other—like a scene in a movie, some multigen saga—had given Janelle a feeling she'd never had before.

She'd envisioned herself in a reel, dressed in a cute retro nurse's costume—Florence Nightingbird, was that the right name?—and strolling from patient to patient, not with pills and compresses but green smoothies and roll bars to protect their backs after ab work.

Janelle could totally rock selfless.

Then she'd gotten real and admitted she had mostly just wanted to be rid of Lark.

Janelle told Kip that Lark had escaped of her own accord, like she'd done at the bookstore, as opposed to Janelle having given her a helping hand. The physics of Lark doing it herself would've been just about impossible; luckily, Kip was too dumb to envision the choreography. Still, he'd been so enraged that for the first time in their marriage, Janelle had felt physically scared of him.

She'd started keeping her phone on her at all times—not that she didn't do that anyway, but making sure to remember the portable charger, even in the house—so she could record his temper fits and threaten to leak the video if he hurt her.

It'd been Kip's desire to raise Lark. Obviously. When he had come clean to Janelle about Talia Bent, he'd said that he had sired a child, actually used the word sired, *as if he were a king. Janelle had gone along with him as she always did. Her mother's biggest regret in life was driving her husband away with what he'd called her "fussing and hollering." Janelle wasn't about to make the same mistake. But it wasn't as if she ever truly wanted a child. On the whole, Kip's dying relieved Janelle of a burden.*

The world was going to be talking about Kip for a long time, even though he would never make another movie. The Ascent had been tracking great even before he and Janelle had left for the East Coast, but things had gone stratospheric after his death was announced. Someone at the trades called the film "Castaway in the woods" and that was that. Oscar rumbles. Oscar quakes.

Kip might win a posthumous fucking Academy Award.

The studio, along with Kip's private publicist, had spun things perfectly.

Kip was a hero, dying in a ball of flames (even though, for some bizarre reason, the car hadn't exploded like it always did in movies) after swerving to avoid hitting someone. And he was a victim, dying at the hands of a vengeful stalker. The fact that those people were one and the same was quietly downplayed. The first story—two for the price of one!—had better legs if the public imagined an innocent in the road.

Oh, and there was a third story too, to address Lark's livestream.

In that one, Kip had to cope with his banshee of a wife, get her the help she needed. The media painted Janelle as a woman who'd fallen prey to misogynistic influencer culture and went nuts before her husband tragically perished. Which was pretty misogynistic itself, if you thought about it. The spliced-together shots of her hair standing up around her face in an electrocuted lion's mane. Her mouth open in a scream that looked like the center of a many-petaled flower.

Eventually, when a garish-enough story hit the news cycle, this would all go away in a poof of dark, bitter outrage. Until that time, Janelle was ducking quietly off of everyone's radar.

Learning to live life as a childless (this time for real) single woman. Not in front of a ring light, devoting every day, every hour, to arduous skin care and nutrition regimens, plus constant hair, wardrobe, and makeup. Without having to fight off the swarms of products that flew at her so fast, it was impossible to choose which to push.

She signed up for an online degree. Janelle had never finished college, but she used to enjoy taking classes in psychology, even all the reading. She went shopping alone; Troy had quit. Once she drove herself up to Uquita in the hills and set out on a walk. Turned out to be easier than the hellish hike she'd taken with Lark and Dr. Shepherd.

Lark.

As invisibly as her daughter had been in her life, so did she slip from it.

Janelle had no girlfriends to talk things over with. To mourn with, if that was the right word. If she'd had any friends, they wouldn't have known about Lark anyway.

Even just basic things like cooking had changed. There was no need to assemble sandwiches out of separately wrapped slices of cashew cheese, vegan turkey, and two precisely matched pieces of low-carb bread—the last freebie she had from a deal with the meal-prep company Slice & Dice—because Lark refused to eat one more quinoa bowl.

Kip's absence created an even more yawning black hole than Lark's; everything had always been about him. But in real life, people who did what Kip had done, died; they didn't just get up and walk away. Janelle had scarcely been able to believe it when she'd seen Kip lying in that patch of dirt. She assumed he would start moving again as soon as the director or AD called, "Cut!"

She hadn't trusted what she was seeing with her own eyes. Movies taught you not to believe anything and to believe everything—all at the same time.

Janelle was now surrounded every day by the hellscape that had stolen her husband and child. It was online and on billboards and on the sides of buses. The title in its jagged font superimposed across a range of mountaintops with Kip's face plastered there too, larger than life, as if he were all four presidents combined on Mount Rushmore.

Seeing the landscape that currently housed her daughter kept Lark real for Janelle. More real in a way than she'd been when they had lived together.

Lark would've been famous by now if Janelle hadn't allowed Kip to override her maternal instincts. Impossible for anybody to steal. Living a life so glorious, she would've refused to give it up. Thrown a fit if told to, even by doctors or therapists or the state.

Throwing a fit wasn't very Lark-like, Janelle reflected. Lark was tough. Badass.

It had taken losing Lark to make Janelle realize her value.

Someday soon, Janelle would get back to posting. Rehab herself and her channel. And when she did, then maybe she'd make a trip back across the country.

A mother-daughter reunification story. Everyone loved those.

It would play so well with her followers.

ACT IV

LARK IN THE WORLD

CHAPTER FIFTY

Lark was in her plush red seat, watching the end crawl, when she felt tears sliding down her cheeks.

"Was this a bad idea?" Shep whispered. "To go see it? We could've waited to stream it at home."

The movie theater was still dark. No one had gotten up yet. People were watching every last second; they'd probably stick around to see who the best boy had been, catch the names of the gaffers and caterer and how SAG-AFTRA had kept the wages from being too low.

Lark turned sideways in the darkened row, tunneling her hand into Shep's.

Shep sat there, looking at her quietly, no hurry to it at all.

"This is the first time I ever felt proud of my dad," Lark said.

She wished she had the same feeling about her mom, but she didn't, not if she were being honest like Shep was teaching her to be. Lark felt glad that her mom hadn't posted, wasn't using everything crazy that had happened to get views. That was about the most Lark could hope for when it came to her mom.

More credits on the screen now, including the book her dad's film had been based on. Lark planned to ask Shep to bring her to Books & Brew to buy a copy. At first, a story was just marks and squiggles on a page or screen. Then it was words, then a whole chapter, and for a while you kept looking down to see how far you had gotten. But after that, something happened. The best she could compare it to was being on a plane. The way the plane went bouncing and jouncing along the runway, wheels touching every bump and lump on the ground, but then suddenly, without you even being aware of it, the whole thing lifted off and it was up in the freaking *sky*. You were flying. That was reading.

The entire audience, including Lark and Shep, roared when the location was attributed.

Filmed in Wedeskyull, New York.

At last the lights came up, and everybody rose. They went out to the old-timey lobby. Popcorn in small buckets, soda in regular-size cups, nowhere near enough kinds of candy. This theater was bigger than the screening room in Lark's old house, but not by much. Out of the corner of her eye, Lark saw someone she knew. She was still getting used to that. She'd go into a store and Dorothy from the police station would be there! But seeing this person was even better.

"Janey!" Lark called.

Janey stood between her mom and dad. His eyes looked different today, less like a wild animal's.

"That's Lark," Janey said to her parents.

The dad nodded. "Did you like Mr. Stratton in the movie, Lark?" He gave his head a weird shake. "I mean, did you like the movie?"

"Yes," Lark said. "I did."

"Me too," said Janey.

"Hey, I can text you now! I'm a real girl." A pause. "I mean, boy."

"*Pinocchio?*" Janey said.

They'd started the game the first night they met. One person said a line, then the other had to guess which movie it came from.

Janey had gotten it right.

Lark smiled. *I'm a real girl.* And now she really was.

ACKNOWLEDGMENTS

For me, every novel begins with a warrior. Someone who faces a battle, the winning of which will improve, even save, lives, including her own.

For all of the real-life warriors and survivors, I hope this book tells some of the truth.

In my past two books, fictional warrior Arles Shepherd has gotten to tell her tale. The character of Arles was ignited by Gracie Doyle, associate publisher here at Amazon, for whose faith and initial spark I will always be grateful. That I then connected with Jessica Tribble Wells, editorial director, is a big part of why this series has gone so deep. Jessica can see through to the bones of a story like no one else. She's an editing X-ray machine. Jessica is joined in her editing exploits by Charlotte Herscher, whose dive into this novel took me to depths I'd never anticipated and helped make it the story you just read.

Editing a book is a multiphase process. Once the structural edits are completed, copy edits begin. To Andrea Nauta, thank you for shepherdship (ha) and steering. Thanks to Angela Elson for production-management magic during a pivotal second round. I am deeply grateful to have worked with Valerie on both Arles Shepherd novels so far. Valerie's feel for the series, and eye for continuity, drew my attention to exactly the right things—many of which I never would've seen on my own. Rachel also has an incisive eye and homed in on words down to the smallest detail. For proofreading that examined every one of these nearly 100,000 words, I am beyond grateful to Jill. I hope I am not leaving out anyone whose additional attentions have benefited this book. Having a production team like this one is every writer's dream—and secret weapon.

Starting a series with Thomas & Mercer has been an adventure in and of itself—if not quite an Arles-level adventure, still something on the high seas. For getting this book into so many readers' hands, many of whom had not yet discovered my work, I am grateful to everyone in the marketing department, a powerhouse of a team. Darci Swanson and others are working constantly to bring this series to life, and their efforts can't be overstated, nor can my thanks.

For this gorgeous second cover—that color, those page shreds!—I owe awe and gratitude to art director Michael Jantze at Thomas & Mercer, and designer Amanda Hudson at Faceout Studio.

I am grateful to have connected with my new agent, Mark Tavani, at just the right time. Mark is a legend in the industry, and had such an immediate sense of what I was doing with Arles—a "character of the heart"—that I knew I'd be lucky to get to work with him. I look forward to this new epoch of writing with Mark by my side.

Behind every release of mine has been the publicity firm Books Forward. I am so happy to have gotten to know Layne Mandros with this book, and to have worked with her and Marissa De Cuir on it.

To Franco and Lucia Vogt, thank you for an outdoors photo shoot that yielded my new author headshots. Franco is a photographer to the stars, and he and Lucia made me feel like one.

I am grateful to every person who has shared their story with me over the years. Writers and others, you all in different ways give me hope.

To Steve Avery, thanks for your help in keeping this story alive from the moment the fictional girl first appeared to me in Surprise, Arizona. You are a great reader and bookish friend; I hope you like how it all turned out.

My first readers are responsible for iterations of this book that got it to the next level—and then the next. Carla Buckley, Karyne Corum, and Stefanie Pintoff are all authors to read or watch for. My mother, psychologist Madelyn Milchman, provided incisive wisdom and a sounding board. My Gen Z'ers, Sophie and Caleb, saved me from myself multiple times, and have deep editorial eyes that go beyond the generation gap and make my work smoother, more substantive, and just plain better. In so many ways, for so many reasons, I would not be the writer I am if my children did not inspire and lift me to new personal and creative heights every single day. And of course, my very first reader, soulmate, and life partner left his imprint on this story in more ways than I can count.

Thank you, all.

ABOUT THE AUTHOR

Photo © 2024 Franco Vogt

Jenny Milchman is the Mary Higgins Clark Award–winning and *USA Today* bestselling author of the psychological thrillers *Cover of Snow*, *Ruin Falls*, *As Night Falls*, *Wicked River*, and *The Second Mother*, and now the Arles Shepherd series, starting with *The Usual Silence*. Jenny's work has received praise from *The New York Times, San Francisco Journal*, and many others; earned spots on Top 10 lists, including *Suspense Magazine* and *The Strand Magazine*; made Best Of lists ranging from PopSugar to PureWow; and garnered starred reviews from *Publishers Weekly, Booklist, Library Journal*, and *Shelf Awareness*, in addition to numerous other mentions. Before turning to fiction, Jenny earned a graduate degree in clinical psychology and practiced at a rural community mental health center for more than a decade. She lives in the Catskill Mountains with her family. For more information, visit www.jennymilchman.com.